THE

ESSENTIAL
REVOLUTION

THE

ESSENTIAL
REVOLUTION

MICHAEL S. McGINNIS, JR.

AWAKEN
VILLAGE
PRESS

Printed in the United States of America.

Editing by Daniel Holloway
Cover and interior design by Tim Murray

ISBN 978-1-7344265-6-4 (paperback)
ISBN 978-1-7344265-7-1 (ebook)

Library of Congress Cataloging-in-Publication Data

Published by Awaken Village Press, Sioux Falls, SD
WWW.AWAKENVILLAGEPRESS.COM

PRAISE FOR *THE ESSENTIAL REVOLUTION*

"In this page-turning novel, it is clear that Michael McGinnis is channeling something unspeakable. This book is a service to humanity and the planet. We are currently at a critical juncture, and we can either choose to evolve into unity consciousness or continue down a destructive path. McGinnis is giving us a roadmap to do the former."

—Sara Yamtich, CEO of Resonate with Sara

"The book is so powerful I had to put it down. While following the transformation of the story's characters, it somehow activated the same changes within me. I was eventually able to come back to it after processing some deep feelings and continued on. The book represents the deep truth around awakening and what's possible for us when we choose our highest path."

—Rah Panchal, founder of Quantum Resurrection

"What a ride! What a journey! This book is a riveting read for people from all walks of life taking all different paths. It's heart-pumping and heartwarming. Its characters bring laughter and tears. But most of all, *The Essential Revolution* offers an intriguing look at what's going on in our world and delivers a creative solution. This conservative grandma loved it!"

—Mer Johnson, retired executive assistant

"New author Michael McGinnis does a superb job of hiding the spinach in the mashed potatoes, so to speak. Transmuting an array of normally heavy esoteric truths into a fast-paced adventure, he delivers a message the world needs to hear."

—Kim Castilla, astrologer

"Author Michael McGinnis straddles the line between the integration of truths in his new book, *The Essential Revolution*. As the reader takes their own journey through the eyes of each of the book's characters, bridges are built from hot, polarizing, triggering drama to deep existential truths. No issue is left untouched, from social justice, through conservative and religious dogma, and out the other side of conspiracy theory. The story weaves a message that challenges every incongruent measuring stick, sacred cow, and sob story until the reader's personal viewpoints are disrobed and stand naked in revelation."

—Christina Luna, author and astrologer

"My wife and I were both immediately grabbed by the book and got lost in the deeper message it held. We started each day by reading a chapter together and then talking in depth about what it told us individually. This book ultimately helped us heal our own wounds and insecurities that were enmeshed within our relationship, bringing us closer together. It offered us another way to look at this crazy matrix we all call life."

—Hans Beunk, founder of Uvita Bali Bosque

"I didn't want to stop reading this book. Every word, every character was like a magic heart opener, a moment of recognition, of coming home. From the minute I opened the book, I was fully immersed in the story wanting to know more. Integrating the lessons into my life became easier as they were told from different perspectives throughout the book. Thank you, Michael McGinnis, for writing the book that forever changed our view of family relations, connectivity with friends, and the interplay of good versus bad. I now know which side to pick. Viva la Revolución!"

—Monique Jurgens, founder of Uvita Bali Bosque

"McGinnis's writing style is easy to read as the book starts off as normal fiction but quickly transforms into a deeper, meaningful piece reflecting the quest for love, truth, tolerance, and forgiveness. It was captivating and had my full attention. A hard one to put down, as it is so badly needed in times like these."

—Marie Simonon

"A gripping, timely, and relevant book in response to what's happening in the world. As an avid reader and someone who studied English literature, what struck me most was the ability of McGinnis to paint the picture in such a compelling way that had me feeling deeply connected to the message and each character."

—Shannon Moran

"Rarely does an author manage to combine a captivating literary style with a fast-paced intricate storyline containing a liberal dose of universal truths and gems of wisdom. While reading The Essential Revolution, it felt like I was spending time with Eckhart Tolle, Perry Mason, Neale Donald Walsch, Carlos Castaneda, Yogananda … all my favorite teachers, including one of my favorite (new) authors: Michael McGinnis. A seminal work of fiction that offers readers a clearly defined up-to-date portrait of the condition of the world with an added bonus: Answers. Solutions. Blueprints to survival. Pathways to escape environmental and social destruction. Meet Dimitri, the new Michael Valentine Smith, who outshines them all (and doesn't need to sit on the bottom of the pool to do it). *The Essential Revolution* is an essential read."

—Steve Fergus

"Everytime I sit down to read this book, I become a better person."

—Monica Mosapor, mother of three

"How the author has managed to bring the main characters to life, in a word, is astounding. I found myself being pulled into the story as certain events unfolded that were not at all predictable. The reader goes along the journey with these characters as countless lessons are being conveyed that have real applicability to the world in which we are currently all living. It's a hard book to put down, and when you do, you long for more."

—David Lema, content creator

THIS BOOK IS DEDICATED TO THE ONE THAT ABIDES BEHIND
THE EYES OF ALL WHO READ IT.

"I know not with what weapons World War lll will be fought, but World War lV will be fought with sticks and stones."
—Albert Einstein

PROLOGUE

MARCUS

Do you remember where you were that day, the day it happened? Like most, I imagine you can recall the exact moment, every detail: where you were, who you were with, and what you were doing. If not, you most likely weren't even alive, because anyone who was could never forget it. Of course, when I use the word *alive*, I am referring not only to the mere physical state of being alive but, more importantly, to the conscious, awakened state of living this thing we call life itself.

Did you experience it over connective holographic technology (CHT), or were you one of the fortunate ones who got to be there, to witness it live as he spoke? If so, how close did you get? One could get pretty close depending on their level of determination. But, in order for me to tell this story, you must know I was the closest, not just on the day the whole world changed but long before.

Now, before I go back nearly two decades, let me tell you what it was like to be there at that moment. I mean right there. Just ten feet away from the most influential human being on earth, giving the most significant speech in recorded history. This was the day we took it all back and solidified our independence once and for all. This was the day we, the collective, or more simply put, humanity, stepped into a new paradigm, a new way of seeing the world through a new set of eyes. We could never go back, nor would we ever want to, and he was the one who led us there. Consequently, those profound words, spoken on that special day, would be the last the world would hear from him.

Six floors up, on the balcony of the massive Ramana Maha Mandir Temple in the Thar Desert of India, perched high above what I can only describe as an ocean of people, we stood. It was said over two million souls made the pilgrimage from across the globe to bear witness to the event of a lifetime. We had chosen that location for security. The newly awakened body of the Indian Government had taken a keen interest in his message and vision.

We figured they could help ensure his safety from the dark forces who were hell-bent on putting an end to his speech. Those who'd run our world with an iron fist for so long were desperately hanging on by their last thread, and they still had the guns. I'd tried to convince him to use CHT only, warning him of the dangers of doing it in public, but he wouldn't hear it. He'd said he just needed to finish the speech and what might happen afterward was of no consequence to him. He was adamant it be out in the open, in the presence of as many people as possible.

Standing tall, he leaned over the podium, pulling himself closer to the audience below. A warm, dry breeze blew toward him as his long, wavy brown hair moved in the wind. His piercing green eyes seemed fixated on all who had gathered, as well as those who hadn't. His voice rolled like thunder across the land, echoing from town to town, city to city, all throughout the world. The deafening roar of the crowd was so loud the building vibrated every time the people were moved by his words. It was then I realized why he insisted on doing it in public. Something was happening, I mean, actually shifting; I could literally feel it. Now, with millions gathered below and billions more connected through CHT, he had humanity's attention and was making the most of it.

Standing there watching, I couldn't help but feel a deep sense of pride. Yes, he was the one speaking, but I knew I'd played a substantial role in coordinating it, just as I had with every speech, interview, presentation, and meeting for the past ten years. You see, I, Marcus Angbo Ogabi, a second-generation African-American ex-cop from the inner city, was right hand to Dimitri Tanomeo, the most influential and famous human being in modern history. But, to be honest, I was more than that. I was his best friend. And, for me, he was a mentor, a guru, a brother to all, a hero, and a leader, one that showed us, ultimately, how to lead ourselves by guiding us to our own internal liberation.

As his speech approached its end, tears rolled down my face. The man who'd once made me cry for the first time in a long time was at it again. I wasn't the only one, though. Anyone who witnessed that moment was deeply moved. How could they not be? It was this man who'd led us to our deepest understanding, or rather our *knowing*, which eventually sparked a global transformation of such magnitude that our planet's most severe ills were healed. This resulted in clean air to breathe, pure untainted water to drink, and organic nourishment for all. There was a substantial overall reduction in the pollution of our oceans, skies, and rivers, a result of the global ecological consciousness born on the heels of his work. The same work that helped us become cognizant of who or, better said, what we truly are. He'd guided us there to that profound state of peace and security, and the world loved him for it. Now he was calling forth our liberation in a way that would change how we would live our lives forever. This speech, this command, for peace and sovereignty would thrust our world into one of balance for all human beings. As of this moment, a new dialogue would be spoken: one of unity, transparency, and compassion.

This day would come to be known as The Summoning.

THE ONE

MARCUS

My partner Sid and I had just sat down for a late lunch at the local Mexican joint when *the call* came through.

The loud emergency tone broadcast from dispatch sounded from both our radios. "Attention units, shots fired at 1152 Nineteenth Street, East Borough. All available units respond. Shots fired at Nineteenth and Crown, fired in the building."

Sid reached down and quickly turned his volume down. "Let another unit pick that up, Ogabi," he muttered while reaching across the table for the hot sauce. His vein-ridden cheeks and sour demeanor told the tale of an overweight, alcoholic police veteran with over thirty hard years on the force.

"That's three blocks away, Sid. We gotta take it," I shot back, raising my hand to my radio mouthpiece.

He looked at his untouched burrito, then at me. His upper lip curled. "Don't do it, Marcus." For a brief second, I considered complying, not wanting to be late for beers and Monday Night Football.

"Sorry, partner. To protect and serve, gotta keep that first. It's all about beat pride, remember?" I turned my back and hit the push to talk button. "Copy dispatch, 3B61 received, en route. We'll be responding code three, back to dispatch."

Keeping my head low to avoid his glare, I turned to grab my tray. He tossed his fork on the plate and stomped out the door.

"Monty's, our favorite. I'm buying after the call, Sid!" I yelled as we got into the cruiser.

"Yeah, yeah, kid, just buckle up," he grumbled, flipping on the overheads and siren. Pinned to my seat, I felt the torque of the V8 Crown Victoria combustible motor of days past as we sped towards the call. A shots-fired call with an ETA of two minutes meant we could very well arrive right in the middle of whatever was going down.

I'd just turned thirty-five, and, with seven years on the force, I'd yet to shoot anyone, unlike Sid, who'd shot three men during his tenure. There was a feeling, which I now know as fear, that would cause me to wonder, or let's call it worry, about when that moment might come. Mental movies of shootouts where I'd ultimately take out the bad guy played so often I wished it would just happen, to get it over with. Those mental movies became yet another component of a day in the life of Marcus Ogabi, a black American cop living and working in Bridgeton.

The tires screeched as we turned the corner. *Just one more block.* We were headed to the heart of the poorest and toughest area in Lincoln County, Crown and Nineteenth, AKA "The Pit." I became hyper-aware of everything, my senses more alive as a cold, familiar numbness crept into my fingers and upper lip. We whipped around the last corner, and I turned my attention towards my gear, checking my vest, gun, and radio.

"Look alive, son!" Sid bellowed with authority as he backed off the accelerator. We spotted a group of young men gathered on the sidewalk outside the apartment building. As we got closer, I squinted, focused on the stoop. That's when I saw *him* for the first time.

Suddenly everything went eerily silent and all movement froze as if time had stopped. I had to shake my head to snap out of it.

"Right there on the stoop. Tall male covered in blood. He's got a gun." I pointed at a tall, young man in his late teens who calmly gazed at us while putting on a shirt. "Go, go, go!" I shouted. Sid hit the gas and the boy took off running. We were within twenty yards of him when he turned down a sidewalk separation between the two apartment complexes that connected to Eighteenth.

"Stop, Sid, stop!" I opened my door with the cruiser still in motion, jumped out, and stumbled into the frenzy. I gained my footing and pulled my gun from its holster as I gave chase behind him. "Police, stop, drop the gun!" He ignored my order, running, pistol still in hand. Breathing heavily, I yelled, "Hey, punk, drop the fucking gun or I'm gonna shoot you!"

He glanced back but kept running. He changed course and bolted to the right, along a small corridor between the back of the building and a concrete wall. I was right behind him in a full sprint. Just the two of us. *No partner, no backup.* A part of me wanted to slow, just let him run. *No one will get hurt that way.* My adrenaline pumped as the same cold, numb feeling in my fingers and lips reached my hands and head as if my body knew the shit was about to hit the fan. Then, out of nowhere, the kid spun around. My gun was already trained on him. We locked eyes for the briefest moment. I remember they were green, clear, and maybe even kind.

"Police, stop, drop the gun!" were the last words I heard myself yell. Then everything went silent again. I felt a thud from my hand region. *Have I been shot? Why didn't I hear anything?* That's when I noticed a stream of smoke rising from the barrel of my pistol.

Suddenly everything returned to normal except the volume in my head, which had been cranked up to max. I stood there, frozen, as the young man, no more than twenty, grabbed his chest and let out a scream of pain so loud and visceral I could feel it pass through my entire being. The cold numbness had now enveloped every cell of my body. I watched in horror as he writhed in agony on the faded, cracked blacktop.

All I wanted was to fall to the ground and suffer for him, but that wasn't possible. I had to stand up and face the situation. Good, bad, right, wrong, justified or not, I had to confront a reality that, at least at that moment, went beyond any rationalization. I had pointed a gun at another human being and pulled the trigger. I had sent a searing chunk of lead to pierce through skin tissue, blow apart blood vessels, and move on to punch holes into vital organs and, ultimately, lodge itself somewhere it had no right to be.

No person or previous event could have prepared me for this. Not my four years in the military or seven on the force. Not my father, my uncle, who were also police, or even my partner, who had shot three men, killing one. Not even the mental movies looping in my mind for years. It was unlike anything I could have imagined. I was all alone on this one.

DEATH = LIFE

MARCUS

Entering the trauma ward at St. Jude Hospital, I trotted towards the emergency surgery area.

Sid and I had been extensively interviewed by department detectives who'd taken my gun and clothing, part of department procedure. Sid had adjusted his version of the truth by stating that, from a distance, he witnessed the perpetrator draw on me first.

"Just stick to the story and it will all work out, kid," he grumbled. "This asshole shot his own stepfather twice, so you don't owe him shit. He's a goner anyways, at least that's what the paramedics said." He grunted under his breath as I contemplated my role in the officer-involved shooting that had just turned corrupt. The victim, the suspect's stepfather, was in stable condition and going to pull through. Unfortunately, the same could not be said for the nineteen-year-old young man I'd shot in the alley.

I'd caught up with Sid just outside the ward where he was talking with the chief surgeon. I couldn't help but suspect he was there in hopes the kid would die. The doctor gave me a nod as I walked up.

"So, Officer …?" He paused, looking at my name tag, not knowing how to pronounce my last name.

"It's Oh-*gah*-bee," I stated.

"Thank you, Officer Ogabi. As I was just telling your partner, the bullet hit the patient's seventh rib and then lodged in his spleen, causing severe hypovolemia. His chances of survival are very low, but we're doing all we can."

Sid's distant voice mentioned something about going to go find coffee. Heaviness invaded my chest as if my heart literally dropped …. It wasn't as if I'd never seen anyone die during my time on the force. But it was different this time. I pulled the trigger. This one was on me.

I took off behind the doctor, through the double doors and into a waiting area in the ward. A woman in her late thirties sobbed uncontrollably. *She must be the kid's mother.* I pressed my fingers against my throat in a feeble attempt to stop the forming lump. Her soiled, ragtag clothing spoke of poverty. Her blackened eye and bruised arms told the anguished life-story of an abused woman living in the East Borough. I secretly hoped it was the work of her son. It was a desperate attempt to alleviate the deep torment of remorse, but my broken heart knew this just couldn't be the case. I wanted to fall to my knees and apologize. I wanted to mend what I had broken and take her pain away. But no words from me would matter, so I didn't attempt to speak any.

There was another person present: an older Hispanic, indigenous-looking woman sitting alone in the far corner. It was hard to tell who she was or what she was doing there. *Maybe his grandmother?* It struck me how unaffected she was by all of it. She just sat there, emotionless, knitting, of all things. But what concerned me most was the look of inappropriate serenity she wore as if all were perfect. I found it oddly fascinating and irritating at the same time, making it impossible not to stare. Yet, even with all of that, I knew she somehow belonged there.

She suddenly pulled her head up from her work with a sigh and looked me dead in the eyes. *This is awkward.* We were locked in a staredown, and I had this crazy idea that, if she continued, she'd know I had done this to her grandson, or whatever he was to her. So, I looked down. When I did look back she had a peculiar smile on her face.

"Hola," she mouthed, in what I imagine was an attempt not to disturb the boy's weeping mother. Confused, I shook my head and gave a subtle serious nod. Then, of all things, she silently giggled.

A bleak silence filled the air and the staff's pace slowed. The boy's mother stood up and faced the surgery room door as the surgeon's staff walked out one by one, their heads down. The distant flatline tone fading in and out in unison with the electric door told me all I needed to know. Every ounce of energy I possessed fell out of me and onto the white tiled hospital floor. The head surgeon walked directly to Dimitri Tanomeo's mother. I watched in horror as she fell to her knees, head hung lifelessly from her shoulders, and a soft moan filled the room.

"We did everything we could" were the last words I heard as I bolted down the hall. Just before turning the corner, I heard the second-most horrific sound of the day. The wailing of a mother who'd lost her son caused my eyes to fill with tears as I darted through the neighboring wards. In my haste,

I ran right into Sid. He knew what had happened by the look on my face.

"What are you worried about, son?" he asked, gnawing at his gum. "He had it coming. Totally justified, just like I said earlier."

I put my head down and moved to pass him. He blocked my exit, put his hands on my shoulder, and stared into my eyes.

"Marcus, pull it together, man. That was good work out there, son. One less, like I always say."

I shoved him aside and continued towards the exit, my vision blurred by tears. I was on the verge of a complete meltdown. I wasn't going to make it to the parking lot. *I'm a cop, no one can see me like this.*

Mercifully, I stumbled across an empty bereavement room. I ducked in, locked the door, put my head against the wall, and sobbed. During the recent hardships of my divorce, I could never cry. I'd begun to wonder if I still could and finally got my answer. I wailed, revisiting the moment during the chase when I thought to slow down, to let him outrun me. I remembered him glancing back at me, what he looked like. He was a tall, fit young man, handsome in a "rough around the edges" kind of way. His brown, wavy hair was long to his shoulders. He was afraid. And though I didn't know what he'd done at the time, I knew he wasn't a hardened criminal.

Overwhelmed by sorrow, one that could only come from the taking of a life, I bellowed, "I'm sorry, I'm so sorry. Please forgive me." My head buried in my hands, I wept for what felt like forever.

In the midst of my anguish, I was startled by a voice whispering in my ear.

"Thank you" was all it said.

I sprung up. The room was empty with the exception of the box of tissues on the table. I grabbed a couple and wiped my eyes.

"Thank you," the voice whispered slowly a second time.

I worried that it was somehow coming from *inside* my head. *Must be from the stress.* I closed my eyes again.

"Marcus, thank you," I heard it say.

My eyes shot open, my attention seized by this bizarre phenomenon. The voice knew my name, it was male, and seemed to have a distinct accent, or at least its own tone. What I mean is the voice was not *mine*, it was clearly someone or something else's.

I'm losing my shit. I gotta get outta here. I wiped my face one last time and opened the door. There was an unusual amount of commotion in the hallway. Doctors, nurses, and other members of the hospital staff were all running toward the emergency surgery ward.

"Dr. Paul D. Jones to Trauma, stat," the disembodied female voice chimed from the hospital intercom. *Same surgeon, same trauma ward.* I began to walk quickly in towards it and, when I turned the corner, I saw Sid standing in the hallway shaking his head with a confused look of disappointment.

My walk became a run. I ran back to the place where a young man named Dimitri Tanomeo had fought for his life and lost. The same place where I felt I'd lost a part of mine.

At the double doors leading into the trauma ward, I grabbed the arm of a male nurse rushing by me. "What happened?!" I shouted.

"The kid came back!" he yelled, hurrying away.

"What?" I ran behind him.

"The kid pulled through. He's back. We don't understand it yet ourselves, but he's alive ... *again.*"

I came to a dead stop in the middle of the corridor. People hurriedly flowed around me. *Am I dreaming?* I hoped with everything it *was* true. I looked down at my legs and willed them into movement. I began slowly as if learning to walk for the first time, then shifted to a slow trot. I stopped just before the waiting area and watched staff enter the double doors.

Now, here's the crazy part. I swear that each time those doors opened, a sort of glowing gold, diamond light radiated from the inside. *No, Marcus, you've just had a hard day. You're seeing things.*

I entered the waiting area where I found myself standing in front of Tanomeo's mother. She was on her knees with her hands clasped together, crying out, "My baby's alive. It's a miracle. My son's alive."

Still feeling like I was in a trance, I looked to the far corner. The older Hispanic woman hadn't changed her composure. She sat, same as before, knitting away with that same grin on her face. She appeared neither happy nor surprised.

I looked down to find my chest moving quickly. I was beginning to hyperventilate and the tears were coming right behind it.

Don't let anyone see you like this. I shook my head, snapping out of the trance-like state, but the emotions continued to flood. I turned to make my way outside for the second time when I saw hospital staff come out of the surgery doors holding up a young female nurse. She was sobbing uncontrollably and having trouble walking.

When I passed them, I heard her say something that would stick with me for the rest of my days: "It was so beautiful. I now see how we are all it!"

I stumbled, glancing back to see her flushed, smiling face covered in tears. That triggered the waterworks in me, and I started moving at a brisker pace towards the exit. I began mumbling, "Thank you, thank you, thank you." I got louder and louder as I neared the exit. "Thank you, thank you!"

I was shouting. This feeling of elation, coupled with the immense relief I felt, trumped all feelings or thoughts of self-consciousness. The glass doors opened in front of me and I burst into the parking lot. I opened my arms wide and stared up at the afternoon sun. I could feel its warmth on my face. It felt like a new day, a new life, as I yelled at the top of my lungs, "Thank you!"

I climbed into my cruiser and sat wondering who I was saying thank you to and what exactly for. No doubt I was grateful for the returned life of this young man, but I was thankful for something else. You see, two people had actually died and returned from the dead that afternoon. I knew that my life would never be the same again.

I dried my face with my sleeve, put the key in the ignition, and, just before I turned it, I heard the voice again. It was clear and, of all the things it could say, what drifted over me were three words I hadn't heard in a long time.

"I love you," it whispered.

Something had just happened to me. Maybe it was good. I wasn't certain, but I sure was curious to find out. This day would be the first day of the rest of my life. For the first time since I was a child, I felt truly alive again.

BENDING THE RULES

MARCUS

"Standard operating procedures, Marcus. Not much I can do about that," my lieutenant stated firmly the following morning as I sat in front of him at his desk. I found myself disoriented after a sleepless night trying to make sense of everything. I still felt the weight of the guilt, but I was also relieved and grateful that the kid had pulled through (or should I say, "come back"?).

"Let's see here," he muttered, flipping through the file. "You've got a toxicology report in the works. The Internal Affairs Division will be interviewing you. It's a clean shoot, so no problems there, right?"

"Yes sir," I mumbled, knowing it might not be one-hundred-percent accurate.

He rattled off a myriad of other things that would follow. I was to be on administrative leave for two weeks, and when I returned, I'd be at a desk job for a while. He talked about the media, how the department was handling them, and strongly suggested that I follow suit. "I have no comment while the investigation is underway" were the only words I was to say.

"I'm ordering a psychological evaluation. Your partner told me you were pretty shaken up by the shooting. So, how are you doing with it all, son?"

I paused for a moment and contemplated how I should answer. Lieutenant Andrew Houser was much more than my superior at work. He was a friend. And not just to me, but my entire family. His wife, Paige, and my wife, Lisa, who I'd recently separated from, were best friends. The truth was, I needed someone to talk to, but the complicated dynamic made that impossible.

"I'm fine, Lieutenant. Really. I'd like to help with the investigation if possible, sir." I tried not to sound too eager.

"Negative, Officer Ogabi," he responded sternly. "You will remain off duty and on leave. You are not to participate in any ongoing investigations surrounding the events of last night, nor are you to go near the crime scene or have contact with any witnesses." He removed his reading glasses and quietly asked, "Are we clear on that?"

"Yes, sir. Crystal clear, sir."

I was walking down the hall to the briefing room when Henry, a fellow officer, shouted from the other side of the corridor.

"Ogabi, good work last night!"

"Thanks, Henry," I replied, wondering what exactly I was being praised for. Surviving a dangerous situation? Protecting the public? Shooting a young man in the prime of his life? Before, had the tables been turned, I might have said the same thing to a fellow officer. But something happened to me after I pulled the trigger and I found myself in a sort of moral dilemma.

Inside the briefing room, all eyes were on me. Several officers made their way over to shake my hand and pat me on the back. I speculated that they were probably relieved that it was a clean shoot and there'd likely be no backlash. Back in those days, there were many questionable and downright dirty police shootings. Numerous officers had lost their jobs. Some even went to jail. There was a level of unspoken solidarity when something like this happened. This unity, originating from genuine concern for a cop, was both reassuring and comforting. Also, within their concern existed a sense of relief, stemming from a kind of self-preservation. An "I'm sure glad he's safe because that could have been me" type of reasoning.

But then I considered that it could be something else, something more disturbing. It goes back to what I was explaining earlier: wondering what it would be like or how would it feel to shoot someone. I knew I wasn't alone with these thoughts. I saw it first in the military with my fellow recruits, many of them chomping at the bit to see action, or engage the enemy. Then there was my own partner, Sid, the oddball who'd at times speak of lowering the crime rate "his way."

I know I could be simplifying a complicated occurrence by leaving out important psychological information that explains this type of twisted thought process. And while this was more a rarity than the norm, my distinct qualification to speak on this lies in the fact that it had just become very real for me. The cause of my current situation could very well have been born from that first, fearful thought—that sick curiosity that caused me to want it, wait for it, then ultimately give into it. Now I was paying for it.

I saw Sid standing by the doorway, arms crossed as he leaned against the wall. He had a strange look on his face. I wondered if he had new information about the Tanomeo kid.

"Hey, Sid, what's up?"

He tried to squeeze out a smile from his bloated, red face.

"Yep, it's your day today, Ogabi. Enjoy it because it's not gonna last. I've shot three, one dead, as you know, and the fame is short-lived, I can tell you that."

I couldn't believe it. He was jealous of the unwanted attention I was receiving. I shook off my feeling of disgust and asked him what he knew.

"Clean shoot, kid. You're off scot-free. Largely due to my help, of course." He gave me a wink. I dropped my head, focusing on my shoes.

"What else? Anything about the shooting at the apartment, the victims, or the perp?"

"Oh, that?" he shot back. "Well, the kid, as you know, is going to make it. They say what happened is nothing short of a miracle, him returning from the dead and all. They're doing all kinds of tests to find out what's what."

"What happened in the apartment?" I asked.

"It looks like the kid got in the middle of a squabble between his mother and her man, the stepfather. He shot him in the gut and the arm, but they're saying the real damage was done to his head and face. I guess the kid pummelled him real good. Stepdad's in the ICU with extensive injuries. They're saying he might lose an eye, and there's the possibility of brain damage as well. The mother's pretty beat up. She's not talking. Says she needs to see a lawyer first."

"What about their rap sheets?"

"All three have them. The stepfather's is a mile long. He's done hard time for battery, extortion, robbery, and attempted murder. Longest stint was six years. The mother's got check fraud and some petty theft stuff, but that was years ago."

I wanted to know more. I was looking for something, anything to help me feel better about what had happened. "What about the kid?"

"What do you think, son? That's East Borough, The Pit. Who doesn't have a record there?" He pulled out a stick of gum and began chewing it. "His is nothing like the stepfather's. He's just starting out, but he ain't clean by any means."

Turns out the young man had been in and out of Youth Authority as a minor, then a short stint in county jail. None of this information was enough to make me feel better about what had happened.

Sid continued, now with a smile on his face. "Of course, he's hit the big leagues now. He'll go away for a long time with all of what happened in the apartment combined with the 'evading arrest' and 'brandishing a firearm at a police officer' charges."

I raised my head. "Here's the thing, Sid, I'm not so clear he aimed at me or if he even had a gun in his hand when he turned around in the alley. It all happened so fast."

The truth was, I hadn't really tried to remember. I suppose I was afraid of what I would come up with.

"Now, Ogabi, don't go gettin' all soft on me!" He lowered his voice and whispered, "I stuck my neck out for you on this one. All you have to do is stick to the goddamned story, and there will be one less punk on the street." He put his hand on my shoulder. "Think about your family, son. We are talking about your career, so get your priorities straight."

I'd heard enough and was moving towards the door when Sid shifted to block my path, a second time within twenty-four hours.

"Son, we are all counting on you to get on board with this thing. There's no turning back now." He checked to make sure no one was nearby and whispered. "Are we going to have a problem?"

I stared back into his eyes. His threatening tone made my blood boil as I pushed past him and stormed out of the building.

I got in my car. The fury was still building inside me, and I was breathing heavily as if I had just been in a fight. The words of hate, corruption, and evil spoken by an empty shell of a man rang in my head. I wondered if those words might be the department's. The "we" he'd spoken of must have been the lieutenant, my father, and uncle. *Are these the world's words?*

I began questioning everything: my life, my beliefs, the department, my family, and even the law. But instead of being defeated or angry, I felt oddly refreshed. I reached down to put the key in the ignition, contemplating if it was even okay to feel these feelings and think these thoughts when the *voice* from the night before returned.

This time it spoke just one word in the faintest of whispers. That one word was "Yes."

HARD KNOCK LIFE

MARCUS

The next morning I slowly drove by the call address. I promised myself I would stay in the car and observe from the street. But within minutes I was breaking the lieutenant's orders, walking down the narrow division between the two buildings where my foot-chase had begun.

The scene of the shooting looked different in daylight—more innocent and much less frightening than that night. Nevertheless, the dark, dried blood, imprinted against the faded blacktop, clearly marked the spot where I'd shot a young man in the prime of his life.

I was transported back to the moment I stood over the wheezing, bloodied young man. I could see him there, lying face-up on the pavement, staring deeply into my eyes. Tears rolled down my face, and I wondered why I still couldn't recall pulling the trigger.

I wiped my eyes and made my way back towards the apartment. I felt a strong pull toward the stoop, where I had seen him for the first time. I knew by entering the crime scene I'd be in direct violation of the captain's orders, putting my already unstable career in serious jeopardy. I let out a sigh of resignation and turned to leave when I noticed an older black man peering through the window of the downstairs apartment. Hesitantly, I approached and was contemplating what to say when I heard myself ask, "Hello, sir. Bridgeton PD. Can I ask you a few questions?" After a long pause, I repeated, "Sir?"

"I hear ya, I heard ya tha first time!" he shouted, opening his door, "I've answered all the damn questions I care to." How many times y'all gotta hear it? I didn't see nothin', nor did Athena. How could she? Been bed-ridden now for years." The door opened, revealing a short but stout, elderly, black man in his late sixties. He had large, rough hands that seemed too big for his body. His face was scrunched together, forging the impression of constant irritation.

"Okay, sir, no problem. Thank you for your time," I said while turning to scurry back onto the sidewalk.

"If you ask me, that boy's stepdaddy got what he had comin' to him," he grumbled, luring me to stay. I turned and took the bait.

"Oh, yeah. Why do you say that?" I inquired, moving closer to his door.

"That sonofabitch been torturin' that po' kid most his life. It's 'bout time he grew a pair and stood up for himself." He waved his hand dismissively. "But I ain't sayin' nothin' and I didn't see nothin' that night. I just wanna make that clear!" He shouted the last part so anyone in the building could hear him.

Sensing he had more to say, I prodded. "Sir, I'd like to ask you a few questions. I'm just trying to get a feel for what's been going on around here in order to understand the motivating factors that led to last night's events." I moved in closer and whispered, "I promise I won't ask you to testify. Strictly off the record."

He stared at me for a long moment, nodded silently, and, after making sure the coast was clear, signaled me to come in.

"So, how about you start by telling me your name so I know what to call you?"

"Cyril," the old man said, "but my friends just call me Cy. I'm the landlord here." I performed a quick scan of his apartment. Of the matching furniture set, one of the sofa chairs had been turned to face the window. Next to it on a small table was an ashtray overflowing with cigarette butts and a half-empty glass of cheap, rose-colored wine. The dingy white curtain was smudged where he'd continually open it, clearly keeping surveillance of the turbulent streets below. Cy was the neighborhood busybody.

"Okay, Cy. My name is Officer Marcus, but you can just call me Marcus," I deliberately refrained from giving my full name. I had crossed a critical line. "Tell me what you know, if you don't mind."

"What I know is a lot," he boasted, taking a seat on the sofa. "I know that kid's been livin' a life none of us would wish for, even on our worst enemy."

"He fought often with his stepfather?"

Cy let out a soft hoot. "Fought? More like had the shit kicked out of him the past fifteen years. Boy's lucky to be alive, I say. Ever since he was little, that fool's been puttin' a hurt on the kid at least a couple times a week. At first, just muffled screams comin' from that apartment up there, sometimes lastin' for hours. Then it got worse. We all could hear it. Beat on 'em so much, musta did some damage. Now he's some kinda retard o' mentally handicapped somethin' o' other, however y'all say it nowadays, seein' how he's walkin' around the neighborhood all slow like. Won't talk to no one but his own damn self. He's just mumblin', laughin' and carryin' on." None of this was what I wanted to hear.

"So he's a mute, but he talks to himself?" I asked.

"Yep. I overhear him sometimes sayin' the agency this and the agency that. He also talks about some imaginary place called Sovereignty Village, or I don't know what. Why, the same day of the shootin', he be across the street over there, his hand on the fence, talkin' to himself for hours. Been like that for years now. Never had no schoolin' and can't keep a job. That bad man musta knocked somethin' loose in there, if you know what I mean." Cy tapped the side of his head.

"Po' Dimitri. He been just livin' day to day, doin' his best to survive. He do what he have to, I suppose. Sometimes when we have leftovers, we leave 'em at his door."

Hearing that Tanomeo was special made me think the court might have mercy on him and put him in a mental institution. *Anything but prison.*

"Sounds rough," I said, shaking my head. "What about his mother? Did she ever intervene?" I wondered how this level of child abuse was allowed to carry on for so long.

"Shiiit, the mother you say? She don't give two hoots 'bout that boy. Or maybe she just too afraid, who knows. That fool, he beatin' on her as well. It's like he takin' turns with them—one day tha boy, then the next, his mother."

"Why didn't anyone ever do something about this? Alert the authorities or something?" I was disturbed by what I was hearing.

His head snapped upward. "Listen here, Officer Popo. You gotta check yo'self. You know where you be right now? You in East Borough, Crown and Nineteenth, niggah. This be Tha Pit. You in the ghetto, boy. Folks here don't 'alert authorities' or get involved in none of that. Folks keep quiet up in here. Especially concernin' someone the likes of that murderin' cracka'. It's all about stayin' alive here in dis hood, niggah!"

I put my hand up in surrender. "I hear ya, I hear ya, Cy. So, what can you tell me about the stepfather? Sounds like a real piece of shit."

"Ah, you don't know?" he asked, throwing his hands up. "This fella here is Eddie The Butcher. Folks 'round here call him tha 'widow-maker,' and for good reason, too. That sonofabitch, he's connected to murders that y'all don't even know about. No, no, no. We all like livin' too much to get involved in that shit."

I'd asked around a bit and understood the severity of the situation. This Eddie character was a cold-blooded killer, a real-life sociopath, and he was connected.

"Just three years back the kid moved down here across from my place so he could get away from it." Cy pointed through the wall to a door on the other side of the hallway. "I converted a storage room into a place for him. Ain't much, but it was a way for him to get out of that situation. Not to mention another hundred-fifty a month in my pocket." He smiled big, seemingly proud of his charitable act. "You wanna hear somethin' real fucked up, Officer … what was it again?"

"Just Marcus, and yes, go ahead."

"Dimitri, he move in, do whatever he have to do to pay me and feed himself. Lord knows he ain't no saint, Officer Marcus. That boy's been in trouble with y'all as well. I'm sure you know that by now." I nodded in agreement. "Anyways, he and I, we go through all of that, and that piece of no-good-shit start comin' down and bustin' into his room just to beat on him from time to time. Now how fucked up is that, I ask you?"

I shook my head. "That's horrible."

A smile grew on Cy's weathered face, and his manner seemed to shift. "But everything changed the other night, oh yes indeed." He stood up straight, his index finger in the air, grinning from ear to ear. "That boy whipped him somethin' good, oh yes he did. There's a new sheriff in town and his name is Dimitri Tanomeo, I say! Oh yes, praise the Lord!"

He was speaking with a new rhythm, almost gospel in tone, seemingly forgetting about anyone in the building hearing him. He clenched his fists and made boxing gestures that were almost cinematic. "That muthafucka finally got his up-n-comin's, oh yes he sure did." He was now in full shadow-boxing mode. "You know, Marcus, I used to be a golden-gloves champion when I was young. Just about that boy's age. That was a long time ago, but I still know a thing or two 'bout the sport, I do."

I waited for him to calm down a bit before I continued. "Cy, do you know what happened in the apartment that night?"

"Shit. I know more than what I told those white cop detectives, I do."

"Would you mind sharing what you know with me?" I asked quietly. Cy looked out the window then came back.

"Hmmmmm, brother, you say this off tha record and all, right?" he whispered.

"That's what I said, and that's what it be, brother," I whispered back. He grinned and nodded, displaying his appreciation that I could speak his language.

"Come take a seat then, and I'm gonna tell you what I saw that night." From his door, he had a clear view of not only the door to the young man's room taped off with yellow police tape but of the stairway leading up to his mother and stepfather's apartment as well.

I sat down and Cy told me everything. "So that night, Dimitri, he'in his room, quiet as usual, when his mama and stepdaddy started fighting upstairs. It was a weekly thing that we all were accustomed to. We could hear the plates and who knows what smashin' against the walls. That went on for a good fifteen minutes. He slappin', she screamin', just like always, folks hearin' it all the way down the street. The boy just stayed in his room, with the door closed, even when she start yellin' fo' help. He knew better—every time he intervened in the past, he'd end up in tha hospital.

"Then, there was a noise like none before. It was a loud thud, but it was the silence that followed that scared the shit outta me. I jumped up, cracked open that door right there just a bit, when I see Dimitri's blow open. He come out wearing only jeans and a mighty pissed-off look on his face. He then flies up them stairs, and all I hear is their door explode and watch as the little pieces of the wooden frame come bouncin' down and landin' right there.

"That's when them two took to brawlin' up there. Every time their bodies hit the wall, the whole building shook, makin' this time different from the past. No, Marcus, this time, it be like an even match, somethin' I neva expected. But then what happened next was the most disturbing thing I ever heard in my life. It be that distinct crackin' sound, you know when one man be hittin' another man as hard as he can over and over again, with no resistance. I knew the boy be gettin' pummeled over and over. I be worryin' for his life. That's when I picked up the phone to call y'all. Then, all of a sudden, the poundin', it just stopped.

"So, I put it down, and went back to the door and cracked it open just a little. I was waitin' to see Eddie come down them stairs, when whatever was left of the door up there blasted open again. I grabbed my baseball bat. I keep it right here just in case that man ever come after me." Cy pointed to an old wooden bat, leaning against the wall. "I just stood there lookin' out and grippin' it tight when I heard the footsteps. I figured he'd killed the poor boy and was now gonna run. I thought about openin' that door and blastin' him in the head when he pass by, but I'm too old for that shit."

Cy's head dropped in discouragement before rising back up with a smile. "So, Marcus, the next thing I see I'll never forget. It was tha boy. Dimitri. He come storming down those steps, his eyes wide open, more clear than I ever seen 'em. He be huffin' and puffin', tha veins in his chest and arms bulging out of his skin. He had this look on his face like a tiger that just killed somethin'. It was a look of victory, I say. And just like that, for the first time in his life, I could see that that boy be free."

Cy shook his head vigorously, holding back the rising emotions.

"I remember thinkin', even if that man upstairs be dead and the kid gotta go away for it, ya know, then so be it. I'm still happy for him." Cy wiped his eyes. "So he gets to his door, right in front of me with blood all over him. His face, hands, and arms … covered in it. But this ain't his own blood—this be the blood of that monster. He took a deep breath, went in, and shut tha door.

"Then there be this long, odd silence, and I look over at the phone, considerin' makin' the call, but then I come to my senses. So, I'm just standin' there waitin' and trustin' in nature to take its course, when I hear some movement up there. And yes, I'm sorry to tell you, it was Eddie tryin' to get to them stairs. But, just by what I can hear, I can tell he be movin' real slow-like, gaspin' for air and all. That's when he turn the corner up there, but, boy, let me tell you somethin', it don't look like him at all. He be completely unrecognizable!

"He just stood up there for a long time leaning against the wall, which be the only thing holdin' him up. Then he spit a tooth out and it come down and land on the last step right by the kid's door. That seemed to piss him off somethin' fierce because that's when he come to take another step down the stairs, still leanin' on the wall, making that bloody smear, before takin' the rest of the trip down head over heels, all the way down. That's when the gun come fallin' out."

"Gun?" I asked.

"Yep, when he be fallin' his pistol musta come out his pants. It just come tumblin' down the stairs, and when it hit the floor, it slid all the way across almost to the stoop."

I breathed a sigh of relief knowing that the gun wasn't the kid's after all. That was the first time I noticed the paradox operating inside my head. A paradox that would continue to work for quite some time. On one hand, I wanted him to be a criminal. That way I could feel good about all that had happened as well as everything that would happen once I went along with Sid's plan. Then, on the other hand, I found myself rooting for him. I wanted to believe he was good, that he'd done the right thing.

"What happened next?" I asked with anticipation.

"Well, that Eddie, he just layin' there on his back starin' up at the ceiling, gaspin' and chokin' on his own blood and whatever else be comin' out of him. I could tell he was givin' it all, just tryin' to muster the strength to pick himself up. He finally made it to his knees and slowly crawled to the gun and picked it up. Then he stood up and made his way to the boy's door, opened it, and stumbled in. The door closed and that was the last I could see."

Cy said that he could hear Eddie mumble something before yet another struggle took place.

"I just knew he was gonna shoot the kid," Cy continued. "And then I heard it ... pop! Everythin' went silent again. That's when I dialed 9-1-1.

"I thought for sure he'd shot the boy. I felt somethin' awful inside me, seeing how he'd just won his freedom from all those years of torture just to end up dead. I was lookin' out the window, waitin' for ya'll to show, when I hear another shot go off. That's when the boy's door open up suddenly and guess who come out? Low and behold, it be the boy, Dimitri, covered in more of Eddie's blood. He musta got the gun from him and shot 'em because he be holdin' it in his hand. He just standin' there, lookin' straight ahead across the street, at I don't know what. Then I reckon he seen tha black and white come rollin' in off of Crown, because he high-tailed his way right outta here."

It was silent for a moment. Cy seemed affected by the recounting and took the break to compose himself.

"That's a hell of a thing, Cy," I said, amazed by the story. "What did you do next?"

Cy chuckled sinisterly. "I snuck out my door real quick-like and spied a look inside the boy's room. Eddie The Butcher be on the floor lookin' real dead. Then I headed back inside, locked my door, and went to tell Athena the good news." He pointed to a closed door which I assumed was occupied by his bedridden wife.

I thanked him, assuring him the information would remain between the two of us. I then asked him for one more favor: that he let me into Tanomeo's room.

I cautiously lifted the police tape as I turned the knob and walked in. "This is a closet at best," I mumbled to myself. There was hardly any light, making it hard to see the chipped grey walls and mold growing in the upper corners. The air in the room felt heavy and dank. It was hard to breathe.

I looked down at the ragged, faded blue carpet and noticed the blood-stains. On the floor in the corner was a thin, worn piece of foam that served as a makeshift mattress. A torn sheet and small blanket rested on top and a rolled-up towel at the head served as a pillow. Next to it, on the floor, was an open pack of Lucky Strike cigarettes with a box of matches stuffed inside.

On the opposite side of the room, clothes were folded in a crate resting on its side. I pulled them out, one by one, starting with the handful of worn and faded t-shirts. I found two pairs of pants tucked toward the back. They, too, were tattered and frayed.

Cut-out magazine photos of smiling children and families covered the holes in the deteriorated walls. When I got to the crates on the other side, I was surprised to see they were filled with books. I took my time sifting through them. Most of the topics, if not all, were esoteric: astronomy, quantum physics, religion, and even philosophy. *These can't be his.*

The more I discovered, the more I began to feel for this person. I was connecting with him. Not through commonality, as is so often the case, but through our disparity. The level of abject poverty he lived in became more real every time I came across one of his very few possessions. The more I imagined what it would be like to live as he did, the more my heart felt heavy. I wondered if I was feeling this out of guilt, as I was about to make his hard life even harder. Or was it that I had food in the fridge, hot water, and a comfortable place to lay my head, while he lived in a musty, moldy hole with a rotting apple, a spoiled carton of milk, and a bucket? I'm not exactly sure why I was so bothered by it. As a cop working The Pit, I'd seen severe poverty, but this was the first time I'd ever *felt* it. It was like, as I stood in that space and held each of his belongings, it was me living his life.

Something etched in the wall close to the head of his foam mattress caught my eye: "I can, and I will, because I am." Perhaps some sort of affirmation. *A lot of good that did him.*

I noticed there was a piece of carpet in the corner of the room slightly detached from the floor. As I pulled it up to reveal old wood flooring, I suspected it could be a hiding place. Opening my utility knife, I wedged it between the cracks of the brown wooden slats until one of them came out.

There it was, a thin, red wooden box hidden within the floorboards. It was held shut by a small lock, so I used my knife to pry off the weak hinge. The box creaked open revealing a large ziplock bag with something soft in it. Opening the bag I could see it was a hand-knit pullover with three buttons leading up to the collar and no tag. The buttons seemed to be made from rustic pieces of cut wood, each one different with a detailed etching on it.

I put the shirt down and a card fell to the floor. I picked it up and read in the dim light:

> Dimitri,
> Le doy este regalo, hecho con amor, para usarlo en tu "día especial."
> Recuerde una cosa, hijo mío:
> Tu puedes, y lo harás, porque lo eres.
> Nana

I brought up the translator on my smartphone to decipher the message: *Dimitri, I give you this gift, made with love, to use on that "special day." Remember one thing, my son: you can, and you will, because you are.*

I took the time to return the pullover exactly as I found it, gingerly patting it down after every fold. This simple shirt, a piece of knitted cloth, seemed to be the young man's most valued possession.

Emotionally exhausted, I got up and walked to the door. I turned the knob but was stopped by an odd sound: a tapping.

I spun around and scanned the room when I heard it again. It was coming from a small window positioned high on the wall. I looked closer and saw a green and red hummingbird hovering just outside. I had never seen one in this part of the city before, and as I walked toward the window, it stayed there as if it was looking at me. *What the hell?* I inched closer. The bird tapped the window once more before flying away.

» » « «

Standing on the stoop, I was surprised to see a small, wooden house directly across the street, sandwiched between a couple of the three-story apartment buildings that lined the entire block. The old house's odd look was enhanced by it being surrounded by a growth of trees and bushes while the other buildings were expanses of gray cement. A colorful garden with a broad variety of flowers bloomed in the front yard and adorned a tiny gated entrance which led to a front patio covered by a dilapidated roof.

The hummingbird was hovering just over the entrance, almost as if it were calling me over. If that wasn't enough, I could swear there was a sort of glow surrounding the whole property. My focus shifted to a person in a rocking chair on the front porch. I strained to get a closer look, and, to my surprise, it was the older Hispanic, indigenous-looking woman from the hospital waiting area, the one who sat there emotionless when the kid died and again when he came back to life. The same one who mouthed "hola" to me, then giggled at the most inappropriate of moments. *I wonder if she is the kid's grandmother?*

My lieutenant's voice rang in my head. *You will remain off duty and are not to go near the crime scene or have contact with any witnesses.*

I considered my job and the consequences of losing it. There would be the wrath of my soon-to-be ex-wife, Lisa, the minute the paychecks stopped rolling in and all the madness that would come with it.

The hummingbird continued circling the front of the house as I realized there were two parts to me: one part was the sane man who knew he shouldn't cross the street; the other just couldn't help himself.

PROPHECY

MARCUS

I stopped at the small gate and cleared my throat to yell when I heard her speak the first time. "The gates are always open, dear one. You just have to choose to walk through them."

What an odd way to invite someone in. I pushed the gate open, straining to see the figure just behind the shrubs. Rose bushes framed the walkway.

"Good morning, ma'am." I pulled my badge as I approached. "I'm a police officer and would like to ask you some questions if that would be alright?"

She ignored my badge and looked directly into my eyes. She wore the same smile as that day at the hospital. "Officer Marcus Ogabi, I have been expecting you. Please come up for a visit if you'd love to, chico mio."

If I'd love to?

I was surprised she knew my name. I suppose the story *was* big news, but I still couldn't help but wonder why she'd been expecting me. I made my way up the rickety porch steps to where she sat, rocking idly, knitting. I went to sit on the wooden bench facing her. "No, over here on this one," she said, and, with the help of her cane, stood and dusted off the rocking chair next to her. "Come on over here and take your rightful seat next to me, hijo." She laughed as if something was funny, but I couldn't tell what it was.

Rightful seat? I stood, perplexed by the oddness of it all. To the side, on the floor planks' worn surface, was a hand-painted pattern: a square encompassing a circle split into four sections. Among the geometry were animals and other crude symbols. The four directions radiated out. At the center were two large footprints. Did they belong to the kid I'd shot?

I was right, she is *indigenous?* Whatever it was, it looked to have been there a long time.

I eased into the rocking chair. We were facing the apartment building across the street, a direct view of the stoop and the young man's window.

I began to rock slowly back and forth, feeling something special. *Is it the porch, the chair, the garden, maybe her?* Whatever it was, I hadn't felt it since I was a child. There was only one word to describe that feeling: home.

For a moment we sat in silence and rocked in unison. *Okay, this is getting weird.* I planted my feet, stopping the rhythmic movement. "So, I'd like to ask you some questions about the night of the shooting." She turned her head to me, smiling.

"No, I don't mind at all, Officer Marcus." Her tone was excited, playful, as if we were to discuss something fun, not the violent acts that ended with her grandson or, at least, neighbor being shot.

"You can ask me anything you want, but you have to agree to just one thing," she said, raising a single finger in the air.

"Oh yeah. What's that?"

Her tone got serious. "You must agree to speak only from authenticity while you are here in my presence." She picked up her yarn and needles and went back to knitting. *In her presence?* Was this condescension or something else?

"Sure, I can do that. I think." I uttered, having no idea what she was talking about. "First off, ma'am, can I have your full name for the record?"

"They say my name is Ana Huya Escavia."

Another puzzle? "Ma'am … Ana … you said they. Who exactly are they, and is that, in fact, your full name?"

"Hijo," she chuckled, "folks call me by many different names, but that would be the name given to me this time around."

I snapped, frustrated by her flippancy. "For me to do my job, I will kindly ask that you take this interview seriously, please, ma'am."

"First, call me Nana, or Ana if you'd like, Officer Marcus," she replied, that same smile on her face. "And second, you have already broken our agreement."

What's her game? "How do you figure?"

"You are not speaking authentically," she responded simply.

"I'm not?" I asked with a raised tone. "To be honest, I don't even know what that means!"

"It means you are not speaking truthfully."

"How? We haven't even started to talk yet!" My reply oozed innocence, but I was worried she might have a point.

She let her bare toes drag against the wooden deck until she stopped rocking. Straightening in her chair, she looked at me sternly. "You said you are here doing your job, did you not?"

I paused and mentally reassured myself there was no way she knew I wasn't. "Yes, I did, that's right," I responded slowly.

"So, you are here doing your job, as you stated before?" She held the smile on her face.

I was dumbfounded. I had spoken to no one about any of it. How could she possibly know this wasn't official police business?

"Ma'am, I am an officer of the law. Would you like to see my badge again?" I fumbled to dig it out of my front pocket, my hands shaking. I knew she could see I was nervous, like a young boy caught stealing money from his mother's purse. She slid back in her chair, relaxing her manner, giving me a short break. It made me feel even worse to know she was playing me while I was trying to play her.

"Hun, call me Ana. And no, I do not need to see your badge. What I do need is for you to try to be honest with me, as well as with yourself for that matter. If you can do that, I assure you we will really get somewhere today regarding your true quest."

My true quest? Do you mean to illegally find out more about the potentially unarmed young man I shot? I shook my head at the ridiculousness of it all before taking inventory of everything I'd said and done that day to ensure there was no way she knew my secret. She spoke again: "When you are ready to state your true motive for being here, I'm ready to listen and assist you in every way I can." Picking up her knitting, she lifted her feet and began to rock again. "So, Officer Marcus, why are you really here?"

I hesitated, choosing my words carefully, replying in an almost scripted tone. "Ana, I am here to interview you and investigate what happened across the street and gather evidence."

She didn't miss a beat, "All true, but what is the evidence for?"

"For?" I asked.

"So far, your statement is true, but in order for there to be complete clarity, would you please enlighten me as to what you are gathering evidence for?"

There was no way I was answering that question. The only option now was to pull the cop card.

"Ma'am, I mean, Ana, from here on out, I ask the questions just like any police officer would and you answer them just like any civilian. Do you think you can do that for me?"

She stared at me for what felt like longer than it was. "Okay, Officer Marcus. I'll play along. It wouldn't be the first time. Go ahead, ask away."

I breathed a secret sigh of relief. "Okay. Great. Thank you. First, are you related to the perpetrator?"

"Perpetrator? Oh, you mean Dimitri?"

"Yes, that's correct."

"Well, Officer Ogabi, then my answer would be yes, I am related to Dimitri."

We're finally getting somewhere.

"And what is your relation?"

"My relation?"

"Are you his grandmother, aunt, or what?"

"All of the above," she shot back, raising her finger for the second time.

My head dropped between my knees in frustration. It was only a moment and I quickly straightened, regaining my composure. "That's impossible. You cannot be all three. So, I ask again: what is your relation to Dimitri Tanomeo?"

"Ah, pues hijo, you see we are all related, as we are all connected. When you ask me a question like that, I must speak from my authenticity."

"Not related," I sternly concluded, acting as if I were taking notes.

"As you wish," she replied calmly.

"I am going to note that you were friends. Would that be accurate?"

She shot up a little in her chair and clapped her hands just once. "Oh yes, Marcus, that would be quite accurate!" she exclaimed giddily.

Oh boy.

"I take it the young man comes and visits you now and then?"

"He finds solace here with me from time to time. And you can refer to him by his name. Can you allow yourself to do that, Marcus? I think Dimitri would like it if you did."

How would he even know if I did? Now it was me that stared at her for an eternity. *Is everything a riddle with this woman?* She rocked effortlessly, absorbed in her handiwork. It was both endearing and worrisome. Was this senility or an early stage of dementia?

"I don't know the young man on a first-name basis, so I'll keep it a bit more formal."

Her feet hit the floor, abruptly ending the rocking. She turned and looked at me directly. "How can you say that, when, in large part, you were responsible for his death?"

Our eyes were locked. I felt a cold numbness in my fingertips.

"You were there. You pulled the trigger. You did that. And you say you don't know him? Hijo, por favor, I invite you to look deeply into this situation with an open heart and mind; there you will find your authenticity."

This is enough. Despite the quickly forming lump in my throat, I stood and spoke. "Listen, lady. I don't know who you think you are, but I'm going to educate you on something! First off, the kid didn't die. Well, not really. I … I mean, he's alive now, and that's all that matters! So I'd appreciate it if you didn't speak to me like that again!" I noticed my pointed finger shaking at the side of her smiling face. She, meanwhile, was once again focused on her knitting.

I started down the stairs. At the base, I turned for a final shout. "Secondly, I was just doing my job. That's what police do, protect and serve. Is there some part of that that you don't understand?" My voice cracked and my eyes began to water. I turned and made my way towards the gate. *Why am I getting emotional over this shit?*

"I understand more than you know, Marcus!" she shouted joyfully. Her voice, faceless behind the vegetation, was that cold person I first saw in the hospital, unmoved even by death. "Protect and serve, you say?" I glanced back to see her silhouette on its feet. "You sure served him up real good, didn't you, papito?"

I stumbled hastily outside, shaking my head in a desperate attempt to clear it. What just happened? Was this woman angry with me for the damage I had caused her friend or was there some deeper meaning behind her stinging words?

"Marcus, wait!" I turned and faced her, the fence and depths of the garden between us. "When you authentically acknowledge and understand the role you played in Dimitri's death, then and only then will you be free of the pain.

"Before you go, let me give you a little clue in your search for the truth and why you actually came here for this 'investigation,' as you've inauthentically named it. There is more than one type of death for humans on planet Earth. You, at this moment, are aware of only one while, at the same time indeed, *at cause* for another. Things are not always as they seem, hijo mio. There is perfection in all process.

"Dimitri is fine, even though you might not be able to see. He is here to be the example of what is possible for all of the world, and you have been chosen to assist him in that endeavor. You are now part of something much grander than anything you could've ever imagined. Bigger than yourself, your job, your family ... and even that thing you consider to be your life. What I speak of is just now beginning to reveal itself. Your instructions will show up when they need to. This is your invitation for awakening, Marcus."

Awakening?

My breathing slowed, my fingers clenching the chain link fence. Was she delusional or was there truth to her words? If she *was* crazy, she possessed a shrewdness I'd never seen before.

"What do you mean, something bigger than I could possibly imagine?!" I shouted. "What kind of example, as you put it, could this delinquent possibly be that would in some way affect the world?!"

Ana responded, "I invite you to experience what it feels like right now to live on a planet filled with love, compassion, and peace. A world of not only sharing in the abundance of this planet's resources but in the collective caring for them as well. A world where all beings are loved through the awakening of unity consciousness. A world in which your daughter, Hope, will not only survive but thrive. *This* is what *he* has been sent here for. To show you all that this kind of world is not only possible but essential to your survival as a species."

How does she know about my daughter? I took a deep breath and let out a long exhale. "That's quite a tall order you've put on this young man. Is he aware of the grandiose plans you have for him?"

"He only knows something within him has changed. It is of great importance at this stage that none of what has been shared here is relayed to him. This includes you meeting me and anything else that comes within these stages of unfoldment. His shifting, as well as his moving into agency, must happen organically so as to not cloud his mind with expectations or unnecessary inquiry."

Shifting? Agency? What's she even talking about? There was a pause. Her shape, hazed by greenery, appeared to be gazing across the street at the apartment building. I walked out and into view. As her silhouette became clear, she glanced at me—only for a second—before shifting her gaze back to the building before her.

"So, lady, you know I'm a cop, right? I have to see things as they *really* are. I'm not sure what world you live in, but if you could see the one I know, you would quickly realize that all of what you just said is impossible. I know this because I experience it, the real world, in real-time, every day—not only on the street with the criminals but everywhere with everyone. The exact opposite of what you spoke of is our reality today. Violence, hate, injustice, and the cruelty and suffering derived from them are rampant. Just turn on the news. It's right there. The world is worse than it's ever been and it's not going to get better anytime soon. It's all around us in the workplace, in our relationships, even in our homes. There's nothing you, I, and especially not a mentally challenged delinquent from the ghetto can do about it!"

At first, I wondered if she'd even heard me. Then that smile slowly returned to her face.

"As I mentioned, there's a perfection buried deep within the chaos you described. Through that disorder will emerge a new paradigm, one that will be recognized across the globe and beyond. The time has come, Marcus. The Phoenix is rising. As hard as it might be for you and others to accept it, Dimitri Cato Tanomeo *is* the instrument. He is the vehicle that will deliver the means to bring this to fruition. He is The One." There was silence as she raised both hands to the air. She bowed her head slightly and shouted, "And so it is!"

Her eyes remained closed and I used their cover to get the hell out of there. I sidestepped, clinging to the little hexagons of the metal fence. My eyes were locked on her hidden pupils. If she opened them, I was sure she'd cast a spell on me.

I guess I can admit it now. … I was afraid. Something about the way she said what she said as if she really believed it. That spooked the hell out of me. I now know what scared me was a deep *knowing*, a hidden truth that my mind wasn't ready to grasp. There was truly something big coming my way.

ALL RISE

MARCUS

Standing outside the courtroom doors, I scanned the hallway in an attempt to identify all the players. Of course, the media was there, several different local stations as well as GNN. I guess beating someone nearly to death, then shooting them twice, then being shot yourself by the police, then dying, and *then* coming back from the dead was considered big news. The reporters tried several times to question me, but I'd been advised to not answer and brushed them off with a repetitive, "No comment."

I saw Sid standing with my father and uncle on the far side of the hallway, all in full uniform. My partner shot me a hearty thumbs up and waited for my response. I felt a twinge of pain in my stomach as I returned a lackluster version of the same.

In the months that passed since the shooting, I'd had plenty of time to reflect on what happened that night. I clearly remembered the kid's gun was, in fact, not trained on me when I'd shot him. In actuality, I distinctly recalled it hitting the pavement before I pulled the trigger. As difficult as it was to acknowledge, I'd shot an unarmed man.

So, here's where it all got tricky and, if I'm honest, downright dirty. In order for my actions to fall under the justified use-of-force statute, the defendant would've had to point the gun at me or have it in his hand as he turned. The prospect of ruining my career, hurting Sid while trying to help me, or even doing time myself all hung on that one important detail.

So, what did I decide to do? I resolved to play along while my partner and others handled the details, transforming my dirty shoot into a clean one. All I had to do was stick to my original statement of not remembering.

Please don't think I hadn't considered coming clean many times. I had. I'd even spoken to my father about it, and all I got from him was, "Just stick with Sid on this one, Marcus." Yes, my own father told me to lie. He somehow justified that my straight life as a father taking care of my child with a respected job was more important than the life of one of the lowlifes on the street. He rationalized that the kid, the defendant, would be better off on the inside where he was fed and somewhat safe from the clutches of his vengeful stepfather. I must say, in a way it made sense to me. At least, I was making it make sense.

While I knew my father's words, as well as Sid's actions, were ultimately for my own good, none of it made it right in my head. Looking back now, it was as if I was on trial. In a way I was. But this was an inner trial. My consciousness was the witness, victim, judge, and jury. And even though I'd resigned myself to proceed with Operation Save My Own Life, I wondered what type of life my co-conspirators and I were actually saving. Living with the burden of regret would be my penance, one that could carry a perpetual life sentence.

On the other side of the hallway, the young man's mother and stepfather sat fidgeting on a marble bench. The cold concrete formality of the Lincoln County Courthouse was a long way from their comfort zone in the slums of the East Borough.

I'd only seen Eddie O'Reilly's past mugshots, but now, after the incident that nearly took his life, he was pretty hard to look at. There was a deep, partially healed crevice that ran from the top of his forehead, past his disfigured nose, all the way down to his upper lip. His unevenly cut hair surrounded the patches of bald spots, exposing several sewn up gashes as well as incision scars from the surgeries performed to save his life. What was not saved, however, was the vision in his left eye, which now remained permanently half shut. I couldn't help but stare as I took inventory of the damages, each one of them representing payment of a long-overdue bill. His stepson, Tanomeo, had turned bill-collector and was now paid in full.

His mother clasped her hands between her knees, yielding to the monster sitting next to her. The short sleeves on her chintzy, blue dress couldn't conceal the fresh bruises on both arms. Her cheap heels clashed with the oversized tan purse that sat half-open on the cold tile floor. I could tell she wasn't accustomed to dressing up but seemed to be making an attempt for this particular day—a day wherein she wouldn't speak up for her son, as she'd requested to be excused from testimony due to the family ties on both ends. The kid would have no one to speak on his behalf, not even the mother he'd saved.

I walked into the courtroom and took a seat three rows behind the prosecutor's desk. I wanted to be able to see the young man without him seeing me. *Maybe he won't even recognize me.* I'd secretly hoped he might have suffered a little amnesia. In all truth, it didn't really matter. The kid was about to be buried by the system, and I was a big part of it. My lying under oath about what happened would make me both grave-digger and pallbearer to a burial that should never have happened.

The bailiff opened the door and the accused walked in. Though he wore a county jail orange shirt and pants, he held his head high. As the bailiff unshackled his feet, the kid scanned the room. Finding his mother, he gave her a soft smile which sent her into tears, covering her face in her hands. After a moment, she lifted her head up to face him, wiping her tears with a handkerchief, and mouthed, "I'm sorry." The shame and sorrow she felt moved through me, and I felt a hard lump form in my throat.

I watched him close his eyes, then open them, a smile returning to his face.

"It's okay," he mouthed and dipped his head and closed his eyes again. I couldn't help but feel admiration. He was a bigger person than I'd ever been.

Then he did something that went beyond explanation. With his eyes still closed, he turned his head in my direction. Suddenly, his eyes shot open, and he looked directly at me with a huge smile on his face. I squirmed as his piercing green eyes burned into me. I looked down at my hands and then back up, hoping the staredown had ended. It hadn't.

Irritated by the developing scene, I shrugged my shoulders, hands turned upward as if to say "What's up?" The grin on his face expanded, and his mood shifted from content to elated.

Oh no, what have I done? I turned away, doing my best to ignore him. That's when I noticed Sid, my father, and the prosecutor observing the whole interaction from two aisles over. I looked back to find the kid bowing at me. He followed it up with a joyful, "Hello, Marcus!"

I was mortified. I turned back to see Sid and the others shooting suspicious looks. I put my hands up and mouthed, "I am just as confused as you guys." Glancing back at the young man, I found him quietly cracking up, amused by the commotion he'd caused. My face felt hot. I wiped the sweat from my brow, knowing that we were in for one hell of a trial.

"All rise!" The bailiff's voice bellowed as the judge entered, drawing my attention from the antics of the defendant. As the judge gave the jury their instructions, I watched the defendant, Tanomeo, who seemed amused by it all, smiling and chuckling to himself for no apparent reason.

It was then that I noticed the person in the chair behind him. It was Ana, the woman in the rocking chair from the old house. *Impossible. How did she just appear like that?* Looking closer, I saw that she was speaking to the back of the kid's head while he sat still, looking straight ahead, occasionally nodding. *Am I the only one seeing this?* Courtroom regulations strictly prohibit communication between the defendant and the public, family or otherwise, during the proceedings, especially when the judge is speaking. *Why isn't the bailiff doing anything about it?*

During the opening statements, the prosecutor painted a picture of a violent, lowlife hoodlum who hated his stepfather and would do anything to get rid of him. This resulted in the several charges brought against him including mayhem and attempted murder. A thug so desperate and reckless that after an unsuccessful attempt to evade arrest, he would aim his firearm at a police officer, only to be shot himself. The prosecutor's name was Pamela Howitzer, and her job was to create a scenario that would convict and sentence the accused to the maximum time possible. By demonizing him, she was doing just that.

Then there was my job, which was to lie. "I can't remember, it's all still a blur" was all I had to say and let Sid fill in the blanks with *his* lies. Our trumped-up charge of brandishing a firearm at a police officer would, alone, add years to a likely already long sentence. The inevitable judgment, on top of his injuries and, you know, dying and all, created a feeling of remorse that was almost unbearable.

Before the trial, I even tried to justify my actions by studying his rap sheet over and over in an attempt to find something to make him a monster. By the looks of things here, he wasn't a monster at all. And although his sheet was long, most of it was small stuff: shoplifting, vagrancy, and a charge of "defrauding an innkeeper" for which he served less than a month in county jail. These were all crimes of survival. "Homeless crimes," as Sid would call them. I then resorted to calculating the crimes I *imagined* he'd committed and gotten away with. I even counted ones he might eventually commit if he stayed on the streets. As twisted as it sounds, it kinda worked. I was ready to lie.

After the prosecutor finished, the judge called the defense to deliver their opening statement. There was just one problem: there was no "they." There was only him. Dimitri Tanomeo had requested to act as his own defense, a move considered utterly illogical and self-destructive in the legal arena.

Tanomeo stood and moved towards the center of the courtroom. There was an air of confidence to his walk, or maybe it was his *way* of walking. He seemed at ease despite where he was. I'd even go as far as to say he was comfortable in what, for most of us, would have been the most uncomfortable of situations.

"Thank you, Your Honor, Madam Prosecutor, members of the jury, and all present today," he announced, politely bowing to everyone in the courthouse. "Today, I am given the most challenging of tasks. You see, I must show you that, during the night in question, when certain horrible, violent crimes occurred, they were not, in fact, committed by the defendant, Dimitri Tanomeo, himself." He paused as the judge raised his hand.

"The court would like to ask if the defendant will continue referring to himself in the third person throughout the trial so as to make note of it on record during these proceedings," the judge intoned.

The defendant, Tanomeo, placed his forefinger to his mouth as if considering the question deeply. "The self-represented counsel for the actual and true Dimitri Tanomeo, who is myself, will continue to refer to the alleged actor of any event that occurred during or before the night in question as 'the defendant.'" The judge stared at him, putting together the hail of words. Tanomeo caught on. "So, that would be a yes, Your Honor."

The judge, as well as the rest of us, paused to study the young man of nineteen who'd just addressed himself as his own self-appointed counsel in a rather literate fashion. So literate, it made me second guess Cy's initial description of the young man. He certainly didn't appear mentally challenged or "slow" as the old man suggested. Crazy, possibly, but he wasn't slow. I glanced at my father. He was already looking at me with one eyebrow raised. In an attempt to show solidarity, I shook my head, signaling my disapproval even though I was, I admit, intrigued.

I noticed Ana quietly chuckling at me. It was as if she could read my hypocrisy.

He went on, "So, you might be asking yourself how the heck is the counsel going to prove they were not committed by the defendant? Surely you will soon see a plethora of physical evidence placing the defendant at the scene with the proverbial smoking gun in hand. DNA blood samples will connect the dots revealing his involvement in these heinous acts that almost killed a man, leaving him disfigured and blind in one eye." He pointed to his stepfather who sat motionless in the back of the courtroom, shooting the defendant, Tanomeo, a cold, dead stare only a genuine killer could possess.

"Just looking at the victim's face," he continued, "the defendant's stepfather, one can concur that the aggravated assault charges, as well as mayhem, seem reasonable. We must consider the brute force and merciless intention one would have to exercise to cause this measure of damage." *Why is he burying himself like this? Either he wants to go to prison, he has something up his sleeve, or he's completely out of his mind. Maybe Cy wasn't that far off.*

Tanomeo suddenly spun and pointed towards Sid.

"Why, we even have with us today one of the city's finest, ready and willing to bear witness to the claim that the defendant attempted to kill one of their own."

Sid straightened up, crossing his arms. His already-puffy, flushed face was getting redder.

"So, back to the original question. How then, with all of this damning evidence, am I—excuse me, is the *counsel* for the defendant going to prove that the crimes in question were not, in fact, committed by him?" He paused for a moment before advancing toward the jury. "By demonstrating that the *true* Dimitri Tanomeo was not present that evening, therefore making it impossible for him to have committed these crimes."

With that, he walked back to his desk.

The judge stared silently a moment. "The court would like to know if the defendant is heading towards a not guilty by reason of insanity plea and, if so, please make that clear for the record once and for all." The courtroom erupted in laughter, forcing the judge to slam his gavel and call for order.

Again, the defendant brought his finger to his mouth.

"As for an insanity plea …" he spoke with a voice of self-assurance and authority. "With insanity being such a complex topic, let us first reveal the actions behind the actions that led to this awful tragedy. Because that is where its own distinct tragedy lies as well. A tragedy I plan to uncover today in this courtroom. So, my answer to your question is no, Your Honor. I plan to leave the delicate distinction of sanity versus insanity in the very capable hands of our astute jury." With that, he concluded his opening statement. The entire courtroom was in a state of utter confusion.

» » « «

Sid was first up to testify on behalf of the prosecution and, of course, he lied, just as he said he would. He started by recounting the events of the evening in great detail. He was truthful right up until the moment before the shooting, at which point the story moved fully into the realm of fiction.

Sid had perjured himself in a court of law. It was a crime that carried a hefty penalty and immediate expulsion from the police force, and he did it without blinking an eye. The defendant remained unaffected, sitting with that same content grin as if nothing could stir his peace.

Moving into cross-examination with the same serenity, Tanomeo approached the witness stand. "You stated you were in the patrol car when you saw the accused pull his gun on Officer Marcus Ogabi, did you not, Officer Prits?"

"That's right. I sure did," Sid fired back.

"You also stated that you were parked nearly one hundred yards from the incident. Would you not agree that your visibility was hindered not only by distance but by the plants located in said alleyway?" The defendant turned over a whiteboard containing a schematic of the street and alleyway where the shooting occurred. Everything was drawn out by hand, right down to the location of the bushes, their heights, and the streetlights and direction of the light they cast. The trial had barely begun, and he was already able to place doubt in the jurors' minds.

But Sid wouldn't have any of it. He stuck stoutly to his story. "I know what I saw and that was you turning to shoot my partner with your gun pointing at his head."

Tanomeo turned and looked at the judge, who promptly spoke up. "I will ask that the witness use the corresponding terminology when referring to the defendant. Do we need to go through this again, Officer Prits?"

Sid crossed his arms and shook his head. "No, Your Honor. I got it."

Tanomeo smiled and jumped right back in. "The two of you have been working together for how long?"

"Four years."

"Not a new partner by any means. How would you say your relationship is with him?"

Sid nodded with pride. "Our relationship is solid. It's a war out there, and we have to rely on one another, watch each other's back."

"Oh yes, I'm sure you do. Would you say you'd do anything for him? Anything necessary to 'win the war,' as you call it?"

I started to feel nervous, knowing where the kid was going. The problem was that Sid didn't. He was never the smartest guy in the room, though, at times, he liked to think he was.

"I'd do anything for my partner. I'd take a bullet for him if I had to."

"Yes, I'm sure you would, Officer Prits. Thank you for making that clear." Sid fell right for it. The defendant had cleverly discounted Sid's testimony by suggesting collusion between Sid and myself.

"Officer Prits, I have another question. Have you ever shot anyone before?"

The first of what would be many objections shot up, as the prosecutor claimed that the witness was not on trial, thus making this line of questioning immaterial. The defendant assured the judge it was indeed relative, and the objection was overruled.

I watched Sid's temperature rise having to admit to "a hoodlum" that he had shot someone. But the defendant didn't stop there. He wanted to know how many and, after a few more sustained objections, the judge ordered Sid to respond.

"I've shot three men in my tenure with the force." The courtroom stirred and the defendant clapped his hands together loudly.

"Hot dog! Three! Wow! I would have thought one, maybe two, but three. … That's a heck of a thing!"

Another objection sounded and the judge ordered the jurors to disregard the last words of the defendant on the basis of conjecture.

"Just a few more questions, and then we'll be finished," the defendant patronizingly reasoned, Sid's face turning redder with every word.

"You can ask me anything you want, punk. Because at the end of the day, I'm going home and you're going to prison." The judge beat his gavel one time, authoritatively, as the jurors stirred in their seats.

"Okay, let's try again. Officer Prits, concerning the three men you shot, what is the condition they are in now?"

"Their condition? They're criminals. As always. Nothing ever changes that." Sid was barking his answers. "You should know, Tanomeo."

Another blast of the gavel and the judge pointed his finger sharply at him. Sid lowered his head and raised his hands in submission as the defendant laughed and shook his head.

"No, Officer Prits. I mean what condition are they in now, in the physical sense, after the shooting. Are they okay? Any damages?" The jurors quietly chuckled. Sid was the only one who didn't get the joke he'd just become the butt of.

I watched the prosecutor toss up objections and the skillful defendant knocked down each one. Ultimately, he'd argued a bit more leeway from the judge and proceeded to rattle Sid's cage like few had before.

"Would you like me to repeat the question, Officer Prits?" the defendant asked plainly. "I can explain it to you more clearly if you'd like."

Livid with anger, Sid took a deep breath. "Of the three men, one fully recovered and the other walks with a limp."

"Excuse me, Officer. You said there were three, but you've only spoken of two. The other?"

Sid's skin tone was now a light shade of purple and sweat—almost certainly alcohol-scented—poured down his face.

"He didn't make it," Sid mumbled before the judge ordered him to speak up. "He didn't make it!" he yelled out.

By now the courtroom was rumbling. Tension filled the air as the defendant, in the role of an attorney, continued pushing buttons, unraveling a man who I had thought unshakeable. "He didn't make it, you say? You mean you killed him?"

"Yes, that's right, I killed him. He's dead. One less, like I always say. Is there anything else you'd like to know?"

Sid had just played into the defendant-acting-as-counsel's strategy. I hoped that it would end soon, as this man, my partner, had reached his limit and was about to explode.

"Well, since you asked ... I would like to know something else."

The judge interrupted: "The court advises you to proceed very carefully. Finish this with as little disturbance to my courtroom as possible."

"Noted, Your Honor."

He went on to inquire about the boy Sid had shot dead. Sid had shot him outside a store he'd just robbed. I knew all about it even though it happened before I joined the force.

"The case against me was dropped. I won. Clean shoot. There's no controversy in that."

"You won? A twenty-one-year-old man, just starting his life, with no priors or gang affiliation, gone. What a victory indeed, Officer Prits."

The judge spoke up to reprimand the defendant before the objection from the prosecutor was even heard.

"I'm sorry, Your Honor. I'll finish up now." The defendant turned back towards the witness. "Isn't it an interesting coincidence that you were the only one to see the shooting in the alley with Officer Ogabi as well as the only witness to your own shooting wherein you were exonerated due to lack of evidence? The only one who can put the gun in the defendant's hand, thus making your partner's actions a 'clean shoot,' is you?"

"Yep, and what about it?" Sid sneered.

"Well, to put it bluntly, you've both controversially shot young men in their prime of life and, in both cases, you were the star witness. I'd say, today, you are showing that you really will do anything for your partner including perjuring yourself."

Sid jumped over the witness stand, knocking the microphone to the floor. Tanomeo simply took a large step back as if the whole thing was planned out in his head. The bailiff struggled to restrain Sid as he spat threatening vulgarities at the young man who had successfully pushed the veteran officer to his breaking point.

"I have no further questions for the witness at this time, Your Honor," the defendant called out while leisurely strolling back to his desk. I looked over at Ana, her eyes on her knitting, faintly smiling and shaking her head.

Who was this young man whose every move seemed calculated and with distinct purpose? I worried that our plan might unravel and wondered what would happen if he was allowed to continue. I prayed that I'd be safe as long as I stuck to my story, my not remembering.

» » « «

I checked under the bathroom stalls, making sure I was alone.

"You can do this, Marcus," I said to my reflection after splashing water on my face. *What you really need is a drink.*

As I dried myself off, my phone vibrated in my pocket. I pulled it out to see Lisa's name on the screen. *That's the last person I should be talking to right now.* Bad news from her could only hurt, not help.

I turned the phone off and took one last look deep into my eyes. "Piece of shit," I mumbled as I threw the paper towel in the trash and walked out.

» » « «

After a short recess, wherein the judge met with the defendant in the holding area, the prosecutor called me as her next witness. I could feel the defendant's eyes on me, smiling, as I walked past. While being sworn in, I wondered what kind of punishment lay ahead for me in the afterlife as I prepared myself to break my promise "to tell the truth and nothing but the truth, so help me God."

As I stuck to the story. I told how I'd seen the defendant, gun in hand, on the stoop. Then, in detail, I went over the foot chase down the alley. I was surprised at how easy it was to lie. At least the words came out easy. It didn't help that, on the inside, shame hung on my shoulders like a dark, damp coat. I thought about my daughter and what kind of person she'd grow up to be. I wondered what she'd think of me, at nineteen, the same age as the kid, knowing I'd just lied about something that would gravely alter his already tortured life. Hell, I knew what she'd think right now at six and it wasn't good.

Once the prosecutor had finished, I remained on the stand for cross-examination, sweat beading on my forehead. Tanomeo slowly rose from his chair and walked towards me. He was looking into my eyes again, this time with no smile. "Officer Marcus Ogabi, nice to officially meet you. I have wanted to make your acquaintance for some time now. Too bad it has to be under these most unfortunate of circumstances."

"Let's get to the questioning, Mr. Tanomeo," the judge interrupted. "And remember what we talked about in the holding area."

"Yes, of course, Your Honor." He answered humbly. "Officer Ogabi, you said you don't remember anything after the point that the defendant stopped running in the alley that evening, did you not?"

"That would be correct." I knew to say as little as possible, so as not to fall into the same trap as Sid.

"How is it that one can stop remembering an event so important? Important not only to one's own internal *knowing,* if you will, but also important in that these facts could greatly affect the future of another human being's life?"

I looked towards the jury, avoiding his eyes as much as possible. "I couldn't tell you. I just forgot. Like I said before, it must have been some kind of shock due to the traumatic experience."

"Traumatic indeed. You must have really gone through a lot that evening." He chuckled and, without turning around, boldly pointed back at the prosecutor, anticipating the objection.

As the judge sustained his objection, I studied the jurors' faces. They all stared me down as if they'd figured me out.

"Sorry, Your Honor. So, Officer Ogabi, let's talk about what you *do* remember. How about that moment just before the defendant stopped running. Do you recall what was going through your mind?"

I paused a moment, then responded with the truth. "I realized that it was just you and me. Excuse me. The defendant and myself. I knew whatever was going to happen was probably going to happen very soon."

"Okay. May I ask if you were feeling any fear at that moment?"

"Fear? Yes, I believe anyone in my position would have felt some kind of fear. It's that fear that can keep you alive," I answered.

"Yes indeed. And sometimes fear can also cause us to make errors, is that not so, Officer Ogabi?"

He was trying to box me in, as he had done with Sid. "Yes, I imagine it could."

"One more thing, Officer. What were you feeling as you watched the defendant 'writhing on the ground screaming in pain,' as you put it in your previous testimony?"

"Objection, immaterial to this case!" the prosecution shouted.

"I'm going to let it through," the judge said earnestly. "Officer Ogabi, please answer the question."

Now, what was I supposed to say? If I said I felt nothing, I would be a monster in the eyes of the jurors. If I told the truth, I might fall into some kind of trap. I figured I had lied enough for one day.

"I felt bad for him. I wanted him to not feel the pain he was feeling."

"Thank you, Officer Ogabi, for that bit of honesty. I have no further questions."

TRUTH BE TOLD

MARCUS

Blood DNA and other physical evidence put the defendant in the apartment where the violent crimes were committed. Add to that being in the alley, gun in hand, and running to avoid capture, and it was all very damning. All the prosecutor needed was a motive to solidify her case. That's what she hoped to get from Eddie The Butcher O'Reilly, the only witness to what happened that night in the apartment building.

All of this was hard to watch since I knew the truth. In a fair world, both Cy and the kid's mother would testify, showing a very different side of a very tragic story. Then there was my lying, which made an already-biased situation worse. The system's purpose was to solve crimes and bring about justice, and with the limited information it had on this one, it was about to fail miserably.

While being sworn in, Eddie The Butcher peered at the defendant. It was plain to see that the visceral hatred towards his stepson stretched back in time, well before the evening that left him permanently disfigured.

The prosecutor asked the witness to recount the incidents of the evening when he was found by the police on the floor of the defendant's apartment beaten to near death.

"The last thing I remember I was walkin' down the stairs. I musta fallen or somethin', ya know?" he stated sarcastically in a street accent.

The judge intervened, telling him he was obligated by law to give true testimony only, as the contrary could land him in jail.

"Yo, Your Honor, really, I don't remember nothin'! If I did, I'd gladly tell ya."

But I knew different, just as the judge and the prosecutor did. Even though Eddie was subpoenaed as a witness, forced by the power of state law to testify, there was no way he'd ever say a thing. Eddie came from the same streets as me. There, he's what is known as "being connected." Connected to an alliance of men who run those streets, recognized by most as the Mafia. When there's a problem, it's taken care of directly or within the group. They live by a code, and in that code nothing—and I mean *nothing*—is handled through the legal system. At the end of the day, this man, Eddie The Butcher O'Reilly, would just as soon be locked up for perjury than assist the enemy in obtaining their goal in any way. To do so could cost him his life.

The prosecutor had to push him in hopes he would break. She moved over to her whiteboard.

"You say you received these damages to your head and face falling down a flight of stairs. You don't remember a thing. Maybe you can explain to the court how it is that, according to the forensic evidence, you were actually in your upstairs apartment when you received the initial damages to your head and face. Then, somehow, you appeared in the defendant's apartment with two bullets in you." She paused for a moment so it could sink into his damaged skull. "Would you care to reconsider your testimony, keeping in mind that you are still under oath?"

Eddie scratched at one of the scars on his head, looking confused by her words.

"Listen here, lady, I don't know nothin' about your forensic evidence or your time chart on that board right there, but what I do know is this: sometimes I drink and, when I do, I get drunk. And when I'm drunk, I don't remember half the shit I do. That night, all I remember is I fell. Who knows what happened before or after." He smiled. "Yo, there's somethin' happenin' here that's really interestin' to me. ..."

"What's that?" she replied.

"Well, you here pressin' me and pushin' with threats of goin' to jail and all. But what I notice is that when it's one of your own up here, *a white colla'*, forgettin' shit just like I do, well then it's *no problem*." He paused and looked at the jurors. "That's pretty fucked up in my humble opinion, right?" The courtroom rumbled as the judge loudly scolded the witness for his use of profanity.

The prosecutor asked about his relationship with the defendant, his stepson, and if he could think of any reason he might have been motivated to hurt him.

"My relationship with D? Well, it's a bit complicated. We don't always see eye to eye. As far as him doin' somethin' to me goes ... naw, D's not capable of hurtin' no one. He's soft. Always been that way. Got too much of his father in 'em. Why he'd cry himself to sleep at night, sad because he never really got to know his old man."

He looked at Tanomeo. "I told him it was better that way. His father was yellow, a real candy ass." His heartless and cold-as-ice tone confirmed the things Cy had told me about this man. "And believe you me, I've tried to toughen him up. You know, get his father out of him. But when a boy's soft, he's just gonna stay that way."

I looked at the defendant's table. The young man remained impervious to the insulting words of his stepfather.

"No more, for now, Your Honor." The loud slap of a file tossed against the desk sounded throughout the courtroom as the prosecutor plunked into her chair.

The judge called for cross-examination. The defendant, head down, approached the witness stand, avoiding eye contact.

"You stated earlier, during the prosecutor's questioning, that you couldn't recall what happened that night. You were so drunk that you couldn't remember, is that correct?"

"That would be correct, Dee Dee." Eddie turned to address the jury directly, laughing, "He hates it when I call him that. I only use it when he acts like a little girl, like now."

The judge gaveled and instructed the witness to stay on topic. The young man, seemingly not affected by the insult, continued calmly. "Since your drunken stupor, were you able to remember beating your wife on the night in question?"

The prosecutor objected, claiming the witness was being badgered. The judge overruled and asked Eddie to answer.

"Do I remember beating my wife, your mother? No, I do not. But you could just ask her. She's right over there." He pointed to where the defendant's mother sat biting her nails. "Oh, wait a minute. No, you can't because she requested to not be asked to testify. Mmmm ... I wonder what that means." He sniggered. "It's like we've got a mom here, and she don't want to testify in her son's trial. I gotta ask, where's the motherly love?"

I saw the jury exchanged glances as Eddie laughed. The judge put his finger up in warning and Eddie continued sinisterly, "So, no, I can't seem to recall beating on her. What else you got for me there, sonny?"

"What about the defendant? Do you recall ever abusing him in any manner?" Tanomeo asked.

Eddie looked around and loudly whispered, "Well, you know, sometimes when a boy gets out of line, you gotta discipline him a bit."

"Could you describe for the court what 'a bit of discipline' looks like?"

Eddie looked around the courtroom. He was growing irritated with his stepson's questions.

"'Looks like,' Dee Dee? What happened to you? Actin' like a big shot. Talkin' about yourself like you ain't here?"

"The witness will answer the question," the judge ordered firmly.

"I had to give you, or 'the defendant,' an occasional ass-kickin' here and there at times. That's what it looks like."

Tanomeo didn't take his eyes off his stepfather. "What I would like to know is, how does your definition of 'a bit of discipline' fit into the systematic torture of a young boy starting at the age of five and continuing into his late teens?"

You could hear a pin drop as all eyes turned on Eddie. "Before you answer," Tanomeao continued, "please, if you would, could you explain to the court what kind of human being considers this an occasional ass-kickin'?"

That's when Tanomeo did something none of us there ever expected or would soon forget. He turned to the jury, raised his hands over his head, and pulled off his shirt. A series of gasps erupted from the jury box, followed by loud murmurs as he slowly turned, presenting something to the courtroom none of us had ever seen in our lives.

The judge loudly beat his gavel, ordering the defendant to cover. But it was too late. There we sat, most of us heartbroken, looking at what appeared to be over a hundred cigarette-burn scars covering his upper torso. Only then would Cy's words become real for me. *Muffled screams coming from the apartment up there, sometimes lastin' for hours.*

After the courtroom returned to order and the bailiff helped the kid put his shirt back on, the judge threatened to hold the defendant in contempt if he pulled another stunt like that again. After apologizing to the judge, the defendant continued with his questioning of the man who'd just become a monster to every person in the courtroom.

"I ask the witness, could you please explain to us all what a young boy could do, or how he could be, so 'out of line,' as you put it, to deserve one hundred and nine of these types of 'ass-kickin's'?"

Eddie The Butcher sat unmoved, stone-faced. The prosecutor didn't bother to throw any objections, only fumbled through her file box on the floor. The defendant's mother sobbed alone while the women in the juror's box passed tissues to one another.

The defendant adjusted his shirt. "If there is to be no answer from the witness to my inquiries, then I have nothing further, Your Honor."

The courtroom went dead quiet, all attention directed at the witness stand.

"Yo, I got nothing more for ya. That kid will say or do anything to save his own ass. We're done here. I invoke my right to the fifth amendment so as not to incriminate myself in any matter, within this trial, or any other possible future trial."

The courtroom remained silent. We all, including the judge, watched in disturbed awe as this low-level street thug somehow knew the rules of the game, how to play it, and, ultimately, take himself out of it.

I looked over at Ana. Like before, she sat knitting, immune to it all.

The judge called a recess, and I quickly exited the building. My father and Sid were waiting for me at the end of the hall. I acted as if I hadn't seen them and turned to take another way out. I just wanted to be alone.

» » « «

Reconvened, I watched in disbelief as the stenographer read back the previous exchange and the judge instructed the jury to disregard a large part of it. He said they were there to try the case against the defendant Tanomeo only and they were to remove those moments from their ultimate decision. *How can you make someone unsee a thing they just saw?*

The judge asked if either side wished to recall any witnesses to the stand.

The defendant glanced at me while Ana, again illegally, whispered in his ear. I did my best to become invisible, sinking my hands deep into my pockets, literally crossing my fingers. *Please don't call me back up.*

"I'd like to recall Officer Marcus Ogabi to the stand, Your Honor," he said, looking directly at me with a smirk on his face. I glanced over at Ana, who had the same smug smile though her eyes stayed on her knitting.

Sitting at the witness stand, the judge reminded me that I was still under oath. I began to feel nauseous.

"Marcus Angbo Ogabi. Did I pronounce that right?" The defendant asked, accentuating my middle name.

I nodded.

"Your name. It comes from the Nupu tribe in Africa, your ancestry, is that correct?"

I paused, puzzled that he'd even heard of the virtually unknown, long-lost tribe. "Yes, that is my ancestry, but how do you—"

He nodded. "I have some familiarity with them and their belief system. Excuse me. Their system of *knowing*. Are you aware of the great text The Itatagohbe Nanbar? A sort of bible of the Nupu?"

I was in awe. The kid had more than just a little familiarity with the subject. He knew the distinction between a belief system and the Nupu's *knowing* of the truth.

"Yes, I am quite knowledgeable regarding the lineage as well as the customs of my ancestors," I replied. "My grandfather was a translator of the great text, as his father was the n'ganga of their tribe. My grandfather began showing me the path of our people when I was nine years old and continued until the day he died."

"Ah yes. Nine years old is when the Nupu introduce their children to yaninga. I assume you are aware of that word, Officer Ogabi?"

The prosecutor jumped in with another objection, arguing that this had nothing to do with the case. I took the opportunity to glance at my father. I found his eyes were already on me, wide open, sharing in the disbelief. *Where is this kid going with this?* I knew us both to be thinking.

I faintly heard the judge say he'd allow it and came back to the witness stand.

"Yaninga, or *ninga* for short, I was saying, Officer. Do you know that word?"

I took a moment, searching my mind for the exact translation. "Yes, if I remember correctly, it is the word for 'honesty.'"

He nodded. "Well, yes, but the word's actual meaning is a bit more elaborate than that. I will be paraphrasing here, so forgive me ahead of time. The word actually breaks down to the concept of the blissful state of living a life in complete authenticity, i.e. heaven on earth, which is the natural order of all life itself. The teaching goes on to explain that, by living this way, one can deter *ubaya* from settling in. *Ubaya*, as I'm sure you know, is the fall of humankind."

"Yes," I stammered, not fully over the shock. "In other religions, it would be considered the darkness, evil, or living in hell."

"Precisely," the defendant beamed. "The teaching tells us that ubaya comes to visit all people in the false illusional world of matter or the physical world. This false world, ubaya, exists in the shadows and appears only when one chooses to live outside of yaninga, one's complete authenticity, or perhaps a better phrasing is 'our true nature.' So, yes, Officer, according to the text, truth and honesty are at the forefront of the teachings and, essentially, the gateways to peace on earth."

I simply stared at him. I was stunned by hearing this short, precise description of the great text. The text my grandfather once proudly followed, taught to the family, and would share with all others who were curious. It was like meeting the one other person in the world who spoke the same language as you.

"How did I do?" Tanomeao asked with a grin. *This kid's not only smart, he's cocky as well.*

I didn't know what to answer. "Yes, very accurate" was all I came up with as I hid my shaking hands under the table.

The judge chimed in, "All very fascinating indeed, but what does any of it have to do with this trial, Mr. Tanomeo?"

"All will be clear soon" is all he told the judge before repositioning himself to stand directly in front of me.

"Officer Marcus Angbo Ogabi, I invite you to go back to the evening in question. To the alleyway where you and the defendant, myself, saw each other face to face for the first time. Please take a moment, close your eyes if you'd like, and do your best to remember. And more than anything, I invite you to speak from your authenticity. Because, Marcus, if you accept your grandfather's teachings, then you know that the only way out of ubaya is through yaninga."

I closed my eyes and, at that moment, something happened inside. My body felt electric as if every one of the hairs on it were standing on end. It was like getting the chills, but beyond any chills I'd ever experienced. My mind became completely lucid, something I hadn't remembered experiencing before.

I went back to the scene with Ana on the porch that day. I remembered her use of the word "authenticity" while trying to convince me to speak the truth. I opened my eyes and looked at her. She was sitting straight up, her eyes penetrating deep into mine. She wasn't smiling.

This is no coincidence. I remembered my grandfather who I loved so much: a great man who never lied to anyone or spoke a negative word, ever. He lived life in a way that was respected by all who knew him. "If you ever find yourself in ubaya, Marcus, just be true and speak only from your heart. From there you will find your way back home," I remember him telling me once.

Everything went into slow motion as I looked over to my father. His head was down. He too had been affected by this young man. A stranger who seemed to speak of truth and wisdom just as my grandfather, my father's father, once did.

My father raised his head and did something I hadn't seen him do since I was a child. He placed the top of his four fingers under his chin and looked up at the ceiling. It was the sacred petition of *yaninga* for the guidance of mind, a customary ritual used by our ancestors. Until now I'd forgotten all about it. My uncle looked at him and did the same.

I closed my eyes as a single tear, one of both joy and sorrow, rolled down my face. This young man had just given me the chance to redeem myself, not only publicly but on a personal level. Then the voice returned with its simple affirmation: yes.

When I opened my eyes, I found Tanomeo standing before me with his eyes closed. He opened them, nodded, and returned to his chair as if to say "the stage is yours."

I straightened up and cleared my throat. "After carefully calling to mind the events of that evening, I am now able to recall all of it with absolute clarity. Earlier I stated there was a moment wherein the defendant stopped and turned, at which point I shot him. I would now ask that it be noted by the court and jury that the defendant had already dropped his gun before he turned. In the confusion and fear, I pulled the trigger, ultimately shooting an unarmed man. I would like to take this moment to apologize to the defendant for my actions as well as for any pain and suffering those actions might have caused until now or in the future. I would further like to apologize to my family, my partner, and the department for my error and for any backlash that has or will come from this regrettable action."

I saw my father nodding in approval. His tear-filled eyes glistened under the fluorescent lighting as I touched my fingertips to my chin and nodded back. At that moment, in my *knowing*, I'd done the right thing.

A silence filled the court as everyone held their breath. Tanomeo slowly rose and walked to the center of the courtroom. He faced me, placed his hands together, and gave me a full bow. As he stood, he mouthed the words "thank you."

» » « «

There was a short recess and, as I took my seat for closing arguments, I noticed Ana had disappeared. *Strange.*

The prosecutor restructured the charges, dropping the brandishing of a firearm at a police officer. Her voice blurred as I recognized the newfound feeling of lightness within myself. But, while my coming clean might have released the stress of worry and guilt, there was still a hard road ahead. Covering my rent, my bills, child support, all of it was now in jeopardy. I imagined the inevitable hostility that would come from Sid and others that thought like him. Then there were the potential legal issues—issues that could make *me* the defendant in a jury trial. Yet, as strange as it sounds, I had no fear. It was as if, in the doing of what was right, I'd freed something in myself. And, I gotta say, it felt pretty good.

When Tanomeo, acting as his own counsel, addressed the court for the last time, he gave it his all. With his closing statement, he did his best to explain an esoteric concept centered around the idea that when one commits a crime, he or she is not the one performing that action per se.

"I believe the easiest way for you to understand this is by imagining that there are two personalities in one person. Two possibilities, so to speak." He stood tall in front of the jury. "The first and highest possibility is the true, unconditioned person who is alive and experiencing the happiness and joy in life. The second, the lower one, is conditioned by negative past events and lives a more challenging life. This occurs because everything that happens is a reaction to some other action that has already taken place. Then that reaction becomes an action that creates the next. Thus, the cycle continues. Essentially the past events in our lives set the stage for our current reactions and how we live life going forward. The level of awareness one has determines to what extent he or she will be influenced by these past actions, thus continuing or ending the vicious cycle."

I looked around the courtroom. Despite the dancing language, the people were hanging on his every word. This young man had the same gift as my grandfather: the ability to captivate listeners.

His words, or rather the meaning behind them, were similar to The Itatagohbe Nanbar. I compared his explanation of the "unaware personality" to ubaya, the dark spirit, which is believed to literally hide in the shadow of every human being past the age of nine. The only way to keep it at bay is to recognize its ability to appear in others as well as ourselves. This recognition creates *huruma*, which translates to "compassion," the great killer of ubaya.

"So," he went on, "how does this relate to the case? Let's look at the antithesis of awareness. We could say unawareness, but let's use 'unconsciousness.' The acts that were carried out by the defendant, myself, on said evening were, in fact, due to unconsciousness, the absence of *knowing*. Triggered by past events coupled to the current circumstance, the defendant, with his narrowed perspective and lack of compassion, had no choice but to commit the insensible acts powered by the lower self.

"Ladies and gentlemen of the jury, the true Dimitri Tanomeo would never hurt anyone in the aware, compassionate state you see him in today. He now possesses a deep *knowing* of his stepfather's position in all of this. Through compassion, the defendant is now able to put himself in his stepfather's shoes and see how this man's unaddressed pain could cause the lower self to arise in him, committing violent acts against the defendant, his mother, and possibly others.

"I would like to now state for the record that I, Dimitri Cato Tanomeo, the defendant in this case, acting as his own counsel, do not hold Edward William O'Reilly accountable for any wrongdoing that may have been committed against myself, or, as I must say, the defendant. At my stepfather's core, in his highest, unconditioned state, there is a gentle and kind person."

The silence in the courtroom was interrupted only by the creak of wood as the jurors stirred in their chairs. They were uncomfortable with the proposed exoneration of a stepfather's vicious acts against this boy—this boy who was now a man choosing to forgive and release what no longer served him.

"Kind members of the jury, I have no choice but to forgive. But you see that's really not the whole truth. If I say I forgive, that means that something happened *to me*. And, if I'm honest, I can tell you that something actually happened *for me*."

More stirring. Even I wondered where he was going with this.

"Through this experience, I am able to see my part in it all. I am the cause of my lack of compassion. I blamed my stepfather and held a grudge. Now, standing in front of you today, I know he was doing the best he could at the time. The tools in his toolbox were limited, as were mine. One could say that forgiveness is a result of taking responsibility for everything that comes our way. Therefore, forgiveness is actually born from compassion. It's what comes with being *at cause* in life, if that makes any sense."

At cause, that must mean being completely responsible for.

As strange as it sounds, it *was* making sense. I could see that the only way to forgive was to understand the other side of what was happening, which made forgiveness ultimately a moot point.

"Only when we are able to do this, see ourselves in others, can the vicious cycle be broken. I speak not only of my family but all families and relationships. For as long as we live in an unaware, unconscious world, the only reaction to the *unaware cause* can be one of the same. Through my choosing to abide in compassion, might I remain in the highest and greatest place of my two possibilities.

"I stand before you today, fully cognizant that this notion of forgiveness through compassion might be a foreign one. So please allow me to make one thing clear: I am not using it, nor the aforementioned law of cause and effect, as an excuse for my actions or any unconscious act committed by another human being. What I am here to tell you is that only through the genuine acceptance of these principles will any of us ever be free from the never-ending pattern of misery which plagues our world today."

He stopped and scanned the jurors, making eye contact with each of them.

"I had told you at the beginning of this trial that I had quite the challenge ahead of me in proving to you that the defendant, the true Dimitri Tanomeo, the one you see speaking in front of you right now, did not commit the horrific acts. Have I been successful? Only you can answer this. But before you do, please allow me to ask you something. As you have all sat there this morning listening to this somewhat unknown, or at the very least unpracticed, concept, has it in any way resonated with you? Was there, at any moment, a feeling or inner voice inside you, no matter how faint, that said yes to these ideas?"

He paused. Several members of the jury leaned forward.

"If so, then allow me to call on that voice now. That inner voice. The true you. I call on it to take heed as I reinstate my plea of innocence, not only for the defendant in this case but for all cases, criminal or otherwise, across the planet. Hear me now, as I plead not guilty by reason of insanity for anyone and everyone who has ever in their life spoken an unkind word, thought a hateful thought, or performed an odious act. Guilty we are not, but responsible are we indeed. You see, today I call on forgiveness born from accountability. Because we are all responsible for creating a world where these acts are even possible."

He stood up straighter than ever and raised his voice. Somehow, he reminded me of Ana.

"Because only through the recognition of our role in all of it lies our redemption and, ultimately, our freedom. This, my friends, is the road back home where a reunion awaits us all. Here our inner voice rejoins with its truest and highest self, ready to create a new earth by neutralizing the dark forces that currently control it. This voice of love will call forth peace, not only in our own lives but for all lives on this planet." He paused again, but this time to look at each person in the courtroom. "Kind members of the jury, your honor, and all others here today, this is your call to action. *This* is your invitation for awakening." He smiled, dropped his head, and gave us all a slight bow.

You could hear a pin drop.

"The defense rests, Your Honor."

I wondered if there were others like me who were struggling with what he'd just done. He'd spoken not to free himself from punishment, as he clearly took full responsibility for his crimes, but to give a message. There was a part of me that didn't like it, using the courtroom to grandstand. It wouldn't be until much later that I'd discover that the part of me that didn't like that and was maybe even offended by it was the little me that believed I should stay small in the world.

The truth was, I couldn't tell whether he had made his situation better or worse by delivering this message. One thing I did know was that the young man I had just observed speak with such a high level of intelligence, clarity, and charisma was not the same person described by Cy the landlord that day in the ghettos of East Borough. Something had clearly happened to him, or, dare I use his own words, *for* him.

» » « «

It took one full day for the jury to come back with a verdict of guilty on the sole charge of aggravated assault. It seemed, as I had earlier predicted, that the jury couldn't unsee what the defendant had shown when he removed his shirt. The same went for the judge, who handed down the lowest-possible sentence. In the end, the defendant, Dimitri Cato Tanomeo, was sentenced to five years in a state prison just two hundred and fifty miles from the East Burrough where he'd grown up.

THE VISIT

MARCUS

The blowback from my shooting an unarmed man was getting worse every day. It had been three weeks since the trial, and Sid still hadn't spoken to me. I'd officially been demoted to a desk position, and my overall job security with the police force hung in the balance. I hate to admit it, but I was beginning to think that telling the truth wasn't such a good idea after all. I'd find myself staying up late, watching TV until the wee hours, attempting to divert my attention from the thoughts of doom and gloom orbiting the new uncertainties of my life.

One night while dozing in front of the television, I had the strangest, most vivid dream. Ana, the lady from the house and courtroom, was in it. She was standing on her porch, her hands on the railing just like the day she called me out. But this time, instead of her yelling at me, she shouted to what looked like millions of people in front of her.

"The voice of the awakened warrior will be heard by all, and he will be known as The One."

The loudness of her voice jolted me from my slumber. While rubbing my eyes, I noticed a presence in the room. I sprang up, startled to see a blurred figure sitting in the leather chair in front of me. The flickering TV light revealed my unwanted visitor: Ana.

I breathed heavily. *What is she doing here?* She sat, expressionless, gazing in my direction, eerily looking through me. I felt locked in place, paralyzed. *Am I still dreaming?*

I was working on calming my breathing when she finally looked down at the knitting resting on her lap. She lifted her work up and let it unspool from her outstretched hands. It was some type of small blanket. She held it up and studied the back before her eyes darted back onto me with a chilling stare. She turned the small blanket around, fully displaying it to me. Across it were the words: "VISIT HIM."

My heartbeat quickened and my heavy breathing returned. I found I could move, but when I stepped toward her, my shin found the edge of the coffee table. I reached down to quell the pain, and when I looked back, she was gone.

It must have been a double dream of some kind. I stood staring at the seat of the chair, resisting my next move. *I've gotta know.* I reached over and touched it.

"Oh, shit!" I shouted, feeling the residual body heat on the worn leather. I frantically touched the sides of the chair, confirming the difference in temperature. "Oh, come on, now!" I yelled, as I plopped myself down on the sofa, realizing that she had, in fact, been there while, at the same time, couldn't have been.

I made my way to the kitchen, grabbed a bottle, and sat down at the small table. I gazed at the cognac swaying back and forth like a syrupy brown ocean, waiting for its captain to set sail. I closed my eyes and took a gulp, my first step towards relief from the madness. *Who are these people and how did they get into my life?*

The trial was over, there was nothing more to discuss. Yet there I was sitting at the table, contemplating whether or not I should visit him in prison. *Maybe clearing the air wouldn't be such a bad idea.* Still, the absolute absurdity of it all had me spinning. I mean, I shoot this guy, he dies, and then comes back to life. Next, a crazy old lady tells me I've been chosen to help him with something I don't understand. I lie at his trial only to later tell the truth, which causes me to lose my partner, other friends on the force, and possibly my job. Then, while waiting to discover the fate of my seemingly dismal future, that same crazy old lady visits me in my home, or maybe through a dream, only to send a message in her knitting that I am to go and visit him in prison.

How did you get here, Marcus? I downed the rest of my drink in one swallow. "Fuck it, I'm going!" I shouted, slamming the glass down on the table.

» » « «

As I was walking through the parking lot at the correctional facility, I wondered what I might say to him. *Hello, Tanomeo. Your surrogate*

grandmother, or whatever she is, came to visit me in my apartment, conse-
quently committing a B&E, and gave me the message that I should come to
visit you. None of it made any sense.

Upon entering, I recognized one of the prison guards. Jim Devic was a
fellow recruit from the police academy but couldn't pass the physical agility
test. Old Jim was too heavy to get over a six-foot wall, so he settled for a job
at the prison. We caught up a bit, and he'd seen the news coverage of the trial.
He joked that there were always jobs at the prison.

"You never know. I might be calling you someday," I said and we both
laughed.

He thought it was odd for me to visit the prisoner I'd shot. I couldn't really argue with that, so I ended up giving him an abbreviated version of the
story, leaving out the ghostly visits and voices in my head, and he nodded
along. Physically, Jim was built like a bear, tall and heavy, but he had a big
heart to match that physique.

He told me he knew inmate number 52066 and referred to him as "quite
the character." He had heard through the prison grapevine that Tanomeo
was being looked at. He didn't have many details other than it had to do
with getting in the middle of something between another inmate and the
Deuce Five, a brutal Aryan gang known for raping younger weak males at
Carlton. I asked him to keep an eye on the kid and he agreed. We said our
goodbyes, and I headed for the visiting area.

Even with a couple of dozen visitors and convicts sitting in numbered
plastic chairs and tables, the large visiting room still felt empty. Hearing the
double clack of the gates, I moved my hands down to my lap, just in case
they started shaking at some point.

The CO opened the main door and Tanomeo walked in. He wore the
same big smile he'd sported at the courthouse and which would become a
signature of his. True to form, he thanked the guard who opened the door
as he walked in.

I'd found a space away from the others, and when he saw me, he shouted,
"Hello again, Officer Marcus!" My mouth must have been half-open as he
trotted around the tables to take a seat on the other side of me. *What's with*
this guy? I was dumbfounded how anyone could be so energetic and happy
in prison.

"Hello, Mr. Tanomeo," I said, using my best formal voice. "I imagine you must be surprised to see me here."

"No, not really. Stranger things have happened in my life. Please, call me Dimitri if you'd love to."

If I'd love to? Where have I heard that?

"Okay, sure, Dimitri. How are you doing here?" I said nervously.

"Well, let me ask you this, Officer Marcus: how do I look?"

I studied his face. While he was a tad bit paler and thinner than the last time I'd seen him, he was somehow glowing as if something was radiating from inside him.

"You actually look much better than I had imagined. And you can leave out the Officer and just call me Marcus."

He nodded while looking around. "I have to say, Marcus, I feel pretty great right now."

At the time, I felt agitated by his statement. Something wasn't adding up.

"Oh really, is that right? You expect me to believe that you actually like it here?" I was trying to pull some truth out of him.

"First, I don't expect anything from anyone, especially when it comes to what you believe or don't." He lowered his tone and pushed his head as close as he could to the yellow limit line running down the middle of the table. "Secondly, would you categorize me as crazy if I told you I did? You see, Marcus, I love it wherever I am."

I took a long, hard look at him. "To be honest, yes, crazy is how I would categorize you. You're a first-timer in a level-two lock-up, kid, a fish."

He laughed so loud the guard gave us a look. "I'm not saying challenging moments don't exist for me in here, Marcus, because they do. As they do everywhere, for everyone. The difference is in my perception of them and how I choose to handle them once they arise. I've literally changed the way I see them and what they will mean to me. Does that make sense?"

I sat there, baffled and, at the same, time perturbed. Mainly it was because the guy sitting in front of me, stripped of every bit of freedom, seemed somehow better off than I was in my life on the outside.

"But look where you are, man!" I quietly exclaimed, holding my hand in the air.

He cracked up again, this time louder than before, ignoring the stares from the others who were curious of laughter in a place where normally there was none.

"Marcus, you're not getting it. And it's my fault in not explaining it correctly. It's true, a part of my physical freedom, at this moment in time, is on hold. If you were to ask me if I'd rather be free to run down the street or visit with my mother, my answer would be yes, of course. But right now that's not possible, so I am choosing to be in full acceptance of my current life situation. There is no resistance in that. To put it clearly, I am saying yes to the *is-ness* of the present moment."

I needed a break from the intensity of the young man who spoke words I didn't understand but felt somehow might be true. Several tables over, I spotted a tattooed skinhead visiting with what appeared to be, judging from her trashy look, his wife. He was shooting threatening glares our way.

"So, how about you, Marcus?" he asked, changing the subject. "In regards to the adjustments in your new life? I've followed some of it in the papers: the recent changes in your role in the police force, the legal issues, and everything else that has shifted after the incidents we shared together."

I didn't know how to answer, or maybe I just wasn't ready to. All I could come up with was "Well, how do *I* look?"

He smiled sheepishly and whispered, "To be honest, you look like you might be going through a tough time in your life."

What could I say? The guy could see it somehow. "That would be a fair assessment. My new life is a bit of a struggle right now, to say the least."

"Well, feel free to share if you'd like. Unless, of course, you want me to go on explaining the virtues of prison life and its many rewards," he winked.

"No, no, please don't," I said, putting my palms up in surrender as we both laughed. It was strange having someone invite me to talk about the problems in my life, especially him. "Yeah, my new life. … Well, that's another story."

"Another story. I'm sure about that. We all seem to have our own unique story about what is ailing us in life," he said with an air of confidence.

"I would say that's true. There almost always seems to be something wrong in our lives. I'm going through one of those times right now," I said.

"Well actually, right now, you are here with me and everything is perfect. We are here just talking and everything is good, no? If I really wanted to make a point, I could remind you that I'm in here and you're out there."

I considered his words. "I hear what you are saying and it makes sense, but I still feel bad about what is going on in my life outside of here. "

"That's because you have brought the goings-on of your life into this place where they don't exist. The problematic stuff is not occurring right now, at this precise moment, anywhere. Is that not correct?"

"No, that's not really correct, because just a week ago—"

"Wait, Marcus. Let's get clear about something. A week ago is not now. It's a week ago. It's the past. Am I right or am I right?"

"Uh, I guess so."

"Uh, you guess so? No, Marcus, it is not happening now. You are only able to project a mental image of whatever happened in your head. It's called a memory. What's worse, you give those memories power, just as most do, by thinking about them, giving them your energy. You carry them around with you, and this is why you, and the rest, suffer. Let's give that a moment to sink in."

He looked down at his hands and fiddled with his fingers, waiting for I don't know what. That was the first time I noticed there was something odd about the way I related to him. I was a cop being schooled by a prisoner. Equally, while his words didn't really make complete sense, there was a part of me that stayed and listened, knowing there might be something to it.

"You know," I said. "I'd rather talk about the exact issues at hand because some of it has to do with you, and I'd like to clear some things up if that's okay."

He looked at the clock on the wall and nodded. "Yes, I agree. The point I was trying to make could take more time than the good people here at Carlton State Penitentiary will allow for this visit, so go ahead. Tell me."

"Well, to be honest, I seem to have more problems now than ever before."

"Really? Now more than ever? When would you say this all began?"

"After the incident in the alley. After that night, my whole life changed." I explained about Sid, my downgraded job, and the threat of losing it. "I have a daughter to feed and bills to pay. On top of all of that, I'm feeling guilty about what happened. I mean, I know shit happens and all, but this is just crazy."

"I can understand that. Certainly, I can. Tell me something, Marcus: do you ever ask yourself why you might be in the position you are in now?"

"Every single day," I scoffed.

"And what do you come up with?"

"Well, it's a bit hard to admit. Especially seeing how you are the one asking." I could see he was amused, smiling and nodding as if he knew what I wanted to say.

"Ah, Marcus. Do you think there's something you could say that would offend me? For that matter, do you believe there is anything anyone could say or do to me that would hurt or bother me?" *Hmmm, interesting question.*

"Maybe I couldn't offend you, but I am sure there is something that bothers you. There must be someone out there that could say something that would upset you."

He laughed some more. *How can this guy be so happy here?*

"I'm going to tell you something that you might not understand at this moment, but I like to plant seeds for the future, so here it goes. ... Once you know who, or rather *what,* you truly are, then and only then will you be completely untouchable in this world. In my current experience here on earth, I know what I am beyond my body, name, or description, whether that be a son, a prisoner, or a man. Now, because I know this, nothing can affect me unless I allow it to, or perhaps a better phrasing is 'choose' it to." He paused. "Knowing this beyond any doubt, gives me the strength to deal with what's coming, not just here in this prison but on the outside as well.

"You see, Marcus, everyone on this planet will soon be put to the test. We will have to choose between continuing to live in fear and remain in the clutches of dark forces or rise to the occasion of the *knowing* of our eternal true power, the one that lies beyond the illusion of darkness. This power I speak of is inherent and lives not only in but through each and every one of us." He got quiet and leaned in conspiratorially. "You see, Marcus, we are It, the capital 'I' it."

What? I was trying to put it all together. "You're right, Dimitri. I don't understand a damn bit of it. And my 'i' was a small one, FYI."

He chuckled, "You will someday. Now, tell me your troubles, my friend."

» » « «

I told him everything. He eased back into his chair as I admitted that even though I knew coming forth and telling the truth at the trial was the right thing to do, I was beginning to regret it. "It's just that all the problems that came with it have wreaked havoc in my life."

His head tilted to one side as he smiled, gazing at me like a child in wonderment.

"It might help to reconsider if what you said is accurate about not having any real problems before."

"Yeah, there are other issues. Ones with my mother, who's always comparing me to my successful younger brother. Then there's the situation with my ex, which seems to be a never-ending saga of its own. If that's not enough, I seem to be suffering from late-onset alcoholism. I guess you have a point, but it seemed like that all disappeared when our thing happened. How's that even possible?"

"Let me suggest that those other problems, those stories, have not disappeared. Rather, they have taken a back seat to the new, more intricate, juicier ones. This is what we do as humans so that we can prolong our suffering through the creation of lasting drama around the past events in our lives.

Something wasn't adding up. "Why the hell would I, we, or anyone want to do that? It sounds insane!"

"That's exactly what it is, Marcus. It's why our world is in the situation it's in right now. Pretty much every conflict, whether it be between husband and wife, a couple of friends, members of a family, or two nations, originates from some type of drama that is not taking place at that exact moment."

I shook my head from side to side, in an attempt to make space for what I felt could be a newfound truth. *Could it be that simple?* I told him of the drama hurled at me from Lisa and her mother, usually centered around money and their belief that I didn't do enough when it came to providing for our daughter.

"Is it true?" he asked bluntly.

"Man, I am barely making ends meet. I'm upside-down on my mortgage, I've got alimony, child support, my rent, and car payments. All of it on a beat cop salary. It's just not working, especially with her wanting more and more. My career advancement to detective was going to save me. Now it'll be a miracle if I can even keep my job. Shit, it's no wonder I drink."

There was no laughter from him this time. Just a calm smile which triggered a feeling of intense guilt deep within me.

"Sorry," I stammered. "Didn't mean to bitch about my life when—"

"Oh, it really doesn't work that way for me, Marcus. It's all relatively the same at its core. It just appears that one life situation is worse than another. At the end of the day, it all comes from the same place and, from there, transmutes into human suffering."

Now, it was my turn to gaze at him in awe. "But what happened to you was so bad. How can you just be okay with it?"

"There was a time when I wasn't okay with it. A time when every punch, burn, cut, and wound, whether verbal or physical, was etched into my mind more vividly than the scars on my body. Each one of them a reminder of how my stepfather, my mother, and even the world had hurt me. I carried this around for years until I decided it was time to hurt back by stealing, fighting, and, ultimately, seriously hurting someone. Where did all of that hate, drama, and ill will get me?"

"Well," I said with a shy smile, "not to be the one who answers rhetorical questions or anything, but it got you here in Carlton State Penitentiary."

He went on to explain that none of the things he'd done to others reversed the things that happened to him. All the lashing out was ineffective at the end of the day. It was making sense logically, but how could he be truly okay with all that had happened. His answer, as hard as it was to get at the time, would eventually change the way I looked at problems for the rest of my life.

"Let's take my story. You might say, 'How terrible all of those things were that happened to you, Dimitri. What a shame. Look at where you are now.'"

"That's exactly what I would say," I said.

"Okay. Now let's imagine there is another opinion, another possibility that someone else might say, 'How wonderful. All those things happened *for* Dimitri. What a blessing. Just look at where he is now in his creation of a beautiful life.' Can you see the two available options?"

I shook my head. "Yeah, so in a way, you are sort of mind-fucking your-self into believing something that's not actually true."

"Not exactly," Dimitri smiled. "It only looks that way coming from your current perspective. You see, what's true for me in my perspective is distinct because I am steeped in my knowing of this truth. From this place, I choose to speak the latter of the two options into existence for myself."

"I'm not sure I completely understand."

"Let's go back to what we went over earlier. Here we are, sitting at this table at Carlton just talking. And, at this exact moment, there are no issues, correct?"

"Yeah, I guess. If you put it that way."

"What other way could I put it? If the moment of right here and right now is perfect, then you have nothing to stress over. Right now anyways."

"Wait a moment, Dimitri. I just got finished telling you about the shit-storm of a life I have."

"You did. And just as I had explained to you, minutes before, none of these issues are happening right now. They have either happened in the past or may happen in the imagined future. *You* are causing them to occur right now in an imagined mental movie matinee made solely by and for you." He pointed his finger at my poker face. "I bet you watch reruns of your movie while you're driving, eating, working, and trying to sleep at night. How am I doing so far?"

I could feel myself heat up. While he was right, there was something about him minimizing my problems that irritated me. "Listen here, what you are suggesting is that these issues are nothing. That I should just not care about them and they will magically go away. Let's remember that it's not just me. I have a kid. She could potentially end up starving to death if I don't get something worked out."

He chuckled, probably at what he believed was my exaggeration, but none of it was amusing for me.

"Okay, okay, let me come at this from a different angle. I'm not sure if you noticed or not, but today, here in the visiting room, we have one of our illustrious members of the Aryan gang, the Deuce Five with us. And it appears that he has taken a keen interest in me." He pointed without looking at the Aryan who was still staring us down.

"Please stop pointing at him," I whispered sternly. "Yes, I did notice, but it seemed like you didn't."

"You see, Marcus, that's just it. I see his stares and I hear the talk in the yard. I know there's some issue with them, but there's none with me. If I ran my program like you, I'd be losing it, not being able to sleep, running movies in my head of them hurting me or me hurting them. Could you imagine how our visit would be if I let his glares intimidate me? It would look a whole lot different, don't ya think?"

"If the tables were turned I don't think I would've had the focus to say what you've said, knowing that something was going to happen to me."

"That's just it. I don't know what's going to happen. None of us do. That's because it hasn't happened yet. If at some point something does go down, I'll handle it just as I would if I was walking around worrying about it. Possibly even better. What I do know is I am here with you, talking, and everything is great."

I can't deny that. He stared at me staring at him. *How can I ever stop myself from worrying?*

"So, let's take this staying-in-the-present-moment thing to a whole different level," he continued. "What do you see in your head when you imagine not paying your bills? How does that affect your world?"

I told him I imagined Lisa losing her shit, screaming, crying, and carrying on. She'd say things like, "See, I told you, you're nothing but a loser, Marcus." I pictured myself living in my car, then losing that to the bill collector. Ultimately, I imagined myself homeless, living on the street. And my daughter: I could see her looking malnourished, in ragged clothes, the kids at school laughing at her.

"You think about this often, Marcus?"

It was strange to actually think about it, to quantify it. "Yes, I do. Nearly every day."

"Wow! Every day. What a thing!"

I couldn't tell if he was condescending or serious. "It's a hard life, I told you that. Do you see what I mean now?" I said smugly.

"I do. I see that your incredible imagination is making your life a living hell."

I just shook my head. He clearly wasn't able to see my reality.

"Tell me," he continued. "Of all of those things you imagine could happen, how many of them have actually occurred?"

My pause was long enough to serve as an answer, which made him smirk. "That's what I thought."

"But they could at any time," I countered.

"If they were to happen, when would they happen?"

"What kind of question is that? They'd happen later, in the future."

"No, the moment of the future never comes. In truth, the future doesn't exist. Think about it. We never wake up in the morning, yawn and say, 'Ah, it's tomorrow finally,' do we? No, and that's because everything happens in the now, the only moment that truly exists."

Somehow that makes sense.

"Okay. I get your point, but that still doesn't prevent things from happening."

"That's correct. It doesn't. Just as you said earlier, *caca* happens. Things will always happen, that's just the way life is. I will explain the reason for that another time. But here's the deal: when they do happen, you will handle them just as you always have, in the now, because it is literally impossible to do otherwise. I mean, you could try, but that would be futile and downright insane."

There was something in me that needed to find a hole in his theory. "But one has to be prepared in life. We can't just go around singing Kumbaya to one another. We've got to be ready for whatever comes our way."

Now, he was the one that paused. I rested back in my chair, feeling quite smug in my presumed victory.

"Kumbaya, my lord, kumbaya," he began to sing loudly. "Kumbaya, my lord—"

"Stop that, really," I whispered, dropping my head down, which just made him laugh.

"I just wanted to show you that we indeed can sing Kumbaya." He laughed a final burst before getting serious. "Marcus, there's a difference between taking an umbrella with you on a clear day in case of a surprise downpour and going outside talking about how bad the weather *could get* while walking around under an open one. Abiding in thoughts of some possible future event, or ones of the past, for that matter, is insane and toxic to yourself and those around you, not to mention all of humanity on an energetic level. By doing so, you are prolonging the madness that plagues our world today. Obviously, you are not alone in this, as nearly everyone is doing the same."

I was truly deflated. *Can't I win just one rally here?* I couldn't tell what I felt worse about: not being able to stump him or finding out I was at fault for a messed up world.

"So, Dimitri, if it's such a crime, why is everyone doing it?"

He explained it had become what he called the "indistinct norm," that it had been going on for so long, no one even noticed it. He said if we continued living outside the present moment, causing conflict both internally and externally, our existence on earth would eventually come to an end. The blaming of others, according to him, was the root of it all—be it a neighbor, mother, ex-wife, stepfather, politician, country, or world that failed us. It was imperative that we free ourselves from the cycle of victimhood to reach our internal and, eventually, external liberation.

"As we continue to crank the sprocket that rotates the wheel of misery, the faster it turns. And the faster it turns, the harder it is to get off. Hence, what we are left with is a collective that continues to spin out of control. Even though there are forces at work trying to hold us in this pattern, there is still a way to get back home to peace and harmony. Strangely enough, we are being pushed in that direction through our suffering. In the same way, you, through your own suffering, are just beginning to come back home as well."

His words had taken a prophetic tone. I could sense his utter focus.

"However, it is of the utmost importance that we hasten our pace before it's too late. Those forces that wish to hold us in this pattern are ramping up their game. At the same time, conditions for us to live on this planet deteriorate more and more each day."

What forces is he talking about? There was no way I was going to ask. Not only did I not want to open another can of worms, but I was also kind of afraid of what he might say.

I glanced over and saw that the skinhead's visitor had left. He was going out of his way to walk in our direction on his way to the prisoner's exit. *This isn't good.*

With the guard's back turned, he kicked the bottom of Dimitri's chair and whispered, "Get ready, punk. Your day's comin' soon." His evil smile exposed crooked, yellow teeth. I'd seen men like him before in the street with nothing to lose. In prison, he had even less. He was dangerous. I planted my feet firmly, ready to jump.

"Hola, buenos dias, Earl." Dimitri slowly turned around and smiled, unfazed by the threat hovering behind him. I clenched my fists in my jacket pockets.

Earl stood staring down, hate seething out every pore of his racist body. Dimitri turned back around to face me, another careless move. Readying myself for a brawl, I jolted up in my chair, sending the loud screech of rubber against concrete echoing throughout the room. Earl shifted his focus in my direction. I stared straight into his wicked, racist eyes, the kind I'd experienced more than once in my life. I held his gaze, knowing I couldn't back down.

Earl shook his head and smiled, unlocking his glare. He glanced at the back of Dimitri's head, then the table, then back at me. The standoff was over, the danger passed. He'd given in.

As I relaxed again into my seat, the guard turned around, immediately noticing the situation. "Move your fucking ass, Earl, or you're going straight to the hole!" he shouted, placing his hand over the red panic button he wore on his utility belt. Earl continued through the exit, still shaking his head as the metal door closed behind him.

"What are you doing? Are you crazy?!"

"I'm using my Espanol. There's a very special person I converse with using her second of three languages. While I'm in here, I'd like to keep it going. Don't want to lose it. I've been sitting next to some Sonoran Mexican fellows in the yard, eavesdropping on their conversation. Seems to be working, don't you think?"

"I think you're fucking crazy, is what I think!" I blurted while wiping the sweat from my forehead. "That guy could have shanked you right here!"

"You said he 'could have,' did you not?" he asked, cool as a cucumber, not a bead of sweat on him.

"Yeah, and he could have."

"But he didn't. Yet you sit thinking, not only about a past event that didn't happen but also about what could have happened. You're worse off than someone living in victimhood mentality if that's even possible.

"What if I had snapped back at Earl with some harsh words? Would that have helped the situation? What if I had just said nothing? That might indicate that I'm fearful, and you know I can't do that in prison, right? You see, Marcus, I hold no fear, nor do I possess any harsh words for him or any of my other brothers in this place. What else could I do but speak to him kindly?"

I slammed my hand against the table. "He is not your brother. He wants to kill you because he hates you and others who are not like him." I was pretty livid by this point, and maybe that's why my filter slipped. "What are you anyways? Your mom's white, but you clearly aren't. Are you half-black or what?"

Dimitri ignored my question, filling the space with his usual smile.

"Maybe he hates me, maybe he doesn't. I wouldn't know, nor do you. Only his highest version knows. Maybe what he really wants is peace in his life as all humans do at their core. What if he loves me so much he's just playing a role? What if these experiences are necessary for him to get to the place where he knows that love? It's in my knowing this about him, and all others, that I'm able to recognize them as brothers and sisters. And I do mean all of them, amigo." I stared at him for a moment in disbelief.

"Yeah, I'm not sure I'm ready for that level of knowledge, just yet."

"Few are. But you will be, and so will they."

Who is this guy and what planet is he from?

"So, speaking to a white supremacist in Spanish and all, do you think that was the wisest move?"

A sheepish grin spread across his face and he whispered, "Oh, he'll get over it." He leaned in as if preparing to tell me a secret. "Marcus, you should probably know something about me. I like to stir things up a bit. You know, rock the boat now and then. I believe it's the best way to change things. So, when the opportunity arises, I do just that." He sat back in his chair.

"Besides," he went on, "it's good for him. Gives him something to think about. I'm here to give them all just that."

"Give who what?" I asked.

"Them, something to think about." His voice carried a level of seriousness I hadn't heard before. "That's why I've been put here on this planet at this point in time. To shine the light on everything that needs to be looked at, from the dark forces and what they're up to inside Carlton and beyond. I'm here to help expose the distortions, the darkness that abides in each of us. To give each man in this prison, and, later, every person in the world, the opportunity to consider a new possibility for him or herself. This new possibility will shift the global, collective perspective in such a way that we'll all finally see what's behind the curtain of Oz ... and beyond."

Where does he come up with this stuff? But his words had transported me to the day I first met Ana. *He is here to be the example of what is possible for all of humankind.* It all sounded so crazy but somehow believable at the same time. Maybe it was just that he believed it so fully that it became contagious.

He looked to his left and then to his right before whispering, "And if we have to ruffle a few feathers to do it, then so be it. I mean, what else are we gonna do, right?" He winked at me and laughed out loud.

Wait. We? Who's we?

Before I could ask, the guard yelled out that visitation would end in five minutes, which prompted Dimitri to ask me for a favor on the outside. He said there was a gift he'd been given, one of great personal value to him. He told me where it was hidden, and I acted as if I'd never seen the beige, hand-knit shirt concealed within the floorboards of his dismal room. He asked that I pick it up and keep it safe.

"Visitation has now ended. All visitors please exit out the white double doors. Inmates remain seated until further instruction!" the CO shouted.

"I guess that's it," I said, taking my time getting up. I stalled, letting the others leave before me. As odd as it seemed, I liked him. And what he had to say, even though it was hard to hear, hard to swallow and digest ... I liked it too.

He bowed with his hand over his heart and said, "Until next time, Marcus."

As I approached the door, I heard him yell behind me, "Marcus!" I turned around and, in the most heartfelt tone I'd ever heard, he said, "Thank you!"

"No problem. I'll stop by and pick it up on my way to work."

"No, not that. You know ..." The CO cleared his throat, signaling me to keep moving.

I was walking backward as he stood up, looked directly at me, and shot me the finger gun. Then he winked and again mouthed "thank you."

Even though he hadn't spoken, I could have sworn I heard it this time. That's when it clicked. *Holy shit.* I stared at him, frozen. *No, it couldn't be.* But it was.

I recognized it. The voice from that evening alone in the hospital. *That was his voice.*

With my hands now on top of my head, I saw him chuckle at my new-found discovery just before my vision blurred. *He's here to change it all.* The words of the once-thought-senile Ana rang in my ears as the riddle of Cy's portrayal of a halfwit simpleton had just been decoded. I now knew *something* happened to him that night I'd shot him. Dare I say something ... supernatural? As my vision returned, I stood there fixated on the fearless young man who possessed no stories of what should or could have been. He then simply walked away, in presence and at peace with everything and anything that might come his way. That's when a feeling engulfed me—a feeling I'd never felt before, but I can only describe in one word.

Hope.

PRODIGAL SON

ZACH

"Zach, you've certainly done it now, son. This time it's the real deal." Those were the words of one of the richest men on the planet as I took my last look at the free world out of the prison bus window.

After a long desolate straightaway of cattle fields and corn crops, the bus turned the corner, and I saw Carlton State Penitentiary for the first time. *It's a fucking city made of concrete.* My head pressed against the glass. *How did I let this happen?*

I felt my stomach sink as we pulled up to the entrance gate. There were hundreds of inmates enclosed by two rows of barbed wire fencing. This place was nothing like where I'd served the majority of my first sentence. These were hard men, doing real time, unlike myself, a young, skinny computer programmer who DJ'd at other rich kids' parties. I'd never seen a place like this. Nothing with a yard this big, this serious. The shit was about to get real, and I knew I wasn't ready for it.

After processing, the other new arrivals and I picked up our "fish kits" at the laundry post and made our way towards the cells. We had to pass through the dayroom where hardened inmates played cards and watched TV. Stepping aside, I let the others go before me. I soon found out that was a big mistake. As the last one, I stood frozen, trembling in front of those who should've never seen me tremble.

"Fresh fish!" someone shouted. "Come on, baby, don't be afraid!" another yelled. I gripped my things tightly to my chest and walked forward. My biggest fear was being turned out, and by the look of some of these guys, I knew it could happen in Carlton.

"Wooooo, she's a nice one!" I heard someone shout as I locked eyes on my final destination, the hallway on the other side that led to the cells.

"Oh, suga,' gotta get me a piece of that, no doubt about it! I call firsts on that one!"

"Bullshit, Earl. Richy Rich is mine!" another responded, making nearly all of them laugh.

Oh shit, they know. I knew there were chatty guards in every prison who leaked info to inmates, like gossiping schoolgirls at the prom, but still hoped I'd get a pass.

Nearing the end of the gauntlet, I felt the tap of someone's spit land on the back of my head. My eyes filled with water as I prayed the worst had passed. That's when I felt someone grab my ass. "No!" I yelled, spinning to take my last steps of the nasty ordeal backward.

Once I was out of the dayroom, I looked down and watched the drops fall onto the white lines painted on the concrete floor below. The echo of laughter bounced off the hard, battleship-grey walls, delivering the jolt of a new, dark truth. I was in hell and there wasn't anything I, or anyone else, could do about it.

You've really fucked this one up, Zach.

You see, with my original case, I'd pled out, and my father, using his connections, got me set up as a trustee with a job in admin at Silverton Men's Colony, a level-one minimum-security fire camp. I had it made, living separately from the general population with decent food and other liberties. But, like everything else my father had ever done for me, I had to destroy that as well.

I stopped to dry my eyes before turning the corner into cell number 111. In prison, the name of the game was to not let anyone, especially your new cellmate, see your emotions. Ever.

I should just go in and crack him right off the bat. I'm not going to be anyone's bitch.

Who was I kidding? The only fighting I'd ever done was with my twin sister, Tess, and Super Street Fighter 2 (if that even counts, and I think it should).

Probably a hardened criminal just waiting to violate his new celly.

I got my shit together the best I could and walked around the column. That's when I saw *him* for the first time. He was just sitting there reading, but I remember *strength* was the first word that came to mind. It wasn't just physical, though he obviously had that. There was another kind of strength that came through him. I know that doesn't make sense, and, believe me, all of it just scared the shit out of me at the time. What I didn't know was that this strength would put the world back together one day.

I took a deep breath and marched up to the doorway.

He glanced up at me. "Hey, fish, welcome." He waved his book, signaling me to enter before going back to his reading.

"Hey," I uttered coldly, a failed attempt to play the badass I could never be.

"Come on in. I'm Dimitri. Top bunk's yours." He had a lame, innocent smile like a little kid. That, combined with his helpful manner, didn't fit his rugged look. *He's playing me.* I tossed my fish kit onto the top mattress and continued to the back of the cell and blew my nose on my sleeve. I tried to slow my breath while assessing the damage, which was mainly mental.

I looked around the cell, trying to steer my attention away from the exposed stainless steel toilet sitting dead center at the back of the six by nine cubicle. There were two photos on the wall, both of a once-attractive, white woman now riddled with deep creases running down her face. She'd obviously had a very hard ride. *That's gotta be his mother, maybe he's human after all.*

I was confused to see a stack of books behind his cot, mainly because he didn't look like a guy that reads a lot. I covertly tried to make out a few of the titles: *The Power of Now, Sacred Economics, A Course in Miracles,* The Bhagavad Gita, and even The Holy Bible. I'd only heard of the Bible, but the others seemed like they could be righteous somehow as well.

I don't think rapists read books like that.

"Looks like you got the red carpet treatment, didn't you there, Zach?"

What the fuck. Does everyone know? I shook my head.

Paying for protection was out since all my accounts were frozen by my father. I was on my own, and I knew the key to staying alive, with my manhood intact, was to trust no one, especially not this guy who could snap me like a twig before busting my cheeks.

I touched the back of my head and was quickly reminded of something I would've liked to have forgotten about. "Fucking animals," I whispered to myself.

"An insult to the animal kingdom, wouldn't you say, Zachary?!" he shouted in a Shakespearean accent, shooting his hand into the air. I looked at him, then did a double-take. He then switched to a quiet, humble voice, "Here ya go." He tossed me a small towel.

Is this guy crazy or is he just trying to get on my good side so he can have his way with me later?

» » « «

After a completely sleepless night imagining my new cellmate attacking me in my slumber, I walked alone in the prison yard after breakfast. That's when I came face to face with the real and present danger.

"Penny for your thoughts, pretty fish." The sappy voice made my mouth dry up instantly and the dread of my darkest fear flooded through me. Before I even turned around, I knew I was fucked.

His somewhat toothless smile, set against a weathered face with a large boil next to a blackhead-ridden nose, made it all the worse. He was about forty, my height (five-nine or so), but he was stronger than me due to the training rituals he and his gang, The Deuce Five, practiced on a daily basis. From the neck down, his jailhouse tats told the story of white pride, evil forces, and his eternal love for someone named Dorthy Jean. There was another tattooed guy with him, who was taller, bigger, and dumber looking, if that was even possible. Both of them had shaved heads and wore clean white shirts.

"What's up?" I mustered as I looked around the yard, realizing I was all alone.

"Looks like you're what's up, suga'. We just wanted to welcome you to this fine institution. My name is Earl and this here is Pete. We're kinda the hospitality committee 'round here. It's Zachary, right?"

"Zach, yes." I hid my trembling hands in my jacket pockets as he explained the importance of having friends in a place that wasn't so friendly. I knew where he was going and wanted nothing to do with it. "I-I-I-I'm okay," I stuttered, "really. Thanks. I-I gotta get going." I stepped to the side to leave, but Pete moved in front of me, blocking my way.

"Listen, guys, I don't want any beef here, so could you just let me go?" At this point, they knew I was terrified.

"Beef, you say? You don't want any? How would you know if you've never tried?" They both laughed and I regretted my choice of words. "Let me just explain how this works. You see, Zach, I choose you. That means you're mine. No one else can have ya, and as long as you come and see me now and then when I send fo' ya, no one else will bother you. I can protect you. And I gotta tell ya, Zach, there's some real bad characters in this place."

Said the toothless hillbilly rapist.

That's when the dark reality, that I was all alone, sank deeply into my psyche. "No, man, I'll just take the risk, you know. G-g-go it on my own, thanks," I stuttered.

"Ah, Zach. I'm sorry to hear you feel that way. But here's the thing: it wasn't just them I was gonna protect you from. You see, I'm so sweet on ya, I'd say you're gonna need protection from the likes of me if ya don't play ball, if you know what I mean. You just run along now, Zach. I'm gonna let ya think on it a bit." I began stepping backwards. "The next time we talk you can give me your answer. Either way, this thing is gonna happen. Bye bye, suga.'"

» » « «

For nearly two weeks I stayed as invisible as I could. I got a job in the kitchen and planned my every move carefully, avoiding the places where he and his gang hung out. Then, one Thursday, while heading back to my cell from the kitchen, I saw them on the other end of the block heading towards me. My mouth dried up again and I sped up, ducking in just before they got to me.

"Whoa, what's up, Zach?" my cellmate inquired. He was sitting on the edge of the bed reading. *Always with the reading!* I spun around, but before I had time to explain Earl was leaning against the metal doorway.

"Honey, I'm home," he announced smugly.

"My answer is no, Earl!" I shouted, knowing I had nowhere to go.

He nodded to Pete, signaling him to keep watch.

I glanced at Dimitri, who'd somehow gone back to his reading. *What's wrong with this guy?*

Earl stepped in and stopped just before passing Dimitri. "Beat it. Me and your celly have a date. We gonna have us some fun."

He took another step before the stomp of a large foot against the concrete wall rattled the whole cell. It rattled Earl's momentum too. He looked at the size-twelve shoe planted firmly into the wall, then at the owner of it. "Do you know what you're doin' there, punk?"

"Oh yeah, I know exactly what I am doing—not only now, but pretty much always," my cellmate, who'd just become my biggest hero, answered in an oddly inappropriate, cheerful tone.

"Do you know who I am?" Earl asked.

"I do. But the question is, do you? I'm sure that if you did know, not so much *who* but *what* you actually are, you wouldn't be here trying to get all up inside of Zach."

Ewwww. I shuddered.

A bizarre silence took over the cell as we all stood there dumbfounded by what he'd just said. "I'm not sure what you're getting at here, mutt," Earl finally spat out.

Finally closing his book, Dimitri said, "Let me explain. You just walked into this cell without being invited, and we all know this isn't acceptable behavior here at Carlton. Let's do this: why don't we start over again, with you turning around and walking out the same way you came in. Then, you can turn around and ask for permission."

This guy's gonna get us both killed. I could see Earl processing being spoken to like a five-year-old. Even Pete glanced back to see what he was going to do.

Dimitri continued, "So, as far as the fun you have planned with my cell-mate goes, I think it would be wise if we ask him how he feels about it, don't you?" He stood up, never taking his eyes off Earl. "Zach, would you like to have some alone time with Earl? He says it's going to be fun."

Fuck no, dude!" I shouted. Dimitri shrugged his shoulders.

"Sorry, Earl, it looks like Zach's not interested in any fun today."

Earl's eyes, seething with hate, locked onto Dimitri's for the ultimate staredown. "Son, you just signed your death warrant." Earl signaled for Pete to pass him a shank.

All I could do was imagine my cellmate lying on the floor, bleeding out, while this yokel had his way with me. Pete was kneeling down and pulling up his pant leg when someone shouted there was a CO in the area.

"Looks like God granted you another day, mutt." Earl snarled.

Dimitri looked around the cell, smiled, then nodded, "Yes, it appears *she* did. Good observation, Earl."

Confused, it took a couple of seconds for Earl to respond. "Mutt, you done fucked yo'self real good on this one. We're leavin' now, but you might want to get yo' affairs in order." I was feeling some shameful relief that Earl's predatory focus had moved away from me to a more murderous one with my cellmate when he smiled at me. "Now, suga', don't think for one second I'm forgettin' about ya. We're gonna meet again real soon, darlin'." With that, he spun and exited the cell.

He'd only been gone a few seconds before I was taken over by a horrified rage.

"Fuck you, Earl," my voice cracked like a fourteen-year-old's. "You inbred, hillbilly, fuck! Come here again and we're gonna beat your racist ass!"

Dimitri slowly turned and I instantly regretted my words. *What the fuck have you done, Zach?* I glanced down at my pant leg and noticed I'd pissed myself.

"Bro, that was intense. Thanks for having my back. You didn't have to do that." *But I'm sure glad you did.* I grabbed my jacket off the top bunk to cover myself. I searched for the words to remedy my cowardly threat, a threat issued behind the shield of the six-foot gladiator who now stood frowning at me.

I have to smooth this out. "Hey, I'm sorry about blurting that out and including you in it. I didn't mean to ruin your world by you having to worry about them coming at you now."

"Well, Zach, you haven't ruined my world in any way. And as far as fearing them coming at me, I have none of that. It's just that it's ultimately not true. I imagine me fighting anyone is probably not going to be part of the equation—if something were to occur, that is."

"First off, dude, there's no *if* in any of this. They *will* come. They're The Deuce Five. They don't fuck around and you're on their list. Secondly, how's it even possible that you won't fight back? Look at you, man. You look like Akuma from Street Fighter 4. You could kick some serious ass in this place. We can capitalize on that, but we need to stand up to those guys when the time comes."

"Kicking ass and capitalizing don't seem like activities I want to participate in during my experience here." He sat back down on his cot, reaching for his book. "For now, I'm just going to go back to my reading, if that's alright with you?"

"Ah yeah, dude, you do that," I muttered as the full weight of Carlton World, as the inmates called it, instantly returned to my shoulders. And now I had to deal with the guilt of involving Dimitri in this whole mess too. But I soon found out that this guy, my cellmate, was much more than the low-life thug I'd pegged him for.

RESISTANCE = PERSISTENCE

MARCUS

It was surreal, this new thing. To see, to witness, the thoughts in my mind as they came. I'd be at my desk job, reminiscing about my time on the streets working the beat, and then, moments later, I'd be worrying about being fired even though I still had a job. The mere fact that I could observe these thoughts as they came made it clear that they were not my own. That observation, in turn, removed me as the supposed owner of these thoughts, causing them to somehow instantly vanish.

On my way over to pick up the shirt for Dimitri, I reflected on how much had changed in my life since meeting him. I became close to my wife, Lisa, who I'd been separated from for quite some time. It seemed we were on the path to working things out and becoming a family again, but there were still things getting in the way. I could see how being out of the present moment affected us. Just the day before, while laughing and singing along to the radio with Lisa and my daughter on our way home from getting ice cream, we pulled into the driveway and I could see the wheels turn in Lisa's head as she studied our neighbor Leif. He was washing the new car he'd bought for his wife a month prior. Lisa pushed the off button on the stereo, putting an abrupt end to the fun.

"Hey, not cool!" Hope said loudly as her mother grabbed her purse and stormed into the house.

"What's up?" I asked once we were inside and away from Hope. *Like I don't know what's coming.*

"I was talking to Paige. She told me there was no way you could make detective with this on your record. What are you going to do?"

I felt myself heat up. I went through the list of not-so-nice words I'd end up calling Lisa if this went much further. Lisa worried about money, about not having enough of it. She believed that if she had designer clothes, a better car, or a nicer house, she'd be happy. Typically this made me furious. But now, with my new understanding of what was really happening, it was easier not to be triggered by the words that came unconsciously, or "unpresent momently," out of her mouth. Instead, I felt for her. I could see myself in her as she fell into her mind's trap of past/future madness. Dimitri referred to this as having compassion for another.

"I'm sorry, Lisa. I'm doing the best I can. We are good right now. Hope's good, you're good, I'm good, even Lucky's good." I pointed at our overweight orange tabby, belly up and asleep in the middle of the family room floor.

"Why did you have to shoot that boy? It's destroyed our lives!"

I stayed calm and simply said, "I'm sorry."

She carried on with her rant. I allowed whatever was happening with her to exist, without resisting it. It was downright magical, miraculous, how my staying present and full of compassion could literally transform who she was to me. I could be there with her, in the moment, rather than focus on our past and be triggered by it.

I know it seems crazy how quickly this was happening and all, but as long as I stayed present, I felt good. I was appreciative of what I learned from Dimitri that day at Carlton Prison and was happy to keep my end of the bargain.

» » « «

As I walked up the stairs and on to the stoop, I saw Cy. True to form, he was peering out at me through the window. His door swung open before I even had the chance to knock.

"Whatcha know, it's Officer Marcus again. How's life been treatin' ya there, son?" He was in much better spirits than the last time I saw him.

"Actually, life's treating me pretty good," I answered, realizing this was the first time in a long time I had said life was good and meant it. "And you?"

"Takin' it day by day. Ya know, that's tha best we can do down here in The Pit." He motioned for me to come inside.

I sat down while Cy poured lemonades in the kitchen. He seemed eager to tell me about how Dimitri's stepfather was now relating to others in the building.

"It's like he's humbled or somethin'. He seem just like another person, hardly ever arguin' and threatenin' folks like he did before. And you know that be makin' my life much easier. Come to think of it, I almost never hear him fightin' with his woman either. Truth be said, I don't know exactly what's goin' on in that man's head, but he different now and we sure like it."

Cy looked at me with a big grin on his face. "Tha Lord be workin' in mysterious ways, don't he, Officer Marcus? He can take a bad situation and make some good from it. Hallelujah, I say to that, I do."

"Mysterious, indeed, Cy. Mysterious, indeed," I said, remembering the young man in prison who showed me that there was perfection in all process. He'd told me that everything is happening to serve us, even though it might not appear that way at first. I wondered if what Cy was saying was true. If it was possible that Eddie was, in fact, helped by the incidents of that evening.

"Officer Marcus, you in there?" Cy asked, snapping me out of it.

"Yeah, sorry. I was just contemplating it all."

"Ah yes, it's a shame that poor boy gotta do all that time on the inside and all. Ain't it?" Cy turned away from me and looked out the window. He hid it well, but I was pretty sure he was tearing up.

"Like you said, the Lord works in mysterious ways."

He nodded and turned to sit down again. "Amen to that. Amen to that, I say."

It didn't take much for Cy to toss me the keys to Dimitri's old place. "You go right ahead there and get whatever you need fo' 'em. I left his room just like it was before. Just bring me back that key when ya done, ya hear?"

Upon entering the room for the second time, it seemed even more dark and dank than it did the first. I lifted the floorboards and there was the shirt, just as I had left it.

» » « «

As I walked to my car, I kept glancing across the street at the lush, immaculate garden that kept the front porch and house hidden from the view of passersby. I told myself I didn't have the time for a visit and that I would come by another time as I pulled out my keys, unlocked the door, and got in.

There was a part of me that wanted to speak to her. There was also a part that was afraid. Not because I thought she might do something to me. It was something else, a force of some kind, that drew me away from her and, strangely enough, drew me in. I thought back to the day we first spoke and how I left, almost running away in fear. I wondered what it would be like to go back and talk again, after my visit with Dimitri, after all I had learned.

"Next time," I said out loud as I reached for the ignition.

Before I could turn the key, a green and red hummingbird appeared just on the other side of my windshield, hovering in place, staring directly into my eyes. "Come on now," I mumbled in disbelief.

I slowly moved my head forward and rested my chin on top of the steering wheel. Its wings vibrated loudly, hovering back and forth just inches from the glass. I was amazed at how its physicality worked in unison with every movement. *Okay, I get it.*

I looked up in the sky, took a deep breath in, blew it out, and said out loud, "I couldn't make this shit up if I tried."

» » « «

"How nice of you to join us again, Officer Marcus. Please come on up!" Ana's voice bellowed onto the street from behind the bushy vegetation.

How does she do that? I opened the metal gate, its squeak announcing my journey through the maze of thick foliage leading to her porch. I found her sitting in the same chair as our first meeting, rocking slightly, while knitting away, the feeble wood under her quietly creaked with every sway.

"Como estas, hijo?" she asked with a thick Latin accent.

"No muy bueno, ahora." I said, taking a crack with my bad Spanish. "What's going on here, Ana?" I calmly asked in surrender.

She attempted to appear naive. "Well, it's a blanket, I just started—"

"Stop. You know what I mean. This is getting to be a bit much to handle."

"Really? What part of it all is a bit much?" she asked innocently.

"How about the phenomenon of a half-wit street kid being transformed into some kind of genius, or prophet, or I don't know what? Oh, and don't forget the part where I shot and killed him, only to have him return from the dead to speak to me telepathically. And how about our late-night encounter where you directed me to visit said genius in prison via mystic knitwear. Last but not least, there's your little green hummingbird friend that you sent to draw me here not once but twice."

"Huitzil," she said.

"What?"

"His name is Huitzil."

"Whatever!" I shouted, though she didn't seem to notice or care about my frustration.

"Mmmm, si entiendo, hijo. You've created many situations, and I can see you want some answers. My question to you is, are you ready to hear them?"

"I didn't create anything. I would venture to say that you actually created the last two and were most likely involved in the first as well."

"You seem to have your mind made up about a lot of things."

I paused dramatically, hoping to drive the importance of all this home. "I know what I saw."

"What you saw? What you experienced? What comes through the limited perspective of the five senses is hardly reliable. The complexity of this goes beyond what you are ready to hear, but I'll gladly give you what I know you can handle at this moment if you'd like."

"I'm all ears."

She placed her knitting project on the table and said, "You see, Marcus, the human race has reached a tipping point. Last time you were here, you said the world was worse than ever, and, in a sense, you were right. But beyond that seemingly eternal cloud of suffering, the light is shining through, just as the sun breaks through the clouds on a gloomy day. People are taking a new interest in healing themselves. They're doing this not only on the physical level but deep inside as well, asking the important questions about their suffering. Have you noticed what I am speaking of?"

"I have a friend who has gone to some intensive workshops," I replied. "Something to do with resolving past issues. He swears by it.

"Then there's Donna from the department. She's gotten into meditation and practices something she calls mindfulness. I noticed her diet is pretty strict. No animal anything. She even went to a ten-day meditation retreat where no one spoke the entire time. For most of us in the department, it seemed odd, but, if I'm honest, I'd say she seems pretty content.

"But here's the weirdest one. A friend of mine from my AA group went all the way to South America to drink some kind of tea with a shaman. I'm not sure what happened there, but this guy has done a complete one-eighty in every way. He's mended some seemingly unfixable family issues going back to his childhood and gotten back together with his wife. On top of it all, he hasn't touched a drop of alcohol since his trip, and that was over four years ago. He claims to have, how does he say it, 'lost the desire to put anything in his system that takes him away from the natural beauty of life itself.'"

"Yes, Marcus. That's exactly what I am talking about," Ana said excitedly, a smile growing on her face. "Meditation and similar workshops and programs are very helpful and can be a great bridge for something even more intensely profound, but only for those who are ready, like your friend Peter."

Did I say his name?

"Okay, but that's only three people out of hundreds that I know. You are making it sound like it's some kind of movement or something. I guess if you throw all of the people doing yoga into the mix, then what you said makes sense."

"For the most part, that's something entirely different from what your three friends are experiencing, at least here in the west. As you might have noticed, many who have joined in the yoga craze are there for the physical aspect. They become fit, flexible, relaxed, healthier. There is nothing wrong with that. It's just another experience in the physical, and that's beautiful.

"True yoga, the science of yoga, is a principle with a practice that can lead one toward inner awakening and unity by detaching identification with the construct of body, mind, and desire. Through this practice, one can attain liberation from the false sense of self, the cause of all human suffering. A large percentage of yogis of the west, teachers and students alike, don't walk the path of unity consciousness."

Interesting.

"But those three friends of yours are diving into their own consciousness and seeing their own muck. It's a form of shadow work. This is where one takes responsibility for the ills of their own life, knowing they are able to shift them by breaking through the imagined limitations of their own internal dialogue. This allows the dismantling of the programming and will enable them to see they are, in fact, in union with all that is. They can then begin to operate from a heart-centered existence. Humans today are so caught up in the mind. That's done by design, of course, to keep you trapped in fear so you cannot know who and what you truly are. That's why you treat each other the way you do. As if there was actually another."

Again, interesting, but I'm not buying it.

"Programming," I inquired. "You mean, like in a computer? Because if programming has happened, then there must be a programmer. Is that what you meant by it being done by design?"

Ana seemed to have completely forgotten her knitting. She was engrossed in the knowledge she doled out.

"Let's just make sure you are clear on what I mean by programming, first. If you were born on planet Earth, fraudulent mental and energetic conditioning is part of your makeup. Period. It started with what your programmed parents and others told you when you were young and then the deeply flawed education system took over from there. This conditioning, whether you know it or not, is the cause not only of your personal downfall, Marcus, but that of humankind as well.

"Would you not agree that most people are unhappy with their jobs, their relationships, their life in general? Have you ever asked yourself why? All this running around chasing money, trying to survive, worrying about the future. How about the perpetual search for love, trying to find that perfect partner. Can you see how it more often than not leaves one wanting? Do you ever wonder why people have addictions to drugs, alcohol, social media, shopping, food, sports, exercise, sex, work, or just staying busy in some way or another?

"There is a deep undercurrent vibration that has a grip on you all. It comes as an internal voice that is so ingrained that it seems normal—so normal that it goes unnoticed. This voice tells you you are right and others are wrong. It tells you that in order for you to survive, you must win, have, or be more than another. This voice has you believing there is not enough money, love, safety, or well-being.

"I tell you this: ever since you've believed that voice, you have been kept small and weak. You align yourself with the dark entity, the programmer, the one that set this up. It lurks in the shadows and has taken human form only to position itself in such a way that you are all dependent on it. It is now planning its next move. To use fear to herd the cattle towards an even more enslaved existence."

Equally concerned and put off by her comments, I asked. "If this is true, what's the solution?" She paused for a moment.

"Why, young Dimitri is. That's why you're here, Marcus."

I slid back in the chair. That day at the prison I knew there was something special about Dimitri, but this ... this was hard to digest.

"He is the spark," she said calmly, confidently. "The rest of you, as you join, will bring about the solution. This programming, as well as the programmer, with all of its perceived power that's endured millennia, engraved on every aspect of the human condition—its days are numbered. With your help, Dimitri is going to expose the greatest lies ever told, and, once he does this, everything will change."

"With my help? I still don't get how I'm involved in this. What am I supposed to do?"

"Like I told you before. You will understand what needs to be done when the moment comes. All who are involved will, including Dimitri. But I think it is important that you know, hijo, that the time is coming soon. The darkside is amping up for the final showdown. Their first wave of deception will be rolled out to instill panic into everyone on this planet. That is how they will control you, through your fear. This will spark a crisis that will cause the *already* crumbling financial system to fall, bringing humanity to its knees. Their aim is chaos in the streets, forcing the herd to voluntarily walk right into its trap. But as the weakened, injured cattle move in that direction, you all will step up and bring back equilibrium to the masses."

Her intensity shrank to a tiny smile. "I mean, what else is there to do, right?" she whispered.

Wait. Where have I heard that before?

Very little of what she'd said actually landed for me. I was especially stuck on the "you all will step up" part. I had a real problem with people telling me what I was to do, and I actually *could* think of other things to do with my time.

"I don't appreciate you predicting my future." Now it was my time to preach. "I don't believe anyone can see what's ahead, not even me. And you're speaking as if I don't have a say in any of this. Last time I checked, the freedom to choose is a major component of being alive. I'm just not sure if I'm ready for all of this right now, Ana."

She smiled and looked back up at me. "It's not *as if* I'm predicting your future, Marcus. I *am* predicting it." She then laughed, bowed her head, and extended her hand towards me, while condescendingly saying, "If it makes you feel any better, I graciously invite you to choose to do whatever it takes to snap out of it and step up." The smile left her face, "The window for human survival on this planet is closing every day as mass pollution and devastating agricultural practices derived from greed permeate your earth and pollute your water and air as well as your spirit.

"Speaking of your polluted spirit, let's talk about how you treat each other: The incessant pointing of fingers to whoever or whatever you're blaming this week for your failures and limitations, be it a difficult childhood, partner, masculinity, race, president, or whatever unfair card you believe you've been dealt. That vile sniveling that scorches the possibility of global unification as its toxic off-gases fuel the raging fire of polarization. All of this held in place by those who act solely from their own moral turpitude. Then, to calm your self-inflicted suffering, you fill your gullet with poisonous food and drink fed to you by the same dark entity that brought you into this situation in the first place.

"Of course, once your body or mind has had enough abuse, it contracts a disease, ailment, or mental illness, a last-chance message for you to clean up and come back home. So, what do you do? You go back to your co-conspirators of misery, those who have taken human form—those who own you, feed you, print the money you believe you earn. You go back to them, and they give you their drugs, not to heal you, but to mask the symptoms while another condition is being nurtured deep within.

"This is the cycle of insanity that has been designed to enslave you by the slave masters as they hide behind your supposed leaders, who continue to grow the war machine, now in its most precarious state ever. And you just sit here, Marcus, as the trembling fingers of madmen rest on the buttons of mass destruction, just waiting for the *wrong moment* to end it all, and you say you aren't ready?" She shook her head in disgust.

"So, what I say to you now is, *get ready, then, hombre,* because the world *is* ready. It's never been more ready. You all have fallen enough, the bottom has been hit. Humankind will either shoot back or be annihilated, it's one or the other. So, I'm sorry you're not comfortable hearing this, but quite frankly, I don't give a damn about your comfort level right now, I've got bigger fish to fry, hijo."

She calmly picked up her knitting as if this kind of conversation was a daily occurrence.

I walked to the corner of the porch. It was as if my feelings and thoughts were being yanked from one side to another. On the one hand, I felt violated as if I wasn't in control. On the other, I was honored by being included in this potential madness that might not be so mad after all.

Ana was suddenly standing next to me. Caringly, she pointed at the painted pattern on the floor. "Venga amor. Stand in the wheel of love and make your declaration of who you are in this world. *Step into agency* along with Dimitri and the others to come. Enter the village! Answer the call!" I noticed the footprints had almost completely faded from the center. "Come and speak to what is already accomplished in the quantum, chico mio."

What's with this village thing?

"No, gracias," I said, turning my back. "I don't know what that means and really don't care to know right now."

I wondered how this great feat she spoke of would even take place. What would Dimitri do to cause such an extensive change, especially from prison? How could I even help? Where would I find time for my revived relationship, my job, and the other things I liked to do in the little free time I had. And what the hell was "agency"? I noticed there were two voices in my head. One that wanted to help in a cause that seemed too good to be true. Another that weighed in for me, my family, and their well-being.

I turned to find Ana gazing at me seriously. "Do not waste another thought. You need not explain anything to me, only I to you. With your permission, I will now address the two voices in your head."

What? How did she know about the two voices?

"Okay," I mumbled, hoping that it was just another strange coincidence.

"You are wondering what Dimitri could do and how he could do it from prison. The *little you* has doubts concerning your participation in such a grand endeavor. Diga me, hijo, how am I doing so far?"

Immediately, the feeling of nausea hit me as I stared down at the tattered wood floor. *Jesus Christ, she can read my mind.*

She reached over and patted my arm. "Yes, I can. But at this moment, Jesus doesn't have much to do with it. I'll continue. Try not to interrupt with any new thoughts, comprende, hijo?

"Dimitri will do what he was sent here to do, first through his example. Then, as he rises to become the highest version of himself, he will take humanity with him, one individual at a time. The majority of his work will commence once he is released, but while he's inside, he'll hone the tools that have been given to him. Your question around how he might reach so many is a valid one, as a revolution of this magnitude must involve a tremendous amount of awakened warriors to stand up to what's coming your way. At this moment, I can only tell you that something of this scale can only be accomplished through the use of technology, but in a form quite different from the one *they* are planning to use against you all very soon. Yes, technology, the very thing that has helped split wide open the cracked hull of this ever-sinking ship you call the human race, will ultimately aid as a major part of the rescue boat that will save you all."

She slowly pulled a bag of peanuts out of her pocket.

"Cacahuates?" she asked calmly, cracking their shells.

What the heck? "No, gracias," I muttered.

"As far as your role," Ana said between bites of peanuts, "it's one of la mas importante de todos. You have been chosen to take care of him, and you need not worry now about how this will occur or what you have to do. It will all happen organically, in accordance with a well-defined but surreptitious plan. All that will be required of you is that you trust."

I felt sick to my stomach, a condition of nervousness I'd had since childhood. Normally I kept it in check, but mind-reading grandmothers and trained hummingbirds were getting the best of me.

She tilted her head to one side, studying me. "Estas bien, hijo?"

"I'm okay," I sputtered as I brought my fingers to my mouth and glanced at the stairs. "Is there anything else you have to say?"

"Yes, thank you for asking," she said, putting away the peanuts. "There are two voices in you. But which *is* you? The one who worries about tomorrow, money, your relationship, and all the heaviness of the world? Or the one that heard the truth and felt honored to help in a cause too good to be true. Which one are you? Or perhaps I should ask, which will you choose to be? Will you be at cause for something greater than those things you want in your life? Are you ready to sacrifice your earthly desires for a new world, a new way?"

I shot across the porch, down the stairs, and vomited in her garden. Wiping my mouth with my sleeve, I turned back to see her standing at the railing.

"I think I've heard enough today," I said, my voice cracking under the pressure of her overwhelming presence. Not waiting for her to reply, I scurried down the path towards the gate.

"Marcus Angbo Ogabi!" She shouted in a voice that paralyzed me beneath the greenery. "You think you know what your destiny is? A husband to Lisa, a father to Hope? One of the city's finest, patrolling East Borough in your Crown Victoria, drinking with your buddies after your shift? Only I know your true destiny. The role I've chosen for you is much grander in that it will safeguard humanity's right for others to enjoy these things. It is so grand, chico, that if you knew, your reaction would be much greater than purging on my lilies."

I looked up at her one last time as she stood up straight with both of her hands on the railing.

"So, Marcus, I call on you, the true you, your highest version, the correct voice. I will do this by only calling forth your unbridled volition in this most sacred of matters."

"No," I shouted, trembling. "I didn't sign up for this. This is something that's more than I can do. Hell, I don't even know what that something is. If you can hear my thoughts, then you know this is not for me. I'm a cop, raised by a family of cops, and the last thing I want is to be part of some kind of revolution. I respectfully decline your offer. I am leaving now. And please don't send the hummingbird after me."

I turned and made my way to the gate. I could hear her chuckling as I fumbled with the latch. I started walking, then ran up the sidewalk to my car.

"My understanding, you say!?" she yelled. "Understand this, hijo. My repertoire doesn't end at mental telepathy, hummingbirds, and late-night visits. Nos vemos pronto, hijo mío, nos vemos muy pronto!"

SINS OF THE FATHER

ZACH

Saying I had issues with my father would be a huge understatement. I despised him. A greedy billionaire who stepped over whomever and whatever he had to, to get more or to be more. For Terrance Markland, our planet, along with its resources, existed solely for his use, a means to an end, an end that, as far as I could tell, would never come.

It wasn't until high school, where I excelled at mathematics and computation, that I met some activist kids who'd show me who he really was. They spelled out what his companies were really up to and how they did it. That's when I began to rebel against him with the little power I had. I'd argue my point with him every chance I got, but he, as well as my mother and sister, always brushed it off as just a phase I was going through. They'd tell me I should be thankful for his hard work, that it set up the lifestyle we had. It was all bullshit in my eyes.

Later in life, I enrolled in the country's top university where I was quickly labeled a mathematical tech prodigy. I was set to win the Turing Award and graduate early and top of my class, when I devised my three-prong plan of revenge against Terrance. I'll gladly go into the details another time, but let's just say it was the third prong that landed me in prison and humiliated my father so much. It permanently wedged a stake between us.

》 》 《 《

After the Earl and Pete incident, I began to open up to Dimitri about my childhood. He'd just listen and nod as if he grasped the weight of my dilemmas and the drama that went with them. He did that until the day he simply said, "Whenever you're ready to end this, I believe I might be able to help you."

"End what, D?"

"Your incessant blaming of others for the things you find difficult in your life." His couldn't-care-less stare and ice-cold words made my head jolt backward.

Find difficult? "Like I have nothing to be pissed about. Have you been listening, bro?"

"I have, *bro*," he said, mocking my tone, "and you have plenty to be pissed about if that's what you are choosing for yourself. You know, to stay pissy. Come to think of it, I've been thinking about nicknames for you. You gave me D, now it's my turn. Yours can be Pissy. Yeah, Pissy Zach. PZ for short. I like that. What do you think, PZ?"

Livid, I jumped up and faced him. "Not funny, Tanomeo. Choose, you say? I have chosen nothing. The things my father did, he really did. I didn't ask him to do them."

He smirked at my attempt to be bold. "Maybe so, but it's how you perceive what happened and what you choose to make of it. That's what you might want to look at. Have a seat there, bruiser."

I stayed put. "Excuse me, but there's only one way to perceive bad things. Bad is bad, and my father, because he did, does, and always will do bad things, will always be a bad man. Pretty simple stuff here, wouldn't you say?"

He flashed his usual goofy, innocent smile. It was like a baby that's impressed by the most ordinary of things.

"Simply flawed, yes," he chuckled, "Your father's acts are just acts. They don't define who or what he really is. There is no such thing as a bad person. There might be people who do bad things, but ultimately that doesn't make them bad."

I paused, giving his bizarre theory a moment to sink in, and realized I didn't like it. "You know that concept doesn't hold any weight in the real world, don't you?" I said.

"What is the real world, Zach. Could you explain that to me?" he said with what appeared to be genuine curiosity.

"Well, you know," I started, "we all know what's good, bad, right, and wrong, and in this world, we use a concept of morality to dictate what those things are. What my father does is clearly bad in the eyes of our world and especially bad for me."

As I schooled him, I got a strange feeling he knew more than he was letting on. He reached over, grabbed a notepad and pencil from his storage box, and sat up, ready to take notes.

"Okay, come on, Zach, sit down and tell me all the things your father does that are bad, as you put it."

"You better get another pad for that." I sat down on the floor and faced him.

"Go on now, I'll write small." He winked.

"Okay, where do I start?"

"Start with your childhood."

I told the tale of my shitty childhood, starting with how my father, with his big career and celebrity status, never had the time for his kids. Then, when I was nine, he had a fling with another woman, crushing my mother's spirit, leading her into a state of deep depression. Since then it's been nothing but wine and Prozac for her, leaving my sister and me to be raised by our nanny. We were kept out of the way in the east wing most of the time. As I got older, I cut my emotional ties with both of my parents, disgusted, not only by his now in-the-open infidelity but also by her lack of courage to leave him.

I concluded my rant by saying, "On top of it all, he assumed I'd just take over his tech company after I graduated from the prestigious Carnegie Mellon."

Dimitri stayed busy writing until I stopped speaking. "Okay. And that last one. He assumed something. Oh, that's just terrible, Zach. Really."

"Well, I guess you don't have to put that one down," I confessed.

"No, Zach, I'm getting all of these atrocities on paper so we can look at each one of them," he said flippantly. "What else ya got for me?"

"Well, the greedy bastard owns several companies that are responsible for the destruction of our fragile ecosystem. His factories deplete the ozone layer as they spew greenhouse gases and other contaminants into the air. As if damaging the planet and its atmosphere wasn't enough, he's also guilty of a shitload of human rights violations. Slaving away in horrific conditions, thousands of laborers in several third world countries turn out senseless products to feed the endless cravings of a materialist society—all of it under the flag of his corporate empire."

"Is that it, Zach?"

"Um, there's got to be another one," I uttered as Dimitri looked at me attentively. "Oh, and he's a money whore. Write that down as well," I announced happily, pointing at the pad.

"Mon-ey wh-ore," he repeated slowly, his head tilted to one side. "Never heard that one, but wouldn't you say it falls under the category of greedy bastard?"

"I guess you're right about that."

"Well, we've got quite a few here, and if you think of anything else, just let me know. So, take a look." He showed me the pad where he had listed the things my father had done. His writing was nearly illegible, and he must have noticed the look on my face as he responded shamelessly, "Oh, my writing's never been very good." He laughed and said, "I didn't go to Carnegie Hall University."

"That's Carnegie Mellon, D."

It was true that he'd never really been to school but, with the little time he did spend in one, he'd learned to read, and he would do that voraciously, devouring books to the tune of three a week.

I studied the list:

Left kids with nanny in east wing
Has sex with other women
Assumed something
Works to make a lot of money
Uses the planet's resources
Depletes ozone layer

"Whoa, D," I protested. "You're missing all the shitty stuff I told you about? 'Works to make a lot of money?' That's not how I said it. I told you he was a greedy bastard and ruthless businessman that spends all of his time chasing money. And 'has sex with other women?' He's a fucking man-whore, bro."

"Maaaan … whore. Another new one. I didn't know there were so many compound words with whore in them, but I digress. So, Zach, what I've done is written down what actually happened. Just the facts, the physical act only, without any description of what you or anyone else makes of those acts."

"The deleted scenes you've edited out have meaning. You get that, right?"

"Yes, I do, and let's start with that."

"With what?"

"What you just said. Meaning. That's where we can begin." He pointed.

"Let's take the first one: 'left us with nanny.' What does it mean when some-one leaves their kids with a nanny?"

I gave him a confused look. "What do you mean, what does it mean? It means he's an asshole for not raising his children correctly."

"Okay, but what word would you use to describe someone who does that? If someone leaves their kids with a nanny because they are too busy, what do we say it means?"

Where are these questions coming from? I stared at him for a moment, not understanding why I had to spell it all out for him. "Okay, Dimitri, if you don't take care of your kids properly, if you leave them with another person to raise, that's being ir-re-sponsible, and that is bad. Copy that, amigo?"

"Perfecto, now we're getting somewhere." He began to write again. "So, just to be clear, one is irresponsible if they raise their kids with a nanny?"

I scrunched my brow. "Well, the way you say it, it sounds like it's not a big deal."

"Really? Then let's dive in a bit deeper. I'm sure you can come up with more meaning around 'leaving the kids to be raised by a nanny,' can't you?"

"Well," I paused, giving it some thought, sure to have an ironclad answer. "A person who does that surely doesn't love and care about their kids. I mean, any father who does that, you know, raises their kid wrong, is bad in my book."

"I might say that one would have their kids raised by a nanny because they love them and want what's best for them, but what do I know?"

I let loose a burst of sarcastic laughter. "Not my father. That's not why he did it!" I snapped.

He threw his hands up. "Whoa, calm down there, amigo. I hear you. Let's move to another one. This time you choose and pick out the worst of all, will ya?"

I yanked the list from his hands, wanting to find anything that would strengthen the case against my father. I scanned, trying to decide between his greed or mass destruction of the planet. I chose greed, seeing how it was the root of all his evils. I handed the notepad back to Dimitri, pointing to my choice.

"The money!" he yelled out. "Yes, such an important one for so many people these days."

We went on and completed the same exercise. First, he asked me what it means when someone chases money, and I told him that they are greedy, shallow, and unsatisfied. I told him it meant we, as a family, weren't enough for him, that he loved money more than he loved us, and that was wrong, thus making him a bad father and a bad person in general.

"I want to find one theme word that describes everything your father's done or hasn't done," Dimitri continued. "Like what it means to you, Zach. If we look at the list from the top down, with the first being you were left with a nanny and it meant he was irresponsible, et cetera, what did it mean, ultimately, to you?"

I looked at the list while scratching my head. "To me personally?"

"Yeah. Many people in the world can act in certain ways, but everything he did made you feel something—something about the way he shows up for you."

"Well, to be honest, it feels unfair."

"Perfect. Let's look at the rest of these. Could we say that him having physical relations with other women would be unfair as well?"

"Absolutely, and we'd be right," I stated with confidence.

"And if we looked at the rest of stuff on the list, we could probably come back to it being unfair in some way or another, right?"

I glanced at the list. "Yeah, if I break it all the way down, I feel he's been very unfair to me and my family."

"Perfect, we have our word and it's 'unfair,'" he said and wrote the word at the bottom of the list.

Left kids with nanny in east wing **irresponsible, unloving, uncaring**
Has sex with other women **doesn't love mom**
Assumed something **lame**
Works to make a lot of money **greedy, unsatisfied, shallow**
Uses the planet's resources
Depletes ozone layer
Unfair

"But there's much more to the story," I mumbled, pretty miffed by the lack of content needed to slam my father.

"You just said it, Zach, right there!" he shouted. "The word 'story' ... that's exactly where I'm going next."

I shot up. "I didn't make this up! It's not a story. These things really happened, dude!"

"I know *something* happened, but there's a difference between what actually happened and the meaning you gave to it." He took the pad back and repeated to point at what he wrote. "You see, he did what he did in the physical sense, and then we have what you say about it, what it means to you personally. *You* made him making a lot of money mean that you and your family are not enough and that he loves money more than you, which ultimately makes him bad. From there you can say that all of his actions are unfair, as you put it."

He waited for my response before showing me the pad again, which only pissed me off more. I pushed it out of my face. *He's making light of my situation.* But if I'm honest, what was really bothering me was that I was questioning my own thought process.

He turned and straightened up, now looking at me more directly than before. "The word 'greedy,' do you know what it means? I'm talking about the true definition?"

What a question. First, this guy minimizes my father's evil doings, and, now, he's questioning my intelligence. "You do know I was labeled a technical wunderkind at the age of twenty, right?"

He smiled, but I could tell it wasn't for my achievement but rather the blowing of my own horn. That embarrassed me, so I decided to make a joke.

"D, let's just put it this way: If you were to open the dictionary and look up that word 'greedy,' you'd see a picture of T. W. Markland."

He let out a loud chuckle. "I'll stick with the Merriam-Webster definition if that's okay with you."

"Whatever, dawg. You do you."

"If my memory serves me correctly, the exact definition of the adjective 'greedy' is, 'having or showing an intense desire for something, especially wealth or power.'"

"Señor Terrance to the tee," I shot back.

"Okay, so I am now going to ask you something, and I invite you to be authentic and honest in your answer."

I rolled my eyes sarcastically. "I'm pretty sure I can do that."

There was a long pause as he looked me in my eyes before saying, "Have you ever been greedy?"

"No. Never. Not once," I snapped, not even having to think about it.

"Take a moment and think about it again," he smiled.

I gave it some thought. I always had money but never wanted more like my father did.

"No. Honestly, I can't think of a time," I responded.

"So, let's get clear about the definition: an intense desire for something."

"And what about the rest of it? You know, the wealth and power part. Let's not forget the most important part of the definition," I reminded him.

"No, I didn't forget, but the core definition is exactly as I said it. The word 'especially' is an adverb; therefore, it can't change the subject. I imagine, being the wunderkind of the Mellon patch, you must understand this."

I laughed, "Okay, that was good."

"So, I ask you again, have you been greedy?"

"Doesn't change a thing. No," I responded.

"Really?" he answered sharply. "You've never had an intense desire for anything? Sex, food, cars, or maybe *fame?*"

He'd made his point. It was clear he knew about my reputation, most likely through the prison rumor mill. I had wanted fame more than anything at one point in my life, and, to be honest, I still did. I desired it so much I figured out a way to break out of a low-security prison by hacking into their system and changing my release date. At the time it seemed like a good idea because I knew it would catapult me to the top of the cyber hacking elite where I'd garner a whole new level of celebrity. What I didn't realize was that I'd end up in this shithole with inbred Aryan rapists and dickhead guards. I guess I thought my father would get me another deal, but instead, he stepped out of the picture and the judge made an example of me, sending me to the real deal, Carlton. Now, here I sit in a cell with a violent hood rat turned saint, who was pressing me to be uncomfortably honest with myself, and I have to admit, I didn't like it.

"Come on, Dimitri. You can't compare that to the level of greed my father runs on. It's just not fair."

"Fair you say? We will talk about what's fair later, but for now, I can compare it because it's just another side of the same coin. You had a deep lust for fame, and your father has a deep lust for wealth and power. One is not better nor worse than the other. Does that make sense?"

"No, man, it doesn't. Terrance's greed has hurt many people. His overseas factories cause pollution. The people working in them live in squalor while he sits in his big chair smoking Black Dragons to the tune of over a hundred grand per box.

"Do you know why I'm a wunderkind?" I asked, feeling the usual pride I felt for the statement. "Because I have a special talent for computer systems. It's a gift, and I use that gift for good. I learned the truth about what my father does way back at the boy's academy. I knew he was evil even then. And then, at university, I joined some protest groups and really found my people. My calling. I became a true activist, or, in my case, a hacktivist."

"That must have been difficult to put yourself through such a costly education. I mean, how did you do it at just sixteen? And then there's college. How many jobs did you have to work, Zach?"

I struggled to think of something clever to say, to save face, but ended up sitting in silence.

"I'm going to make some tea," Dimitri said casually. "Would you like some?" He walked in humble victory toward the tiny electric stove in the back of our cell.

I was frustrated and more than a little pissed off. "This is bullshit."

"The only bullcaca here is what spews from your mouth when you try to defend your position of victimhood!" He'd spun around and was now pointing his finger at my face. "The great perpetrator of countless crimes against humanity, Terrance Markland, and his legendary, greedy-for-fame son, Zachary. What a pair, the two of you!"

He was laughing, heartily and without irony. He truly found it funny. "So, we've got a guy just chasing money like a mad dog, seemingly unaware of all of the damage he's doing, at least on a conscious level. I mean, he might know that it's hurting others as well as the environment, but he apparently doesn't care right now.

"Then there's you, who *does* know and who supposedly *does* care but still participates. You use his blood money for your schooling, your pleasures, your own greed. Maybe not right now, because you've been cut off, but that was daddy's choosing wasn't it? Why if he hadn't done that, you'd be guzzling RC Cola and chomping on nacho cheese chips from the commissary right now."

His green eyes penetrated deep into me as I realized he was right. "How's that little dose of reality sitting for you, Zachy boy?"

I looked down at my hands, emotions stirring. "So, I'm bad too then. Is that what you are saying?"

He handed me a cup of tea and sat on the floor to face me. "For me, the bad, if you want to use that word, is in the blaming of others. It's just so hypocritical, Zach, in every circumstance. We've all experienced being greedy and all of us have done some not-so-nice things to people. Seeing this in yourself will allow you to have compassion for him as well as others. Through compassion you'll find that there is no bad, there's only *what is*."

I covered my face with my hands. "I'm confused, D. I've been pissed about this for so long, I don't know how to be unpissed. He still abandoned us to chase money, he cheats on my mom, and does so much other sucky stuff. What do you have to say about that, Doctor Phil?"

Dimitri gave me a confused smile. *This guy doesn't know who Dr. Phil is.*

"I'd say we can narrow it down to just one word, as you said before. Your father is 'unfair,' right?"

"Ah yeah. Unfair. I'd say that sums it up," I mumbled cautiously.

He cleared his throat and asked sternly, "Have you ever been unfair to anyone at any moment in your life, Zach?"

"Fuck you, dude! I knew you were gonna say that!" I shouted as he laughed so loud it echoed outside our cell and into the hall. I watched as he clapped his hands, amused by my frustration. I scooted to the edge of the cot, placing my hands on my knees and looked down at the floor.

He remained silent, letting me have my moment as a big truth set in.

"Does this make me a monster?" I eventually asked.

"No, brother. It makes you human," he whispered as he patted my foot. "You can transcend that humanness right now by letting go of that anger, by seeing yourself in him. Forgive yourself first and, with that, he's automatically forgiven. See how you both did the best you could with the tools you had at the time. You can look at this as your invitation for awakening, Zach."

Awakening?

He got silent again as if he knew something was coming into me. And it was. Clarity. For the first time, I saw the similarities between my father and myself. Another person might have not used his money if they didn't feel good about where it came from, but I did. I wasn't bad. I, like my father, was just doing my best.

He had more to say on the subject and guided me to see that my father had done some great things as well. His slew of products helped people do their jobs more efficiently, sleep better, and feed their babies. His tech company created software that revolutionized the way people lived and did business all over the planet.

He explained how, indeed, a great imbalance did exist, but it was up to us to take responsibility for our part in it. We had to recognize that, in an esoteric sense, we are the ones who created that imbalance. Only after we recognized that, would we be able to stand up to those who tightly held the reins of the old system—a system that needed to die so another could take its place.

I took a deep breath and looked at Dimitri, really fully seeing him for the first time. That was the moment it truly sunk in. There was something different about him, something special. At the time, I didn't know what it was or if it was something of great significance. I could just feel he was good in the purest sense of the word.

"I don't know what to make of all this. It's a little embarrassing to say, but I kind of feel like I need to cry or something."

"Congratulations. And good work, Zach," he said, putting his palms together at his chest and giving me a slight bow.

"What are you congratulating me for?" I asked.

"For being man enough to acknowledge you need to cry."

"But men aren't really supposed to cry, D. I think you've got it backward."

He laughed. "No, Zach, the programming within you has it backward. Your internal system knows when it's time to release stored emotional energy. Holding it back comes from a narrative that's simply not true. These things and others will come to you as you continue to 'confront the dragon to get the gold.'"

Goosebumps erupted across my arm.

"Chicken skin never lies!" he yelled out, pointing.

I laughed with him. *This guy's a trip and a half, but I think I'm getting it.*

"So, I'm gonna decide for myself it's not a good idea to show my emotions in this place, and any crying that needs to be done should be done in private."

"I'm with you on that. And while you're at it, don't let any of the other inmates know that you were upset about having been raised by a nanny. Something like that might get you shanked in here."

» » « «

Later that night, we lay in our bunks in the near dark. I watched a moth flutter in the fluorescent light that leaked in from the walkway outside our cell door. My brain was still racing, thinking about what Dimitri had said and the change he'd sparked in me.

"Hey, D," I whispered. "Are you asleep?"

"Not anymore," he answered good-naturedly.

"What did you mean this afternoon when you said 'inner work'? Is there more to do?"

I felt him roll out of his bunk. He patted my arm and made his way to the back of the cell, where I heard him put the kettle on. *Why is he heating water?*

"For the most part," he said, "if you are in a human body here on planet Earth, there's still work to be done. To become your best version, you need to deprogram years of input as well as output. Only then can you move into the really great stuff. That little thing we did this afternoon is just the beginning. If you stay on the path, as I'm pretty sure you will, considering I have you as my captive audience, you will reach heights you've never dreamt possible."

There was so much to take in with this guy, and I started to feel a bit lost. "Path? What path? Where is it and how do I get on it?"

Even in the darkness, I could tell he was smiling. "I'm talking about the chosen path toward your inner awakening and transformation. We have all come here to do this. You can choose it for yourself right now if you wish. Of course, it's got to be natural and happen when you are ready. But be aware, hanging around the likes of me could very well propel you in that direction."

"We've all come here to prison for this?" I asked, lost again in his words. "As far as I know, I came here to do my time. I never got the literature on the 'path option.'"

His laugh rang through the blackness. "No, we came to planet Earth for it. Now that you mention it, to prison as well, but that's a deeper discussion for another time."

"Yo, D, very cool, all of it, but I'm not sure about going on any path and transforming myself. This already is a lot for me to digest."

"We'll see," he said smugly.

"I'm wondering why I still feel something around my father. I mean, I understand the logic you shared, and I want everything to be good between us again someday. The thing is, when I picture myself with him, it feels uncomfortable, just like before. Maybe even worse."

"What's happened is you've fixed it in your intellect. Mentally you understand the truth around what really happened. Once you cry, you will begin to remove the stored emotional energy. But there's another energetic aspect. This is where the unease still lies."

I considered what he was saying, but it sounded odd to me. *I better get used to him talking like this, I guess.* There was the quiet sound of metal touching as he moved items in the darkness.

"I don't get it," I said. "The lingering discomfort of what I'm feeling has something to do with energy?"

"No, Zach. It has everything to do with energy because everything *is* energy. It's a big discussion, and when the time is right, I can explain something about how the universe works in relation to the energy that it is. What's important now, though, is that I show you how to remove the energetic block with your father, to heal it."

"I'm all ears, D."

It got quiet again as he moved back onto his bunk, then whispered, "It's so simple that it's going to sound ridiculous. All you have to do is …"

That's when I heard the jingle of an overloaded keychain at our cell door.

"Inmate Markland, front and center!"

The keys belonged to Officer Tanas, the most corrupt CO in Carlton. Whatever he wanted, I knew it couldn't be good. The lights came on.

"We need you in the kitchen, right now, Markland. Let's go." I looked to see him open the door before placing his hands firmly on his hips.

"But, Officer Tanas … the kitchen is closed. If there's something to do, I can do it in the morning."

"What works is if you get your skinny ass moving down the hall with me, that's what works. This isn't a fucking country club, Mr. Zachary fucking Markland. Your rich daddy has no pull in here. Let's go."

What he lacked in height, he more than made up for in dickheadedness. Everyone knew he brought in drugs for the Mexican mafia as well as being their go-to boy when they needed help pulling off dirty deeds.

Dimitri slowly rose from his bunk. He was calm. Well, calmer than me anyway.

"What happened in the kitchen, Officer Tanas?" he asked with a steady voice. "Some kind of mess or something, I imagine?" I watched him stare into the guard's eyes with an intensity I'd never seen before. For a moment they seemed to be locked, and I could have sworn Dimitri's eyes vibrated. *That's weird.*

Tanas changed his tone, sounding more humble with almost a touch of fear or nervousness in it.

"Yeah, but it doesn't concern you, inmate," he said quietly before looking at me and shouting. "Let's get a move on, Markland!"

Dimitri closed his eyes and turned toward the stove and spoke to what seemed to himself, "Yo entiendo. Gracias, Nana."

"You okay, inmate?" Tanas asked.

Dimitri snapped out of it. "Yep, I'm great, thanks. Just a type of meditation I like to do when it calls me."

Tanas shook his head. "Tanomeo you're one weird motherfucker. Always in here wasting your time meditating and reading. You need to get out and make some friends. You never know when you're gonna need the backup." A sinister grin grew on his face.

I noticed Dimitri was holding his thermal cup as he quietly replied, "You're probably right about that one, Officer Tanas."

After climbing from my bunk, Dimitri pushed the cup into my hands. "Zach, take this tea with you for your sore throat." He was staring directly into my eyes.

What? I don't know what you're up to, but I'll play along. "Okay, thanks."

"Oh god," Tanas snickered, "this is good. How does it feel, Tanomeo, to be at the service of Country Club Boy here? I bet you never knew you'd just be one of the help for the Markland family."

What an ass. I don't even like country clubs.

Dimitri looked up and smiled, "Interesting choice of words there, Officer Tanas. 'At the service,' yes. And if you'd like to define me as 'the help,' I'd say you have no idea how right you are."

I walked out of our cell and headed toward the chow hall with Tanas. I felt the side of the cup in my hand. It was scalding hot.

INTERVENCIÓN DIVINA

ZACH

We got to the kitchen door and Tanas unlocked it. I entered first while he stayed outside, pacing.

"You gonna come in and show me what I need to do here, Officer Tanas?" I asked, waiting for instructions.

"Go on to the back, by the sink. There's a big mess there. Get working on it, and I'll get the lights."

Go back alone? Prison rules don't allow inmates to enter a freshly unlocked kitchen without an inspection by a guard first. I made my way to the sink area, straining my eyes in the darkness looking for the spill. I put the thermal cup on the countertop and kept looking.

Something didn't feel right. "Officer Tanas, you there? I can't find it if I don't have the lights on." Still, there was nothing. I began to walk back toward the entrance when I saw someone just inside the door.

"Officer Tanas, is that you?" I squinted again, trying to make him out.

"Hello, Buttercup." My stomach sank and my head began to spin. I saw the taller figure of Pete move behind Earl as he switched on the lights.

I began slowly moving backward, toward the dish area, and they proceeded in unison with my every step.

"You know you can't escape boy. It's a dead end back there, and there's nowhere for you to go."

It was true. There was no way out, but I continued backward in an attempt to buy time.

"I want you to know somethin'!" Earl shouted from out of eyesight. "Once we take care of your boyfriend, Tanomutto, you know, in the most permanent of ways, I'm gonna have Tanas transfer you to my cell. Or I to yours, it don't matter either way. You see, Zach, I neva' been with royalty before, so you're gonna be my queen and I'm gonna be yo king. Maybe ya daddy might give us a nice weddin' gift or somethin'. He can send it straight to my wife. We got us five kids, and a bit a' cash could really help. Whatcha think about that, sweetness?"

I frantically looked from side to side, hoping to find something to protect myself with. There was a huge, electric potato processor on the table, way too heavy for me to do anything with. Beyond that, there were just plastic dishes, some utensils, and sponges. I desperately started throwing anything I could find in his direction. That's when Earl popped his head around the corner and smiled.

"Honey, I'm home!" I threw another cup, but he pulled his head back and it sailed by, just missing him.

"Now, you are really starting to annoy me here, son! There's two ways this is gonna go down. The easy way is you just calm the fuck down and try to enjoy it. If not, Pete and me are gonna rush in and put a hurtin' ya! Either way, we gonna do what we came here to do. It's your choice now, boy!"

My back was literally up against the wall now. The only way out was through them, and I knew that wasn't happening. I also knew I didn't want to get the shit kicked out of me on top of the rape. For the first time in my life, I wished I were dead. My shoulders slumped and I started to cry. I dropped the plates and cups and heard them bounce loudly on the concrete floor.

I was weeping loudly when Pete stuck his head in the room, making sure I was calm. I watched them both charge toward me.

"No, please don't!" I cried, my hands covering my face, not wanting to see what was coming. I could tell by the tone of their voices that it was all business from here on out.

"I'm up first, Pete!" Earl ordered.

"I know, I know," Pete answered back.

I felt my body go cold. Pete was the first to reach me, grabbing my right arm violently, making me hiss in pain.

"Fuck!" I yelled. I was so weakened by fear that I had no fight in me.

Earl followed, seizing my left wrist while gripping my shoulder with his other hand. The room spun. My heart pounded and I began to hyperventilate. I collapsed and heard Earl say, "No, no, sweetness. Stay with us."

When I came to, they were holding me up, talking about getting me bent over something. They spun me around and pushed me onto the prep table. I heard cutting boards and utensils clank on the ground as Earl readied himself behind me.

Pete kept hold of my wrist, stretching my arm out while pushing firmly down on the back of my neck, forcing my head down onto the metal surface. I could feel the cold of the stainless steel against my left cheek as I stared at the broom handles and mops I used every day leaning against the wall. The strong odor of onion reminded me that I hadn't used bleach to properly clean the table before my shift ended. For some reason, those things triggered an even deeper sadness in me, and I began to cry even louder.

I thought of my mother, of how much I wished I could be with her. I thought of how much I had tried to hurt my father, and yet he was always there for me. I wanted to apologize, but it was too late. I knew that after what was about to happen, I would never be the same again. The Zach my parents knew and loved would no longer exist.

"No, please, no!" I screamed. When that didn't work I tried shifting gears, calming my voice in an attempt to reason with them. "Really, guys, please don't. I'll pay you anything you want. My father's rich as fuck."

They carried on preparing for the task at hand. I lifted my head to look back at Earl. He looked back at me and said, "This hand stays here on the table," and released my right hand. I kept it there as he ordered and returned the side of my face back down on the stainless steel countertop while he moved behind me. I could hear him pull down his pants. I was shaking so much I couldn't control any part of my body. I felt the warmth of my own urine run down my leg.

Earl pressed his body up against me. I could hear his panting as he reached under my shirt to feel my lower back and side. I cringed and writhed, trying to avoid his touch, but it was useless. Then the smell of his hot, wretched breath made me gag, twice. On the third, I threw up on the table, and I saw Pete pull back, then bust out laughing.

"Now what's so damn funny Pete?! I'm tryin' to have me a moment here!" Earl shouted.

Pete looked at the floor like a scolded child. "Sorry, Earl. It's just that this is the first time I seen a famous person throw up, and me havin' that thought and all made me laugh."

My vision began to blur as he groped the outside of my pants, moving upwards toward my backside. I began slipping out of consciousness again.

Out of nowhere, I heard a voice in my head say, "Zach." I opened my eyes only to see fuzzy colors and shapes. "Zach, the tea!" the voice said loudly.

My vision returned and there it was, two feet from my free hand sitting at the top of the table: the thermal cup.

I felt Earl's fingers grip the top of my pants firmly as he began to pull them down.

"Earl!" I shouted.

"What is it, punk?" he shot back, frustrated, holding tight to the back of my pants.

"Does your sow of a wife and the five little piglets know you're nothing but a hillbilly rapist that forces himself on kids in prison?"

There was an odd silence, neither of them believing what they'd heard. I took three short breaths and, with a burst of energy, lunged forward and grabbed the cup with my free hand, flipped the lid off, and tossed the hot liquid onto Pete's face. He released his grip immediately and fell to his knees.

I pulled my foot to the middle of Earl's chest and pushed as hard as I could, boosting myself further onto the table. Now on my hands and knees, I started crawling frantically toward the doorway. Earl, with his pants around his ankles, stumbled to grab my foot while Pete screamed in agony.

"I've got him, Pete, get up and help me."

It was do or die. Everything went into slow motion as I used my free foot to push the one-hundred-plus-pound steel peeler off the table and onto Pete's foot below. I heard the bone break and Pete howled in agony.

Earl exploded with anger, pulling me off the table and to the floor. I landed hard on my back, knocking the wind out of me. He pulled off one of his pant legs to gain stability and straddled me. I struggled to move. There was a half-naked redneck straddling my stomach, his arms flailing as he pummeled me with punches. I used my hands and arms to protect myself, deflecting some of the blows, but they kept coming. From the corner of my eye, I got a glimpse of Pete moaning on his back holding his leg up.

The punches slowed as Earl wore himself out. "Zach," he said wheezily. "I'm going to have to kill you here today, right now." I shook my head back and forth, the blood from the cuts on my face spilled into my eyes.

"No, Earl. No, you don't. Let's just stop now. Enough damage has been done," I said as both of us huffed and puffed.

"Zach, I just want ya to know somethin'!" Earl shouted.

"What?" I asked as my voice cracked in terror.

"I want you to know, I'm still gonna fuck ya while ya bleedin' out here on the floor."

He twisted his head around to look at Pete, all the while making sure to keep his weight on me.

"Give me the shiv, Pete."

This was it; my life was over. I was going to die in the kitchen of this rundown institution at the age of twenty-two. Tears rolled down my face as I relaxed my body, knowing. I closed my eyes and began to detach, Earl's voice growing distant as he yelled to Pete.

Then everything went silent, and I knew it was my time. I felt the presence of the blade over my head. *Here it goes.* I scrunched my eyes together, dreading the inevitable.

Forever seemed to pass .... *Why hasn't he stabbed me?*

I slowly opened one eye. My head jolted back, stunned by the sight of a size-twelve dark blue prison-issue slip-on next to my head. Inside of it was the foot of my cellmate.

I opened my other eye and turned, looking straight up at Dimitri as he stood, hands on hips, staring into Earl's eyes.

"I just wanna know one thing," Dimitri said, using a Southern accent just like Earl and Pete's. "Which one of y'all decided to have a party and not invite me?"

Earl, shiv in hand and still naked from the waist down, jumped backward off of me. I remained on the floor, looking straight up at the fluorescent ceiling lights, relieved to be alive.

"Hey, Zach," Dimitri said quietly. "I need you to get up. Can you do that, brother?"

"I think so," I answered. My voice sounded exhausted.

"Whatcha think you doin' there boy. I'm not finished with him yet," Earl said nervously.

Dimitri took a step, straddling me, a foot on either side of my stomach. *He's shielding me.* I was now looking at the back of him. He stood tall and straight, his hands still authoritatively on his hips.

"Step back, motherfucker!" Earl shouted.

"Zach, slide backward through my legs and stand up. Do it now!"

I scurried backward and used the table leg to get to my knees. I panted loudly. For me, at least, the danger was gone.

"We gonna kill you. You know that, dontcha, boy?" Earl shouted at Dimitri.

"Zach," Dimitri said.

"Yeah, bro?" I answered.

"It's time for you to get back to the cell. I'll be back soon."

"I can't leave you here, dude," I said.

"I'm not asking," he said, looking back at me as I moved slowly to a standing position. "Go," he whispered.

I walked slowly through the doorway. I was making my way toward the exit door through the kitchen when I realized I didn't want to leave him there alone. I made my way to the closed service window and peered through a small space between the frame and the wood shutter. I could see the back of Dimitri still standing in front of Earl, and I could hear everything.

"So, what are we gonna do here, Earl?" Dimitri asked.

"Well, mutt, first I'm gonna fuck you up, then figure out how to get back to my sweetness in the very near future so we can finish what we started. Either way, Tanomutto, you're both dead."

"So, you're gonna fuck me up? I should let you know you can't hurt me. I am what you might call 'unfuckwithable.'"

What a badass.

"It amazes me what someone will do for a piece of ass these days, Earl. Being sneaky, paying off guards, only to roll around on the ground getting all bruised up. For what? So poor Pete over there can have a burnt face and broken foot? So you can end up half-naked with a shiv in your hand? All to have sex with a young man who doesn't want to have sex with you?" He paused, looked around for a moment, then continued, "Just so that you didn't come all this way for nothing, why don't you take me instead?"

Dimitri reached down and pulled his shirt off. Earl's head snapped back, obviously affected by the sight of Dimitri's scars.

"Oh, do you like my tats?" Dimitri cooed. "They're a bit different than yours, aren't they? I got all but one when I was a little boy. There's a total of one hundred and ten of them. I make it a point to thank each of them every day." He reached for his waistband.

"I don't want nothin' like that with you!" Earl scoffed.

"But you wanted it with Zach. What's the difference? I'm not going to resist or anything. What is it that you don't like about me? I'm starting to feel a bit insecure here, Earl."

"You've got other things to be worryin' about right now," Earl said.

"Oh, it's the scars. If you want I can put my shirt back on and just take off my pants."

Earl lunged forward. Instead of defending himself, Dimitri opened his arms wide, exposing his midsection. He stood tall, his face toward the ceiling. He began making a loud, resonant, continuous tone that seemed to come from deep inside him.

Earl paused momentarily, not knowing what to make of this, then plunged the shiv into Dimitri's stomach. My jaw dropped, but there was no reaction from Dimitri. Not even a flinch.

Suddenly Dimitri's left hand swooped down and grabbed Earl's hand, the shiv still tightly grasped in it. Then Dimitri's other hand darted to grab Earl's free hand and pulled the Aryan's hands together, holding them tightly, the knife still plunged deep inside. The chanting sound stopped as his head turned down to look into Earl's eyes.

"Yes, Earl, this is what you wanted. And now you have it!"

Earl twisted frighteningly, trying to escape Dimitri's vice-like grip. Then Dimitri stepped forward, causing him to stumble back against the refrigerator.

"What the fuck are you doing, mutt? Let go of my fucking hands!" Earl ordered desperately as Dimitri pressed his body closer, the shank still buried inside of him.

"No, not just yet, Earl. I want to show you something. Can you feel where the blade is right now?" He gave a nod toward their bloody hands, encouraging Earl to do the same. Earl swayed back and forth, frantically trying to break free.

"Earl, stay with me here. I want to explain to you what's happening." Dimitri said, as I had a perfect view of Earl's terrified face. "At this point, the blade has cut through the skin and into the muscles of the abdominal wall. It's just millimeters from entering the retroperitoneum. We just need to go a little bit further. Are you following along, Earl?" He then pushed himself toward Earl and into the blade. "There it is, that was the pancreas we just hit, and I'm pretty sure we nicked the ascending colon as well. Exciting isn't it?" he whispered.

What the fuck?

Earl had given up struggling. Dimitri had his undivided attention.

"You're a fucking freak, man. Just let me go," Earl cried as most of the life had left his face.

"We're not quite finished here," Dimitri answered. "You see, Earl, this so-called damage that we've caused together, for me, is really nothing. I'm gonna let the doctors do what they do, but ultimately, it will be me who goes in and heals this thing at what many will say is a seemingly miraculous pace. And I guess that leads right into my message for today. We all have the power to heal ourselves. The people of the world just don't know it yet.

"Speaking of healing, Earl, you've sure got a lot of work to do. Whatever happened to you, what makes you do these things to other human beings, is something that can be healed if you are ready. It will require that you go way back and look at everything in your past. Once we address and heal our past issues, our traumas, then and only then may we stand in our own power. From there we can alter not only our own lives but the lives of others as we join in agency for a new earth, a new way."

Agency, I like that.

"I know this all must sound a bit crazy, but I want you to know what's possible for you, so I'm going to give you a little glimpse. Normally, I wouldn't do this, but seeing how Zach and I have so much work to do, here in this prison and beyond, we really can't be bothered by any more of your antics. So just this once."

I don't know what he's talking about, but I bet it's gonna be good! I stood in suspense, wondering what ass-kicking was coming for Earl while, simultaneously, wondering what D meant by "work in this prison and beyond."

"No man, I've had enough. I can't feel my hands anymore, please just let go." Earl cried, his head hanging in defeat.

"That's precisely what I'm going to do, and so will you, for about one second."

"What the fuck are you talking about?"

"Letting go. The key to liberation." I quickly pulled my head back as Dimitri glanced behind him and all around the room, making sure there was no one else there. I returned to watch when I heard him speaking. "This is what it's like to be free. You can only get here once you completely let go, in your life, so this is just a glimpse. Just know, for you to return to it someday, you'll have to do your own inner work. For now, all you have to do is surrender. You ready, Earl?"

"Please, I don't want this," Earl shouted. "I'm not ready."

"Oh, you're ready. You just don't know there's something to be ready for."

He gave Earl a nod and, with lightning speed, released his grip and shot both hands up, clenching the sides of Earl's face.

Dimitri's large palms seemed to be holding up Earl's dangling body, his bloody fingertips cupping the back of Earl's head. "Surrender!" Dimitri shouted, and Earl's body began to shake. The lights flickered, and Earl let out a blood-curdling shriek.

Dimitri released his hold, and Earl collapsed into Dimitri's arms. I heard the shank clang to the floor as Dimitri lowered Earl's body to the ground. Earl looked to be catatonic, his eyes wide, clear saliva oozing from his mouth. He came back slowly, fighting to catch his breath. As he regained himself, a joyous smile slowly came across his face.

"How, how, did you ...?" he stammered. "Oh my god, was that what I think it was?"

"Just a glimpse of the Truth, Earl. That's Truth with a capital T. A glimpse of what you really are. The rest will be up to you," Dimitri said as he knelt to help Earl with his pants.

"We are all it! It's inside of us! No, it is us! I thought it was up there somehow." Earl beamed. "That was amazin'. What did you just do to me, Tanomeo?"

Earl teared up. "Man, I'm sorry, really I am. Please forgive me. Can you do that? I need to know you forgive me!"

"You are forgiven, Earl, as I, too, ask for forgiveness for my part in all of this."

Earl stared up at Dimitri in amazement. "Thank you," was all he said. Every hair on my body stood up, as a strong rush of buzzing energy passed through my spine.

Tears welled up in my eyes as well. *Who is this guy crouching on the floor to help someone who just tried to kill him? What kind of person apologizes to someone who'd just stabbed him. How was it that he didn't feel any pain? What was this glimpse, and how did it turn Earl into a happy, blubbering mess?*

Dimitri turned to leave, and I took that as my cue to get the hell out of there and bolted through the main door and down the hall.

As I snuck through the walkways, getting closer to my cell, an elated voice reached me in the prison grayness. I knew it belonged to a white supremacist named Earl Mills.

"I love you, Tanomeo!" echoed down the halls. Little did I know, they were the last words I'd ever hear him speak.

» » « «

Waking up the next morning, I felt the skin of my forehead stuck to my pillow. There was a slight sting as it detached, and I opened my eyes to the sight of dried blood on the low-grade fabric. I spun as fast as my aching head would allow and scanned the bottom bunk. Dimitri had never made it back.

"Wake up, ladies!" the guard yelled as the lights went on. I jumped up, put my clothes on, and quickly made my bed.

The latch sounded and I slid the door to one side. I had just turned to brush my teeth when I heard the jingling keys again.

"Shit!" I yelled, startled to see Tanas standing in the doorway. "Whoa, whoa, what do you want?" I asked loudly, my hands raised in nonresistance.

"What I want, you little, rich fuck, is for you to keep your fucking mouth shut."

"Not gonna happen, you sadistic piece of shit," I said calmly. "You're going down."

An evil smile came to his face. "I think you need a lesson on how things really work here." He put his hand on his club. There was no way I could handle another traumatic event so soon on the heels of the one experienced with Earl and Pete. "You see, you're a fucking prisoner, a nobody. I, on the other hand, am a respected CO that's been doing this job for more than ten years, and—"

"That's because you're a fucking loser, Tan-*ass*." My temper combined with my fear got the best of me.

He stared at the ground. That was the second time I'd really regretted what I'd just said during my stay at Carlton. He nodded and returned with a smile even more sinister than before.

"That may be, but only in your eyes, you spoiled little fuck," he whispered, pulling out his club. He got right in my face and placed the tip of it on my chest. "At the end of the day, it's your word against mine. After your bullshit whining is heard, they'll believe me. After that, I'll make your life a living hell. Earl and Pete were pussycats compared to who's next in line. The boys I'm talkin' about will run a train on you seven strong."

I gulped, and I'm pretty sure he saw it. "Okay, just leave now," I breathed, my voice cracking.

He came in even closer, whispering in my ear. "I was actually imagining the call. You wanna hear it? It goes something like this: 'Mr. Markland, this is Officer Gene Tanas calling from the correctional facility, sir. I'm afraid I have some bad news. Your son, Zach, has died from blood loss due to a perforated colon. It seems that he'd been intimate with several different men in his block. Sometimes it takes a lengthy prison stay for young boys to come out of the closet. So sorry for your loss, sir.'"

He smiled, showing his perfect white teeth. He tapped his club lightly against my chest and walked backward to the door.

"You didn't see anything and you don't know anything. You play ball, and you might make it out of here a virgin." He slid his club back in its belt ring, gave his keys a shake, and walked out.

I let out a huge sigh. He was right. I wasn't gonna say a word. I was just a prisoner. One who'd tell a story that would eventually be ignored and, then, I would pay for telling it. That's how prison works.

» » « «

To make matters worse, I heard through the prison grapevine that my cellmate, the man who'd saved my life, had sustained major injuries and was going to be in the hospital for at least a few weeks. I felt terrible for him, but, at the same time, I was worried about Earl and Pete exacting their revenge on me.

For the next few nights, when the lights were out and the cell door was closed, I'd bury my head in my pillow and let out the tears. For the first time in a long time, I was able to feel again.

I realized that I was responsible for the struggles in my life, and the only way out was to take full responsibility for it all. Not just for the way I saw my father but all others that had supposedly done me wrong. By going through this, I was becoming liberated. I recalled Dimitri speaking of my "programming" that day. I could tell a big chunk of it had been lifted.

I know this will probably sound crazy, but this newfound feeling actually made me feel mentally, emotionally, and physically lighter. This was by far the most memorable and profound thing I had ever experienced. I was able to let go, and, by my doing that, I could experience what it meant to be alive for the first time.

THE BOTTOM

MARCUS

I could feel something wasn't right as I walked into the room. I'd been back on patrol for only two days after a three-month stint behind a desk, and here I was again in my lieutenant's office. The department chief and legal representative sat on either side of him.

"Sit down, Marcus." The flat tone of Lieutenant Houser's voice confirmed my suspicions. "We've got a situation here, son, that we need to talk to you about."

My stomach churned as I took a seat facing him. I always felt sick when someone told me that they needed to talk to me about something, work or personal.

"These things are never easy for me. I know you know how much I respect you and the other Ogabis on the force, but …"

Right then and there, with the word "but," I felt the life force drain from my entire body. From there on everything was muffled. I heard the distant sound of his voice talking about racial tension and political this and that, all of it leading back to the shooting of an unarmed man. What I had spent weeks worrying about had come true—I was being let go.

The chief spoke about the opportunity for me to retire early instead of being fired. There was a folder with info on the limited severance package. "We know you might need some time to digest all of this, so go ahead and take this with you, and let's meet again tomorrow morning, same time. Son, we never really know why these kinds of things happen in life, but I'm sure you'll land on your feet." He shook my hand and left.

"If you have any questions about anything in the folder, please feel free to call me, Officer Ogabi," the lawyer said quietly and handed me her card.

I gave a somber nod as she followed the chief out the door.

It was just my lieutenant and me, alone. "How are you doing there, Marcus?"

I shook my head in disbelief. *How am I supposed to be doing after losing my career as well as any hope of a better life for myself or restoring my family?* "Well, sir, I hoped we'd turned a corner on this thing."

"I'm sorry, Marcus. You know it's all politics with the chief and the mayor. I did everything in my power to keep you on board." I nodded as he put his hand on my shoulder. "Thank you for all your great work here and for being a truly standup officer for so many years. I'm sure you know that Paige and I love all the Ogabis and want what is best for you, Lisa, and Hope."

» » « «

Once home, I looked over the severance package and saw that there was actually very little money left after paying all the new bills after Lisa and I split. A separation can crush a man, not only emotionally but financially as well. *At least I have her back in my life.* I pulled out my phone and dialed Lisa. I needed some comfort.

When we were younger, she'd always be there for me, no matter what happened. Now, with her sensitivity around money and with me losing my job, I questioned whether I was doing the right thing.

"Hey, Marcus, I'm glad you called. I need to talk to you about something."

No, not those words again. A fresh knot tightened in my stomach. *This can't be good.*

I tried my best to be present, like I had learned from Dimitri that day at the prison, and not let my mind wander, but it just wasn't working.

"Marcus, are you there?"

"Yeah, sorry. I'm here."

"There's no easy way to say this so I am just going to come out with it. I met someone. His name is Alberto, Beto, and I like him a lot. I want to move in with him."

What did she just say? "When the hell did that happen?! I thought we were doing really good. We all went for ice cream the other day. I mean, you and me, we even had sex the other night, remember?"

"Come on, Marcus."

My ears suddenly began to ring, and I felt a cold numbness pass through me. *How is it even possible to receive so much devastating, life-altering news within a two-hour time frame?*

Her voice dimmed, as I went into that same trance-like state I'd been in at the station. When I came to, she hit me with the worst part of the news, and that was that Beto lived in the small town of Fuller, four hours west of East Borough. She was taking Hope with her.

We argued for almost an hour, with her telling me about Beto's money, nice home, and the private school Hope would be attending.

"Haven't you ever wanted anything more for yourself, Marcus?" she asked breathlessly. "Remember when we were young and you would say you wanted to change the world. Have you done that by being a cop, following in the 'Ogabi tradition'? I married you because I believed in you. I believed you were going somewhere in life. But that didn't happen."

"It's all I've ever known," I mumbled as a lump formed in my throat.

"Look at your parents. Their relationship fell apart just like ours did, and they didn't even have the biracial challenges. Do you think it's been easy being married to a cop? Can you even imagine what I had to go through after the shooting, all the questions that were hurled at me? Do you know how hard it has been for me to stick up for you with all of the bullshit you pulled: not remembering, then remembering you shot an unarmed boy."

"Man. He's a young man," I responded weakly.

"Whatever, Marcus!" she shouted, and it got so silent I thought she might have left.

"I know this might be hard to hear right now," she finally whispered, trying to imitate someone who cared, "but they say everything happens for a reason."

"You mean a better financial reason for you, don't you, Lisa?"

She gave me another blast of silence before answering. "You know what I'm most happy about, Marcus? I get to see my daughter with a father figure who's more interested in his family than going out and getting drunk with his buddies and watching sports."

What's wrong with watching sports?

In the mayhem of my rampant thoughts, I blurted out, "You know all of this wanting more and more puts you more in the category of a prostitute than a good mother. Maybe you should look at that, Lisa."

I instantly regretted it. I could feel the hate seething through the phone before she even spoke.

"Only a jobless loser talks about something he can't even afford! Go cry to your mother, Marcus!"

I threw my phone across the room, where it skittered across the kitchen counter, causing Lucky to jump out of his bed.

Sitting alone at the kitchen table, my anger turned to deep sadness, the kind where you want to cry but can't. My world had fallen apart. All the things Dimitri had said weeks earlier rattled around in my mind, none of it making sense anymore. I'd lost my career, and Lisa was gone forever. I thought about my daughter, Hope, how she'd changed after the split and realized that she, too, must have seen me as a loser.

In a flash, it all became clear. *They're right.* I now regretted my decision that day in the courtroom. *What sort of man risks his family's future for a street kid?* There was a tightness around my heart. It was as if something had dropped out of me, something I would never get back. That thing, call it spirit, or mojo, the thing that got me out of bed every day eager to better my life for Hope, Lisa, and, in a way, for the world, had been crushed. I had truly hit bottom. There was no way up.

I looked over at the kitchen cabinet where I kept my personal thirty-eight hidden in a box of prunes. I imagined Lisa crying as my father broke the news of my suicide. I remembered the many times she'd said she would never leave the old neighborhood. "Fucking liar!" I yelled as Lucky looked and walked in my direction. *Four hours away.* The furthest I had ever lived from my daughter was fifteen minutes.

All I wanted was to make Lisa pay.

I looked down at the purring cat rubbing his head on the side on my leg. *He's hungry, loser.*

I got up to feed him. "You're just like Lisa, Lucky," I said as he followed me, meowing. "You only want me for what I can give you. When you want something, you're nice, then, once you have it, you forget I ever existed. But I forgive you because you don't know any better."

Tears ran down my face as I dumped the entire bag of kibble into his metal bowl, watching as it overflowed onto the tile floor. "That should last you until they find me."

He ignored the food and walked outside through the open slider. *You're talking to a cat.* Even stranger was the manner in which I was doing it. It brought me back to my visit with Dimitri and how he taught me that we all have stories. I was telling mine to a cat named Lucky. *I'm so pathetic.*

I grabbed the box out of the cupboard, pushed the prunes aside, and pulled the pistol out. Sitting back at the kitchen table, I grazed the stainless steel barrel with my fingers, still sobbing loudly.

I activated the cylinder release latch and the chamber fell open. I read the back of the shells: FEDERAL 38 SPCL. *That ought to do the job.*

I jerked the pistol to one side, closing the chamber and put it to my temple. My hand tightened around the black rubber grip as the tears rolled uncontrollably down my face. My finger began to squeeze the trigger. *This is the only way out.*

Lucky moaned a long meow. I released my finger as he walked briskly back into the house with a small bird in his mouth. Normally, I'd try to save the poor creature, but that day was different.

Looks like there will be two deaths at the Ogabi residence today.

I put the gun back to my head and looked at the box of prunes resting in front of me. I noticed the brand: Colibri.

Colibri. What an odd name.

I recalled how much Hope hated prunes, hence my reason for hiding my gun with them. I realized I didn't like them either. *Does anyone on this planet like them? And why am I thinking about fucking prunes right now?*

I put the gun down and pressed my hands against the sides of my head in deep contemplation. *What's going on here?*

Then it hit me. It wasn't my talking to the cat or my questioning of the world's prune consumption while holding a gun to my head that was odd. It was that I was able to *see myself* having those thoughts. Just like Dimitri had shown me how to witness my thoughts that day in the visitation room, I was, almost involuntarily, observing them come now.

The noticing of my thoughts confirmed that there were two entities at play. There was the me that was in deep pain, talking to the cat and having odd thoughts about prunes, and then there was the me that watched and wondered why I was having those thoughts. How many me's were there in my head? Even more important, which one was the real me?

Who am I about to kill?

The part of me that was observing the thoughts as they came in was fine. It wasn't upset that it didn't have a job. It wasn't losing it over its ex moving away with its daughter. And, as far as I could tell, it sure as hell didn't want to kill itself. I knew I better figure out which one I really was before committing a double murder of sorts.

I remembered Dimitri telling me about the middle way and that any extreme emotional state, high or low, was usually an indicator that one was not in the state of presence.

I replayed the events that had just taken place, remembering the dismal image of a future without my daughter and wife. Combining that with thoughts around the impending doom of living in abject poverty makes for a mental movie that no one wants to star in. Everything was and had been fine at that moment, outside of my head at least. My projecting into a future that hadn't even happened yet caused the emotional turmoil that nearly cost me my life.

Damn, if I could just remember to stay present always, just remain in the knowing that this moment is all that we ever have, my life would be so much easier. I remained still as another epiphany came in.

You just did it again, Marcus.

I could see that getting down on myself for not being present was, in fact, an act out of or away from being present in itself. The thought "if I could just remember, my life would be so much easier" came from a projection of the future as well as a falling back into the past in a way.

I reveled in my newest insight surrounding a seemingly complex but simple truth. *I am good right now. I'm already there. There's nothing that should or shouldn't have happened.* I just needed to keep my thoughts in this time, this present, only.

Goosebumps exploded across my arms and an electricity traveled the length of my spine. I placed the pistol back in the box and slowly brought my head to rest on its side, staring at the cube-patterned wallpaper.

Lucky returned, now bird-free, and glared upward, past me. I heard a loud humming and looked up to see a green and red hummingbird hovering over my head. My heart pounded as it lowered itself in front of my face before turning and buzzing out the door.

I took a deep breath and replayed the recent events of my life. From hummingbirds and prunes, to mysterious encounters with old women, all the way to the words of a young man I'd unjustly shot. I thought about how that young man's words ultimately saved my life.

I exhaled and whispered, "Thank you."

AS LUCKY WOULD HAVE IT

MARCUS

Lucky pawed at the ringing phone. *Still looking out for me, old friend?* Like most animals, he was aware something had happened that afternoon and was doubling up on paying attention to me.

"Hello, this is Marcus," I said into the receiver while scratching Lucky behind the ear.

"Hey, Marcus. This is Jim at Carlton State Prison. How are you?"

It took a second for the cobwebs to clear. *It's James Devic who couldn't make it over the wall in training.* He was the last person I was expecting to hear from at that moment. *Has to be about Dimitri.*

"Marcus? Is this a bad time?" he asked after my silence.

"Hey, Jim, sorry about that. I was thrown for a moment. No, it's not a bad time at all. And to answer your initial question, all I can say is I'm alive. How about you?"

"I'm alive as well and doing pretty good. But I don't know if I can say the same for the kid here, inmate Tanomeo. I told you I'd let you know if anything happened with him and it did. Seems he's gotten himself into some kind of a mess with a couple of the Aryan Deuce Five boys. He got cut up real bad, took a shank to the gut, pretty serious. This sort of thing requires at the very least a month of hospitalization, but, Marcus, he was out of the infirmary in just five days. Doctors have never seen anything like it. Granted, he's not completely healed, but he's walking around. He's a different breed, this one."

You have no idea. "What happened exactly?"

"Well, no one's talking. The kid's not saying a word because, get this, 'he doesn't want to put his brothers at risk.' And that's a quote."

"Yep, he said something similar that day I saw you there. I guess he's in the shit now." I was concerned about the kid, but apparently he didn't seem too concerned about himself.

"I'm not sure that's the case. Something happened during the attack. No one really knows what exactly, but one of the former leaders, a guy named Earl, is acting, uh, peculiar."

The Aryan guy who tried to hassle us. "This guy Earl, I know who he is. He was in the visiting area threatening the kid when I was there. Real thug."

"So this thug, now j-cat, has been admitted to the mental health ward. Supposedly, he asked to go there. Said he wanted to expand his horizons. Also said he was God or some crazy stuff like that. There was such a change in his behavior, the medics thought it'd be wise to send him in for an evaluation. He's kinda gone from a violent racist to a harmless nut job if that makes sense."

"Jesus, Jim, I'm not sure what makes sense anymore. If you had any idea of what's gone on around this kid with me, you honestly wouldn't believe it."

Jim grunted a vague understanding. "How's everything else going for you these days?"

I decided to be honest about the newest link in the chain of events surrounding the shooting. What I remembered from the academy was that Jim was a good, honest man and seemed to be genuinely interested, so I told him that I'd lost my job, and at first, I was a little spun out. I left out the part where I had a gun to my head.

"So, what's your next move, Marcus?"

"You know, this thing has happened so fast, I haven't had the time to even think about what's next."

There was a pause on the line. I figured Jim didn't really know what to say. I know I wouldn't have.

"Marcus," he finally said, and he sounded earnest, "I don't remember much of growing up in a religious home. I chose to rebel against pretty much everything my parents pushed on me, but I do remember a passage from the Bible that's stuck with me. I can share it with you if you'd like."

I took a deep breath and sighed quietly in resistance. "Go ahead, Jim, what else do I have to lose?"

"Well, it says, 'God works all things after the counsel of his will.'"

Lucky looked at me and I looked blankly back at him.

"Jim, I have no idea what that means."

"Well, I think it means there is some bigger reason for everything that happens. Like I said, it's one of the only lines I remember, but it's always helped me when things get funky."

"My ex-wife said something very similar, just after she'd rolled out a new, very harsh reality to me. But, to be honest, I don't know what kind of god would ever put anyone through these types of situations. The whole 'God's plan' thing never sat well with me, seeing the type of world we live in and the suffering folks go through and all."

"I understand what you mean," he said. "I think a lot of people feel that way."

"I appreciate the call, Jim. I had better get going. God wants me to find a new job, so I need to get to it."

"Will do. Oh, and there's an opening here at Carlton for a correctional officer. You'd be a shoo-in. Good benefits and all the overtime you'd want. I know you've been over there your whole life and your family's all there, but I thought I'd throw it out there."

I sat there in silence.

"You still there, Marcus?"

"Sorry, I'm here," I answered slowly. "Yeah, Jim, thanks for thinking of me. I'll keep it in mind."

"Okay, then. Until next time, over and out."

The line went dead. I scrambled to my laptop and pulled up a map of the state. *This would be too much of a coincidence.* Lo and behold, Carlton Prison was a thirty-minute drive from the town of Fuller.

WAKE-UP CALL

ZACH

"What up, D?!" I shouted as I jumped off my bunk, landing hard on the concrete floor. I wanted to hug him, but lack of confidence and concern for his new injury made me settle for grasping his shoulders.

"All good, Zach. How're things here in the sacred cell?" Him referring to our cell as sacred felt off.

"Mellow, just like you like it." I didn't want to lay the Tanas visit on him quite yet, but he hit me with his suspicious gaze. *Can he tell I'm lying?*

"Good to hear." He slowly lowered himself onto his bunk.

"Word on the yard says you were supposed to be in the infirmary a long time. It hasn't even been a week! What's up with that?"

"There's a lot of work to be done here, so I decided to become a conscious component in my own healing." He lay back on his cot.

"Okay, I'm not even gonna ask you what that means, but what's the work you're talking about?"

He sighed and said, "To be of service in the transformation of the lives of the men at this prison and beyond."

I figured that transformation, at least in the way he spoke of it, was what I'd experienced with him during our talk. He certainly had a surety and confidence about declaring his mission. I think that's what amazed me most. He carried zero doubt around any of it. It reminded me of the man I idolized growing up: my father. A man who turned everything he touched to gold.

"You remind me of Terrance sometimes. He talks like you. With conviction. Whether it's taking over a billion-dollar company or a woman he wants to slay, in his head, he knows he can do it, and he's usually right."

"First off, I find it unsettling that you call your father by his first name. But, yes to the other part. It's just manifestation 101."

"It's an old habit," I shrugged. I'd started referring to my father as Terrance back in high school when I first became angry with what he was doing in the world. "I've heard of manifestation, but how exactly are you gonna make this transformation happen, especially on the scale you're talking about?"

"The same way your father does. You see, Zach, before it's even begun, he's experienced it as a completed event in his mind."

"Sounds accurate."

"I'll do the same. And, on top of that, I'll feel what it feels like to have accomplished the feat, literally in my body, even before it takes place."

I nodded, even though the whole part about the body didn't make much sense.

"I imagine it will work even better for you because what you're doing is good. What he does mostly isn't."

He turned to look at me, "It doesn't really work exactly like that, Zach. I mean, there is *energetic alignment*, but that's a discussion for another time. Just remember, there's no such thing as a universal concept of good outside of its judgment-biased, subjective form. Many would say what I am doing is good, that it is good and right to help these people because everyone deserves a helping hand. One could also say it's bad to help after all the harm they've done, and that would simply be their subjective viewpoint."

"I see where you're going, but it's hard to grasp, seeing how I've been raised to think differently."

"I know. The programming," he said, nodding. "But if you continue to look at both sides, you can see how they are each right, which, if you think about it, makes them both wrong at the same time. It's all subjective, personal to the individual. Things are neither universally right, wrong, good, or bad. They just simply are. All of it is an equal part of creation. Zeroing in on my own individual subjectivity, what's right for me, what works for me, is the best way I've found to live life. Being in service to the whole is what feels right and good. From that standpoint, I could call a thing good or bad, but it would be so only from my individual viewpoint. It's the same for what doesn't work. It's only *bad* for me."

I think there might be a hole in your theory. "But if many people, hell, most of them, say a thing is good or bad, then it has to be, doesn't it? That's what makes the world work."

"Then I'd ask you, is it working?"

"Is what working?"

"The world. Does it work? Really?"

I'd never really thought about it that way. "Well, kinda?"

"Are we kinda thriving as a global population or are most just getting by? You know, just making it through another day?"

He's got a point there.

He continued, "Also, just because there's a consensus around a thing doesn't make it universally right or wrong. Consider this: When two countries go to war, how do we determine which one is truly right and which one is wrong?"

"Well, clearly the one with the higher moral ground."

"Really, Zach?" he snapped as I took a seat on the floor in front of him. "Who decides which has the higher moral ground? They are both right and they are both wrong because each believes they are right and the other is wrong. Therefore, both are neither.

"Imagine the suffering that has been and will be caused by this misconception. Look at our world, Zach. Notice how every war, every dispute, has been waged from this false belief."

I was pretty baffled by it all and not comfortable with my presumed ignorance.

He sat up straight and patted me on the shoulder. "You're getting it, don't worry, amigo. It's just programming, and it will all go away. It just takes time and inner work. Now, back to your point about manifestation and it working better for me because I'm doing something you call good."

I nodded. *I'm sure this is gonna blow my mind too.*

"With your new understanding, or, I hope, your new *knowing*, you can get that the law of manifestation works the same within all human action equally. Everything is possible, whether you are operating from a negative space or a positive one. You can create anything you want as long as you are sure beyond any doubt that you can, in fact, do it. The proof is in everything we do. We are manifesting constantly."

I took a moment, trying to find another hole in his theory. "So, those who live in poverty and misery, the ones who were born into it, what's up with that?" I asked.

"Yes, poverty driven from a very broken monetary system rooted in greed and fear plays the major hand in it, but there's still a vicious cycle at play wherein we the collective have agreed upon an inner as well as outer dialogue that keeps us stuck in it. We've lost our way, so to speak. For now, I say we stick with me showing you why it's been such a challenge to get out of this or, let's say, change what currently is. From there we can talk about how we're going to shift things, you and I. Of course, this would mean coming up against the dark forces, so to speak. Exciting, no?"

He did seem genuinely excited. *But ... dark forces?* "Us?" I asked warily. "You gotta mouse in your pocket or something, D?"

He busted up laughing so hard I jolted backward. "That's if you're in, of course, Zach. I mean, what else is there to do, right?"

I must have looked like such a jackass, staring into his eyes, unable to speak. I honestly didn't know how to answer him, mainly because I didn't understand what he meant by me being "in." Also, I had no idea who or what the "dark forces" were exactly or how he could be so gung-ho to go up against anything with a name like that in the first place.

Time to change the subject. "You've said that word 'collective' more than once. I'm not sure what it means."

"It's the majority of the people on the planet. It coincides, in this context, with the word consciousness. The collective consciousness is the shared view of most. A sort of agreed-upon understanding, if you will. You could also describe it as the current level of awareness in most people. These understandings, handed down through generations, are so limited and downright corrupt that they've basically held the collective awareness hostage for thousands of years. With the help of the dark forces, of course."

More dark forces stuff?

He paused to look at our cell doorway, and then leaned into me, whispering. "Now here's the good part, Zach. That old, vile, unholy, global agreement that hasn't been questioned or challenged for who knows how long is about to become null and void. This I promise you." He sprang back up and cheerfully asked. "Copiado, amigo?"

I wanted to ignore the "dark forces" stuff, but I was getting my head around the collective. "So, if I were to put it into my own words, I'd say that the collective consciousness is locked into some kind of old programming. Would that be accurate?"

"Perfectly accurate," he said, pointing at me.

"So, that day we talked about the collective's viewpoint on crying, that it's wrong or a sign of weakness in some way. That's just another example of it, right?"

"It is," he answered happily, seeing that I was putting it together on my own. "The only reason you believed that crying was a sign of weakness is because you heard someone say it."

"I've heard several someones say it," I interjected.

"And at some point, you chose to make that part of your internal voice."

"My what?"

"You began to internally speak the words of others to yourself. Their words, their truths, have become your own. You had unwittingly taken on the collective's false view of what it means to cry, not to mention a lot of other stuff."

"The thing is, Dimitri, I don't ever remember choosing this."

"It was handed down to you when you were young. And because you wanted answers and you wanted to be a part of the tribe, so to speak, you accepted it. You chose alright, just unconsciously. How could you do otherwise with the limited tools in your toolbox at that age?"

"It all ties back to that toolbox of yours, doesn't it, D?" I have to say, as strange as it was, I was getting this far-out concept. "There's a lie behind a lot of stuff," I said, shaking my head in awe.

"The words of the collective programming are corrupt, so it's time to clean up the toolbox and replace what needs replacing, which is pretty much all of it."

"Why has it been so hard for the world to change? Why haven't we been able to change the tools in the toolbox of the collective?"

"Because," he said, "the words we speak to ourselves create our reality. Most would say having abundance for all people of the world, living a great life, or awakening prisoners to their true potential are things that are out of reach. If the majority is saying that, you can see how that old, common dialogue would become ours collectively. Those voices have joined together and literally manifested the idea that us moving toward a co-creative partnership with the earth is out of reach. So, if us living within a *sacred gift economy* is to remain out of reach, what is left in its place?"

I drifted off, calculating it all.

"That's a question, Zach," he demanded.

"Yeah, I know. I'm not really sure what those measures, which sound pretty good by the way, entail. But what's left—poverty, misery, injustice, impossibleness—is all that can remain in a world that's told itself good stuff isn't possible."

"I couldn't have said it better myself."

Him saying that made me feel pretty good. "And you, me, and everyone are somehow responsible for all of it?" I asked. "All the gnarly stuff as well as the awesome?"

"The good, the bad, and the fugly, amigo. Subjectively speaking, of course. One could even argue that we came into this, we didn't have a choice, and that would be true to a certain extent. But we are all responsible for its continuance, even those who suffer deeply. Just the way we talk to ourselves about the things we don't like keeps the old system at play."

Okay, now I'm lost again. "Sounds like another deep concept that I might not be ready to grasp quite yet. How can any of us change the way we think when these things are actually happening? I turn on the news, I see what I see. I almost get raped by a couple of booty bandits. How am I supposed to not feel what I feel or know what I know?"

"We can change all of it. Everything can evolve out of its current state and into a beautiful one. We, all of us, have the power to make that happen by changing our perception of the things we experience. We can shift our internal dialogue, our inner voice, to make those things mean something entirely different. Just like we did with your father."

I nodded.

"So," Dimitri continued, "let's take what happened with Earl and Pete and what you made that mean.

"That's easy. I made that mean it sucked."

"Could it mean something else?"

"Like they are both assholes?"

He laughed. "That's not exactly the direction I'm going. Could we not say they've probably both had really hard lives?"

"Judging from Earl's teeth, or lack thereof, I'd say that's likely."

"I know you're trying to be funny, but you actually have a point. If his teeth were knocked out by someone at some point, wouldn't—"

"Meth. Probably meth, D," I interrupted.

"Or he lost them due to the use of methamphetamine. Either way, wouldn't that indicate he's had a really hard journey?"

I crossed my arms. "So what. That doesn't mean he had to turn into a rapist, does it?"

"In this case, it actually does mean that, because that's what happened."

The inside of our cell got very quiet, as what he'd just said wasn't what I wanted to hear. I thought about how to respond. "That right there was the lamest thing you've ever said, and you don't say many lame things, so I'm gonna give you a pass this time, Tanomeo."

His laughter echoed down the hall, mixing with the chaotic sounds of the prison block. "Did your father," he asked, his smile disappearing, "putting you with a nanny and doing all the crap he did, mean you had to turn into a whiny, intolerant activist that got himself sent to prison just so he could show the world he was a somebody?"

Ouch.

"I guess I had that one coming, but it's not the same. I didn't have to become anything. They were just the choices I made, albeit not the best ones."

"The fact that you did what you did means that you had to do exactly what you did. Could it have gone differently? Could you have understood your father better? I guess in a parallel universe perhaps, but in this one, it simply is exactly as it is. Now, as far as the future goes, and how you'll react next time, it's for you to decide.

"Also, the only difference between what you've done in the past and what Earl did was the act. The acts themselves were different, but they both came from some event in the past, right?"

"Wait, you are actually comparing me to a rapist?"

He nodded and smiled, "Yes, I guess you could say I am. How does that feel for you, Zachy boy?"

"Not cool is how it feels. So what if Earl the Rapist had actually succeeded? I can't imagine you'd be singing the same tune right now, would you?"

"Imagine again, Zach. I'd be singing it even louder so that you might hear me when you *really* need it."

I wish I could hit this guy. "It's not the same. I didn't hurt anyone."

"So, seventy-five thousand people without power for half a day in the dead of winter didn't cause some, if not much, distress? How about what your father felt with you going against him the way you did. Not to mention you blaming your own mother for being cheated on and not leaving when she wasn't ready. Do you think that might have hurt her?"

Uh, that stung. He put his hand on my shoulder and whispered, "You've raped, Zach, just in a different way. Until you realize and accept this fully, you will remain at cause for a world where rape, hurt, and suffering can even exist. You must see yourself in Earl. Then and only then will you be ready not only to change your life but help others change theirs in this prison and beyond. You, me, your father, mother, Earl, and the other seven billion-plus are all in this together. Each one of us, doing the best we can with the tools we have in our own very limited, individual toolboxes. Knowing this, not just understanding it, creates compassion, and that compassion will reward you with a beautiful life."

Each prisoner and their crimes flashed across my mind. There were extortionists, murderers, drug dealers, and thieves. *Am I, are we all, just like them?*

"Yes, baby yes!" I heard Vinny the Italian yell from down the hall.

I guess I just got my answer. Synchronicity's a bitch. I didn't like what he was saying, and he could see it.

"I guess I should disclose something right now. I'm not here to tell you what you want to hear, Zach."

"Ah yeah, that just became very clear, dude."

"I'm here to tell you what you need to hear in order to wake the eff up, amigo, but only if you want to hear it."

"'Wake the eff up,' who says that? Feel free to cuss, D, this is prison, I can handle it."

"I'd rather not, it usually doesn't suit me."

I nodded smiling, "Whatever, you do you. So, about helping you help many of the guys in this prison …" I said, still trying to wrap my head around it. "Do you really believe it can be done, and how could I even be of assistance? I've never even heard of the stuff you're talking about, let alone fully accept most of it."

He looked at me, his eyes radiating trust. It made me believe in myself. "There's a reason we've been brought together here in this place," he said. "In this cell more specifically."

Now it was my turn to rip on him. "Tell me you're not one of those who believes there's a reason for everything and all that shit."

"I don't *believe* in it. I don't believe in anything. I only know. Believing is for those who are uncertain, those who are not ready to know the truth."

I want to know.

"But in my world," he continued, "I choose to know exactly what it is that I am going to know. This is just another way I create and manifest my reality."

He's so advanced in this shit.

"As for the things I don't know," I said, "how about I just believe in them? That's the best I can do, bro."

He gave me a thumbs up. "Believing is a beautiful thing, and, for most, a necessary way to start."

"So, how can I help," I said with a shrug.

His calm, knowing smile told me he'd already chosen to know I'd be in. "Thanks for coming aboard."

» » « «

We rapped for close to an hour, finding that my place was in the orchestration of a program we would set up together for the inmates. Dimitri had never gone to school, so his writing was terrible, and he had zero organization skills. But where he lacked, I excelled. As a computer programmer, my abilities were in the coordination, management, and administration of systems, making what we wanted a piece of cake.

"Hand me a shirt, will ya, Zach?"

As he changed, I stared at the large bandage over his newest wound. I knew it'd eventually join the others as another scar among many. His body had wounds that would become scars, but in his mind, all was pristine.

What an idiot I am. My life's been a cakewalk compared to this guy's.

"You know, what you did for me … I owe you, that's for sure," I said. "I'm here for whatever you need. It's my moral duty."

He waved his finger. "Everything I do, I do because I want to. Every movement I make is a calculated action. From that action, there is an equally intended reaction. If you're going to be in, you have to be in because you want to be. Moral duty is just egoic caca. Let me put it this way, through your helping of others, you must feel that you're helping yourself. From that place, we will move mountains, my friend."

That one literally gave me goosebumps all the way to my face.

"I love your confidence, bro. Not exactly sure where it comes from, but it's inspiring."

"Thank you for the acknowledgment, and in regard to where *it comes from*, that's a topic that might take some time for us to arrive at, but we will get there, I promise. And let me just say that whatever you see in me that inspires you is merely a reflection of the true you, Zach—the one who loves all that is and is down for this righteous cause just because it feels right." He slowly stood up and faced me, adjusting his shirt.

"This is just the beginning. What you'll be part of here in this prison will eventually extend beyond these walls. The message I'm here to deliver will reach every corner of this planet and change everything." He put his hand on my shoulder, "This *I know*."

Again with the goosebumps. How many times can this happen in one day? "I still don't know how you plan to do that, you know, the whole 'every corner of the planet' part," I muttered, which made him laugh.

"Like they say, 'only the illusion of time will tell,'" he answered confidently.

"Uh, I don't think that's exactly what *they* say."

"Well, I added the 'the illusion of' part."

"I figured that. You do know that makes, like, zero sense, right?"

"Well, to me it does, and I know it will for you at some point in the future."

There was something I'd been wanting to ask him ever since he walked in the door.

"Dimitri ... the day Tanas interrupted us, you were about to finish up with something about my father and how to repair what had happened."

"Oh, yes. It's actually so simple it's ridiculous," he said inching his way toward the door.

"You're killing me here with the suspense, D."

He stood in the doorway and whispered with a smile, "You need to apologize. It's the only way out."

"What?!" I shouted.

"Sorry, Zach," he laughed, bolting out of the door.

"Fuck you, dude!"

I could hear him laughing all the way down the hall.

INSIDE JOB

MARCUS

By now I had a pretty solid grasp on the difference between policing the street and working on the inside of a prison. The truth was, I preferred the street. On the outside, the criminal element shows up here and there and you deal with it accordingly. On the inside, it's everywhere all the time. It was almost as if I was a prisoner myself. But that was all about to change.

When I first got there, I was thrown into the fire with eight weeks at Carlton's level-four maximum-security J-block. The worst of the worst. I learned it was commonplace to do that with new guards. They believed if you could handle that, you could handle anything. Then, one Monday morning, I learned I was being transferred to the level-two medium-security block H. *His* block.

"Marcus, how are you doing, buddy?" Jim said, greeting me with a handshake just outside admin. "Looks like we're going to be working together in H-block."

"Sure looks that way. And thanks for your help in getting me this position."

This was the first time I could genuinely thank him for saving me. I was living close to Hope, and with all the overtime, I was able to get back on my feet.

We walked to the admin cafeteria where Jim pointed out that there were two celebrities doing time at Carlton. One was the Mexican mafia La Eme's very own Joaquin Flores. On the outside, he was a high-ranking member of the Mexican gang La Familia. After years on the inside, he'd moved up to General and took his place as the shot caller for the largest gang in the system and now, consequently, had the keys to Carlton.

You see, in prison there are two sets of rulers. There are us guards—the zookeepers, if you will. We make sure the prisoners get from point A to point B: the yard, chow hall, the day room, and their cells. We step in with discipline when necessary, but ultimately the inmates have their own set of rules designed to keep order in a place where there'd normally be none. While the warden could be considered the one running the zoo, Joaquin

Flores was the alpha beast who ran what happened inside the cages.

Jim gave me his physical description, which didn't sound so beastly: five-foot-nine, about one-sixty, thirty-eight years old with no tattoos, wore thick horn-rimmed eyeglasses, was quiet, polite, and read a lot.

"Of my twenty-plus years as a CO, he's probably the most interesting gang leader I've ever run across," Jim stated, sounding unexpectedly impressed by someone who, in my mind, wouldn't deserve it.

"He doesn't sound like much."

"I'll tell ya, Marcus, it's hard to explain. It's his level of institutional sophistication that sets him apart. He's intelligent in a calculated, disciplined sort of way. Don't get me wrong, at the end of the day he's a coldblooded killer, but you'd never know it by looking at him. It's almost like he's not a prisoner. When you're around him, he seems like an equal." Jim shook his head, "That didn't make any sense did it?"

"I know what you mean. We had some pretty buttoned-up OGs running the streets in East Borough. Who's the second?"

"The second what?" He asked, then laughed, "Oh, that's right, he's an easy one to forget. Zachary Markland. You ever heard of him?"

"The name sounds familiar, but I can't place him."

"The name should sound familiar. He's of the Markland dynasty. His father is Terrance W. Markland."

"Oh yeah. He's the kid, the cybercriminal that hacked his way out of the level-one detention center upstate, right? I heard about it on the news. Damn. Hard to believe he's in here with these guys."

"Originally, with his first charge, he pled out. His father pulled some strings and got him an easy gig as a trustee, an inmate clerk at a low-security camp. But the kid couldn't help himself. Hacked into their system and shortened his release date by six months. He would have gotten away with it but after he'd been released, the prison camp upgraded their system, found the discrepancy, and voilà, welcome to Carlton."

"All of that for six months? That doesn't make sense."

He laughed again. "To us, it doesn't, but to a spoiled rich kid living in the shadow of such a powerful father, it might have been the only way to prove himself, and in a way, he did just that."

I shook my head in bewilderment. "I guess Terrance W. couldn't pull any more strings on that one."

"The judge had to make an example of him. His father cut him off. I reckon the esteemed Mr. Markland didn't like his home being raided and being threatened with a harboring charge. They found the kid hiding in the wine cellar. Terrance didn't even know he was there."

"I saw that kid on the news. He couldn't weigh more than a buck forty. Kind of a pretty boy. How's he faring?"

"Well, let's just put it this way: If it wasn't for his celly, he would've already been turned out by now." Jim smiled, "I'll give you one guess." He looked me in the eyes and waited for my response.

No ....

"He's locked up with Tanomeo?" I asked in disbelief.

Jim nodded.

"How did that happen?"

"I made the decision while on placement duty. It was more of a gut feeling than anything. Neither of them was cliqued up, so I figured it might work, and it has."

We grabbed coffee. As we sat down, I asked him if there was anything else I needed to know about Carlton.

"Listen, I couldn't tell you too much on the phone, but since the warden's got me showing you around and all, I feel it my duty to give you a thorough briefing." He declared with a smirk.

Jim was the only person at Carlton that was aware of my concern for Dimitri, he also knew to keep it between the two of us. Over-familiarity with an inmate can get you fired in prison.

Jim filled me in on a few more details. I was surprised to find out that what disturbed Jim the most at Carlton was a guard named Gene Tanas. According to Jim, he was a manipulative sociopath who had dirt on the warden, giving him dangerous power he used for his own gain.

Jim looked at his watch and got up. "Let's roll, buddy. There's something I'd like you to see."

» » « «

We were walking in the direction of the chapel.

"You taking me to church, Jim?" I asked, laughing.

He smiled as we stopped at the door. "Not exactly."

I could hear a loud, familiar voice speaking with conviction and authority. It was a voice I'd last heard as a visitor to Carlton. We entered and there was Dimitri, holding court in front of dozens of sitting inmates.

Two prisoners stood facing each other. There was a visceral tension between them. One was a young, stocky, heavily tattooed Latino in his late twenties. The other, an average-built, taller white male in his mid-thirties.

Dimitri glanced in our direction, and a quick smile fluttered across his face but only for a second. I was taken aback that he wasn't more surprised to see me there. He went right back to the business at hand, as I could see he was working.

"So, Espinoza, what's this nonsense about respect?" Dimitri asked.

The Latino man, triggered by the question, puffed up and got in the other man's face.

"Ain't no bullshit. This fuckin' *guero* be cuttin' in front of me in the chow line yesterday. This shit's for real, holmes. We gotta take care of this one."

"Wow, he cut in front of you at chow? Now, that is some serious caca. What do you think? You gonna stick him for it? Yeah, maybe you can kill him, then go after his family?" Dimitri's sarcasm caused a small rumble of laughter. Others crossed their arms at his devaluing of their most sacred of concepts.

"Well, fuck you then, *güey*! Now you disrespectin' me as well!" Espinoza shouted at Dimitri with his arms out. "You want some, Tano*guero*?" A few Mexicans in the crowd shouted and laughed at Carlos's derogatory play on words, although not entirely accurate, with Dimitri's ethnicity being questionable, at best.

Dimitri held his hand up in the air. "Okay let's slow it down before it gets weird in here. Remember, this is a sanctioned, nonviolent zone. Let's at least *respect* that rule, boys."

He turned to the other man. "Frank, is what Carlos is saying true? Did you get in front of him at chow yesterday?"

"Yeah, I did," Frank answered calmly but sternly. "He was hangin' back talkin' to some of his people, holdin' up the line, so I walked in front of him. He seemed cool with it at the time, but this mornin' he came at me with some words. You know how it is, D. I'm not gonna back down. Can't be doin' that in here. Gotta maintain respect."

"There's that damn word again: respect." Dimitri's voice had a quiet authority. "Do any of you know what it actually means? Go ahead and sit down, you two. I think we need an English lesson before we move forward."

He went to the whiteboard and wrote the word "RESPECT" in large letters. A young, thin white male sitting on a chair just off to the side handed him a dictionary.

"That's Zachary Markland," Jim whispered.

He looked different than on TV: paler, thinner, and had a shaved head now. Dimitri never had to ask for the dictionary. It was just handed to him, already opened to the correct page, as if they'd done this a thousand times before. The Markland kid seemed to know his every move.

"What is this?" I quietly asked Jim.

"It's called the Early Release Program."

"I don't get it. What does that mean?"

"Don't worry, you're not the only one." Jim covered his mouth and whispered, "You should've seen the first day. Just about every inmate in the block showed up thinking they were going to reduce their sentence somehow. After some harsh words and a riot nearly erupting, just five out of a completely packed chapel remained. That's them in the front row there."

"Why is it called that, then?"

Jim paused, trying to recall something. "'Your friend' says he's here to help them release themselves from the prison of their mind. The word 'early' implies that a person doesn't have to wait an entire lifetime trapped within the confines of their thoughts. He says that one can be released from it here and now, but it's an inside job, meaning you've got to do it yourself. I'll tell ya, Marcus, at first I had no idea what he was talking about, but now that I have been around several of these sessions, believe it or not, it kind of makes sense."

"I've heard him speak more than once, and each time, I have to admit, I got something out of it."

I stood listening to Dimitri's strong voice. I looked at Jim, "This kid practically just got here and is already making shit happen?" I looked down at my arm and noticed I had goosebumps. What I didn't know was that prison history was being made at Carlton Penitentiary. The Magnificent Seven, as they would later be called, had begun what would be the greatest prison rehabilitation experiment ever executed.

Jim nodded and motioned for me to follow him toward the corner of the room. As I walked over, I looked at what he'd written on the whiteboard.

RESPECT

Definition: a feeling of deep admiration for someone or something elicited by their abilities, qualities, or achievements: Example, the director had a lot of respect for Douglas as an actor.

He finished and turned to address the crowd. "So, brothers, I'm confused here. Do any of you see a connection between this word and its exact definition and what Carlos is wanting from Frank?"

He looked around the room, the men remained silent. He turned and focused on Carlos Espinoza, now sitting in the first row. "Let me direct this inquiry to you, Carlos. As you can see, the definition of the word 'respect' denotes a deep admiration for someone elicited by their abilities, qualities, or achievements. Can you please show us how you have displayed any of your abilities, qualities, or achievements while demanding this thing called respect from Frank? I mean, at least Douglas here in the example was probably a good actor." The room laughed as Dimitri pointed to the board. But Carlos wasn't laughing, sitting silently with his arms crossed. "Maybe, just maybe, you have confused the word respect with another word, and that word would be 'fear.'"

I wondered how Dimitri ended up in a chapel giving courses that, as far as I could tell, had little to nothing to do with Jesus and the cross. "Who's letting this happen?" I asked. "Is the warden aware of it?"

"He's aware of it alright. Inmate Tanomeo fought for this, Marcus. The warden and the other suits came at him with all kinds of reasons he couldn't do it, but he was resilient. When they quizzed him on which religion he would speak from, he told them that his teachings were spiritual in nature and all religious teachings are similar at their nucleus. He somehow showed that Buddhism, Judaism, the teachings of Christ, as well as many others are all intertwined and eventually point to the same core message. Every time they threw something at him, he answered back with a valid argument making his case. He also seems to know a thing or two about the law, and in the end, the warden didn't have much of a choice. So, it's five days a week, two hours a day. That's what he gets.

"Carlos, you gotta know something, brother," Dimitri was saying. "As long as you confuse respect with fear, you will never have what you crave." He was standing directly in front of the man, with his hands on his hips. "So, let me break it down for you. This thing called fear, well, I for one will never have that for you, and if that's what you want from people, then all I can do is invite you to look at where that might be coming from."

He walked back to the middle, addressing the whole group. "Here's the interesting thing, guys. If you go deep and ask the pertinent questions, you can see that your desire for another to fear you is actually coming from fear itself." Dimitri scanned the room, looking into each man's eyes.

"Fuck that, holmes. I ain't afraid of nothin'!" Carlos yelled out. A few of the inmates laughed.

"Oh, you're not? Are you sure about that? Once again, Carlos, it's just an invitation to take a look. That's all. Oh, and just so you know, you're not alone in this. Every man in this room, including myself, as well as every person on this planet has been, as many still are, ruled by fear in one way or another."

"Yo Dimitri, getthefuckouttahere," a young Italian American blurted out. "How do you know that everyone is fearful? Just like Carlos over there, I ain't afraid of nothin."

"How do I know this? That's a great question, Vinny, thank you." Vinny the Italian smiled proudly as Dimitri addressed the room once again. "Let's do this. I invite every one of you to take a look at your own situation. Let's use the crime that put you here. I say that whatever it was that you did, you did out of fear." He paused as many of the confused men shifted in their seats, while others crossed their arms.

"Oh, you guys don't believe me? That's fine. Let's play a game. For those who are willing, shout out your crime, and I will show you how fear played a role." Dimitri scanned the room, but no one said a word.

"Come on, what are you guys worried about?" he said, smiling. "We all know what each other is in for, anyways."

"Grand larceny and bank robbery!" one finally shouted.

Dimitri shot back right away, "In some way, you were fearful that you didn't have enough. Pretty simple, no? A desire for money so strong that it leads you to commit a crime of that magnitude could only come from the core emotion of fear. Next!" he shouted, egging them on.

"Attempted murder!" another yelled.

"Who did you try to kill?"

"I caught my wife with a man in our bed, so I beat him with a bat," the man answered. The crowd roared with laughter.

"Perfect. You were afraid that your wife was loving another man. I'd say at the center of that, you were fearful of her leaving you." The man didn't react. "I'll take it one step further, Lyle. I bet your parents didn't stay together when you were growing up, did they?"

Inmate Lyle shook his head.

"What made them split? Divorce or death?"

"Divorce. But what does this have to do with me knocking my ex-bitch's lover in the head with a bat?" A few laughed again.

"How old were you when they divorced?"

"Nine," Lyle answered.

"At nine years old, divorce is hard on a kid, right?" Dead silence filled the room. Lyle sat motionlessly. "Of course it is. It's always tough on a child when a parent leaves. So, guys, do you see where I'm going with this? Many times there is a deep-rooted event that took place when we were young that is the actual cause for our current pain. I call it 'past pain.' In Lyle's case, when we become overly attached to someone, it's usually because we have lost someone earlier in our lives. That past pain was so bad that we will do anything not to feel it again, even hurt or kill another human being."

Dimitri stepped back, opened his hands, and without hesitation said, "Give me one more!"

This guy's on fire.

That's when it clicked for me. My anger and jealousy with Lisa was fear around her leaving with Hope. It was a product of the past pain originating from my parents' divorce more than twenty-five years prior.

"Yo, what if you're innocent?" Vinny the Italian blurted out. The whole room, including Dimitri, busted up laughing. Next to me, Jim shook his head.

"Okay, Vinny," Dimitri asked, "what are they falsely accusing you of this time?"

"Yo, they say I ran a heroin ring. I'm in the appeal process," he replied confidently.

"Of course you are," Dimitri smiled. "The nerve of some people, huh, Vinny?" The whole room busted up. "So, this falls under the same category as the first one in that it comes from lack, or like I said earlier, the fear of not having enough.

"Ask yourself right now if you would willingly contribute to the destruction of a person's life by selling them poison if you already had all the money and everything you ever wanted or needed." I saw a few of the inmates shake their heads. "Only by being inflicted with the fear of lack would we even consider the risk of being sent to a place like this, right?"

"Yo, there's people all over the world hurtin' each other because they don't have enough then," Vinny announced.

Dimitri nodded. "You're absolutely right, brother. There are millions and millions of people who own, run, have shares in, or work at companies that commit hurtful acts every day. Whether it be through polluting our planet, our health, or our minds, these folks unconsciously fill their pockets, feed their children, and make a living off of the pain and suffering of others.

"We can take this beyond business. All of it, every ill and degradation, every bit of greed and destruction, all arguments, and every war has come from fear. You don't have to take my word for it, guys. All you have to do is trace each one back like we just did. If you do, you are sure to find it there, lurking in the shadows."

I studied the faces of the men in the room. Some were nodding in agreement, others sat up a bit in their chairs. I could see that by including people on the outside in his rant, the mood shifted.

"Let's get back to the true meaning of respect, shall we?" Dimitri said, returning his gaze to Carlos. "We can now see it's an entirely different thing than fear. So, as I stand here in front of my brother Carlos, I must be completely honest. I have to give credit where credit is due."

"I'm all ears, holmes," Carlos snapped back as he uncrossed his arms and put his hands up, still keeping the hard act in play.

"There is something he *has* done today that I do admire and is worthy of respect from every man in this room." Dimitri looked again at the group, "Can anyone here tell me what Carlos as well as Frank have done that would earn them actual respect in accordance with its true definition as written on the whiteboard?"

Finally, a hand went up and a middle-aged black man shouted, "I'd say it's because both of these guys came in here to work out their differences instead of throwing down. They deserve respect for that!"

"Right on! Thank you, Malik." Dimitri clapped his hands like an excited kid. *I wonder if he knows how strange it looks when he does that.* "Remember, guys, that this is something not widely accepted in prison. So we can admire their courage and that quality within them that wants a better way for themselves. Are you guys following me here?"

A surprisingly powerful "Yes!" sounded throughout the room.

"Beautiful!" he shouted. "And finally, what would we call this stepping out of an old pattern?" He looked again around the room and slowly pointed to the last word written on the whiteboard. "We'd call that achievement, wouldn't we? Moving from one way of doing things to a better one is defined as an achievement, and I think we can respect these men here for that as well."

I looked over at Carlos as a couple of the men sitting close patted him on the back while another gave him a fist bump. Carlos, obviously caught off guard and not wanting to lose face, just nodded proudly.

"Can I get you both back up here real quick? Our time is almost up, and I'd like to have some closure on this."

Both men got up and walked to the front of the crowd as Dimitri continued, "I would invite all of us in this room to remember that the truly powerful man is the one who is not affected by the words of another. Nor is he troubled by trivial bullcaca like cutting in line or walking through the supposed wrong side of the yard due to some gang affiliation crap. He doesn't get rattled over someone using a toilet that's supposedly been designated for a certain race or any of the other two hundred weak-ass reasons beefs get started in this place. A truly powerful man knows when to say he's sorry and is not afraid to do so. That is power born not from fear, but from humility. We can acknowledge our brothers in their humbleness, thus giving them the respect they truly deserve."

Just like that, boom, they were all on board. Chairs shifted and a "right on!" belted out.

Dimitri looked at both Carlos and Frank and took a couple of steps back to let happen what needed to happen. The tension in the room grew as they stood for what seemed to be an eternity. Finally, Frank stepped forward, "Hey, Carlos, yo sorry for cuttin' yesterday, bro." Frank extended his hand. It took a moment for Carlos, but he finally nodded and shook Frank's hand.

"All good, holmes," Carlos said coolly as others in the room gave a short clap. A couple even hollered out in approval. "Word!" one of the black prisoners shouted. "Odele, Carlos!" another Mexican exclaimed.

Zachary Markland handed Dimitri a piece of rolled-up fabric.

"Anyone ready to take the stand today?!" he shouted, pointing to what appeared to be four white prison-stock bandanas stitched together with intricate drawings on them.

Where have I seen something like that before?

There was silence. Dimitri looked at Carlos and Frank, and both shook their heads declining his offer.

"Thank you guys for coming up today," Dimitri said as he shook their hands. He bent over and maneuvered the square of fabric, looking up at different points in the room. He stood at its center and took a deep breath.

Ah, it's the wheel of love. The same as on Ana's porch.

"I, Dimitri Cato Tanomeo, hereby stand in the already accomplished awakening that's happened in this prison. I thank Divinity in advance for the completion of this miracle. I stand for justice and love within these walls, knowing that it already exists without me even saying so."

He stepped off, picked up the fabric, and folded it gently.

"Okay," he said. "Thank all of you for being here, for having the courage to look at yourselves, and to consider a new way. Every one of us in this room can respect each other as well as ourselves for that, right here and right now." He placed his hand over his heart and gave a slight bow.

Several short, powerful claps followed. It was clear the majority of the group was pumped up by what they had just seen. I admit I was one of them, though I couldn't show it at the time.

"Guy has got some juice, doesn't he?" Jim asked as we watched the men walk up and thank him.

"No doubt about that. He's pretty controversial with what he's saying, going against the inmate's system of respect," I answered. "It's hard to believe he hasn't been checked for any of this."

Jim took off his glasses and pointed them at me. "You know, I've thought the same thing. I reckon it's got something to do with how bad he beat his stepfather, Eddie The Butcher. You know he did time in here as well. One of the baddest OGs I've ever known in my twenty years at Carlton. Then, there was what happened with Earl Mills from the Deuce Five. There's a mystery around this kid, and no one's had the cajones to test him ... yet." I nodded in agreement.

"Marcus, I'm gonna hit it. Can you make sure they clear out of here? There's an AA meeting at the top of the hour?"

"Yeah, sure, Jim. I got it."

I stood by the door as the other inmates walked out.

"We're gonna need more notebooks. A lot more. I'm not exactly sure how to make that happen," I overheard the scratchy voice of Zachary Markland say.

"You'll make it happen, Zach," Dimitri whispered. "I have great confidence in you, amigo. They will show up as we need them, I promise."

As the last inmate left the room, Dimitri turned and gave me a smile.

"Officer Marcus Ogabi! Please come over and join us," Dimitri called out excitedly.

I walked over slowly, not exactly knowing how to manage the awkwardness of now being a prison guard and him a prisoner.

"Hello, inmate Markland." I gave him a nod, then turned to Dimitri and formally said, "How are you, Tanomeo?"

"I'm great. Zach and I are working with the prisoners. I'm showing five others how to do the same. I noticed you got to see the tail end of our session today. What did you think?" he asked with the enthusiasm of a young boy.

There was no "what are you doing here?" or "I'm surprised to see you." It was as if it was no big deal. *Maybe he knew I was coming.* "I think it's great if you can help these guys. I also think you need to make sure you don't offend anyone or any system that is already in place."

"As far as offending someone goes, it would be a great opportunity to find out what it was in that person that could even be offended. Taking offense to something is a co-creation. There are no victims.

"And as far as offending a system, well, that's just silly. A system cannot be offended. Only challenged, shut down, or accepted and utilized. I'm here to challenge and eventually shut down every system that's flawed at its roots. To be clear, I'm not talking about just here at Carlton."

He took a dramatic pause before whispering, "Were you able to take care of that thing we talked about last time, Officer Ogabi?"

Zach's head turned toward Dimitri with a confused look. I was still digesting the "taking down the system" part.

"Yep, I got it." I finally answered. Zach's head spun back to me.

"Wait, you guys know each other?" he asked.

"Officer Ogabi and I have some history," Dimitri answered. "We go back. Not way back, but enough."

"Wait a minute. Ogabi. I've heard that name before," Zach said, tapping his forefinger to his forehead trying to remember. I wasn't gonna volunteer any information. "Oh snap! He shot you, dude! You know him? I mean, you know him like *that?*"

Dimitri looked over at Zach with a hint of seriousness in his eyes. "It appears that's the case, doesn't it? Now keep your voice down. Remember, we're in a chapel. Have some *respect,* will ya?"

Zach laughed at the irony. "This guy thinks he's a comic, Officer O. Can I call you that?" I stared at the billionaire's son. He also seemed too happy for a place like this.

Another strange character. "Let's just keep it Officer Ogabi, Markland."

"Okay, I can do that. So, you guys are cool and everything, huh?" he asked, pointing to us both.

"Zach, you are so observant, it astounds me sometimes," Dimitri said, grinning.

"What a trip! You know, that he's here and all, talking to you like no big deal." A perturbed Dimitri shrugged his shoulders, but Markland couldn't help himself.

"So, what was it he took care of for you?"

"Damn, inmate. You sure ask a lot of questions," I said sharply.

"It's a shirt, Zach." Dimitri said. "Officer Ogabi was kind enough to do me the favor of going back to my old place and pick it up for me. A shirt that has a lot of sentimental value. Of course, he did this before he was a CO here."

Zach lifted a cup of water and took a drink. "I've got a whole bunch of whys, hows, and what the fucks going on, but I'll just keep them to myself for the moment. But since he's down with helping, maybe he can help out with what we were just talking about."

When did I say I'm down to help?

Dimitri smiled, "Like I just said, Officer Ogabi did that before he was a correctional officer. Now he has to carry himself in here as a CO first. We can figure out how to get those on our own."

That was the first time I saw the discipline in Dimitri as well as his ability to know that I had to keep mine. He knew I had a job to do and that it was important to keep the inmate/guard relationship intact. He then checked the time on his bare wrist, signaling to me it was time to leave for my own good.

"Okay, Tanomeo, Markland, as you were," I said with authority. "And just one more thing," I said, turning back as I walked away. "What is it that you two need so badly?"

Zach looked over at Dimitri, who gave him a nod of approval.

"We need notebooks. Many, many notebooks," Zach said.

"Oh yeah?" I asked, "Why do you need so many notebooks? What's wrong with that big stack of them you have over there on the floor?"

Zach shook his head and laughed, "No, you don't understand, boss. We need many more than that. D here has big plans for this place."

"Big plans?" I asked.

"Well, Dimitri says that we are gonna ... how did you say it, D? Transform the prison from its current state into something that works."

Zach waited for a response, which I didn't have, so he chimed in again.

"He means the inmates, you know. Like, help them change their lives and shit."

"Like you guys were doing today?" I asked.

"Well, in reality, D's the one who's doing it all. I'm just assisting where I'm needed in the organization part of it."

Dimitri's hand shot up to interrupt. "Which is just as important as what I do. This is a team effort, and one part is not more important than the other."

That was the first time I saw him acknowledge another who helped him get his message out, and it wouldn't be the last. Even many years later, after he'd reached the pinnacle of great fame, he'd still wholeheartedly share the spotlight.

"So, what do you need so many more pads for then?"

"Because we need to document everyone's individual experience, their personal issues, breakthroughs, and just basically where they are in their process. I'm creating a system so I can gauge each prisoner's level of awareness in regards to the issues in their life and how they react to them," Zach answered, as I watched Dimitri flip through the pages of a notebook, seemingly not interested in this part of our conversation.

"For D, this is just the beginning of what is coming. He says many more will be joining, and we have to be ready to receive them."

This guy really has high aspirations. "So, how many do you see coming on board?" I asked.

"How many are there?" Dimitri calmly asked, never looking up from the notepad.

I figured he was asking me, seeing how I was the only one there that might have that answer. "Well, here in this block you have—" His hand shot up, interrupting again. It felt odd, my stopping mid-sentence as if I'd taken an order from an inmate.

"No, Officer Ogabi. How many in the whole prison?" he asked bluntly.

I stood in silence. Zach raised his eyebrows, then looked down. I just stared at him not answering. We all knew there were thousands.

He nodded. "So, as you can see, we need many more and somewhere to store them all."

"You can't possibly believe you can reach that many men, right?" I asked. It sounded ridiculous.

That seemed to stop him dead in his tracks. He just gazed up at me with a confused look. "Well, of course I do." He looked back at his notebook. "I plan to help all who are ready. And you know what? If they are here, in this place, I'd say they're ready."

"Why's that? And when you say 'ready,' what exactly do you mean?"

"Well, not everyone's ready to look at their caca," he replied. "You see Officer, many have not hit their bottom yet, and in most cases, that's what's needed for them to be ready for a change. I should be clear that I am speaking not only of the prisoners here at Carlton but all the people of the world."

He laughed. "It's funny if you really think about it. They are prisoners as well, they just don't know it, yet." Zach looked straight ahead as if he wanted to be invisible. "There will be holdouts, those who are content where they are, not just in their current physical surroundings but in their mental, emotional, and energetic state. They will find my words intolerable. But, yes, most will come, and most will awaken and transform."

Now Zach was smiling like some kind of groupie, buying everything his cellmate had to sell. He shouted, "I mean, what else is there to do, right, D?!"

Again? They fist-bumped. This would be the first time of many I felt left out.

I knew there was a part of me that liked what Dimitri said and another that was offended that any one person had the audacity to believe they could make such a difference. Only later would I learn it was just the part of me, which wasn't the real *me*, doing its best to keep myself and the world small.

"Oh, it doesn't stop there. D's got bigger plans. He sees Carlton like the first sovereign, awakened village. You know, like it takes a village to awaken the planet," Zach said with enthusiasm. "Carlton is the village that will—"

Dimitri's hand shot up once again.

"You've shared enough, Zach. Let's not scare Officer Ogabi away too soon. He just got here."

Zach laughed, "You sure didn't have a problem telling me all about it, did you, dude?"

"That's because I knew you weren't going anywhere. You are literally my captive audience."

"You've got to watch out for this guy here, Officer," Zach said as he stacked the notebooks in his arms.

"Well, carry on then."

As I walked down the hallway, continuing my rounds, I wondered where this was all going. We had an out-of-touch-with-reality nineteen-year-old guru, a hip computer genius turned convicted cybercriminal, and me, a middle-aged, nearly divorced alcoholic ex-cop turned prison guard, together in a strange new environment. It certainly had the appearance of the beginning of a very new life.

HOUSE OF MIRRORS

ZACH

One afternoon, alone in our cell setting up the notebooks for the first five participants, I contemplated D's approach to this growth process. He felt that the first thing they needed was to observe their patterns, the ones that sabotaged their lives. Not so much what they did to get into prison but more the thoughts that were holding them in mental bondage today.

Every limitation, problem, or lingering issue arises from a past memory of a challenging occurrence. He insisted that the first step was digging up what happened. As he would say, "All of us have something that happened. We are blinded by our past experiences. How can we ever expect to live in peace and harmony when this moment is being seen through the eyes of what happened, the eyes of our pasts?"

I had gotten to a place where I knew this to be the straight-up truth, but for whatever reason, I couldn't hold on to it at times.

"Yo, D, why is it that I keep forgetting these things? The important stuff you taught me about my father and my relationship with him. I catch myself still pissed off, blaming him for my troubles and all that. It almost feels like a trap I keep falling back into. You sure your system works, bro?" I asked while laughing and patting him on the shoulder.

"Sure it does, as long as you are willing to work it. It's the only way to keep yourself out of the trap," he answered.

"Work it? Work what?"

"You have to work on this thing, Zach. You have to consciously bring it into your new mental dialogue."

"I thought I had," I said, frustrated. "Usually when I learn something, I get it. It's there and that's the end of the story. But this is different and I don't know why."

"It's because the story is an old one—one that's been around for thousands of years. The story of victimization is actually a program of sorts, and it's been in you and just about every other person on this planet for a long time.

This is not like learning a new mathematical technique at school. This has to be dismantled constantly. Think of it as being in a house of mirrors, you have to call it out as not your own every time it shows up. This helps you internally confirm that it is no longer your story. Then, at some point, you have to choose a new story."

"How the hell do I do that?"

"First, you have to understand one thing: There's no such thing as a happy victim."

Simple, but profound.

"Then," he continued, "you start realizing there is a voice in your head that is not yours. It's the one that blames and falls victim to the past. Your true voice, the one that *is* yours, is the one that just a moment ago asked why you keep blaming and falling into the trap."

I gave him a curious look while trying to add it all up in my head.

"I know it seems odd," he went on, "this idea that you have more than one voice inside of you, but, over time, you will be able to spot it more easily. The more you begin to notice it, the more it will become a practice for you. You will become an active participant in shifting your inner dialogue, the voice in your head, away from the clutches of the false self, the one that blames. And to answer your next question, you do that by just observing it talking, much like you just did but from a place of knowing that it's not your own. You can even give it a name. Maybe something like Richard, AKA ... you know."

I cracked up at his lame joke. At the same time, I could see how if I just pointed out the other voice when it showed up, it would be very clear that I wasn't the owner of it.

"Okay, so it's Dick from now on. How long do I have to do this?" I asked.

"Once your inner dialogue has been handed back over to the true self, the mirroring will cease. This is how true liberation is attained. Basically, that means you'll do it until there's only one voice being spoken, yours."

True liberation. That sounds pretty good. I wondered how far I was from it.

"Okay, so all of what you just said leads me to believe there's a lot more to this thing, more than what you've already shown me."

He laughed and clapped his hands. "You're quick with this stuff. I like that. Yes, there's more, but for now, you just need to apologize."

I didn't like where this was going, and he could see it.

"Your corrupt internal dialogue started a long time ago when you were young. It happened during the original uncomfortable, or call it traumatic, incident when you discovered that your father had done this and that. At the time you had no choice but to take cues from an unconsciously sick world that told you they were bad things, that they shouldn't have happened, and that he was a bad man. This was the important moment: when you told yourself, 'I blame my father for X.' This was the moment an imprint was formed in your mind. There are different terms for this within different practices, but I like the term 'mental imprint.'"

I thought about the implications of what he was saying. If true, it would mean most people in the world would be filled with these mental imprints. "The thing is, Dimitri, I blame many people for things, not just my father."

"You have many imprints, as do most," he shot back without missing a beat.

"So, could you explain why I need to apologize to my father then?"

"Because he seems to be the biggest actor in your play or, rather, your plague. The issue you have with him is the biggest in your life. He's the one you blame the most. The original one."

"But how and why would apologizing to him help me with anything?"

"As the powerful human beings that we truly are, we must take full responsibility for everything we have created in our lives. You created the blame around the issue. The problem is yours. He was just doing the best he could with what he had at the time."

I started to interject.

"Before you try to disagree with me," he said, "I'll ask you to take a moment of self-reflection and notice how you are ultimately at cause for all of it. Just ask yourself, who seems to always be there when there's a problem with anything, you know, when you are blaming? Once you get that answer, as the newly compassionate and understanding human being you are today, you will see that you must make amends. Asking forgiveness from the person you've made wrong removes the imprint while paving the way to your own internal liberation."

As hard as it was to admit, I got his point. But I was still unclear on how apologizing would remove the imprint from my system.

"Imagine it, Zach. The so-called victim apologizes to the so-called culprit. This unlikely and even uncomfortable experience born from love and compassion has the ability to shock the imprint right out of one's mind.

Introducing the counterintuitive incident of apology, where there normally wouldn't be one, counteracts the original trauma imprint causing its power to diminish or even vanish."

"Okay, dawg," I said. "It all sounds very interesting, but how do you remove the memory of what happened?"

"That's exactly what this is all about, memory. Everything that comes from anywhere but love is a distorted memory and always based in fear. What you are doing here with me is evolving from a past memory narrative into the choosing of a new truth. The truth that we are all ultimately One. Once you own this, you won't have a problem with the memory anymore. You will be liberated, from that issue at least."

I could see how taking absolute responsibility, then energetically releasing old patterns through the counterintuitive event of apologizing could return equilibrium to any broken relationship. The implications of this were earth-shattering, limitless. But I still had questions.

"I'm not sure what my father would think if I apologized to him, D. He knows what he did, causing all the issues in our family. He'd probably think I had lost my mind."

"It's not important what he says or thinks. His reaction doesn't matter, really. This is for you to clean up things inside of yourself and your energy with regards to how you see him. When you recreate another through your perception of them, you recreate not only yourself but all the people of the world."

Jesus, where does this guy get this stuff?

"Let me get this straight," I said. "In any situation where one has done something to another, no matter how horrific, the victim needs to apologize to the other who did the thing to them? Is that what you are saying?"

"Well, no one needs to do anything. They can just stay in their misery, as most do. You see, one can't really progress or, let me put it this way, will not be free to soar if they are weighed down by their past. They can just sit and stew, consciously or unconsciously, about what someone or something did or are still doing to make their life the way it is. But ultimately, yes, that's exactly what I'm saying. It's the fastest way I know of clearing up stored negative energy around any situation.

"Of course, that person, the supposed victim, has to get it. They have to be conscious of their part in the destruction of any and all relationships affected by the past incident or incidents in question. If they are just saying the words, which is very common with pseudo-spiritual people, it won't work. So, I guess the real question is, do you want to remain common folk or become an extraordinary human, Zach?"

"Nice peer pressure in the midst of a heavy concept," I laughed.

"I gotta give it my best shot," he shot back, goodnaturedly.

"I can't imagine many people could do this, taking responsibility for their own involvement at that level. Especially if the shit that was done to them was gnarly, extreme trauma. How could they even get there? Forgive maybe, but what you are talking about … I don't know, bro."

He nodded. "Many can't get there. Their ego won't let them, so they stay stuck in their wound, focused on what happened to them. Most don't even know they're doing it because it's so deeply embedded. They merely exist in this world, causing sickness not only in their minds and their relationships but in their bodies as well.

"As far as forgiving goes, that isn't what this is about. Forgiving will happen but it will occur innately after taking responsibility. It comes second. It's more like a result of accountability and compassion."

No one thinks like this guy.

I waited a few seconds before playing the devil's advocate. "Why can't one just say 'I forgive you' and be done with it?"

"Well, first off, there's nothing to forgive once you are free. If one still has something to forgive, then they will carry the story with them, a story that ultimately isn't true. You see, we want people to be empowered enough to move beyond their story and into the space of *knowing* that whatever happened actually happened *for them* instead of *to them.* From there, and only from there, is anything of any great merit possible."

He reached over and grabbed my shoulder. "This is about recognizing the truth that everything just *is* and living in full acceptance of that truth."

This is all pretty heavy, but I think I'm getting it.

"What did you mean about how all this ties to sickness in the body?"

"The refusal or inability to clear up the energetic blockage around the issue is nothing more than a form of resistance in and of itself. This resistance to what is can, and usually will, manifest itself in the form of physical illness. It's The System's last-ditch effort to wake you up. Can you see how important it is for the individual to take responsibility, because if they don't who will?

How does the cycle stop? Only they can heal themselves, no one else. By the way, that's System with a capital S."

"Why a capital S?" I asked.

He smirked and whispered, "I'm going to let you come to that one on your own, but here's a big hint ... it's *that* important."

I thought about all he'd said. "You do know this sounds crazy to a normal person, don't you, D?"

"So, now you're normal, Zach? Like a setting on a washing machine. Good to know."

» » « «

We got a little time in the prison yard every day. It wasn't much, and it sure didn't feel like wide-open spaces surrounded by all that razor wire and chain link, but it was nice nonetheless.

Dimitri and I walked together along the perimeter. The feet of thousands of prisoners, following the same path as us, had worn a dark trail into the grass.

My mind was still wrestling with the concept of apologizing for harm done to one's self. On one hand, the idea of apologizing to and then asking forgiveness from the person who'd done something to me seemed bizarre, but, on the other hand, it somehow made sense. Except for one thing ....

"D, earlier we talked about asking for forgiveness. I get it, but before that, you also said there's nothing to forgive, remember?"

"There isn't if you are awake," he said, "*if* you are truly in your full knowing. But you cannot expect the one to whom you are apologizing to be where you are, so out of a kind of courtesy, you ask them for forgiveness. This is part of the practice, Zach."

I nodded, my eyes focused on the path we walked.

"The next step is to take it even further," Dimitri said, "by bringing forth yet another counterintuitive move: *thanking* the other for this situation."

My head snapped back in confusion. "Why would I wanna do that?"

"Because the situation, your blaming, uncomfortable as it's been, has brought you to a deeper truth, brought you back to yourself. These problems or complaints of ours are actually gifts, especially when we reach the truth about them. Do you not feel like a whole new person after all of these revelations?"

"Yeah, I actually do," I admitted. "It just seems a bit strange to say 'thanks for the problem.'"

He nodded in agreement.

"To be clear, you are not necessarily thanking the other for the problem, because it was never real to begin with. It's more like you are taking the counterintuitive thing to a whole new level, an additional shock to the system, above and beyond the first one wherein you apologized. This double whammy can bring forth deeper clarity, not only in the mental field but in the energetic as well. You are actually thanking the higher self or selves, the one that sent or created the thing that got you there. You are saying thank you for their part in your realization.

"This part is a bit esoteric and this is not the time to get into it. But let me just say this: the true you, the one that can witness the voice in your head, the one that wants only the best for you, is brilliant and powerful in ways that you couldn't possibly imagine. It is so intelligent and wonderful that it sent you these difficult issues knowing they could help you return to your true nature of love, joy, and peace."

"I think you're right, D. This isn't the time for that level of esotericism. And please don't ever say double whammy again, either."

He threw his head back and laughed.

What blew me away was that he'd spoken the truth. I didn't know how I actually knew it was the truth, but I just did.

He quickened his pace, and I could tell that he was done speaking for the day.

"Let me get this straight," I said, as we completed our final loop of the yard. "If I say I'm sorry, ask for forgiveness, and thank the problem as well as the person, I'm set? Is that what you are saying?"

"That's what I am saying. Of course, it helps if you know it will work. Not *believe*, but *know*. There is a difference. For now, if you can only believe, then so be it. But once you do this thing and it works, you will know. And when you know, you can then leave belief behind. Belief is for those who don't know."

I pulled my journal out to jot it all down.

"One more thing," he said as we neared the end of the walk.

"What's that?"

"Say 'I love you' at the end."

"Why do I gotta do that?" I moaned.

"Because that completes the cycle. And because you do."

"I do what?" I asked.

"Love him. You may not realize it because you are just now discovering, or remembering actually, but you do, Zach. You love your father and anyone or anything that brings painful opportunities like these to you."

"But all I have to do is go through this apology process with my father and that's it?"

"Yes, until you need to do it again."

"Do it again? This isn't just a one-time thing?" *This is beginning to sound like a lot of work.*

He grinned and shook his head, "The program that causes you to blame and think negatively about yourself, another, or anything runs deep. Very deep. It will require repeating the process every time a thought of that nature arises. It's referred to as 'cleaning.'"

"Cleaning?"

"Well, that's what we are doing. But the system does have its own name: ho'oponopono."

"Ho'oponowhato? Why did you name it that?" I asked, holding back laughter.

"I didn't. The Hawaiians did," he said. It's their ancient practice of healing, or correcting."

We were at the doorway leading out of the yard and back into the dense walls of the prison building and, eventually, our cell. I stopped as he continued inside.

"Wait, so it's not yours?" I said sharply, surprised.

He turned to look back at me. "Well, what I just shared with you was an altered version of it. I reworked it to utilize within victimhood situations like the one you have with your father. The actual practice uses the same four statements but goes further into a deeper, universal, more esoteric truth. One day this mantra—I'm sorry, please forgive, thank you, I love you—will be used to save the world. I'll explain it to you fully when you are ready. But no, ultimately, it's not mine; it's all of ours, Zach."

"It just seemed, the way you were talking, that you invented it. So it's not original then, is it?"

"Original? What is original exactly? Every word we use, every thought we have emanates from something we have seen, heard, or experienced before. All that incredible wisdom out there at our disposal, waiting for us to utilize it so that we may transmute it into our own inner space of knowing—it all existed before us. It was all known before us. It's not always necessary to reinvent the wheel, Zach."

Can't argue with that.

He walked into the building, leaving me considering all of the people in my world who could use this *cleaning*. My mother and her issues with her own father and the dark secrets that no one talked about. *Could this be why she's always sick?* My sister and her feelings of being left out of my father's business visions and all the suffering that causes her. The world and all of its bullshit. Could this Hawaiian method really heal all?

VICTIM NO MORE

ZACH

I have to admit, the Early Release Program grand opening, when nearly every inmate in our block left pissed off, shook me a bit. But D had a completely different way of seeing it. As they were walking out, many throwing looks and words at us, he assured me that all was right in the world and that those who stayed would become the core group. He was right. In the end, there were just D, myself, and five others.

Much to my dismay, D lamely dubbed us the Magnificent Seven. There was Malik Abdul Ali, AKA Tyrone Henson, who was slapped with "a nickel" (five years) for strong-armed robbery. John White Eagle, in for six for grand theft auto. Carl Plowman, with a class three embezzlement charge and maxed out with a dime. Robert McKenna was doing a bullet (one year) for possession of an illegal firearm. Lastly, there was Chuck Clemans, who got railroaded with a twenty-eight-year sentence for multiple attempted murder charges after shooting at the home where he'd just been jumped and beaten.

It was pretty dope watching D do what he did with me in the privacy of our cell out in the open with the others. Hearing it repeatedly would eventually give me fluency in the concept.

He'd just finished helping Robert see a deeper truth behind a horrible upbringing wherein his uncle had sexually abused him for years. The fear of speaking his truth had Robert grow up feeling powerless, which drove him to severe alcoholism and homelessness. After an hour of Dimitri's words, he was able to see his part in the very complex web of hereditary family trauma. From that place, he was able to capture the greater truth, the bigger message, and Robert was set free.

Dimitri invited him to practice Ho'oponopono with his dead uncle, explaining that it didn't matter that he wasn't here in the physical form. What mattered was for Robert to let go energetically. Robert told us that he needed to do it with his mother as well because he always blamed her for letting it happen.

Needless to say, there were some emotional releases happening and, while most of us were moved by watching Robert go through the process, there was one who wasn't. Malik just sat there with his arms crossed.

"Do you have a question about this, Malik? Is it connecting for you?" Dimitri asked.

Malik nodded his head arrogantly. "More of a comment than anything, I'd say."

"We'd love to hear it," Dimitri offered.

Malik sat up in his chair, still keeping his arms crossed. "Well, I can see what you are talking about on a personal level, and it's great that Robert was helped. I can even look at my own situation with my wife and the problems we've had and see how this thing might work and all. But what I can't see is how this works within a specific race of people that have been held down by another for generations."

"Could you be a bit more clear on this, Malik?" Dimitri asked.

"If a whole ethnic group has suffered at the hands of another one, then this idea of one taking responsibility can't possibly apply. We can't possibly just forgive that. There's irreversible damage that has affected my people and always will. Especially when it's still happening on the scale that it is today. I don't expect you to know much about history, especially when it doesn't affect you."

"So, let's talk about slavery," Dimitri started, "one of the many evils of civilization. Something that's been around since the times of Babylon. Now, I take it you're referring to African and African American slavery, which started in 1776. Many believe it was abolished by Lincoln in 1863 with his creation of the Emancipation Proclamation, but that's just not the case. It actually ended when the Thirteenth Amendment to the Constitution was ratified on December 6, 1865."

Malik faintly nodded his head, humbled by Dimitri's knowledge. "But that is only part of it," Malik barked. "What about the injustices toward blacks? Until recently we weren't able to vote, not to mention all of the other forms of unjust treatment we have received by the white devil."

"So, what year were you born, Malik?"

"1963. Why?"

"Well, seeing how blacks were finally given the right to vote with the signing of The Voting Rights Act by Lyndon B. Johnson in 1965, I was just wondering who you wanted to vote for when you were a one-year-old and couldn't because of the racial inequality brought on by the white devils at the time."

Malik sat silently staring at Dimitri with a look of disdain.

"You see, Malik, I'm here to talk about how you are being affected today, right now, at this moment, as we sit here in this chapel. How do the injustices of the past affect you in the here and now?"

Malik was notably getting more pissed off by the minute. "You want to know, Tanomeo? I'm affected by all of them. Every white man represents the hardship of my people."

Dimitri nodded and smiled. "Okay great, now we're getting somewhere. I'm just curious about something. What do you think about prejudice? Do you like it, dislike it? Or are you neutral?"

Malik looked at Dimitri like he was crazy and threw his hands up. "Don't you get it, Tanomeo. That's exactly what I am talking about here, prejudice. It's the disease that has plagued the black man for hundreds of years."

"Okay, so you are against it? You don't like it?" Dimitri asked calmly.

"Of course I am against it! I hate it. I always have, ever since I learned what the white man was up to behind his shiny, white-toothed smile."

Don't smile or even open your mouth, Zach. I'd never been around a black man that was this angry at white people before.

"Maybe we should kill all of the prejudiced people in the world. What do you think about that as an idea, Malik?" Dimitri asked.

I watched as he shifted uncomfortably in his chair, taken aback by Dimitri's suggestion.

"I didn't say that."

"No, I did. But in your world that might be a remedy to this rampant global prejudice issue."

"That's a bit harsh, no?" Malik humbly asked.

"I'd say so, but I thought it might work in your world. Okay, how about we just throw them all in prison for the rest of their lives. That's better, right?"

Malik narrowed his eyes. "I'm not sure if you're being serious here, Tanomeo, but if you are, how could we ever know which were the ones who were racist?"

"You've got a good point there. That's a tricky one for sure." Dimitri nodded, looking up at the ceiling contemplatively before looking straight into

Malik's eyes and calmly saying, "Well, I guess we could just start with you, couldn't we?"

Malik shot to his feet, standing over Dimitri in a threatening manner.

"You callin' me a racist, Tanomeo?"

"Absolutely. If the shoe fits and, as far as I can see, it's fitting rather nicely," Dimitri answered. He gave a nod toward his chair, indicating for him to take his seat.

Malik hesitated for a moment before slowly lowering into his chair.

"That's better," Dimitri said gently. "You see, I'm here to call it like it is. You might not like what I have to say, but I am going to say it. If you want to continue talking about what happened in the past, then you will never be able to move ahead. This is your invitation for awakening, Malik." He paused to let his words set in. Malik wasn't buying it, so he went on.

"What's the first thing you think when you meet a white person? Do you ever say to yourself, 'they don't like me,' 'they think they are better than me,' or 'I don't like them'?" he mocked in a whining voice.

"I invite you to listen inside to what that internal speaking says to you about white people. Take a look at any projections about what they think of you or black people in general. Consider the poor me, victim bullcaca attitude you've been running for God knows how long. Take a look at the damage you are doing not only to yourself but the rest of the black community and humanity as well.

"And if you are going to tell me that many others feel the same way, then all I can say to you is that there are many asleep people in the world. You, as well as they, are contributing to the low vibrational frequency on this planet. Yes, I said vibrational frequency. I'll explain it another day."

He paused for a moment. I might have been the only one in the room who understood vibration, but I was stuck on the bullcaca comment. *Why does he still refuse to cuss?*

He went on staring directly into Malik's eyes. "But just so we are clear, you are at cause for racism and prejudice, not only because of your own bigotry caused by your projections but mainly because you give so much energy to racism by recognizing it, talking about it, and thinking about it every day of your life. What's it going to take, Malik, for you to stop holding humanity hostage through your racism?!"

Malik was visibly humbled by Dimitri's rant. "First of all," he said quietly,

"I don't dislike all white people, and maybe I shouldn't have used those words to describe them. I had never thought of myself being prejudiced like that. I'm not sure what to make of it."

"What you can make of it is that we all have prejudice to some degree. We are all pre-judging others as well as life's circumstances. That's just what we do. You will pre-judge until you stop pre-judging, the same as the next person who will do it until they don't anymore.

"I don't think it makes much sense to call it wrong; it just is. If someone doesn't like you because of what they think they see with their eyes, don't worry about it. It's just something they don't like in themselves. It's their loss anyway, Malik, because you're great! You can't get rid of ignorance just because you don't like it. Just like you can't make a donkey be any less of an ass until he's ready to evolve out of his jackasshood."

The entire group laughed at that one.

"Brother," Dimitri continued, "I'm here to empower others, so I do not recognize the possibility of inequality for them. For me, it doesn't exist. And while things may seem skewed in one direction or another, and we can certainly call that inequality, I don't give it any energy. Instead, I like to look at it all as just different experiences for different people because that's all it is. And, if you really think about it, it's as if those unequal experiences were magically put here to bring us back together. Like what's happening right now in this chapel."

Damn, that's heavy!

Malik sat staring down toward the center of the circle, resisting and in deep contemplation at the same time.

John White Eagle, the Native American, raised his hand. "So, what about what happened to my people? The eradication of millions of innocent women and children, a whole race and its culture, virtually wiped out in the blink of an eye. What do you have to say about that? What do you have to say about genocide?"

"What do I have to say about it? I say that it happened and nothing else. It's the past and it's done. Just like Robert's situation with his uncle, mine with my family, and slavery for that matter," Dimitri answered.

Kinda makes sense.

"But what about the residual effects? Lack of schooling, drug and alcohol addiction, poverty, and all of that?" John asked.

Dimitri nodded his head in agreement, "If those things exist, then they exist. And if they were a result of something that happened, then so be it. Once we call something wrong, we step into the cycle of victimhood, thus giving up our inherent power to change things. There's a lot of issues that can be looked at and shifted in this world, but we have to clean our own house, internally, before we can even begin the discussion of true change.

"But, let me ask you all something: Are there Native Americans, people of color, and members of other ethnic groups who have pulled themselves out of adversity and made something of their lives? Do you think they did that by bitching about what they don't have, crying about the shitty hand they'd been dealt? Of course, they didn't. We've got to put this separation thing away, on all fronts, because the anger you carry will eventually lead to more violence, destruction, and polarization. Nothing positive can come from that, I assure you. The changes you want for your people are the changes we want for all people of the world, and the only way to get there is through awakening. I say we start here, in this chapel, today."

He looked at each of us individually to see if we were getting it. We were.

"I'm here to be part of the solution, not the problem," Dimitri went on. "I'm looking for strong men who can stand in their power, ready for what's coming toward us in this world."

We all remained silent considering his words.

"Guys, this new inner conversation that I am inviting you to join is one of taking responsibility for the way you see the world right now. From that place, you can stand in your own power as the great creators that each of you are and change what needs changing, and to both of you, know that I know there's a lot that needs to be changed. It's just that only from there, that healed place, will you be able to freely create a new life, a life worth living." Dimitri got in Malik's face. "You want to help your people, then wake up and step up."

Malik got up and walked out of the circle, clenching his fist.

» » « «

The group took a quick water break to clear the air. Malik paced back and forth at the opposite end of the chapel the whole time.

As we retook our seats in the circle, Malik leaned over the back of his chair and focused on Dimitri. "What if I said I know what you are saying is the truth, but I can't accept it? Damn!"

"Come back to the circle, and I'll explain why you're struggling, Malik," Dimitri said.

Malik slowly took his seat. He seemed calmer.

"How long have you been blaming white people for?" Dimitri asked.

Malik gathered himself. "When I was about nine. I used to hear my mother talk about it. She was from the South, so she was affected and stayed that way till the day she died."

"Let me suggest that there is a part of you that knows what I speak is truth, and that part is the real you. Then there's the part of you that feels the need to hold on to the anger and blame. This is the you that you believe is you but is not really you."

"Say what?" Malik asked.

"Let's just focus on the part that can't let go. There's something inside you that wants things to stay the way they are, right?"

Malik looked up and asked, "Yeah, how did you know that?"

"Bear with me. Let's just say there's a voice in your head that doesn't want things to change. It's fearful because it knows that this change, in particular, will lead to its own demise or at least a dramatic lessening of its power. You see, right now you believe you are an advocate for black rights, a fighter for racial equality, or whatever wording you use to describe yourself in your head or to others. And because you actually believe this, your mind has formed an identity around it. How am I doing?"

"Whoa. Then maybe this is why ..." Malik stopped with his mouth wide open. "Never mind."

"No, say it. Whatever is coming up, it's important to recognize it," Dimitri stated.

"Okay. When I stepped away from the circle, I wondered what my brothers and sisters would think if I changed my tune about the whole racial thing. I thought it was pretty ridiculous to even worry about such a thing, but it didn't make the concern go away."

"Amazing. You have just identified the false self at work. Remember when I said there's a you that you believe is you but isn't really you?"

"How could I forget?" Malik sneered.

"So, that is what I am referring to now as the false self. When the thought came in around what your friends might think, that wasn't you that had that thought. It only seemed like it was you because you have never been aware of the voices. You were the one that noticed it was a ridiculous thing to worry about in the first place. It was the true you that wondered why it didn't go away even after realizing its ridiculousness. To put it simply, you were the one that observed what was said and knew something was off. Is this coming through, Malik?"

"It's starting to, but I'm still a bit unclear on the name of the false self. How can it be 'false' when I'm experiencing it?" Malik was now fully engaged.

"There are many words used to describe what I just referred to as the false self. The ego, lower self, shadow side, ego-mind, the little me, and even Satan if you know what JC was really saying when he spoke of it. All of these point to the same thing, and it is what is currently inhabiting the mind of most people.

"The lower self, through years of collective programming, has us believe that we are small. Then we are convinced by the same programming that having a title makes us bigger than the little me we inaccurately believe we are. An advocate of this or that, professor of whatever, mother, father, veteran, CEO, survivor of cancer, victim of abuse, president of whatever, or anything that gives us a false identity which we believe validates us. We like this because, in the little me's world, we were nothing before, and this newly given title just turned us into a something."

His words brought me back to how important it was to have the title of "the world's most renowned cybercriminal." My motivation to gain this status outweighed my own freedom. I actually believed I was less of a person before I shut down the electricity of an entire city, forever cementing my status with that lofty title. The part that really tripped me out was how meaningless it all felt less than a week after attaining it.

"Furthermore," Dimitri continued, "if a thought came in concerning the fear around what your people might think and, at the same time, there was the recognition of how ridiculous it seemed, which one of the two thoughts, the two yous that had those thoughts, is the true you? Are you the one that had the ridiculous thought, or are you the one that noticed the thought come in and had the wherewithal to name it ridiculous?

"That is the million-dollar question, Malik. You can only be one because it would be impossible to be both. I mean, you can't have a thought and be the one that notices it come in at the same time, can you?"

It took a minute for him to contemplate it all. "No, you can't, can you!" The penny had finally dropped, and he began to laugh out loud, for the first time in a long time, I imagined.

"So, Dimitri, I am not the one who is actually being ridiculous, right?"

"You are not."

"Then I'm the one that noticed it was ridiculous, right?"

"That would be you. You are the one who witnesses the thoughts. You are the awareness that is behind all of it."

Malik's eyes widened. "Oh shit, that's exactly true! I am the one who is aware!"

"Yes. And even more to the point, you could just say 'I am awareness.'"

"I am awareness," Malik repeated slowly with a huge smile on his face.

Everyone in the room was beaming, blown away by the whole process. Everyone, that is, except Carl Plowman, the prison's intellectual, AKA The Professor, appeared unimpressed as he sat with his arms crossed.

"What you are talking about is the ego. I've studied it in all of its variables and possibilities, but where's the physical proof of it?" he asked.

His voice even sounds like a professor.

"Tell me, Carl, does light exist?" Dimitri asked.

"Of course it does," Carl scoffed.

"Show it to me. I mean, we can all agree that there truly is a thing called light. So prove it to me."

"Okay, well," Carl mumbled, letting out a nervous laugh. He then began pointing in several directions inside the room. "It's just there. It's everywhere."

"Let me help you," Dimitri said and made his way toward the chapel doors where the light switches waited.

"This is dark," he said as he switched off the lights. "This is light," he said and turned them on.

"So, did I just prove there was light?" he asked, retaking his seat. No one answered and he didn't care.

"It's kind of the same with the ego. In Malik's experience, there were two opposites at work. I know it's a subjective thing and we couldn't be inside of him having the experience, but each one of us can become aware of it within ourselves. So, Carl, your proof is in your own experience. Once you have that moment where you witness the voice of your mind in action, putting you always in the past or future, you will have proven the existence of it."

"True dat!" Malik shouted while extending his hand. "You're all right, Tanomeo."

Holy shit. This was kind of a big moment. Here we had the leader of the Nation of Islam and, in his case, an outspoken opponent of the white race with his hand out to someone who had at least some white in him.

Dimitri shook his hand and tried to pull him in for a bro hug, but Malik backed off. Dimitri laughed out loud and said, "No problem, Malik. You've come a long way today. Baby steps, right?"

"Word, but I will take the stand," he said with a smile.

"Yeah, baby. That's what I'm talking about!" Dimitri shouted while rushing to get the mat, not wanting Malik to have a change of heart.

Dimitri unfurled the wheel of love and lined up the directions using the marker we put on the wall for due south. Malik walked into the center, stood on the square of cloth, and did his thing, adding a ho'oponopono at the end for good measure. Just like that, he was transformed into a different person, right in front of our eyes.

I sat back in my chair and let it all sink in. Malik surprised me with a pat on my back as he walked back to sit in his. I was proud of my cellmate, the wizard who'd waved his magic wand and started changing the world one person at a time.

» » « «

In the weeks to come, Dimitri worked with each one of us in the group sessions and, one by one, the miracles kept coming. Breakthrough after breakthrough were experienced as each one of us had our lives changed forever.

It wouldn't be long before the Magnificent Seven became more magnificent than ever. This is where I had to step up my game. Once the group grew, largely by word of mouth, or maybe by example, it became a bit more complicated to keep up with everyone's process, but I managed.

I requested that all new members bring a notebook that they handed over to me on their first session. However, there were some issues with that. Though you could buy one at the commissary, many of the prisoners didn't have or were not willing to spend the little money they had on a notebook. That's when something very interesting happened.

Early one evening, Malik and Carl showed up to our cell. They knew about the issue surrounding the notebooks and offered to buy as many as they could with their own money. This was a rare occurrence. Prisoners trade their commissary items and such but donate ... almost never.

Dimitri had tears welling up in his eyes. "Wow, guys. What is occurring today, here in this cell, is the beginning of something really big. I just want you to know that. You are the first who have stepped forward in a way that many would have trouble doing."

"To be honest," Carl interjected, "Malik had to nudge me a few times."

We all laughed at his honesty.

"Even still, thank you for that. This is the first step in a shift that will continue all over the world, wherein others give freely what they have to assist their brothers and sisters in their own awakening. I know that might sound strange to you, but you just made it very real for me, and from the bottom of my heart, I want you to know how much I appreciate it."

Dimitri put his hand over his heart and gave them each a slight bow. The two nodded and smiled in appreciation before turning and leaving.

"Now that was a surprise," I said, pulling up my own notebook to record what just happened.

"This is what happens when humankind awakens, Zach. Better get used to it. This is just the beginning."

I'd become accustomed to him speaking in broad terms. He was a great dreamer, and I had stopped questioning him about his grandiose declarations when I began to see things really happen.

The most surprising thing about that encounter was Carl stepping up. He had been the only one of the original six that didn't seem to have a noticeable breakthrough. He would almost always have an intellectual dispute for everything that was taught.

I casually asked Dimitri what he thought about it.

"All of us have blockage of some kind. Carl's mind-ego is, or was, so strong because he's full of knowledge. The ego loves to use knowledge, as well as other traits, to create an identity for itself. Once a person steps into the realm of an ego identification based on knowledge, they will usually believe they know everything. Once that happens, as the saying goes, 'it's a wrap.' Luckily for Carl, it appears his heart was touched at our session, and there has been a shift."

"Okay, but how is that you have a lot of knowledge and that hasn't happened to you?"

"There was a time, before the incident, when I had a lot of knowledge, just like Carl. The difference is that I never made it mean I was more than another. Due to my upbringing, I truly believed I was nothing, so it was impossible for it to have gone to my head. Then, as you know, something happened and that knowledge was transmuted into experiential wisdom."

"Well, since you brought it up," I said, "are you ready to tell me about the incident yet, D?"

"All in good time, amigo. For now, let's talk about notebooks. We need to be ready for what is coming."

"Should I even ask how you know this?" I asked.

His eyes went far away. "Let's just say that very soon there will be an incident in this prison. They're coming and we have to be ready."

BLOOD IN, BLOOD OUT

RONNY

When ex-Carlton Prison guard, Marcus Ogabi, asked me to tell you my story, I didn't want nothing to do with that shit. But, after everything that happened, I knew it was important I did.

To start, I need to tell you that when you join our *clica*, La Familia, it's no joke. It's forever. You know, like when you hear the *vatos* say "for life," they really mean that shit because it's blood in, blood out, for reals.

I was one of the lucky ones. I made it out alive. I disrespected the code, which got me green-lighted, but here I am today telling my story. Maybe it will help other vatos that may already be in the game or are thinking about jumping in.

First off, if I would have stayed in, I'd either still be in prison, dead, or banging with the homies on the street. And none of that shit was how I wanted to roll for the rest of my days.

Of the six years I was down in Carlton, five of them I acted as first lieutenant to one of the baddest shot callers there's ever been. Joaquin "El Capitan" Flores was cold and calculated and made for that shit because he'd come up in life. His father, brothers, and even his sister were in it. Rumor has it that his great uncle was the OG that started La Eme way back in the day.

The first day Dimitri Tanomeo walked into Carlton, Joaquin felt something was up. You know, like he just didn't like him or something. At the time I didn't know what it was about, so I just kinda forgot about it. But a month later when Tanomeo had his first meeting, Joaquin sent one of the soldiers, Creeper, to check it out. When Creeper came back, he told us what was up.

"The vato is mainly talking about some kind of self-help shit or something like that, ese."

"Oh yeah. How many were der, holmes?" Joaquin asked.

"Small group, *carnal*. Less than ten. There were a lot more, but they got pissed and left."

"Si, y porque, Creeper?" I asked.

Creeper laughed. "Most of the fools that showed up thought it had something to do with reducing their stretch. The thing is called ERP, like Early Release Plan or some shit."

"Any bangers with him?" Joaquin asked while cleaning his fingernails. He did that when he wanted to show he wasn't tripping on something but was.

"No, holmes. This white boy, or mulatto, whatever he is, he ain't rolling in any car. Solo este negro, Malik, was there. You know, from The Nation, but he ain't nobody."

"Okay Creeper, I want you to keep an eye on him for me," Joaquin ordered.

"Do you want us to fuck him up, carnal?"

"Que vato, did I say I want you fuck him up!? Just watch the fool, ese. I'll let you know when I want something done. Now, get da fuck outta here."

With Creeper out of the cell, Joaquin could ask me the questions he needed answers to but didn't want the others to know he was asking. "What do you think about him, Ronny?"

"Who, Tanomeo? I don't think about him, *ese*. He's just another fish doing his time."

Joaquin laughed. "That's why I've got the keys to this place and you don't, holmes. I see the shit coming before it even happens. That's my gift."

It was true. Joaquin always knew who'd burn him and who was loyal. He even knew when shit was gonna kick off in the yard before it went down. The vato could just feel things like that. "Whatchu thinking, Joaquin? He ain't gonna rise up and take over, hermano. He's not even affiliated," I laughed. I was the only one who could talk to him like that.

"Chinga tu madre, güey," he laughed with me, but only for a second then got serious. "Yeah, I know, carnal, but der's something about this fool. I'm not sure what, but we need to watch him."

I didn't agree because I couldn't see the threat at the time, but an order was an order. I gave him our handshake and nodded. "We can do that, tranquilo hermano." I got up, threw him a sign, and walked out of our cell.

It wouldn't be too long before I found out how wrong I was. As Tanomeo's thing got bigger, we'd bring in less money. At first, I couldn't see how the two were related, but one day, when I was alone in our cell, I spied in on a cell toss next door. It was Freddy Archibald, a piece-a-shit junky/

sometimes dealer who would steal from other inmates to pay his debts. I could hear everything from our cell and grabbed my mirror so I could see the shit go down.

"Listen up, inmate. We're going to find it, so why don't you just tell us where it is and we won't tear up all of your crap in the process," CO Devic said while frisking Archy out in the corridor and another was already inside his cell going through his shit.

"Okay, can I tell you something, boss?" Archibald asked as Devic stopped the frisk.

This is when I figured he was gonna fold. *Chicken shit, cobarde.*

"Go," Devic said.

Then the white boy said something I wasn't expecting to hear. "This might be hard for you to believe because you've only known me as a dope fiend all these years, but I'm telling you now, I'm done with that shit. Been straight for months, hand to God." The white boy even put his hand up which made me silently crack up a little.

"Good story, Archibald. Palms out, bend your head down and run your fingers through your hair."

"Okay, officer, but what I'm telling you is true."

"I haven't seen you in any of the AA meetings lately. Come to think of it, I've never seen you in a meeting," Devic said. He was a pretty cool CO. You know, as cool as he could be. He was, like, fair and shit and I respected that. He was the only CO I respected.

"Yeah, that's true, but where you might have seen me was at the ERP meetings. I haven't missed one since I started going, close to four months now. That program's helped me work through all the heavy shit I went through as a kid. I've given up being a victim to my past, and now I've got no reason to escape the present moment with dope." Devic started laughing. He wasn't buying it, but it was kinda making sense to me because we hadn't sold anything to Archy in months.

"I tell you, officer, my mind is clear. The words I now say to myself, you know, the ones in my head, are pretty positive ones. I can do this because I now know that life is just that, it's positive, or at least it can be if I choose that, and that's what I'm doing. I've chosen sobriety for myself. I'll be out in six months and nothing, yo, I mean nothing, is getting in the way of my new life."

I saw Devic backup to check him out. I put the mirror down for a minute to give it some thought. I had just figured he was getting his shit from the blacks, but he did look different. I put the mirror back and saw CO Ogabi come out of the cell. He was shaking his head. He couldn't find anything. None of us in the LF liked this negro Ogabi. There was something about him that wasn't right, like he was hiding something or some shit like that.

"So, what are you going to do when you get out?" Devic asked.

"I'll be getting out with my GED, then I'll be off to study real estate appraisal. My uncle's been in it for years. When I was young, I would go with him on jobs. I figure, if he can do it, so can I."

"It seems like inmate Tanomeo's words are working for you?" Devic asked quietly, you know, like it was some kind of secret, like Devic believed him.

"If I'm honest, I'd say his words have become my own, in a way."

Who is this huevon, and when did he start talking like this? He was like confident and shit. Something had changed in him.

"I was thinking the other day that just the money I'll save from not using will really help with the cost of the appraisal course."

Devic pulled Ogabi off to the side, toward my cell. I pulled the mirror away and got my ear as close as I could to the bars without them seeing me.

"Do you see this, Marcus?" Devic asked.

"Yeah, he's speaking like Tanomeo does. It's kind of haunting, but in a good way, I guess." Ogabi answered.

"Look at his eyes. No black bags under them. Do you see how clearly he speaks? This isn't the same Freddy Archibald I knew before. I've known this guy for years, and he's never looked this good. He's definitely clean."

From that day forward, I started to pay attention to what Tanomeo was up to. I watched him like a hawk, but I never told Joaquin what I'd seen and heard. I kept it to myself, and I don't really know why.

But it didn't really matter because later Joaquin would figure all this shit out on his own. One day when it was just us two at the handball court, he let it out.

"Don't you see it, Ronny? The more these guys listen to this fucker, the less they want to buy our shit, gamble, or do anything we're into."

"I'm not sure if I'm stupid or something, carnal, but I don't see how this is connected to us." Now, I was straight-up lying, because I knew where Joaquin was going and didn't want to face it.

"That's because you don't understand what he's doing. He's helping them get rid of their addictions and shit. Our thing needs for them to stay just like they are. You know, all fucked up. We should have made a move when he first got here."

This was the first time I'd ever seen Joaquin really trip about something.

"Yeah, holmes, I see it now. You're right, but what can we do about it?"

He looked down at the blacktop, like he always did when he was trying to figure some shit out. "Fuck, Ronny, we don't have a choice. We need to do it, holmes."

I bounced the blue handball a few times, trying to be cool when I wasn't feeling cool.

"Is that a green light, jefe?" I asked, confirming the order. He paced back and forth. I smacked the ball with my hand. It bounced hard against the concrete wall then came fast at Joaquin's head, and without even looking, his hand shot up and caught it.

"Yeah, it is, but I'll let you know when. It could be a minute. This fool's gotten too popular. They kinda love him and shit, you know? Der's too much at stake, Ronny. If we fuck up, we lose this whole thing." He had a point, Tanomeo had become a somebody at Carlton. To pull something like this off, it would have to be planned by someone smart as fuck, someone calculated. Fortunately, or unfortunately, depending on whose side you were on, that's where Joaquin shined. "So, yeah, Ronny, it's a green light, but I'm gonna call the shots on all of it. Don't say nothing to the crew yet. You got that, holmes?"

And just like that, a hit was called on the most peaceful vato in the whole fucking prison. In the past, when he'd tell me to get some fool, it never felt good inside, but with Tanomeo not being in the game or nothing, it felt even worse. I mean, I didn't even know what that motherfucker was teaching, and it still felt like I was gonna be taking out Saint Francis or some shit like that. So I had to call up the evil inside of me and ask it to bury that shit deep, that part that felt something.

ENTANGLEMENT THEORY

MARCUS

Over time, I'd gotten to know all the players. Among the inmates, we had dealers, thieves, prison punks, hustlers, booty bandits, gays, snitches, holy rollers, kiss-asses, and shot callers. My job was to develop relationships to gather information with some and keep an eye on others.

I also learned about the guards and their temperaments. In many cases, they were as bad as the prisoners, if not worse. Corruption, petty gossip, cruelty, nepotism, politics, and basic stupidity were just some of the qualities that my new colleagues possessed. Luckily, I had Jim, who'd just been made captain, to help guide me through it all.

One would think the reason for gathering intel from prisoners was so I could perform my duties as a guard to the best of my abilities, and to a certain extent, that was the case. However, I found myself calculating how some of these individuals, especially the key players, might relate to Dimitri and what he was creating in Carlton.

And he was creating a lot. It was hard to tell how many were enrolled in ERP at this point—maybe half the block. Depending on when one had started, there were three different levels, each with its own meeting time and location. He was stirring things up, and I felt the unrelenting need to watch his back.

By this time, I'd seen so many of his sessions, and I was completely on board with what he was doing. This created a struggle in me. My job was to be an authority figure to all of the prisoners. Fair but firm. But internally, my attention was always on him.

I tried to be where he was and watched how the other inmates looked at him. His celly, Zach, was almost always by his side. Then there were the other five men who'd been with him since the beginning of ERP. In the mess hall, many wanted to sit next to him. One of the inmates would always be there to take his tray and remove certain foods he didn't eat, which he would give to one of the others in exchange for a share of their vegetables, fruit, beans, and bread.

The group would sit at the same table every day, and the empty spaces there would fill quickly, as well as the nearby tables. Many wanted to be close to him, at first, I figured, to hear words of wisdom, but he rarely spoke about the deep issues outside of the sessions in the chapel. Instead, he'd mostly joke and laugh with the guys. Sometimes he'd just be silent.

I observed the inmates that weren't interested in his words as well. Most of them would keep their distance and not pay much attention to him. There was one that did pay attention and, unfortunately, that inmate was Joaquin Flores. He'd always make sure he had an unobstructed view of the kid and his table and would study Dimitri closely at chow time. Joaquin made no errors, so there was a reason he had such a strong interest in Dimitri. I knew it couldn't be a good one, so I kept watching *him* watch him.

I'd eavesdrop on staff conversations in the program office, trying to get a read on what my co-workers thought of Dimitri. I'd keep a keen ear during our daily briefings, always interested in what was being said by the warden and others about the odd young man who was helping the prisoners at Carlton change their lives. I was beginning to feel like a spy. Unbeknownst to me, things were about to shift in a big way, eventually turning me into a full-blown double agent.

There were mixed feelings within the staff about what inmate Tanomeo was up to. Most were neutral and didn't really care as long as he wasn't caus-ing trouble. There were only a couple of us that were impressed with what he was doing, mostly Captain Jim Devic and myself. We'd talk about him at times and were, quite possibly, the only staff members who truly wanted what was best for him. There was a covertness to our conversations that was never addressed, which made it a bit uncomfortable at times. However, it felt good to know I wasn't alone.

On the opposite end of the spectrum, there was the one person I truly despised at Carlton, Gene Tanas. The first time I laid eyes on him, I knew he was no good.

What bothered me most was his hatred of the kid, which I never quite understood and he never tried to hide it. There were several times I'd be watching over a session when he'd walk in and just stand there with his arms crossed, sneering at Dimitri. He'd even make insulting remarks under his breath loud enough for the prisoners to hear.

His opinions of inmate Tanomeo were, however, just the icing on the cake. This incredibly corrupt corrections officer was a deeply disturbed individual. Narcissistic by nature and a borderline sociopath that, in my opinion, would make for a better inmate than CO.

He was one of those short, always serious, white guys that spent his free time in the gym. His full head of dyed black hair looked almost plastic it was so perfect, and when he walked, he kind of bounced as if he was trying to gain inches. I'd caught him, more than once, staring at a picture of himself on his cell phone. He couldn't have been older than forty-two, but who knows with the botox and overly whitened teeth.

It was rumored that he made an extra hundred thousand smuggling in drugs, payphones, and who knows what else for La Familia. At first, I couldn't believe it could be that much, but when I did the numbers, it made sense. One of the female guards, Brenda, told me he had a tanning bed in his living room which, according to her, looked as out of place as his altered uniforms did, oddly hugging his small, fit frame.

One morning, while sitting in the briefing room listening to the warden ramble on about prison policy surrounding sexual harassment, I stared him down.

"Warden Shady, I think it's high time we address the situation with prisoner 52066." It was comical how he tried to make it more dramatic by using Dimitri's inmate number every time he'd bring him up.

The warden lowered his head to see above his reading glasses and asked wearily with his Southern drawl, "What'd he do now, Gene?" It seemed he'd grown tired, like the rest of us, hearing Tanas whine about the same thing for months.

Tanas shot out of his chair like a shameless school tattletale. I caught Jim, who was standing behind the warden, discreetly rolling his eyes. I bit down hard on my cheek, trying not to laugh.

"Well, first of all, this thing he's doing is against prison policy. He's having public meetings in the chapel. As you know, the chapel is solely to be used for religious purposes. You're a God-fearing man, Warden Shady. Isn't that sacrilegious or something?"

The warden slowly removed his glasses and raised his head from the document on the podium. "No, son, I don't know that we only use the chapel for religious purposes, because we also use it for AA meetings, band practice, and lord knows what else!" It was the first time I'd seen him lose his temper. "And I'd be much obliged if you wouldn't bring my faith into question ever again, Officer Tanas. That is, if you like your job and all."

I straightened in my chair, enjoying the forbidden fruit of seeing Tanas scolded, both happy and shameful at the same time.

Unfortunately, it didn't even faze Tanas. "Yes, sir, but just one more thing. The attitude of the inmates that are participating in that ERP program. They've become sort of ornery, sir."

"Ornery. How's that?" the warden snapped.

"I believe they are becoming too independent, making them hard to control."

I wanted to speak up, but couldn't. The last thing I needed was my cover blown. I looked at Jim. His eyes were closed. He wasn't about to jump in either.

I scanned the briefing room, hoping that at least one of the others would say something in the program's defense, but no one spoke. Most were either staring at their cell phones, crunching on chips, or dozing off. For them, the job was nothing more than a paycheck. They didn't care enough to even pay attention, let alone get involved.

"Let me just check the stats here?" Warden Shady said as he flipped through his files. "Says here overall infractions are down since this program began. That's drug seizures as well. Hell, even overall health has increased according to the reports from medical. So, what in tarnation are you talking about, son?"

"Warden, that all may be true, but the prisoners are getting a bit uppity. I'm afraid that we could lose our grip if this thing goes any further," Tanas griped.

"Hold yer horses, Gene. Let me read the report aloud so you all can hear it. 'In summary, my overall assessment of what inmate number 52066, Dimitri Tanomeo, is attempting to do is a positive one. The Early Release Program (ERP) is designed to help prisoners heal the emotional wounds caused by past troubling and traumatic events, restoring their spirit so they can become productive members of society once they have left as well as during their imprisonment at Carlton. In my professional opinion, this program has the potential of becoming a valuable addition to the overall strategy in regards to this institution's rehabilitation process as well as greatly reduce negative stats and grow positive ones.'"

He took his glasses off and closed the file. "That was signed by Doctor Gabe Matera, who we all know as the lead psychiatrist here at Carlton. So, tell me, son, how is it that this program that a trained professional not only approves of but recommends is a problem?"

"I can just see something coming, that's all," Tanas focused in on our superior, wanting him to take the bait.

"Because they've become uppity and hard to control, you say? Well, let me just be real straight here, son. You know I'm running for office in this election, and the last thing I need is a problem with any of them damn civil rights organizations. This ain't like the old days. I gotta be mindful of every move I make. Not to mention, if the prison stats keep improving like they are, well, that can't hurt my campaign none." He finished with a wink to us all.

The warden came from an era where the prisons were run on the good ol' boys' network. Now he was trying to exist in a new world that was changing faster than his sixty-something-year-old mind could keep up with. Becoming governor would be his last hurrah, his ticket out of the prison and into politics where that network still thrived.

"You might just have to deal with the uppity inmates. If they are too hard for you to control, well then, we'll just have to find someone who can."

Tanas stood and made his way toward the door.

"I'm finished talking about inmate Tanomeo and his program. I don't wanna hear another word about it, ya hear?!" the warden yelled as Tanas pushed open the double doors, raised his hand, and gave a thumbs-up just before the doors closed behind him.

That was disrespectful.

» » « «

After the briefing, I walked back to the cellblock with Jim and asked him about what we'd just witnessed. He told me he didn't know a lot, but he'd heard through the staff grapevine that Tanas had something big on the warden.

"It's got something to do with the fraudulent use of funds," Jim said. "You've seen that huge patch of unused land just on the other side of the north end of the yard?"

"I heard there was supposed to have been a whole new set of cell blocks built there but the plan got shut down," I said.

"That's right. Something happened to the money for that project, according to the grapevine, that is. It's a big mystery, but it could have something to do with someone receiving kickbacks from the contractors. What is for sure, Tanas was so close to the warden back then that he's probably got something solid on him, if that's what happened, of course."

"So, all that stuff about Tanas losing his job?" I asked.

"It's all a show. Warden Shady throws that threat at him at least a couple of times a year. It's been going on a long time and where's Tanas? Right here, job intact. Nope, he'd have to be caught red-handed in something big with no way out, and I don't see that happening any time soon."

As we walked, I thought about how strangely the world worked. I considered the corruption that surrounded nearly all men in positions of power and their abuse of that power. I had seen it in the police force and the military. Positions were filled by those who were incompetent, incapable of walking in honesty and integrity themselves. They were given the power to lead others and used it for nothing more than personal gain.

"Well, maybe that earful he just got from the warden will make him ease off of the kid and his program," I said, trying to find some light in a very dark tunnel.

Jim laughed. "You don't know Tanas. He's just gonna keep pushing. Our only hope is that someday someone with some real power will push back."

LOSS OF OWNERSHIP
MARCUS

Within the ERP, there were still the original six below Dimitri. All of them were now teaching the curriculum to others themselves, with the exception of Zach, who seemed to be notetaking constantly. Dimitri had begun to teach meditation to a smaller group of inmates, ones who'd been in the program for a while. When he wasn't doing that, he was coaching the five teachers, helping them hone their skills.

I remember watching some of the original crew lead their first sessions. Dimitri would stay in the room, sometimes jumping in to add content or answer questions when needed. They did a good job of getting his message across. They spoke the words he spoke. They were good at what they did, but none were as good as Dimitri. He was the master, no doubt about that.

I would say Malik was a close second. He knew how to speak to people and was becoming a great leader in his own right. It was natural for him, seeing how he was already the head of the Nation of Islam clique, which he had recently shifted from a black-only gang to an open group, welcoming all ethnicities. Even the soldiers of the NOI under him were regularly attending ERP sessions.

Of course, ERP wasn't perfect. Some of the students would leave the program, never to return. Others would still get into trouble. We'd catch them with drugs, fighting, or stealing. But many, perhaps even most became model inmates.

Sometimes, while I was observing sessions, Dimitri would shoot me a nod or a look, especially when making a point pertaining to something we'd gone over during our visit before I started working at Carlton. We both knew there was a connection between us, but we also knew how to play our roles. I hadn't really outright helped him at this point, but I did watch over him. For instance, when he moved about the yard, I'd make sure no one was on him.

One afternoon he was called to the infirmary for a routine check-up. I was on duty, and Jim ordered me to escort him.

When I approached his cell, Markland was standing in the back, facing Dimitri's bunk with a notepad in hand. I wondered how he was so gung-ho about the whole thing but still not qualified to teach. He was too into it all—a real kiss-ass in a way. I wanted to be into it at that level. He knew things I didn't, and this made me feel less than him. What made it worse was that he seemed content, and I clearly was not. I'd gotten some great lessons of my own while standing guard at the ERP sessions, but I wanted more.

I was envious of the prisoners who stuck with the program. Their growth was palpable, and I wanted to be where they were. I could literally feel the difference being in block H compared to the other blocks. The noise level was lower, and there was less fighting and aggression. It wasn't calm by any means. It was still prison, but it was calmer than any of the other cell blocks at Carlton.

"Officer Marcus, come on in," Dimitri said quietly with a smile that said he was genuinely happy to see me.

I popped my head in the doorway. "Actually, I'm here to escort you to the infirmary. You've got a check-up due, Tanomeo."

"Oh, really. It's that time again?"

"Let's go!" I said loudly, playing the part.

He stepped out and began walking in front of me. "I figure we've got an eight-minute walk if we slow it down," he whispered. "Now's the time for whatever questions you have for me."

I was taken aback by his boldness. This was the first time since my arrival at Carlton he'd spoken to me like that.

"Questions? What questions would I have for you?" I asked, finding it hard to drop the role.

"You don't have any? Is that what you are saying? I can see you're struggling. We're seven minutes away. Walk a little slower."

Is he actually counting?

He slowed his step, and I had no choice but to slow mine. *The audacity of this guy.* There was still part of me that thought I needed to be a guard and even a stronger part that couldn't admit I had questions for a nineteen-year-old convict.

"Life's great. I moved closer to Hope, so I see her more often. We cook together, sing karaoke, laugh, and watch movies. What's not to love?"

He gave me a look that only he could. Then I gave in.

"Well, alright," I whispered. "I stand guard at the sessions, and I hear what you and the other guys are saying. It makes all the sense in the world, but I'm not applying it to my life. There are moments that I do, but then I go right back."

"Give me details with not too much explanation," he ordered, speaking faster than I was comfortable hearing from an inmate. I shook my head and let it go.

"I'm still drinking more than usual, especially on days off when my daughter's not with me."

"What's bothering you? What's going on?"

I paused. I didn't want to admit my jealousy about Lisa's boyfriend.

"The clock's ticking, Officer Ogabi."

"I'm still jealous of Lisa's relationship with her boyfriend."

The words were barely out of my mouth before he jumped on them.

"You need to take responsibility for the jealousy and every story you have around her and him. All of it. What's his name?"

"Uh, Beto, but I don't even like to say his name. He's caused me so much pain, taking the woman I love from me."

"First off, you don't love her. Not really. You might think you love her, but you don't. You might want her or even believe you need her, but this is not love. When you really love someone, you love them without any conditions. You love them without any in-order-to's or any as-long-as's. Take your daughter. I imagine you love her no matter what. There's nothing she has to do for you to love her, and, no matter what she does in the future, you will always love her."

I quietly chuckled at the ridiculousness of the comparison. "Yeah, but that's different. She's my kid."

"It's only different because you have been brought up in a world where romantic love means you possess someone. Possession is ownership and you own no one, Marcus. The sooner you get this, the sooner your life will flow easier.

"After hearing that, you can see how Beto took nothing from you, nor did he cause you any pain. The pain was the vehicle that brought you to discover this truth about unconditional love. You'll know you truly love a woman when all you want for her is to be happy. Just like you feel with your daughter."

I shook my head, "That's a hard one to grasp."

"Maybe, but it's the truth. Once you can honestly confirm that you have created this whole mess in your mind, you need to then apologize."

"Oh no, I've heard you talk about ho'opon something or other. I'm not sure if I'm ready for that one."

"It's called ho'oponopono, Officer, and if you don't resolve this, the thoughts and emotions around jealousy and envy will increase, causing your life experience to become even more torturous than it is now. You'll attempt to drown out those thoughts and emotions through drinking or some other addictive pattern, which will only make matters worse once the temporary numbing effects are gone." He was speaking so fast it took me a moment to catch up.

"Sounds like I have a lot to look forward to," I said.

"Only if you choose it to be so. You are the only one who can fix this." He glanced back at me. "What else, quickly? You can process later."

"I also wonder why the guys who are the most down and out seem to do the best in your program. Like Robert, or *Pruno*, as he's known. That guy drank nearly every day. He's sober now, seems happy, I can see it. Then there's Freddy Archibald. Same thing there, but with drugs."

"It's because Robert and others, not just substance addicts, have, for lack of a better term, hit their bottom. Most people have to hit a bottom before they can bounce back. Remember, it's not the alcohol that is causing you to drink. It's the diseased thoughts of what your mind is saying that's causing you to do it.

"Those destructive thought patterns, which nearly everyone carries, cause painful emotions of suffering. But, Marcus, it doesn't have to stay like that. This can be your bottom. But only you can make that call for yourself. No one else can do it for you. It's happening to most people all over the world in different ways. Whether it's the pressure of hate, fear, envy, sadness, greed, loneliness, or jealousy that's building inside of them, it's the same. That feeling of being on the verge of exploding is what most are going through; they just mask or numb it in different ways.

"But you see, it's there as a message that it's time to declare you've hit bottom and that you're finished living a life of torment. It's telling you it's time to come back home. You can start the process of bouncing back before the toxicity of your emotional baggage causes a physical ailment that pales in comparison to what alcohol can do."

I sighed and remained silent, trying to assemble it in my head. I recalled him explaining at an ERP meeting how compulsive activity is born from the overactive, unconscious mind as it strives to fill a void that never existed in the first place. At the time, I didn't relate any of it to my drinking, which had been part of my life for many years. At this moment, I was seeing it as clear as day.

I also admit I took some relief in knowing I wasn't alone. I thought about how I could see manifestations of this in other people I knew. As Dimitri said, it didn't only show up in substance abuse.

I thought of my mother and how she couldn't be still for five minutes. She called it staying busy, but I could now see that she was obsessed with doing something, anything, all the time. I imagined the root of it was from the divorce with my father, as she'd still make judging comments about him years after their split. Her ignorance surrounding her own suffering was due to the fact that nearly everyone else was caught up in a similar pattern, only with different faces on it. She'd recently been prescribed antidepressants.

Pretty much everyone I was close to was caught in the same cycle. Lisa with her constant search for more stuff. Whether it was money, clothes, or a new man, she was always hunting for something. My brother, who, when he wasn't chasing career advancement, would lose himself in porn and video games. My father was so overboard with his devotion to the force, he almost never left the place. It had become his life, and, when he wasn't there, he was watching sports or drinking with others from the department. It seemed like we were all constantly trying to distract ourselves from ourselves. Even my younger sister had issues with her neck and had to see a doctor due to her constant cell phone use, another addiction. It was everywhere and no one could see it.

Then there was Hope, who just loved to play and be herself. I wondered if she would follow in our footsteps, creating a nonexistent void within herself. I remember the words of Malik in one of the sessions: "Balanced parents raise balanced children." I was ready to do something about it.

I liked what Dimitri said about calling my current state *the bottom* before it wreaked havoc in my life, but I didn't think I could ever do the apology part.

"What else you got for me?" Dimitri asked.

"This last one is just a curiosity of mine. Why did you turn the original inmates that took the program into teachers? Well, except for Markland. I guess he didn't make the cut or something."

"First off, Zach is more than qualified. He knows the curriculum better than anyone. He could easily hold those sessions but he happens to be doing the huge job of organizing this whole thing, and he's doing it all by hand. There are dozens of students that he logs for.

"Now, to answer your question about the five men taking on a new role. There are two reasons I did that. First, a truly great teacher doesn't create more students, he or she creates more great teachers.

"Know that my intention is to bring up anyone and everyone who comes into my field. Because once one can teach a thing, then they own the curriculum, they get it within every cell of their being. If they can get it at that level, then they will live it. And if they live it, they've achieved a certain level of mastery in their lives. That's how we change the world."

We were nearing the admin office. *I've got one more question.* "The first day I saw you and Markland in the chapel, you mentioned something along the lines of you waking up the majority of the men in this prison. Do you remember that?"

"Absolutely, but I never said I was going to wake them up, only they can do that for themselves. What I said was that I would facilitate the awakening of the majority of the men in this prison."

"Either way, at the time you seemed so sure of yourself, and here you are now still far from your goal. How is it that you, with all that you know, deal with that level of failure?"

Laughing he said, "I am so amused sometimes by how narrow the mindset of the average man can be."

I'm an average narrow-minded man? Great.

He continued, "There is no failure in my world, that word only exists for the unawakened. There is still time. I stand by what was said that day, not only within regards to most of the prisoners in block H waking up but to the majority of the prisoners in Carlton. This leads us to the other reason I've brought the others up to teacher status."

He looked around, making sure we were alone. "Soon, something will happen that will change everything. After this, you will see a surge of inmates from H-block come into the program. ERP will spread like wildfire to the other blocks, through these concrete walls with their iron gates, and beyond. And you know what? There won't be a damn thing anyone can do to stop it. And do you wanna know something else?"

"Sure," I said.

"The same thing's gonna happen on the outside, but on a global scale."

"What are you talking about, Dimitri?"

"I'm talking about when the inhumane, supposed rulers of this world make their move."

"What move will that be?" I figured he was talking about the government.

"They will create an atrocious act that will affect ninety-nine percent of humans in a way you won't believe, and I'll be there at the gate waiting for them. That's when we'll roll out our plan and launch the revolution of all revolutions. We will succeed because The Light will always outshine dark."

He sounds just like Ana. Maybe he is insane after all.

"Sounds a little conspiracy theory-ish, but whatever," I whispered.

"You can forget I said it for now if it helps." We'd arrived at the infirmary doors. "Do you remember what I said earlier about apologizing?"

"Yeah," I said apathetically.

"It's not just your ex that you have to say you're sorry to."

"No?" I questioned.

Who else?

"Beto. He's the one. If you really want to mend the sickness in your mind, then this is required. I thought I'd leave you with that, since we're both being really honest today."

What a ...

I bit my lip to keep from saying anything. The thought of apologizing to that guy made my blood boil, and Dimitri could see it on my face.

"Come on now, amigo. At least you've got a front-row seat to the greatest event that's ever taken place on prison soil, and then later on planet Earth." He laughed out loud, not caring about blowing our cover.

"Good luck with the apologies and enjoy the entertainment."

BOTTOMS UP

MARCUS

I was beginning to think time might have a different meaning for Dimitri than it did for the rest of us. It had been a while since we'd taken our walk to the infirmary, and there was still no mass spreading of ERP to the other blocks and beyond, as he had forecasted.

But there was one thing he predicted that did come true: my situation with Lisa. He told me it would get worse if I didn't come clean. I'd become much more bitter, especially after she sent divorce papers. She and Beto talking about tying the knot hurt like nothing else. I guess I wasn't expecting that level of closure to come so soon.

It got so bad between Lisa and me that we couldn't speak to each other for more than a few minutes without a blow-up. What I didn't know at the time was that things were about to get a whole lot worse.

It was Saturday morning, my day to pick up Hope for our weekly visit, and I was still in bed. Unfortunately, it wasn't my bed. Fellow Carlton correctional officer Brenda Ferguson and I had gotten drunk after our shift and ended up at her place. Still a bit drunk, I cranked my car and proceeded to break one of my own cardinal rules: driving inebriated with my daughter in the car.

At the time, it seemed there was no way out. I couldn't call Lisa and cancel because, first, she'd know I was drunk and, second, her plans with Beto would be ruined and she'd lose her shit.

I pulled up to the house and honked while chomping on three pieces of gum. I doused myself with cologne, just in case Lisa approached the car to bitch at me.

The door opened and Hope ran out. I turned around to help her into the child safety seat.

"Do I really have to sit in this thing, Daddy?" she whined. "It's pretty embarrassing. I'm almost eight, you know."

"Yep, you do," I responded. "And to be honest, I wish the law said you had to be in this thing until you were seventeen."

She sighed. "Oh, brother. It's a good thing you're not the one making the laws then, Dad." She had a sense of humor and always said just what she felt. "Maybe someday I can make a law, Daddy."

"What law would you make?" I asked, looking at her in the rearview mirror.

"I'd make a law that made it illegal for men to use too much cologne," she said and pinched her nose.

"Oh, sorry about that. Yeah. Definitely used a little much today," I laughed as we sped away.

We were mere blocks from my place when I heard two bursts of a police siren.

"Fuck!" I yelled out.

"Daddy, you are not allowed to say that."

"I'm sorry, hun. Just be quiet for a moment, please. The police are pulling us over."

"Why?"

"I'm not sure. Just be quiet and let me think."

"There's not much to think about, Dad. You just pull over," she pointed to the side of the road. "Park the car, roll down your window, and say 'what are you pulling me over for, sir?' Just like on TV. Unless, of course, it's a girl, then you would say ma'am and not sir."

I grabbed another piece of gum and frantically shoved it in my mouth as we pulled over. My heart raced as I handed my license and registration to the young officer. This is the first time I'd ever been on the other side of a possible arrest, and I didn't like it one bit.

The officer told me I'd run a stop sign several blocks back as he leaned in to say hello to Hope. As an ex-cop, I knew it was a ploy to secretly take a sniff.

"Mr. Ogabi, have you been drinking today, sir?" he asked.

I knew better than to admit to anything. "No, I haven't, officer."

"Okay, sir, after observing you run a stop sign and pulling you over, I've noticed a slurring of your words as well as a strong odor of alcohol in the car. This leads me to reasonably suspect that you have alcohol in your blood system greater than the state's legal limit."

"I accidentally put on too much cologne this morning. Maybe that's what you're smelling."

He didn't find that funny. "I'll request that you step out of the car to perform a field sobriety test."

I knew I was done for. No matter what I said or did, I would be taken in for suspicion of driving under the influence. My blood alcohol count would definitely be over the legal limit, which would not only land me in jail with a hefty fine and a police record but problems with Lisa that would keep me from seeing Hope for a long time.

"Do you agree to take the field sobriety test now, sir?"

I refused all tests and chose the right to have a chemical test performed at the station.

"It's his cologne, officer," Hope piped in from the back seat. "I told him not to use so much. He didn't see the stop sign because we were talking."

"Hope, please. Not right now."

"Hope, your daddy's going with me to just behind your car. We'll be close by. I need you to stay in the car with your seat belt buckled. Can you do that for me?"

"Yep, but my daddy didn't tell you he's a police officer too," Hope blurted.

The officer looked at me curiously.

"No, I used to be on the force," I said quickly.

"Oh yeah. Where?"

"East Borough."

"Ah, The Pit. I've heard about it. A rough area, yeah?" he asked.

Then Hope leaned forward, "Rough is right. My daddy shot a man who shot his own father who was mean to him. Then the man my daddy shot died in the hospital and came back to life and now they're friends." I dropped my head in despair.

"It was his stepfather, Hope," I said. "And how do you know all this?"

"Mommy told me."

The officer all but opened my car door. "You wanna go ahead and step out, sir?"

As I got out, another police cruiser pulled up and parked behind his. I could make out two people in the front seat, but only one got out. I could tell by his stripes he was a sergeant, and his name-badge read Chavez. He was a tall man in his fifties with a dark complexion and full head of silvery grey hair. He observed as the officer read my rights and then walked back to the cruiser and leaned in the passenger window.

While being frisked, I glanced back to see the sergeant on his cell phone. I was told to turn and place my hands behind my back. I did and I looked at the back of Hope's head. She was oblivious to all of it but wouldn't be for long.

The sound of clicking handcuffs and the tightening of metal around my wrists put me in the shoes of the inmates I'd been in charge of and the people I'd arrested in the past. The alcohol, combined with the overwhelming knowledge of the damage this would bring, caused me to silently weep.

"You can turn around now," the officer barked.

When I turned, the sergeant was right in front of me.

"Mr. Ogabi, I'll be needing the phone number of a legal guardian so your daughter can be picked up. If there is no one, we will have to call CPS," he said sternly, looking me in the eyes.

I gave him Lisa's number, trying to wipe tears with my shoulder. I prayed Lisa would answer the phone. The last thing I wanted was Hope driving away with a stranger from Child Protective Services.

Oh shit. With Hope in the car, I can also pick up a child endangerment charge. Up to four years! I stomped my foot down and clenched my teeth.

"Can I please talk to my daughter before her mom gets here, Sergeant Chavez? It will likely be the last time I'll see her for a while."

The sergeant closed his notepad. "I'll make the call first." Before he turned, he gave a look of disappointment I'll never forget.

In reality, it couldn't have been that long, but it felt like I stood on the roadside, in handcuffs, for hours. When the sergeant returned he whispered something to the younger officer, who made his way to chat with Hope. The sergeant stayed, looking at me intently.

"How'd she take it?" I asked. He closed his eyes and shook his head.

My chin hit my chest as I stared at the blacktop. I remembered the alley that day when all I wanted was to turn back the clock just a little. Today, just like then, I knew I couldn't. Still, I prayed to a God I didn't really believe in for help I knew wouldn't come. Life as I knew it was over.

"Mr. Ogabi, I'm going to ask you a couple of questions before I let you speak to your daughter."

All I could do was nod. I was numb. He looked to the other officer.

"Hey, Stevens. Will you go over and talk to the senior citizen ride-along?

Tell her we're almost done here."

"Sure thing, sergeant."

"She's a real handful," Sergeant Chavez murmured as the officer passed. He watched until the other officer was out of earshot, then whispered, "Just what the hell do you think you're doing?"

My spine stiffened as my eyes opened wide. "Well, I—"

"Shut your mouth. I'm not finished." He took a step and was in my face. "I know who you are. Is this what you've become after everything? A man who puts his own daughter in danger?"

His words were more powerful than a scolding, angry mother.

"Speak!" he demanded.

What could I say? I was crushed. The only thing I had was the truth. "The kind of man who is tortured by his thoughts, sergeant," I answered. "I'm not making an excuse because there isn't one. But there is a reason and I'm responsible for it all. No one else. Just me. All I can say is I'm deeply sorry, sir."

I could feel his silent glare on me. "Turn around before I change my mind," he spat as he produced the handcuff keys.

I could feel life return to my entire body. It reminded me of the day in the hospital when I found out Dimitri was alive.

"Really?" I asked.

"You're only about six blocks from home, is that right?"

"Yes. On Floyd and King," I answered eagerly, still in disbelief.

"Do you think you can make it six blocks with a police escort and not kill anyone?"

"Absolutely I can," I answered, feeling tears beginning to form again. "But, wait, what about my ex? Isn't she on her way?"

He looked at me with a straight face. "I called my wife. Told her I'd pick our son up from school. Gotta protect him from drunk drivers."

I swallowed hard.

"Get yourself someone to talk to about those tortured thoughts," he said with a strange warmth. "We all have them. And we can all use a hand sometimes. You've hit a bottom here today. I only pray this is your last one."

I stood frozen, stunned by the synchronicity of his words.

"I will. I mean, I do. I do have someone to talk to. I just need to listen more and apply it. I want you to know that I am declaring this the bottom for me."

He nodded and turned back to the other officer. "Okay, Stevens. I'll pull out first. You follow behind Mr. Ogabi."

Hope was writing in her diary when I climbed back in.

"Sorry about that, hun. It was just the cologne. We're going home now." I stared at her in the rearview mirror.

"He was a nice policeman," she said without looking up.

"Yes, he was," I breathed softly. "What are you writing there?"

"I write about everything I learn and everything I see. It's private, so maybe you don't have to ask me anymore."

I could see the exhaust from the tailpipe of the sergeant's cruiser and knew he was getting ready to pull out.

"But there is something I'm supposed to tell you," Hope suddenly offered.

Supposed to tell me? "Oh yeah. What's that, baby?"

The cruiser's turn signal blinked, and the morning sun bounced off the sergeant's windshield hitting my eyes. I looked down and when I looked back the cruiser pulled out slowly.

Hope put her pen down and closed her diary. "I'll tell you, but I don't want you to think I'm crazy," she said.

"I won't think you're crazy because I know that you already are." I laughed but she didn't. "What do you know you are supposed to tell me?"

I could see the shape of the sergeant conversing with his ride-along. I put the car in drive and waited as he pulled slowly by me.

Hope said, "I'm supposed to tell you that you should be journaling about everything as well, especially what *he* says."

As the sergeant and his passenger passed, I glanced into the cruiser. The reflection on the window obscured my view, but, for a split second, I swear I could see the face of the ride-along clearly. In that flash, the face looking back at me was Ana's.

"What the hell!?" I shouted.

"Another bad word!" Hope yelled out, as my full attention was on the back of the head of the sergeant's passenger. *Oh shit, I'm hallucinating again.*

It took every ounce of will to not break formation and pass the sergeant's car to confirm what I'd seen. I glanced back at Hope, who had returned to her writing.

At that moment I knew that this, as well as all the other anomalies of the previous months, would remain mysteries. I could choose to call these mysteries random occurrences, coincidences, synchronicities, or even deep messages. In the end, it was my choice.

OLD DOG, NEW TRICKS

MARCUS

When we pulled up to the house Monday morning, I gave Hope a hug and asked her to have her mother come out and talk to me. I'd sent a text, but there'd been no response.

"I will," Hope said. "And don't forget about writing everything down in the journal like I do."

The front door opened and there was Lisa, almost six feet in heels. She wore a black pantsuit, making her long, natural blonde hair stand out against her well-balanced figure. Her professional style mixed with the fed-up look on her face made for a tense mood.

"There she is, Daddy," Hope cheered as she blew a kiss and hopped inside.

"Make it fast, Marcus," Lisa said as she approached the car. "I've got a job interview, and if you say one word about Beto, I'm gone."

"I'll make it quick," I straightened up and stood directly in front of her. "So, Lisa, I've had a hell of a ride with all that has happened in the last couple of years, and—"

"That's your fault," she said, cutting me off.

I felt the old sting of anger. I was being triggered by her words and, for the first time, I took responsibility for feeling it. Now I knew it wasn't her causing this. I was allowing myself to be affected. I could see she too was triggered before I even spoke.

I was witnessing our cycle in process. I'd trigger her, she'd trigger me, and on it went. I had never looked at it from the outside with a clear head before. Today was the day to break this cycle.

"You're right. It is my fault and that's what I came here to talk to you about." I said in a slightly enthusiastic tone. Her head rocked back in confusion. "I've been blaming you for all of my pain and all my problems. I've been making you wrong and, in my doing that, I've destroyed our friendship."

"No, Marcus you're the one who's wrong here. I—"

"Lisa, just wait a minute." She was so used to the way we were together that she couldn't even hear what I was saying. I had listened to several frustrated men in ERP explain how the same thing happened when they called their loved ones to apologize.

"You must remain in the state of compassion when you apologize," Dimitri would say. "Understand there is a cycle going on within them as well. Keep at it. If they can't hear you, just say what you need to say and be done with it. They will hear your words later, internally, when they are ready."

"Lisa," I continued, "I hope you can hear me right now. I'm saying I'm sorry for everything. I take full responsibility for all the blaming I've done, which led to fights and bad blood between us." She stared at me blankly. "I want to ask you to forgive me. I also want to thank you for everything you've been to me—an incredible wife, a loving mother, and a great friend. But, most of all, I want to thank you for being such a big part of my life and, as strange as it might sound, my growth."

She shook her head.

"No," I pushed, "seriously. All this stuff that's happened between us, I have to thank you for it. It's changed my life. I also need to tell you that I love you."

Instantly something left me. I felt lighter as the pain I'd carried for so long vanished into thin air.

"Are you okay, Marcus?" she asked with more than a note of genuine concern.

"Yeah. I just wanted to say those words to you," I replied, wiping my eyes.

"I'm not sure what to say to all that," she said, still using her kinder tone. I hadn't heard it in years. "You know I'm not leaving Beto, right? You just come over here and say these nice things and tell me you love me and ..."

She went on and I just stood there, not really hearing her words. I was busy seeing her as just Lisa again, not some demon that I'd created within our drama. It was surreal what had happened. It was as if my taking responsibility changed her. What I had just done recreated who she was for me.

"I don't want you to leave Beto. That's not what this is about," I laughed. "As a matter of fact, I probably need to talk to him at some point."

Her eyes got big and I laughed. "Not right now. This is about me cleaning up the things that don't serve me in life. Fighting with you definitely doesn't serve either of us ... or Hope."

She looked down. "You said you love me. Why did you say that?"

"Because I do," I said, smiling, raising my hands up. "I learned what unconditional love is and that I don't have to have you in order to love you. I can just love you no matter what. How could I not? We were together for so long. You and I created Hope and she's perfect. And so are you. I'm not gonna let a little thing like you falling for another guy get in the way of what's true."

She put her hands over her smiling face and shook her head. "Somehow that makes sense, but I'm not sure exactly how."

"I know, right?" I said as we laughed together for the first time in years. "I'm still a work in progress, but it's pretty nice right now. I just have to remind myself of what's important now and then."

"All right, well … keep up the good work, I guess," she said, still at a loss.

"I'll do my best. That's all I can do."

"Take care, Marcus," she said awkwardly, slowly closing the door.

As I got back in the car, for the first time I noticed that I'd grown. I could see I'd shifted to a different place than where Lisa was. She really couldn't get what I was saying. I, on the other hand, had let go of not only the desire but, more importantly, the hope of us ever getting back together. I realized that it was the idea of being in a relationship like we had in the past that I was attached to, and this was no longer possible because we were different people now.

The strangest part was that there was no effort in that letting go. It was natural. I didn't have to try, and there was no pain. I guess I'd had my share of that already.

The oddest part was that I knew something she didn't, and, for the life of me, I couldn't figure out why this was important. Then I remembered the words of Malik at one of his sessions I'd walked in on.

"You see here, brothers," he'd said, "there will come a time when you will notice that you no longer vibrationally align with another. This is when you have to answer a question to yourself: Will I lower my frequency to remain here with this person or do I, for the moment, let them go, in love?"

At the time, those words meant nothing to me. But now, sitting in my car in front of Beto and Lisa's house, they had full meaning. I knew, for the first time in my life, I needed to move on, in love.

» » « «

On my way home, feeling like a new man, I decided to stop by the local natural foods store. Dimitri often talked about the importance of taking care of "the temple," as he called it, referring to one's body and what goes into it. I figured I'd also listen to Hope and look for a journal.

I was surprised to find that there were no animal products, not even chicken or cheese, in the store. I made do with all kinds of "good for you" substitutions that I'd never heard of. I was feeling brave and willing to try something different for the first time.

In the checkout line, I realized I'd forgotten the journal. I left my cart, ran to the stationary area, and frantically fumbled through the pile. *Come on, just pick one.* I blindly grabbed a journal and, as I turned to go, I heard one of the other ones fall to the floor with a slap. There on the cover was a hummingbird. *You've got to be kidding.* I tossed the other one back and ran back to the checkout.

Passing by the cork bulletin board on my way out, there were ads for services offered by the local health community. There were several different kinds of yoga as well as some woo-woo stuff I'd never heard of before—Soul Mapping, Light Code Alchemy, and something called Wokeness Detoxing— none of which grabbed my attention. One, however, stood out: Meredith Jackson's Meditation For Beginners. I'd seen Dimitri teach meditation to the ERP students and knew that, as a guard, if I ever wanted to experience this, I'd have to do it outside of Carlton. With my bags of healthy food and a genuine desire for a new life, I decided to make the call.

» » « «

"Hello," a woman's voice said on the other end of the line.

"Hi, is this Meredith? I'm calling about the meditation classes."

"It is, and what is your name, kind sir?" she asked joyfully, which made me a bit suspicious.

"My name is Marcus. Marcus Ogabi."

"Well, Marcus, nice to meet you. I'm Meredith, but friends call me MJ. The classes are an hour long. I teach a simple practice for those who are just starting out or just want something quiet and easy. There's a session starting in thirty minutes. You're welcome to join if you'd love to."

If I'd love to? A little too woo-woo for me, but where have I heard that before?

"I was mainly just wondering for the future. Maybe I'll come to one at some point."

"That's fine, but you do know, Marcus, tomorrow never actually happens, right?"

Wait, what? I didn't answer, remembering when Dimitri had said the same phrase.

Meredith went on, "Awakening ourselves to our highest version brings us to that place of ultimate joy in life. It's how to change the world."

At this point, I knew this was either another perfect synchronicity or a very pushy, possibly desperate, yoga teacher just trying to make money.

"Yes, I've heard that said before. More than once actually. It's true about it all happening in the present, in the right now," I answered, hoping I wasn't opening a can of worms.

"That's it. Whoever told you that was speaking the truth. So, Marcus, are you ready to change the world? I mean, what else is there to do, right?"

I was going to my first mediation course.

» » « «

Walking up to the quaint, cottage-style house, I admired the sound of the metal wind chimes hanging from the eave. There were several pairs of shoes strewn around a doormat that read *OM SWEET OM*.

Oh, brother. I rolled my eyes and nervously knocked on the door.

"Marcus? Hi, it's so nice to meet you. I'm MJ," said a pleasant, shorter woman in her early forties. I took note of her long black hair as she stepped aside and pointed to my feet.

"Oh, okay," I said, kneeling down to untie my laces. *This is ridiculous.*

I removed my shoes. She stared at my socks and shrugged her shoulders.

"Thank you," she said as I followed her inside, secretly admiring the quality of her long, what looked to be handmade dress.

I immediately noticed how different the house felt. It was beyond just being comfortable. I didn't have a word to describe it because I'd never experienced the feeling before.

Lit candles rested on hand-carved end tables. Colorful exotic rugs covered the parquet wood floor. Tapestries from faraway places hung like artwork on her walls. None of these things were new. Most were a bit worn, in fact. There didn't seem to be any strict order to where things sat, but there was a perfection to the disorder.

There was the calming subtle smell of incense, a nicer, more natural one than Lisa's pina colada version. *How can incense make me feel good?* I paused to have a look at the plush vintage red velvet couch. It looked so inviting, covered in knit pillows, that I had to tell myself to move on.

Then it came to me, the word I was looking for, the one I'd never felt before. "Your house is *cozy*," I said shyly.

She spun around in the hallway and stood to face me with her arms open wide. *Oh shit, she wants a hug.* It had gone from comfortable and cozy to awkward and tense in seconds. I was raised in a home where only family hugged, and that was pretty much only on holidays.

"Ah okay," I mumbled, opened my arms, and moved toward her. She held me close for what seemed longer than normal. I nervously patted her back, trying to signal an end, but this made her hold on even tighter.

She led me to the studio, which was nothing more than a large, cleared-out living room with a shaggy blue carpet and large cushions strewn about. I nodded shyly to the others, who all looked like perfectly nice people. Everyone was white except for me and MJ, who also had dark skin, although I couldn't pin down her ethnicity.

I could tell they felt more comfortable than I did. Not just because I was the new black guy who showed up last. I'm talking about a comfort within themselves. As if they were relaxed in their own bodies. None of the men wore watches or socks for that matter. One of them had a man-bag, but he seemed straight to me.

I sat down and crossed my legs, trying to pull my foot up onto my lap like the others only to find it wasn't going to happen. I was secretly relieved to see the pregnant woman on the other side of the circle couldn't do it either.

"Let's start by closing our eyes and connecting to our breathing by taking three deep breaths inward. When we exhale, let's get all of the air out of our lungs," MJ said quietly. "Okay, deep breath in …"

We all followed her instructions. By the third breath out, when we were instructed to sigh loudly, I felt calmer than I had just minutes earlier.

"Now just connect to your own breath at your own pace. When thoughts come in, don't resist them, just let them come and go while always focusing on each breath you take. Let yourself be the witness of those thoughts. This way you will see that they are not your own."

I was surprised to hear her speak like Dimitri about witnessing thoughts, or, as he called it, "the voice in the head." I found it fascinating how I was able to see the mind speak on its own as I just sat and observed. There were moments I was able to get into a truly thoughtless place, though it only lasted for seconds at a time. It was awe-inspiring to see how powerful the mind was, just as Dimitri had said so many times before.

Afterward, MJ opened the circle for any who wished to share their experience or for any questions. When it was my turn, I nervously reintroduced myself and, with as few words as possible, said that the experience was helpful. That wasn't enough for MJ.

"Marcus, I'm curious to know what brought you here."

"Well, I've been going through some interesting situations lately, and I thought it would be good to start this process—to try to calm the mind and all." I paused and looked around at the others; most were nodding or smiling. This made me feel more comfortable so I went on. "The truth is, there's this guy where I work who helps people with their struggles. I can't really participate fully because ..." I paused again, not wanting to tell all the details, "because I'm working."

"How does he help people with their struggles?" one of the participants asked.

"It's kind of hard to explain, but he uses their problems to show them another way of looking at those problems, and what the inmates—" *Oops.* "I mean, the people, make those problems mean. He's showing them another way to live. Sorry. It's much more in-depth than that and it takes a while to explain. I guess I'm not very qualified to talk about it." I was embarrassed but mostly hoped no one noticed my slipup.

"It sounds like what you are talking about is shifting one's perception," MJ interjected.

"Yes, that's what he calls it. You've heard of it?" I asked, surprised.

"It's one of the keys to living a great life," she answered.

"You said inmates. Do you work at Carlton State Prison?" the man-bag guy asked.

"Yes, I do," I said quietly.

"So, this guy you are talking about. He's teaching the prisoners?" MJ inquired.

"Yes."

"Is his name Dimitri?" MJ asked, a knowing look in her eyes. She smiled as she waited for my answer.

"Ah, yeah, but how do you know his name?" I asked, blown away by her question.

"This area's spiritual community is quite small and word gets around when people do great things."

"He doesn't talk about spiritual stuff. He talks about awakening and liberation of the mind."

She chuckled. "Well, exactly. It doesn't matter what he calls it or doesn't call it. It's one and the same."

It was odd to be in a place where Dimitri was a hero outside the prison. A few people came up after the session and thanked me for my "energetic support" around his work. They used terms like "bless you" and "namaste," things I neither understood nor liked hearing, maybe because I didn't understand them. Whatever it was, the woo-woo stuff just turned me off.

» » « «

As I continued to attend MJ's sessions and my meditation practice grew, the New Age woo-woo stuff bothered me less. My understanding of the terms and what they meant grew. I became friends with MJ and soon realized she was neither desperate nor pushy. She was actually a lot like Dimitri, genuine in her way and wanting only the best for others.

I quickly learned that the things Dimitri taught and knew were also known and taught by others. Not just recently but for thousands of years. I would share what he and the other men in the prison were teaching, and MJ would fill in the blanks where needed.

I was shown that there are no accidents and that everything was working in my favor, even if it didn't seem like it at times. I saw how the simple, open discussion with Lisa created a space that allowed me to find a new practice and meet new people, all of which helped me find peace.

I knew this was only the beginning of something big, but I still had no idea what. I also had no idea what to write in my journal, which I would keep with me at all times just in case something showed up. What I did know was that as long as I continued to work on myself and my issues, things would continue to unfold and reveal themselves when the time was right.

BAIT AND SWITCH

RONNY

"You and Creeper need to be at this thing, Ronny. I want to know what that fool's up to," Joaquin said, pointing to a handwritten sign that Markland had taped to the wall in the dayroom.

ERP IN (NORTH) YARD
TUESDAY
3 PM
DIMITRI SPEAKS OPEN TOPIC
ALL ARE WELCOME

"Okay, Joaquin, but you don't think it will draw attention to us?" He took his glasses and pointed them at me as he gave it some thought.

"I don't think so, ese. Remember, Creeper went there, back in the beginning of it. This shit's open, especially now that he's doing it in the yard for the first time. You and Creeper can just be there. No one's gonna think shit." He looked back to Creeper who was walking tail. "Que dice, Creeper?"

Creeper walked up and looked at us both and nodded. "No problemo, holmes. This vato, he don't care who comes. He ain't suspicious or nothing. I think even you could go and see the shit for yourself."

I shook my head because I knew what was coming.

"Listen, puto, did I ask you to think?" Joaquin snapped. There were certain things that really pissed him off, and a soldier *thinking* was one of them.

"Sorry, holmes."

"Don't be sorry, just don't do it, ese. You leave the thinking up to me. Now, largate, pinche cabrón."

We secretly smiled at each other as Creeper walked away with his fucking tail between his legs.

"So, what you think, carnal?" I was the only one he'd ever ask and only when we were kickin' it solo, just me and him.

"I don't think you should go, Joaquin. But I'll check it out and break it down for you, holmes."

He looked around and paused for a few seconds. I knew something was coming. He then gave me a look and nodded. "Casi, hermano," he whispered while putting his glasses on. We did the LF handshake and he walked away.

Those words combined with that look meant only one thing: that Tanomeo's days were numbered, probably along with other members of his crew as well.

» » « «

Creeper and I watched as dozens followed Tanomeo and the other six towards the north corner of the track. Many of the inmates in the yard laughed at them while others just stuck to their workouts, basketball, and other shit.

We moved to a spot where we could hear what he was going to say, but not right in the middle of the shit, like with the others. When he started, I could see he had a way of talking that pulled in the other vatos. I knew right away that there was something different about him. In a way, he reminded me of Joaquin. You know, people listened to him. The difference was he spoke of positive shit, and, since I'm now telling the truth, there was a secret part of me that liked that, but I couldn't show it. I mean, I wasn't even supposed to feel that shit, so I pushed it down deep and let it die off real fast.

"Okay, guys. Thanks for showing up today. I know this is a different scene than what we're used to, but it's pretty nice to do this out in the open, right?" he shouted. I watched a few of them nod while others, like me, played the part and stood there with our arms crossed.

"I also want to thank Carlton Prison's finest for being here as well, keeping everyone safe. I really do appreciate it, guys." Creeper and I both laughed at him giving props to the pigs that were there.

"What's up with this fool, ese. Is he kidding or what?" I asked Creeper.

"He's a trip, ese. You ain't seen nothin' yet."

"Que vato, eh?" I said while shaking my head.

I looked over at CO Tanas. His arms were crossed too, but he looked pissed off, which I kinda liked. *Hijo de puta.*

I saw El Negro, Officer Ogabi, was there too. I still couldn't put my finger on it, but there was definitely something kinda fucked up about him. Captain Devic was there. He was cool. We all thought he was alright.

"So, today, I thought we might leave it kind of open. There might be questions for those unfamiliar with what we are doing. Also, if there are any questions for those already in the program, that's great as well." No one said shit, so he said, "Let me say it another way. I'm sure there are some of you going through some heavy stuff right now. Maybe it's something on the outside or maybe in here. Let's talk about it. Go ahead and shout it out." Nobody said nothin' for a minute.

"Yo, I got one." It was that little pinche guido, Vincent Palermo. He was doing five-stretch for distribution of H, and his New Jersey wise-guy accent made me wanna pop him every time I heard it.

"Okay, Vinny, whatcha got?" Tanomeo shouted.

"The food in this place. Yo, it's disgustin.'"

We both laughed with the others and nodded our heads, but Vinny turned around and held his hand up, shaking his finger. "Yo, I'm fuckin' serious here, no joke." Then we all shut up. "I want to know how this is even possible. It's a kind of torture in and of itself. I'm surprised all yous are laughin.' Are you not with me on this?"

"I'm with ya on that, Vinny!" one inmate shouted.

"Word!" another yelled as others clapped in agreement. Creeper and I, we didn't say shit even though he had a point.

"Okay, let's talk about that," Tanomeo yelled. It got quiet again. I guess you could say he had our attention. I looked over at Tanas again. He was even more pissed off. You know, even though we worked with him bringing in our dope and helping us and shit, I always saw him as a rata piece of shit that would sell out his own mother for a dollar.

"First off, I agree with you. What they are serving isn't even food in my estimation. It's more like a slow poison that's killing us softly," Dimitri said while laughing at his own joke.

"That's right, D!" one of the inmates shouted as others cheered him on.

Dimitri continued, "Instead of focusing on what we don't want, what we don't like, let's focus on what we want to create. Does that make sense?"

No one said anything right away, then Vinny spoke up.

"No, it doesn't. You know why? Because it's their prison, their food, their rules. We can't create shit here, yo." Tanomeo smiled, like some kind of wise vato that knew something we didn't but was about to tell us.

"There's this little thing called manifestation, and if you would have continued to come to ERP, you'd know a thing or two about it, Vinny."

"Yo, I got things to do in here, knowwhatimean?"

"You got things? Yo, what things?" Tanomeo asked with an Italian accent, playing like he didn't know about Vinny's slinging dope on the inside.

"Things. You know, things." The inmates laughed at Vinny's joke while Tanomeo stepped back and looked at the crowd.

"What if I told you all that every man in here is an expert in the act of manifestation and creation?" He paused and looked at each one of our confused faces.

Again, Vinny broke the silence and mumbled, "Yo, yous can say anythin' you want, but we ain't manifestin' no good food up in here, that's for sure."

We all laughed at that shit. Even though he pissed me off, he was still funny as fuck.

"Only if you say so, Vinny," Tanomeo snapped back. "Only because you say it can't happen, it won't happen."

Vincent looked around at the others, now as confused as the rest of us. "Yo, so now it's my fault?"

"I don't like the word fault. Let's just say you're responsible. We all are, actually, and not just us here in the yard or in this prison. No, brothers, this goes way beyond these concrete walls and fences. But let's just keep it here for a moment." He rubbed his hands together, which reminded me of Joaquin. He'd do that right before we were about to put in work on someone. That's the shit that excited him. It was like they were opposites but the same in some ways. At the time I really didn't get it.

"How many of us have said or thought, 'life's hard,' and really meant it?" he asked.

Only a few raised their hands.

"Pinche maricones," Creeper whispered. I laughed, but inside of myself, I raised my hand with them. It was true, there were many times where I said life's fucked up, you know?

"Let me take that a step further and ask it like this: How many of you have doomed your own existence by participating in some kind of bullcaca self-talk that says stuff like 'I can never be more than what I am now' or how about 'things will never get better' or 'life sucks'?" He scanned the crowd. This time the men just sat in silence. "I'm looking for a show of hands here, guys," he shouted as he raised his own and kept it there as, one by one, nearly everyone's but ours went up as well.

"That's what I thought!" he yelled while nodding his head. "Let's just take it to a more global scale and ask ourselves how many of us have looked at our planet with its polluted air, lands, rivers, and oceans and said, 'Nothing will ever be done about it.'

"How about the corruption-infested systems of government and finance, designed to enslave the people of the world? The system's allowed to continue through our mutual participation, all validated by those six words that, when put together, form the awful phrase that's kept us in bondage for thousands of years: 'That's just the way it is.'

"How long are we gonna keep telling ourselves that? Do we really have to destroy everything: our health, natural resources, relationships with others, and our children's futures?" He had his hands on top of his head. "Look at it, guys. We've all done this. We've created a reality that we don't want. We did that, and we continue to do it. That's how powerful we are!" He then started cracking up. "Don't you see how absurd it all is?"

I have to say, I was impressed at how the vato could state such a grim truth in such a positive and convincing way. The rest of his crew and a few others laughed with him. It was clear that they understood him, but there were still many of us that didn't. I was one of them. I mean, I could see how I'd fucked up my life. I blamed myself for not being there and for not getting my kid out of the barrio before he was shot. I also knew that I was the one who caused mi madre so much pain. But the rest of what he said I couldn't understand at the time.

"Yo, Dimitri, I hear ya," said Vinny. "Don't know if I believe ya, but how exactly does all of this relate to us getting better food up here in this shithole?"

The guys hooted and yelled so loud that it got the attention of the others in the yard.

"Great question. I was just going to reel it all back in, so thank you for that, Vinny." He then looked at the men and asked, "How many of you came up hard? I'm talking poor here. The real thing." He raised his own hand up and kept it there until many others followed.

"Okay, that's the majority of us—besides Zach, of course."

We all busted up, except for Markland. He just shook his head and looked back down at his notepad.

"Tell me something, have you ever seen one of your peeps from the 'hood get serious and really do something with their lives? Someone who really kicked ass."

Tyrone, a black guy doing a six-plus-two for aggravated robbery, put his hand up. "Right here, boo. Ray Ray Washington from tha 'hood, he got himself the whole east side of Samstone locked up. That's the Projects all to himself. He's pullin' at least five hundred G's a year."

"Damn!" one of the inmates yelled out.

"Word!" another shouted.

I looked around at the others chatting and trippin' on what Joaquin makes in a month working both the inside and outside while in a prison cell.

"Orale güey," Creeper whispered, reading my mind as we fist-bumped.

Tanomeo shook his head. "Thanks, Tyrone, but I'm talking about someone who made it in the legitimate world."

Tyrone then raised his hands. "Ah, okay then I'm out." Everyone laughed.

Then Malik, the black dude from the Nation, took a step towards Tanomeo and put his hand up. "I've got one for ya, D."

I could see that many of the inmates called him that. We'd always fuck around and refer to him as "Tanoguero," even though he wasn't really like a white boy or anything. It just sounded funny so we said it.

"There was a kid in the projects who came up harder than any of us. His mom was hookin' and on the pipe. His dad could've been any one of fifty tricks. With no food in his house, he was skinny and malnourished. He had to leave school when he was fourteen to find work, doing odd jobs when he could find them. When he couldn't, he would beg.

"Years later he got a steady job in the construction department of a real estate company that bought, refurbished, and sold old buildings. Over time, he was able to move up the ladder and into sales where he began to make real money. Now, remember, this is a poor black kid from the projects, doing quite well for himself. At this point, he's got a car and a nice rental on the other side of town. But it gets better. This boy, who's now a man, ends up going out on his own and convinces a bank to finance the purchase of his first building. He scratches and scrapes to make it work, leavin' his apartment to move into the deteriorated building he's just bought while he works on it night and day. He finally finishes it up and makes over two hundred thousand in profit. From there, there was no stoppin' him. He repeated the same pattern, buying other commercial buildings and converting them into apartments and penthouses. This cat's name is Edwin Grant of Grant Investments. He's got his face on every bus stop bench in the city."

Tanomeo nodded. "Great story, Malik. How many of you, yourselves, have tried to do something, to break out of the cycle of poverty but, unlike Edwin, failed at it? I'm talking about big dreams: attempted business ventures, failed plans, whatever."

I watched as many of the inmates began to slowly raise their hands. Internally I was raising mine as well. Once I tried to open a taco shop with my homegirl Chema using the money I'd saved from slinging. We wanted it to become a chain, but it didn't make it.

"Perfect, got it," he confirmed. "So, why is it this Edwin character was able to make it while so many of you crashed and burned?"

"He got lucky!" one yelled.

"His circumstances were different. He had an opportunity," another said.

"Let's talk about those. It's got nothing to do with luck, guys. And the circumstances in his life were absolute caca. He didn't have an opportunity, he created one, so that's not it. I want to know why he could and you couldn't."

"Yo, he had a special talent. Somethin' in his DNA," Vinny yelled.

"No, it wasn't in his DNA. I'm pretty sure success in the real estate business isn't passed down."

Vinny threw up his hands.

Tanomeo turned to Malik again, "Did you ever talk to this guy after he had made it big?"

"Yeah, he comes back to the neighborhood once a year during Christmas and gives out toys to the kids. He's one of those guys who'll never forget where he came from."

"That's beautiful. Have you asked him how he did it?"

"It's funny you say that," Malik answered. "My cousin asked him that the last time we were all together, but he didn't say much. Just that he knew he could do it, so he did it."

"Woohoo! It doesn't get any better than that now, does it? That was exactly the answer I was looking for." Tanomeo was clapping like the goofy motherfucker he was.

Malik laughed, "It wasn't the answer my cousin and I were looking for."

He clapped again while laughing, "No, I'm sure it wasn't. But it's so perfect."

He paced back and forth, just like Joaquin, with his hands clasped together. I could tell he was in his head, putting together the words he would use to explain what it was he was so excited about.

"So, let's go over Edwin's words," he said as he put his finger to the air. "'I knew I could do it, so I did it.' It can't just be that he absolutely knew, without a shadow of a doubt, that he could change his difficult life situation to become a multimillionaire, right?"

"Yo, there's gotta be more to it, right Tanomeo?" Vinny piped in again.

"What if I told you that what he said was actually *it*? Nothing else to the story. Just six perfect words." Dimitri turned to write on his imaginary chalkboard while slowly and loudly speaking the words. "I knew I could do it!"

"Yo, fuhgettaboutit. There's no way all he had to say was that and it worked! I call bullshit on all of this!" Vinny shouted as others sounded in agreement.

"You're right there, Vinny. But it wasn't that he just said something and it worked. Malik said 'he knew he could do it.' It was the fact that he knew without a shadow of a doubt that it was possible for him. You all know how to do things. Maybe they're mundane things, maybe some are more complicated, but you know you know you can do them. That's the only way they got done.

"When you were kids, there were things you couldn't do, but then there came a time when something changed and you said to yourself, 'I can do that.' Then it happened. The only way any of this happened was because you possessed the knowing that you could. Conversely, if you knew you couldn't do a thing or even believed you couldn't, and all of us have those limiting beliefs, then you literally wouldn't be able to. That's how powerful you are."

He waited to let shit sink in for all of the fools there. It did for me. I wondered how this guy who was so much younger than me and from The Pit could say the things he was saying the way he said them. He had a real confidence with his words that was kind of perfect. That's when I had one of those "oh fuck" moments and realized he was just doing exactly what he was preaching to us. You see, he knew he could and there he was, just doing it.

This is some crazy shit.

Vinny broke the silence with, "Ah, yeah, right. Yo, just one question though. How does this make me a millionaire and, even more importantly for now, how does this get us some decent food here in this joint?" All the fools there hooted in agreement. I just shook my head.

"I'm getting there. Patience, brother." But patience wasn't happening in Carlton. I saw more than a few walk away.

"The reason Edwin Grant was able to do what he did and others couldn't or can't was because he possessed zero doubt that he could. It might not have been easy. He probably had to be persistent, never give up, and—"

"That's actually true," Malik interrupted. "He told us he had to visit more than thirty banks over a two-year period before he could find one that would finance him."

"Exactly, and it was his knowing that pushed him through resistance, the hard parts.

Those of you who gave up on your dream when things got hard had a doubt that lingered in the shadows of our mind. You may have had all the good intentions in the world when you started, but as soon as there was a hiccup or two, that was it. You were done. By stopping, you only confirmed the doubt's validity, worsening your chances to even step up to bat a second time.

"Maybe you threw out an 'I knew it' or some other self-defeating combination of words like 'I'm not privileged like others.' We call that the victim role, and many know how to play it well, but I digress. That doubt will remain inside your mind, destroying any possibility until you remove it."

"I tried opening a few legit businesses and all of them failed!" Dan Wilcox, a white boy that was in for check fraud and identity theft, shouted from the back.

"You gotta go back to your childhood, Dan. Start there and find when you made a decision around business or money."

"My dad always had money issues."

"There it is. From there you decided that making money, or having abundance, was a difficult thing, maybe an impossible thing."

Dan was thinking it over. "Then how did this Edwin guy make it when he came up worse than me?"

"We'd have to ask him, but if he had a wound around money, which he most likely did have, he probably healed it. He changed the way he spoke to himself around money. Maybe he'd hit such a bottom that he decided he would do anything to change his situation."

Malik raised his hand. "I remember him mentioning he was inspired by a woman he read about that came up hard as well and turned it all around. I think she became a famous chef or something like that."

Dimitri nodded his head. "Great. He was inspired by someone else, and the translation for his internal dialogue went something like this: *I saw that someone else could do it; therefore, I knew I could.* He went from thinking that he could to knowing he could because he changed the way he spoke to himself. That was the key to his shift, guys." Tanomeo started laughing and clapping at the same time. "It's so simple that it somehow seems complex in a way."

He then raised his index finger in the air and shouted, "This is all about you choosing a new reality for yourself. You might have to dig deep and do some real work to find that moment that you chose whatever self-destructive phrase or phrases that killed all future possibilities for yourself and deal with it.

"It comes down to you choosing a new way to speak to yourself. Once you do that, a new world will appear before you."

I'd glanced at Creeper, who was basically shaking his head without shaking his head. He wasn't buying any of it, but I have to admit in some way I was.

Tanomeo then turned his back to us and shook his hands intensely while jumping up and down. I later found out that he was shaking off energy or some shit like that. He then turned back around. "How do we get some good food up in here?" He waited for someone to say something, but no one said shit, just like before. Malik was looking around before he finally grew some huevos and raised his hand a second time.

"Let's see if someone who's not one of the guides can get this," Tanomeo said. Malik nodded and lowered his hand.

"Yo, so it's just like you said, right? We gotta begin by knowing it's possible," Vinny shouted.

"Perfect."

Vinny nodded his head and pushed his lips together like he was proud of getting the answer right.

"Qué pendejo," Creeper whispered. I nodded.

"Here's an even more important question: How many of you know that it is possible to have better food here?" Tanomeo raised his hand and kept it up. The members of his crew did as well, then another three followed. That was it. "Okay. We just need to fix something then. We gotta have a better percentage than that for it to work. Vinny, would you mind coming up here and going through something with me?"

"Why not? What else I got to do today?" he asked as he walked up.

"You didn't raise your hand, why?"

"Ah, because, well, dat just ain't gonna happen, D. You know, us having better food."

"Why is it not going to happen?"

"Because the Bureau of Prisons is just a bunch of cheap bastards. Who don't know that?"

Tanomeo shook his head. "Could there be any other way to have some better food here?"

Vinny shook his head. "No, not dat I can see, D."

"Of course you can't. Otherwise, you would have raised your hand. Let's see if we can change that." He then turned around and pointed towards the first security fence. "What do you see over there, Vinny?"

"I see a twelve-foot chain-link fence topped with zinc-coated, double-coil concertina razor wire."

"I'm not talking about the fence, which you seem to know a lot about, by the way."

"That's because I've been tryin' to figure out a way to get over it for the past three years. Yo, the way I see it, I have a better chance of escapin' than you do of changing the menu in this shithouse." Everyone, even Tanas, cracked up at that one.

Tanomeo waited for the laughing to stop. "But what do you see on the other side of the fence?"

"Yo, I see nothin'."

"You sure about that?"

"Yo, like I said, there ain't nothin' there. Just a big field. Nothin' else."

Tanomeo snapped his fingers. "So there is something there: a big field." He then walked over to his water bottle and took a drink. "Is anyone getting this yet?"

We all just gazed at the field. I wasn't getting it. Then a voice spoke up.

"It's never going to happen." It was Tanas. All of us looked at him, wondering what the fuck he was talking about.

"Hey, Tanas!" Devic shouted, shutting him up as he stood there with his arms crossed again. That's when I got it. This vato wanted to grow food at the prison.

"Crops," someone yelled out from the crowd as Tanomeo's finger shot up.

"That's right. Crops!" he shouted as we all looked at each other, thinking this guy was fucking crazy.

Vinny was still up in front. "Getthefuckouttahere, how's that gonna happen?"

"The first thing we've got to do is to get to a point where we all know that it is possible," Tanomeo answered as he faced the group. "I ask again, how many of you are with me on this?"

Five or more new hands went up.

"That's what I call progress!" He then looked back at Guido Vinny. "Vinny, you still aren't raising your hand. What's up with that?"

"Yo, there's three reasons. And don't think I haven't been thinkin' about it, 'cause I have for about a half a minute or so. One, none us know how, you know, to grow food. Second is that prisons don't let inmates grow their own food, and—"

"Speak for your own self, there, city boy," a voice interrupted from the corner. "I know how to grow food. Raised on a farm all the way up to when I was nineteen." It was Harlan Smith. We called him vaquero. He was serving three for robbery.

"Same here," another hand shot up. It was some other white boy named Wade. "In this climate, we could grow all kinds of greens, vegetables, and even certain fruits."

"Beautiful. Thanks, guys. How about Vinny's second doubt? Does anyone here know of any prisons that have farms on them?"

"My cousin did a stretch back east in a medium-security facility. They didn't just grow their own food but raised livestock as well," that indio, John White Eagle from their original crew, announced.

"Vinny, let's see if something changed with that newest bit of information." He looked at the crowd. "Men, now how many of you know that it's at least possible to have a big upgrade in what we are eating here?" Me and Creeper looked around, many of the fools had their hands up.

"Que vato mas loco. He thinks he can really do this shit, eh." Creeper whispered while laughing.

I just shrugged my shoulders and looked back at Tanomeo.

"I'd like to ask all of you, especially those who had their hands raised, to look over there and imagine that dry, grey, empty field transformed into a lush food farm with greens and colorful vegetables. Imagine yourself, or someone else if that's not your thing, over there working the soil, filling large sacks, and transporting them to the kitchen. Feel what it feels like inside of yourself after this is accomplished.

"I know this request might sound a little strange, but if you could just humor me. It's all part of a bigger process." He closed his eyes for a second and so did the rest in his crew, so I gave it a try. I began feeling kinda happy that we were eating something good, but it didn't last long when I felt Creeper bump me. I snapped out of it and looked at him.

"What the fuck you doing, holmes?" he asked.

"I'm just sleepy. Relax, ese!"

Tanomeo opened his eyes and he looked back at Vinny, "What was the third reason?"

Vinny just stood there like he was afraid or some shit. Then he looked at Tanomeo and tilted his head to his left, towards where Tanas was standing.

"You mean him? What he said?" Dimitri asked as he pointed at Tanas while laughing.

"There's something you aren't seeing here." He kept his finger on Tanas. "Officer Gene Tanas, he's just a guard, nothing else. He doesn't make those types of decisions here. He has a job to do and has to follow rules just like we do."

"Hijole,'" Creeper muttered.

I looked over at Tanas. He was in a staredown with Tanomeo, who was still pointing at him, kinda trying to push him or something. A lot of the inmates were nodding in agreement. Tanomeo turned back to face the group, put his hands up, and quietly said, "Now, whether he actually does his job and follows the rules could be up for debate." Everyone cracked up. Even CO Ogabi laughed a little.

One after another, the crowd went off hooting and shit like that. No one had ever said anything like that, you know, without any fear. It was like we all were in agreement with this crazy fucker Tanomeo, who was fearless even in front of a psycho vato like Tanas.

I looked over and saw that Captain Devic and Officer Ogabi were getting nervous and talking together just outside the group. Tanas had his hands clenched.

Vinny was just standing there nodding. "Well, since yous put it dat way, I guess it is possible, isn't it?"

"You're damn right it is, Vinny!" Dimitri yelled back. "Now listen, I need you to do something when you go back to your lives here. Visualize all of us here, as well as the others in this prison, eating our own food, grown right over there. Do like we did, but longer, while keeping your eyes closed and see us at chow eating healthy, good food. Create the image in your heads of us celebrating as we raise our plastic cups filled with juice made from the berries we've grown, toasting Carlton and everyone and everything that made this possible. We have to see it first in our minds, then feel it every day as if it already happened. If you can do that, the rest will fall into place. This I'm sure of because life is magical like that."

"Yo, I'm down," Vinny said confidently, as he strutted back into the group.

"In summary," Tanomeo shouted as everyone began to move out, knowing the talk was over, "when we want to manifest something, we remove all internal doubt around the possibility of it happening by digging deep into why we think it can't. Then we imagine the thing already done and feel what it feels like to be there. Thanks for coming, guys. I really do appreciate it. And, as always—"

"I don't know why you bother, Tanomeo!" Tanas yelled, causing the inmates to stop. "What do you think you are doing here with these guys? Do you really believe they're ever going to make something of themselves?"

Tanomeo moved his head, finding Tanas through the crowd. "No, actually, Officer Tanas, I don't," he said, cool as a fucking cucumber as he zipped up his coat and adjusted his sleeves. All eyes were on him. "I really don't believe they are going to make something of themselves because I know they already have. These men have taken their current life circumstance, prison, and made it positive. They are turning their lives around right here, now, today as well as tomorrow. It's a long road, but as long as they are breathing, they'll be on it. As will I." He started to walk away, stopped, and turned back at Tanas. "At least, we are here, in our process, doing the work to become better versions of ourselves. That's a lot more than I can say about most people in this world, including you, sir."

The fools in the yard started hooting like we did in school when someone ripped on a teacher. There were even a few fist-bumps. Tanas looked pretty pissed off and was in some kind of sadistic staredown with Tanomeo.

"Are you disrespecting me, convict?" he asked.

"No sir, Officer Tanas," Tanomeo answered while calmly looking at him. "You're doing a great job of that on your own."

Tanas grabbed his club and was moving quickly towards Tanomeo when, out of nowhere, I saw Captain Devic step forward, blocking his path. "Okay, that's enough, Tanas. You've had your fun. We're done here."

Tanas stopped and smiled uncomfortably. "You can say what you want, Tanomeo, but the stats show that the odds are against most of these losers, and that keeps me employed. So I'm good either way."

I looked around at the faces of the other inmates. His fucked up words, designed to bring down their spirits, were working.

"Who the fuck you callin' loser?" Wes, a real deal OG and a respected member from the AB yelled out as others stepped forward. "Yo, what the fuck?" another shouted. I signaled for Creeper to back up. The last thing we wanted was to get caught in the middle of some shit with Tanas. He was a big part of our operation.

"Wait. He's got a right to his opinion, just as we do," Tanomeo shouted, trying to mellow everyone out. "I hold no value for your statistics of the past!" He shouted above the other fools who were losing their shit. "I am only concerned with a new possibility, the transformation that is taking place right now, in this yard, at this prison. And you know what, Gene. There's not a damn thing you or any other evil thing can do about it, because the light always outshines the darkness."

I tapped Creeper's shoulder, and we moved back even further. The shit was about to pop off as some began to whistle, calling others in the yard over. This crazy fucker Tanomeo was about to start a riot.

"Walk away now, Tanomeo, or you're going to the hole!" Captain Jim yelled while grabbing the chest pockets of Tanas's uniform, trying to calm him down.

I looked up at the tower and could see that the gunner was looking down at us. CO Ogabi was already on his radio while Captain Devic was talking in Tanas's ear, "Relax, Gene. There's too many of them and more are coming.

You need to relax. You're putting us all in danger."

"I'm good!" Tanas said as he looked around. There were inmates from the courts and tables walking quickly towards the scene. The gunner grabbed his rifle, and I looked back at Tanomeo. That's when I caught him looking at Ogabi, who was shaking his head at him like they had a secret connection or some shit like that. It got confirmed for me when Tanomeo just smiled and shrugged his shoulders like it was some kind of joke or something. *There's some weird shit between them two.*

"Let's get the fuck outta here, holmes," I said to Creeper as we moved quickly away from the scene. I knew the goon squad in their riot gear would be there soon, but I still wanted to see the guards get fucked up before they made it to them. "This is good here, Creeper. I wanna watch this shit go down, ese."

"Si, carnal. Shit's poppin' off, for reals."

"Okay. Captain Devic, we're dispersing now!" Tanomeo shouted above all the yelling and hoots from the pissed-off crowd. "I want to repeat that my only intention today was to speak about better food for the prisoners and how to make that happen!"

"Motherfucker called us losers!" Big Sam Thompson, a real chingon from the United Black Front, shouted while staring at Tanas and Captain Jim.

"Yo, and said we got no hope in our lives," Vinny yelled back while pulling off his shirt. The little guido was pumped up, pissed off, and ready to throw down. The alarm sounded, and the gunner got into position, but the guards and the inmates were too close for him to take a shot.

I saw Tanomeo say something to Malik who then whispered to the others. They all nodded, except for Markland who took off running. Then Big Sam and several others started running towards the guards. That's when Tanomeo's crew spun around and locked their arms together, creating, like, a fucking barrier between the three guards and the angry mob.

"Oh, check this shit out, holmes. They're protecting the fucking COs," Creeper laughed.

Big Sam got there first and, in the chaos, squared off on Tanomeo, landing a blow on his open chest so hard we could hear it from where we were standing. But get this, it was like Tanomeo didn't even feel it. He just smiled, causing Big Sam to stop and stare at him. I think he was just as confused as we were. The other ERP fools were getting their asses handed to them, but they felt it, for reals.

"What the fuck! Did you see that, Ronny?!" Creeper shouted. "That fucking negro threw a real chingaso, ese. No one could handle it like that!"

He was right. That's when I knew there was something about this Tanomeo vato that wasn't normal. That's when I started asking myself questions. Who was this guy that was smart as fuck but was willing to cause a riot only to have him and his crew take the shit for it? I'd seen Joaquin make moves that didn't make any sense to me at the time only to understand them later. Was this guy like that? Then there was the past shit as well. How did he heal so fast after getting stuck deep in the gut? The rumors of what happened when he was shot. Was there something more to this vato loco? Either way, I knew I had a lot to talk to Joaquin about.

The tear gas landed, and we all dropped to the ground. Two warning shots were fired from the tower, and I pulled my head up and saw the guards pounce on top of Tanomeo, cuffing him and many others.

El viejo, Robert, or Pruno like we call him, got it the worst. He was all jacked up and was spitting blood onto the dirt below his face. I looked over at Tanomeo and saw Officer Ogabi whisper something to him. I could tell he was pissed off. *These fuckers are way too familiar with each other.*

» » « «

Carlton went on lockdown and, back in our cell, I broke it all down for Joaquin while the COs finished up in the yard with the detainees. He listened while just nodding his head as if he wasn't surprised by any of it. Then a loud-ass roar of shouts and hollers lit up the building. I grabbed my mirror to see what was up.

I nodded to Joaquin, "It's him, jefe."

I could make out Tanomeo being led by Officer Ogabi and Captain Jim. Behind them, the others were being escorted by several COs in riot gear. They were on their way to solitary, and the clanking of cups and loud cheers said it all. Tanomeo had just become a fucking hero in cell block H.

Joaquin stood up as the noise got louder. I stepped back so he could be there in front to witness it for himself as Tanomeo passed by our cell.

"Good food, good food, good food!"

The chants got louder as Tanomeo came into our view. He was smiling and shouting in unison with the rest of them. I looked over at Joaquin. He was kind of nodding to himself, you know, like he expected it or something. But if I'm really honest, I think he was maybe jealous. That was the first time I'd seen that in him.

I looked back out through the bars and could make out Officer Ogabi yelling at Tanomeo, "This is what you wanted? All of this, just so you can rot in the hole?!"

The crazy puto Tanomeo just laughed, "There's perfection in all process, Officer. You'll see!"

As they got closer, Joaquin got into character by standing up straight and putting his hands behind his back. Tanomeo was still chanting when he was silenced by the sight of Joaquin staring at him. His face changed, and he got serious just like Joaquin. They locked eyes, and I watched his head twist as they marched him past us.

Joaquin stayed there even after they were gone. He was thinking, so I just stood behind him. I was pretty sure about what was coming next. The problem for me was that I was now asking myself questions about what I thought about the guy and what he was doing at Carlton. I knew that these kinds of questions and thoughts were dangerous and could get me killed.

I heard Joaquin sigh loudly. He then turned around, looked me in the eyes, and gave me the nod.

LOVE OVER FEAR

MARCUS

"You mean to tell me inmate Tanomeo and his boys actually protected y'all after instigatin' the whole thing?" Warden Shady asked in frustration as Tanas and I entered his office at almost the same time. Jim had his back to the door, tending to the warden's plants on the bookshelf. Jim was an avid botanist; no one loved plants more than Jim.

"I wouldn't say he actually instigated the whole thing, Warden." Jim turned as we hung our coats on the rack. He nodded toward the warden, who had his full focus aimed at Tanas.

"Sit down, son," he said. "You wanna tell me what happened out there?"

Tanas sat down stiffly. "Warden, just like I've been saying this whole time, this guy and his movement are dangerous. What happened in the yard is proof of that. Everything inmate Tanomeo does is—"

"Just answer the question." The Warden was getting tired of the Tanas double talk.

"He was telling the prisoners they could grow their own food. Out there, yonder beyond the north side of the track."

Yonder? Really? What a kiss-ass.

"The only thing I did was inform him and the inmates that this wasn't possible and he shouldn't get the men's hopes up. You know how dangerous that can be, promising something to the boys and not delivering."

At his wits' end, the warden pleaded, "And how, pray tell, does this almost start a riot in my prison, Gene?"

I felt hope for the first that Tanas's days could be numbered. Even if he lied, Jim or I could speak up and tell the story the way it really happened. But I didn't know how deep the corruption ran.

Tanas sat back in his chair, crossing his legs, a faint smirk growing on his face. "I guess you just had to have been there, Warden. Sometimes you have to be up close to a thing to truly have a grasp of all the intricate details of the who, what, why, and where of it all."

I could feel my heart beat faster. I knew, just as Jim had suspected, Tanas had something on the warden and was covertly extorting him at the moment.

Jim was staring down at his hands, distancing himself from what was happening.

The warden's mood had visibly shifted. He cleared his throat, "I'll review the tape and see what's what." Everyone in the room knew nothing would be done about Tanas's involvement in the incident. Our warden was being blackmailed by the sleaziest guard at Carlton. It made me sick to my stomach.

The warden asked Jim about the prisoners responsible for the riot and the actions taken. Jim stated the whole prison was on lockdown, and Tanomeo and his crew were in the hole, along with Vincent Palermo and Big Sam Thompson.

Tanas piped in, "It's not enough, Warden. You need to put an end to this ERP business."

I shook my head and sighed, not caring if anyone noticed. *God, I hate this guy.*

"Take away their chapel privileges and prohibit inmate Tanomeo from gathering in groups altogether. We can validate them as gang members and break them up, move them to other blocks if necessary. Hell, if you have to, you can transfer some of them out of Carlton. The key is to separate them from Tanomeo. Without him, their power is gone."

The warden sat quietly, squinting his eyes as if trying to figure something out. "Do you even think about what you're gonna say before you say it?" He looked at Jim and me, then back at Tanas. "I'm serious here. Do you, son?"

Oh, this is good. The feeling of hope had returned.

"You need to cut the head off the snake. It's the only way," Tanas said stoically, unfazed by the warden's scolding. "If you don't like those ideas, say there's a contagious virus loose in Carlton. With just that, we could keep everyone on lockdown. Jolt them all back into submission so they forget about all of this awakening nonsense."

I couldn't believe what I was hearing. I glanced over to find Jim already staring at me with a raised eyebrow.

The warden's response, or at least the motivation behind it, wasn't what I expected. "Need I remind you, I'm startin' my campaign next week. I'll be damned if I'm gonna do anythin' that could draw negative attention to this prison and the way I run it. Jesus, I'm not sure what part of prison stats and their importance to my becomin' the next governor you don't understand, Gene." He motioned for Jim to read the information he had in his file.

"Since the inception of ERP," Jim read, "H-block has seen a twenty-eight percent reduction in overall infractions by inmates. The biggest drop came when the core members of the group outside of Tanomeo, that would be McKenna, Henson, White Eagle, Plowman, and Clemans, began to teach inmates in smaller groups. Additionally, numbers improve in other blocks when participation in ERP increases."

"Twenty-eight percent," the warden repeated. "That's pretty good, ain't it, Jim?"

"That's actually the best we've seen, sir. Ever," Jim answered.

The warden nodded his head and raised a finger at Tanas. "You hear that? The best ever for Carlton. Are you gettin' why we can't rock the—?"

"Excuse me, Warden," Jim interrupted. "It's not only that it's the best here at Carlton. If you look at the data on a per capita basis, it's the best in the nation. Ever."

There was an odd silence in the room. None of us expected to hear that.

Still, Tanas couldn't help himself. "Don't you see, Warden? They got stronger once he showed the others whatever it is he's doing. If this keeps going, we could very well lose control over the inmates. I'm telling you, they must be herded like sheep. It's the only way."

"Hold your horses right there. Give me a damn minute to think about all of this," the warden snapped. The old guy was getting flustered.

The warden looked back at us, a gleam in his eye. "Best in the damn nation, you hear that, fellas? I reckon I'm a shoo-in, alright!" he shouted as he stretched and walked to the window.

Jim was nodding in agreement. *Really?*

The warden stared at the vastness of the land below. We watched the back of his head shaking slowly as he contemplated. When he turned, he had a look on his face that I can only describe as villainous, as if he'd changed into another person.

"No, boys, we have to be careful about how we treat this here situation with inmate Tanomeo. This ERP thing is what we might call a secret weapon. And what do we do with secret weapons?" he asked, looking at each one of us, scrunching his brow when no one answered. "We keep them a secret, for Christ's sake!"

He whispered to Jim, "Who else knows about them numbers there?"

"Just us here in the room, sir. I haven't told anyone else, but they do go public," he answered, not looking at the warden. Jim was a company man and had his company aspirations, but he was also the kind of guy that couldn't look someone in the eyes if he didn't respect them.

"They are public, but what the public don't know is how they got so good. That's what needs to stay in this room until I figure out how to weave it all into my campaign. Are we clear on that, boys?" He pointed at both Tanas and me as he sat back down in his leather chair.

I reluctantly nodded. *This son of a bitch wants to take credit for ERP so he wins the election.* He was so blatant about it. I guess he figured we were all on Team Shady. *Am I the only one who cares?*

He lowered his head as if to tell us a secret. "I hate to say it, but Gene might have a point after all. We've got to take control of this thing. We can't let this movement get any bigger. It needs to stay right where it's at. The stats are so good that they alone, with the governor's endorsement of course, should win me the election. Hell, even if shutting it all down reverses the stats, it won't show until months from now after I'm already elected." I looked over at Tanas who was sitting up straight in his chair with his fingers interlaced.

What a piece of shit.

I knew where the warden was going. He, like anyone in a position of power that thinks of themself first, was about to exert that power in the name of control. The corruptness within him needed to control Dimitri and his crew so everything fell into place without disruptions.

"Here's what we're gonna do: take the rest of Tanomeo's clique out of the hole and anyone else who's in there. I want him alone with no one to holler to. Put them on disciplinary probation with a one-point reduction each. Do the same with the Italian boy and the others. But Tanomeo gets sixty in the box."

Now there was a second man at Carlton I truly despised.

"That level of solitude should make him think twice about pullin' them shenanigans in my prison. I can't have a riot on my hands, now can I, boys?"

We all remained silent. Tanas just nodded.

"That there was a question!" the warden exclaimed.

"No, sir," we said in lackluster unison, except for Tanas.

"No sir!" he shouted late, which made him look like even more of an ass.

"You can't, Warden. And this man can cause one. I can attest to that."

Oh, Jesus.

"The way I see it, keepin' him out of circulation and quiet will let some wind out of ERP's sails while I figure out the best way to make this work to my advantage. Plus, it does sound like he's gettin' a bit too big for his britches. This'll bring him down a notch."

The warden turned to Jim, "Let's have a chat with him on day fifty. He should be more pliable then, ready to work with us instead of against us."

Tanas, feeling pretty smug, proceeded to rat out inmate Markland for exceeding the allowed limit of nine-by-eleven notebooks in a prisoner's cell. This type of infraction was ignored by the COs unless they wanted to mess with an inmate.

The warden ordered a surprise cell inspection not only for Markland but the other five as well.

With Dimitri in the hole, it appeared Tanas was going to push against everyone and everything that kept ERP alive. Unable to have large meetings out in the open or in the chapel, the ERP crew would have to move to smaller sessions in cells.

The warden stood, signaling the end of the meeting. I was last at the door when he said, "Ogabi." I turned. "Did that boy really tell the men they could grow their own food?"

This was my chance to say everything I wanted to say, like the inmates growing their own food was a great idea. It would boost morale while saving the prison money. He could work with inmate Tanomeo, instead of against him. I wanted to remind him that those stats, which he referred to as "his," had nothing to do with him, that he should give credit where it's due. Lastly, what I really wanted to get off my chest was my disgust in how he allowed Tanas to walk all over him, due to some past transgression.

If you weren't such a self-centered political pig, you could do incredible things to help these men.

"Not exactly, sir," was all I could muster.

"That boy is one crazy son of a bitch, that's for sure," he mumbled, shaking his head. "A farm at Carlton. Now I have heard it all."

» » « «

I needed some sage advice. On my break, I rang up the one person I knew could give me that.

"Hello, Marcus," the joyful tone of a truly happy person answered, just as she always did when I called.

I'd fallen pretty hard for MJ. She was always there for me when I was faced with a dilemma. She knew all the players as well as the roles they were playing, so it never took her long to catch up. She loved Dimitri and what he was doing and asked about him often.

However, what I did find unsettling was she had love for the warden and Tanas, who I pretty much hated. She'd say things like, "They are just in their process, dear one. Might we have compassion for them as they are a reflection of something unresolved within ourselves." Or, "They are just as much a part of the great awakening as we are." That kind of talk actually frustrated me. But when things got rough, her advice would calm me.

"Dear one, it sounds like you have a decision to make. You can warn Zachary of what's coming and help save the program, which might make you feel as if you've betrayed your word and your co-workers and, maybe, the public, seeing how they are prisoners and all. There could also be legal repercussions that might put your job in jeopardy, or worse.

"You've come so far on your path, and I want you to know I support you in whatever you choose. I can say that because I trust the purest resolution will present itself while The Light continues to reveal itself within you and Carlton. All you need to do is listen."

How she spoke to me was a bit woo-woo, but, coming from her, I loved it. "Listen?" I asked.

"Remember how Dimitri showed you there were two voices in your head? Maybe you can take a moment when we get off the phone and listen. Ask yourself which voice represents the true you. Remember, one will be fearful and the other empowering, born from love. You will have to choose between the two."

Believe it or not, I actually got choked up and had to take a minute.

"You're right," I finally said. "Thank you, *Mapenzi Wangu*."

"I love it when you call me that, dear one. You are a great man, Marcus, with a beautiful heart. I want you to know that I see you."

I'd just been paid a very high compliment, though I didn't know it at the time. In woo-woo speak, when someone says "I see you," they are referring to the recognition of your highest self by their highest self. The best in them sees the absolute best in you. Your best version. No one had ever told me that, not even my own mother.

"I wonder," MJ went on, "how the amazing Dimitri will do in solitary?"

"If I had to bet, he'll meditate and enjoy the quiet. I'm actually wondering how we'll get him outta there once his time's up," I answered jokingly.

MJ laughed, always a beautiful sound, and said, "You gotta love that guy. He's very special. And I know that you do."

"I do what?" I asked.

"You love Dimitri. You do know that, right?"

The truth was I'd never thought about it like that. He was a man that wasn't a family member.

"Don't worry, you don't have to answer. I just wanted to point out the not-so-obvious," MJ said in a gentle tone. "So, how's Jim?"

"I guess the warden is keeping him busy, seeing how he's in the middle of his campaign. What's strange is that we both know there is a real injustice being committed with Dimitri and ERP, but Jim doesn't do anything about it. It's like, as solid as he is, he's kind of a kiss-ass. There's a lot of talk like 'if I was warden I'd let the kid hold court wherever he wanted,' but there's no action. Especially now when he needs it most."

I heard her giggle on the other line. "Don't you see it, dear one? He's made his decision. He's afraid of losing his bond with the warden because it could impact his career."

"That's exactly right."

"Just like you, he had a dilemma in that he had to choose between fear around the loss of something and love in standing for those who sometimes can't stand for themselves. The real question is which one will you choose, fear or love?"

ONE OF US

ZACH

Wes Stowan
3 years, aggravated assault
Issues: mother left at 2 years old, break up with first love
Main struggle: fear of abandonment, addiction to sex and cocaine

Notes for Wes:

... Reminder that trading one addiction for another is not the way to liberation. Let's find the root of the addictive personality and heal from there. Start by remembering when the imaginary void inside was created by the traumatized child. In that way, we can ...

"How goes it, Markland? What are you writing?"

Startled by the stern, official voice, my pen flew across the cell. I was finishing up an entry in Wesley Stowan's workbook, one of ERP's most disciplined members.

For some reason, Officer Ogabi's presence made me extra nervous this time. It wasn't his twitching or that he'd checked the door twice in the ten seconds he'd been there, but it was more that he was asking what I was writing about. "These are the notebooks we use in the program. I've designed them to work as a sort of a logbook. Each student has a book, and the five facilitators take notes as they coach them through the different stages of their transformational process. You do know what I mean when I say 'transformational,' don't you, sir?" I asked cautiously, not wanting to bruise his apparently-fragile ego. He stared at me like he was trying to figure something out.

"Of course I do. My girlfriend is a meditation teacher, so I know all about it."

"Okay, cool," I answered. *He knows very little about it.*

"You said 'the five facilitators.' Aren't there six?"

"I didn't include D in that," I answered, starting to feel uncomfortable, wondering where his questioning was going.

"Why not include him?" Officer Ogabi asked.

"Because he doesn't look at the books, sir. He doesn't need to."

He glanced again out the door. "I'm not getting you, Markland."

"He remembers everything about all of them. We have a weekly meeting with the facilitators, and they talk about the students, and D remembers everything that's said."

"You're telling me he has a photographic memory? The surprises keep coming, don't they," he said, shaking his head.

"No, that would mean he remembers everything he sees. He can't even remember what he had for dinner last night or what day it is. But when it comes to transformational work, he never forgets any of it." I pointed at the notebook. "By logging their progress, we can meet them where they're at, as D puts it, when new challenges arise."

"New challenges?"

"Yes, Officer. The Universe will continue to throw challenges our way so we can transform them into tools for growth. Once the suffering around those challenges is transmuted, they will no longer be needed, therefore ceasing to arise as often. Because of where we are as a species, there's a lot of work to be done. That means new challenges arise more often. All of this makes it an ongoing thing, as in, for the rest of our lives."

Again he stared at me. *He looks like he's confused or trying to solve a puzzle.*

"Remember when you and I first met in the chapel?" he asked.

"Yeah."

"You seem to know a lot about this stuff now. You didn't seem to know much then."

"Well, sir, I've been stuck in a cell with a master. It was bound to happen sooner or later, right?" I laid the notebook on the bed.

"And the others? Are they as far along as you?"

"Like D says, it's better to try not to look at it as levels. Higher or lower, further or less aren't really accurate indicators. The process is sort of all over the place. Like, there will be things that I have already experienced and learned from that one of the other guys hasn't and vice versa."

"But what about inmate Tanomeo. He must be at a different level altogether." He was still attached to the programmed concept of hierarchy and ranking.

"Mastery is a whole other thing. D would actually argue that there are no masters, but I don't know about that."

"So, how is it you guys are out there teaching if you aren't at this level yourselves. How do you know what to say to the students?"

I could see that he really wanted to understand the process, so I gave him a small sample of how we rolled. "I think what you are really asking is what do we do when we don't have an answer for someone, especially now that D isn't around?"

"Basically," he answered.

"There are two methods we rely on when we get stumped and our IGS is down."

"Whoa," he said. "What's an IGS?"

"Our Internal Guidance System. Each and every one of us has all the answers inside. They exist in our soul, which is the truest you there is. Does that make sense?" I hated to keep checking in with him like that.

His expression shifted from agitated to engaged. "That's like the little voice that comes from empowerment rather than fear, right?"

"Oh snap! You do know your shit, don't you, Officer Ogabi!" I overplayed my excitement a bit and a touch of smugness came in with his smile. "If, for some reason, we're unable to tap into that voice of empowerment, as you called it, then we get together as a group to figure it out."

He nodded his head in approval, which impressed me. "And the other method?" he asked. "You said there were two."

I pulled up the sheet that was folded over the edge of the bottom bunk. "Those notebooks, they're our last resort."

"What's the difference between those and the one you were writing in and all the others spread over your cell?"

"These under the bed," I explained, "the ones marked with a purple line on the edge, they are the ones D and I started with. They have his teachings in them with close to eight months' worth of data. If we need to, we can go to them for the guidance we are looking for. It's a bit of a task, but we just have to be willing to take the time and look for it."

"I see," he said, nervously glancing outside the cell again. "So, these note-books, they're pretty important to what you are doing?"

"They are for sure! These books are everything to the program. Not only for the men currently in ERP but to all those that will join in the future. I'd say, combined with the two separate sets of notebooks, we have the perfect counsel to just about any personal or emotion-based problem a person can have in the world today." I could see his skepticism.

"Every problem a person faces in the world today? That's a hard one to believe, inmate."

"I'm sure it is, especially when you are not as close to it as I've been. There are actually several different tiers to each answer, if we can call them that, for each problem.

"There are some who are ready to hear a more direct truth because they've been in the program for a while or maybe they've done some work before they came to prison. John White Eagle is the perfect example. He's an American Indian who grew up in the Lakota tradition. D spent some time figuring where he was at in the process. After that, John was able to come into the deeper teachings earlier, not wasting time on the things he already knew."

He nodded, but I could tell he still had questions.

"But the teachings of the Lakota and what Tanomeo teaches are not the same, right?" he asked.

"At their core, the essence of the teachings are pretty much identical, as are most ancient spiritual traditions."

"I've heard that before. Not sure if it was from Dimitri or my girlfriend," he laughed.

His guard was down, and we were beginning to just talk, like friends.

There was something about Officer Ogabi that I liked. He seemed like a pretty cool dude. I know D thought well of him, often referring to him as "one of us." I could sense that he genuinely liked what we were up to, even though he couldn't fully express it.

"I bet that's pretty cool to have a partner that's into all of this, right?" I asked, leaning into the new-found friendliness.

"Sometimes it's a bit more communication than I'm used to, or even comfortable with, but it seems to work," he said.

An awkward silence set in. The kind that shows up when there's nothing else to talk about but you desperately want to find something.

"What's that?" he asked, pointing to the TAS mat sitting on D's bunk. "I've seen you guys get on them and talk."

"D calls it el ruedo de amor, the wheel of love. I knew that name wasn't gonna fly in here and he finally agreed. So it's a TAS mat. A "Take A Stand" mat. We sewed together some bandanas, and D wrote these cool figures and symbols. Most of the ERP members are making their own now. It's a cool practice to keep speaking your deepest truth. It holds you accountable."

"But what does it really do? Why the symbols and directions?"

"For D, it has some pretty deep meaning or connection, but he's staying quiet on the origin of that connection." Officer Ogabi stared at it, nodding as if he'd seen it before. I lifted the mat and pointed. "All I know is we line it up with the four directions correctly. D's marked different parts of the facility so we know where due south is, for example, in the chapel and so on. To him, it all means something with the planets, their alignment, and navigation. For me, it's more metaphoric than anything. You stand on it and make a declaration about how you will show up and who or what you will be for the rest of your life."

I held it up and nodded towards the ground. "You ready, Officer?" I asked. He frowned at me and ignored the question.

"Listen, Markland, you know that having this many notebooks in your cell is against Carlton rules, don't you?"

"Well, technically, yes. What, are you here to write me up?" I could feel my defenses rising. *I thought this guy was on our side.* "You're not gonna confiscate them, are you?"

He looked outside again before whispering, "No. I'm here to tell you something, but you have to keep it between you and me. They're gonna toss your cell tomorrow morning. If these are as important as you say, you need to get them out of here. You've far exceeded the limit per inmate, so you better figure it out."

I had so many questions but now didn't seem like the time to ask. *There is one, though.* "Who is the petty fuck that's behind this?"

He gave me a look and a grin that said it all.

"Tanas, that piece of shit," I mumbled. There'd been bad blood between us ever since the Earl and Pete setup backfired.

Officer Ogabi informed me our whole crew was getting raided, so giving the notebooks to the other Mag Seven guys was out of the question. The only option was to give them to each member with their corresponding name. It would take forever, but I didn't have a choice.

I looked him in the eyes. "Thanks for this."

"I know. I saved your ass," he smirked. "Oh. And there's only one thing that troubles me."

"What's that?" I asked, bracing for more troubling news.

"I won't be around to see Tanas's face when he finds out the notebooks aren't here."

His grin grew bigger, as did the one on mine. *Okay. I really do like this dude.*

"Real quick, Officer Ogabi. How's D doing?"

He started laughing. "Funny, I just got word on that. It probably won't surprise you to know that he actually likes it there."

"Oh, that's rich!" I said, busting up.

I put my hand over my heart, bowed my head in respect, and he was gone.

» » « «

John White Eagle and I were alone in my cell, the last stack of notebooks on the bottom bunk. He sifted through them and set aside half.

"I'll bring these with me. These guys are close to my cell," he said.

"Cool, cool. I'll get the rest where they need to go. There's still thirty minutes till lights-out."

"How do you know we're all getting checked tomorrow?" he asked.

"Does it matter John?"

"I just want to know how sure you are, because we might have another problem."

"What other problem?" I asked.

"I received the package this morning. I have the medicine you wanted."

"Medicine?" I asked, drawing a blank before remembering the peyote he'd promised to smuggle in for me. "Oh, that!" I had never taken any strong psychedelic besides acid and molly. I wanted to try it, on John's recommendation, as he'd used it often on the reservation where it was legal. Of course, in Carlton it wasn't.

"Yes, that. I'm going to give it to you now, and you need to think about how to hide it from the guards."

"What are you talking about, bro?" I asked, terrified about taking on another problem just after unloading the notebooks.

"I'm talking about giving it to you now, *bro.*" I wanted to laugh at his bad impression of me, but then he pulled a ball wrapped in plastic out of his sock.

"Where the hell am I supposed to put it?"

"Sounds like they're coming to look for books. I doubt they're gonna do a cavity search." He tilted his head downward.

"Hell no!" I yelled.

"Then I suggest you sit with the medicine tonight," he said in all seriousness. "But remember, it's a long journey best had alone and in silence. Make sure you set your intention and always remember it's going to end at some point." His voice was stoic, without tonality.

"Jesus, John. Thanks for scaring the shit out of me."

"Sometimes people become fearful that it won't end. I feel you should know that. Oh, and I know of no one who has ever died from taking it. Well, not physically, that is."

Oh, that's reassuring.

John was the most stone-faced, humorless person I'd ever known. *Though his seriousness does make him funny somehow.*

"Is it really that intense?" I asked nervously.

"It can be. But intense is gooood," he answered in a deep voice.

"It's just that I've taken other drugs and—"

He put his hand up. "Do not refer to the sacred hikuri as a drug again, Zach, or I will have to take it back."

"Whoa, relax, White Eagle. So, what's hikuri, anyways?"

"Hikuri is another name for peyote, which is not a drug. The things you take from your doctor or what you used in the past at the parties, those are drugs. They mask pain or take you away from it. The medicine of my people brings you into what needs to be looked at. This is about healing, not masking."

"Okay, okay," I said as he did some ritualistic thing, holding the plastic ball in the air before shoving it between the frame and mattress of the top bunk.

"Tókhi wániphika ní!" he said and walked out of my cell.

"Hey, what does that mean?" I hollered after him.

"Good luck!" I heard him yell from a distance.

» » « «

I won't go into much detail about my journey at this moment, other than to say it was very heavy. On top of that, having CO Gene Tanas show up to toss my cell wasn't the best way to end the trip, but the look on his face when he found a whole lot of nothing was priceless. He was like a kid that ran downstairs on Christmas morning only to discover that the gifts were gone. I loved it.

HUMMINGBIRD AND FIRE

MARCUS

Nearly seven weeks after committing treason by helping Zach divert a near-disaster for ERP, I was once again reminded of all the good the program had done in such a short period of time.

While watching over chow one day, I could tell something had shifted.

Where are the other guys? They usually all sit together.

I saw White Eagle at a table on the other side of the room, so I walked over and could hear him teaching a group of men at his table.

I scanned for the others and was surprised to see all of them, with the exception of Markland, were seated, speaking in different areas of the chow hall. They'd strategically separated to reach more inmates.

That moment was a pivotal one I'll never forget. As I stood there, in front of the stainless steel drinking fountain, within all of the noise and commotion of a filled-to-capacity mess hall, I truly understood. The work that inmate number 52066 was doing, had done, and would do in the future was ultimately effective. It was all good, which meant he was all good. I was convinced that the young man who was changing things in Carlton, even as he sat in an emptied-out solitary confinement area on the other side of the facility, was capable of changing the world as well.

I eavesdropped on Charles Clemans as he quietly spoke to several inmates. "What is important here, brothers, is that we are first grateful for the food that we do have. We must see and know that it is good in the way that it nourishes our bodies. If we say otherwise, we are doing ourselves no favors."

It was moments like that one that gave me hope. But I'd be jolted back to reality when I thought about how men like Warden Shady, Tanas, and others thrived by keeping others in bondage. As I got deeper into helping Dimitri, Zach, and their program, I felt more and more upset by what I witnessed around me. After my shift ended, I needed to talk to someone, and there was only one place to go.

When I arrived, she could tell something was wrong.

"Dear one, come in, sit down, and have some tea. You can tell MJ all about it."

I sat down and filled her in on my day, starting with how I'd seen Dimitri being taken from solitary to the warden's office for his fifty-day review. Jim and another guard led him in shackles toward the main building. Everyone seemed to know who he was. Even the guards from the different blocks stopped just to watch the guy who'd caused so much chaos that day in the yard. I knew it wasn't a good sign when he was led back less than ten minutes later.

"Jim filled me in on what happened inside the warden's office. Apparently, Dimitri rejected the warden's order to tone down his speeches, limiting them to once a week, on the basis of his right to free speech and public assembly. He told the warden he should coach his guards on etiquette. Predictably, the warden responded with the threat to keep him in the hole longer if he didn't play ball."

"What did Dimitri the Great have to say to that?" she asked as she sipped her tea.

I laughed. "Get this. He told him that it wouldn't be a problem because he's enjoying the quiet."

"Of course he did," she said, laughing too. "I'm just loving this all, dear one. Did anything else happen?" She moved closer to the edge of her chair.

"He boldly stated his intention for developing large-scale organic food production in the empty field just outside the yard."

"No, he didn't!"

"Yes, he did. And you're really gonna like this next one."

She put down her cup and clapped her hands. "Oh goody, tell me more."

She's taking way too much pleasure in this.

"The warden said," I put on my best warden impersonation, "'Where the hell do you get off telling the prisoners they can have a farm at Carlton, boy? Have you done lost your mind or somethin'?' Can you guess what Dimitri said?"

She thought about it for a moment before blurting out, "'Yes, I have lost my mind.'"

Baffled, I asked, "How did you know that?"

She just winked back.

I told her how Dimitri told the warden that losing his mind was the best thing that ever happened to him. How he explained that the mind-ego, and the thoughts that came from it, were at the root of all suffering. How he recommended that the warden join ERP and that he'd be happy to facilitate a staff version.

All of this made MJ ecstatic. "Oh, the joy of it all, Marcus."

"Not so fast, MJ. It didn't exactly work out so great for Dimitri the Great."

She made a worried face. She was fully into the story.

"The warden gave him another thirty days in solitary," I said, "and shut down ERP in H-block until further notice."

MJ went on to reconstruct the many pieces of the puzzle, figuring the stats had improved so much that the warden didn't care if they dropped because, by the time they'd be public, he'd already be governor. She was right.

"That is just so rotten," she said. "The warden only cares about the stats so he can take credit for them."

"True," I admitted, "but why is he hell-bent on stopping Tanomeo and his program?"

"Because the warden is in all this for one thing: power."

"And money," I said.

"Exactly. They are intertwined in the world of dirty politics and unconscious desire."

I thought about how men like the warden, Tanas, Sid, and others like them thrived on the power they held over other people.

"The warden told Jim that he'd keep Dimitri in solitary for the rest of the year if need be. That he has no problem putting the others in there as well."

She moved to sit next to me on the couch. "We are living in interesting times, that's for sure. This is the duality of things, the light and the dark playing out their roles perfectly. This all may be difficult for us to understand at times, but we can stay in our power by choosing to see it and accept it as it is. This is actually great practice for what's coming."

It had never sat well with me, the whole "accepting it as it is." Then there was the part about "what was coming." That part I flat-out ignored because I wasn't ready to hear it. She got up to get more tea, and I chewed on the subject.

"However, dear one, that doesn't mean we can't take action to change it," she said from the kitchen.

My head turned, "Now you're speaking my language, MJ."

She came back into the living room, tea in hand. "Maybe it's time the public knows about the changes at Carlton and, more importantly, who's really behind them."

I reached over and patted the seat in front of me. "Sit, MJ, sit. Tell me more."

"The media nowadays is mainly spreading false narratives to instill fear in the collective, but we can use it to do good," she said excitedly.

I remembered the ways the department would manipulate the media. On rare occasions, it even backfired on them.

She said that she had an idea of how to make it happen and I wouldn't have to do anything. "You just go back to work and let MJ handle the rest," she smirked and gave me a wink. "For now, let's not talk about it. The less you know, the less you'll have to answer to when the you-know-what hits the fan."

She was a paradox. She didn't want to cuss but had no problem making moves that would rattle many people's cages.

"It's gonna really piss off the warden and create a shit-storm like no other," I said.

"I imagine it will. That's what we have to do sometimes as lightworkers."

"Lightworkers? What's that?"

"It's what I am. You are as well, dear one; you just aren't completely aware of it yet. We are here working for The Light, the goodness in all, and for all. We are here to bring about a change in the world."

"Like Dimitri says he's going to do?"

"Yes, and he's already doing it. So are we, in our own way."

"I'm not sure how any of this is going to change the world," I said. "These things just seem so small in comparison to what you are talking about. I'm not discounting what Dimitri's done for the men at Carlton. It's just that the world ... that's a mighty big place."

"There's so much for you to learn still, dear one." She put her cup on the coffee table. "In order for us to experience the change, it must occur in the micro first. You've told me Dimitri once said to the men, 'You must be the shift you want to see in the world'"

"Sometimes he yells out 'be the shift!' at the end of his talks," I laughed.

"When singular consciousness, your experience, evolves, it moves into unity consciousness, which is your experience knowing it is not separate from other experiences but part of the One that is having experiences through you. So, basically, that level of evolution shows up in the macro through the 'as within, so without' universal law of manifestation.

"I can break it down easier like this: While the big shifts in the individual may appear to be small when viewed from a global perspective, I assure you they're not. They affect everything because you are actually everything, you just can't see it with your eyes. This is how the illusion works, making one unified field appear to be separate. Did that land, dear one?"

The truth was, very little of it landed. I felt like I'd had an overdose of MJ's woo-woo by this time and lay back on the sofa looking up at the ceiling, trying to tune out from what she was saying.

"If you could just see yourself as the hummingbird in the story of the raging fire, you would know that what you are doing has merit," she said as she got up to go to the kitchen.

I swung up and put my hand out.

"Wait a minute? What did you just say?" I asked.

She sat back down. "The story of the hummingbird. Do you know it?"

"No. Is it jam-packed with woo-woo?"

"I can give you the abbreviated version," she said, settling in to tell the tale.

"So, there was a raging forest fire that burned out of control. The animals ran out of the forest, fleeing their homes, helpless against the powerful flames. All but one: a hummingbird. The other animals watched as the hummingbird swooped down to take a few drops of water from the river and fly them back into the forest to drop on the fire.

"'Don't bother. You are too little. Your wings will burn. Your beak is too tiny. It's only a few drops. You can't put out the fire!,' they yelled as the hummingbird passed over them, looking down on the defeated and hopeless animals.

"Then one of the animals yelled out, challenging the hummingbird in a mocking voice, 'Hey, what do you think you are doing anyway?'

"The hummingbird stopped in midair, hovering just above them. Without missing a beat, it said, 'I'm doing what I can.'"

I was speechless and she could see it. "Why don't you go into the meditation space and contemplate that for a while, dear one?"

I nodded and quietly made my way to the studio. I crossed my legs on a cushion and began focusing on my breath. Many thoughts rushed in about all that was happening, but, just like she'd shown me, I let them come and go.

After a little time, I was able to reach the state of no thought.

Though it was a short break from my mind, it was helpful in ways I can't explain. Through the peace, I found that, just like the hummingbird, I, MJ, Dimitri, Zach, and everyone else who participated in this crusade of awakening was doing what we could. We all were doing our part and, sooner or later, the raging fire that scorched the consciousness of humanity would be extinguished by the many hummingbirds that would show up to do theirs.

VISION QUEST
ZACH

The night after Officer Ogabi and White Eagle visited my cell, I went on my first peyote journey, and it was the shit.

Knowing it would last all night and into the next morning, I chose to begin two hours before lights out. I arranged everything to be as comfortable as possible. I had my water bottle and a small plastic bucket in case I needed to vomit, which according to John was a common occurrence during these experiences.

I also set my intention by asking the medicine to reveal how my life might be used to bring about awakening on a global level. I thought about how crazy that might sound to people who knew the old Zach. The infamous hacker who wanted nothing more than to show the world how much damage he could do. The outlandish DJ who threw wild parties, high on ecstasy and other drugs. The outspoken activist with an incredibly unhealthy ego that could never be satiated while pushing the triad of perpetrator-victim-savior agenda, never realizing the damage I was doing. Yes, I had taken a huge turn in my life and was ready to go even deeper.

Sitting on D's bottom bunk, I crossed my legs and thanked The Universe in advance for a deep and safe journey and ate the dried cactus. It had a nasty, bitter taste, which I unsuccessfully tried to wash away with water.

I sat back and waited for close to an hour. Nothing.

At that point, I figured it was a scam or I'd been given too little. As if on cue, I started feeling something in my mouth and hands. It was a strong tingling that wanted to take me over. Thanks to John White Eagle's instructions, I knew I needed to surrender, to allow whatever came up to just be there. I lay down and opened my arms and breathed deeply.

The feeling got stronger by the minute. It became more and more uncomfortable in many ways, but, when I finally let go, there was a peace that I had only come close to in my meditations with D. The difference was, this peace went on, uninterrupted by my thoughts because I wasn't having any.

I'm not sure how long I stayed like that, but at some point, with my eyes closed, I began to see things happening in my head. But that isn't entirely accurate. It was like I wasn't really there, or here, I was somewhere else where the things I saw were actually happening. I wasn't hallucinating—that would imply what I was seeing didn't exist or wasn't there. Everything I experienced was here or there, just not in this here or there. What was clear was that this was a dimensional thing, beyond the grasp of my limited mind.

I found myself in what appeared to be outer space. Or inner space. The deep hollow sound of infinity and the visual perception of an endless galaxy were almost overwhelming. I had to get up on my knees and breath heavily, per John's instructions, in case things got too intense. Feeling the onset of nausea, I opened my eyes to look for the bucket, but I could only see the same thing that I saw when my eyes were closed.

I felt aimlessly around the mattress and finally found the bucket, shoved it under my face, and began to purge.

I could hear inmates in the distance bitching about the sounds of my retching, but I didn't care. They were a million miles away. I was far out in space, but also closer to myself than I'd ever been. All this while throwing up in a plastic bucket on a bunk in a state penitentiary.

I got to the point where nothing more was coming out, but I continued to gak away. John had told me this might happen, that there were negative energetic spirits that might have to come out and to just keep going. Of course, I didn't believe any of this at the time, but I swear I saw a kind of black fog come out of me with every dry heave.

Once it subsided, I fell into an even deeper level of peace and calmness within. It was as if the purging had cleansed me of all negativity. I lay back on the bed and opened my arms and hands in acceptance.

The galactic vision had become even stronger and more intense, and I had grown pretty okay with it. Out of nowhere, an enormous waterfall appeared. The more I looked at it, the more it seemed to get closer and bigger. Suddenly I could see that it was, in fact, two massive waterfalls side-by-side, flowing into each other at the bottom.

I focused in and saw something that absolutely blew my mind. "What the fuck?!" I yelled as I sprang to my knees, my face pressed against the mattress. What had originally appeared to be water gushing down the falls was, in fact, human beings. People, millions and millions of them, flowed constantly as if they were the water themselves. It was there, or at least I was somewhere watching it.

Now, as if floating in infinite space, watching humongous waterfalls flowing with humans wasn't enough, this vision was about to get even weirder.

I wasn't sure how much time had passed. In that state, time didn't seem to exist, correlating perfectly with what D says about time, it being a man-made construct. There I was in the middle of this incredible timeless event when out of nowhere I heard a hushed female voice loudly whisper, "Ground floor."

And just like that, it was over. I popped up and opened my eyes. I could see again. I checked my hands and legs, making sure everything was still there. I was panting and covered in sweat. I'm pretty sure I was in some kind of shock after being jolted back into my body so quickly. "What the fuck was that?" I said loudly.

"Shut the fuck up, Markland," an inmate from the adjoining cell yelled. I had no idea what time it was, but it must have been late.

I buried my head in my pillow, continuing to breathe heavily. "What, what, what, what the fuck was that?" I mumbled, trying to make sense of the most intense experience of my young life.

As I began to catch my breath, I calmed a little. *Ground floor. What the hell does that mean? And who said it?*

I remembered more of John White Eagle's advice. "If you get a vision, there will be a message in it. You need to find what it is, and you do that by processing your experience. Don't worry, it will always come. Just be there, present for it, so it can reveal itself."

The visuals were gone, but I could feel the medicine still working in me. I sat up, crossed my legs, and began to meditate. I was amazed at how easy it was to drop into the no-mind state. There I sat, in thoughtless peace, bringing the experience I'd just had into my consciousness. I contemplated the constant flowing of humans into and down the waterfall and what meaning they might have in reference to the words "ground floor."

It seemed like hours had gone by. I was lying on my back, staring at the underside of my own mattress on the top bunk, when it finally hit me. I shot up and frantically grabbed my notebook. I felt I had to write it down as if I could ever forget the message.

Very soon, an event brought about by the dark forces will take place and cause a vast number of human beings to flood toward and into their individual, transformational awakening. In turn, this will usher humanity into its new paradigm. We must be on the ground floor, creating the instrument that will accelerate this transition on a global level.

That was it. When or how this flood was going to happen or what the instrument was that we needed to create, I had no idea. But the confirmation that something big was on its way, as D had often spoken of, and that we were to play a major part in it was an incredible start.

DESTINY MANIFESTED

MARCUS

A large group of inmates was high-fiving outside the chow hall, crowding around the windows that looked over the yard.

"What's up, Vinny?" I asked. I was getting back into the swing of things at work. MJ had convinced me to take some vacation days. She said I needed to rest up for what was coming.

"Yo, I don't believe it, Officer Ogabi. This is just nuts."

"Move aside," I ordered, and a few inmates stepped away, giving me a view of something that I never thought I'd see and certainly would never forget. In the yard on the other side of the fence in the abandoned field was Dimitri, who, as far as I knew, was supposed to be locked up in solitary. But he wasn't alone. There was Wade Bowman and Harlan Smith, along with Jim Devic, Warden Shady, and the rest of his entourage.

The rush of tingling goosebumps overcame me. I watched the men continue to crowd the windows. I'd never seen them that happy before. *I wonder if they really get this.* Everything that Dimitri had talked about that day in the yard had magically worked, just like he said it would.

I wanted to call MJ and tell her the news but knew I had to wait until my break. I wondered how the call she made to the press was intertwined in all of this. The word "intention" kept ringing in my head, but who's or what's exactly? The intention was set by many that day in the yard and afterward with the ERP guys pushing it. But what was the force that carried it through? What organized all the different components that ultimately put together this complex puzzle? Did it even matter? What did matter was that it happened, and for the prisoners, it was nothing short of a miracle.

I knew Jim would have valuable information and wanted to hear it straight from him.

» » « «

We met for lunch in the program office just after I called MJ, who was thrilled to hear the news.

"Damn, boss. I didn't see that coming." I said, taking a seat. "I'm surprised you didn't give me a heads-up."

"I just found out about it two days ago," Jim replied. "There was no time to do anything but arrange the meeting out there with those directly involved in the first part of the project."

"First part?" I asked, beginning my fishing expedition.

"I wasn't in their meetings, but, from the looks of it, the kid negotiated a full-blown organic food production operation. Starting with planting crops and building a very large greenhouse. Down the line, we'll be moving into animal husbandry, sustainable water management, and who knows what else."

"The warden and Tanomeo met again, after the first one?"

"Yep. The warden called him back in about a week ago. Like I said, I wasn't there, but I guess the warden had some kind of epiphany because, well, Carlton's gonna have its own food."

Epiphany my ass.

"What about the kid staying in lockdown for a year if necessary?"

"It's over. And not just that." Jim said, gnawing on a piece of beef jerky.

"There's more?" I asked.

"Yep, and it's the part that puzzled me the most. The media's coming to do an exclusive piece on the ERP program. They're going to interview Tanomeo and the warden."

"What's so puzzling about that?"

Jim dipped his head down and whispered. "First off, Shady wasn't planning on exposing the stats to the media until we got closer to election day. And he sure the heck wasn't going to give any exclusives. He needed this out on all four networks as well as online. And he never planned to talk about ERP. It was just *his* stats that were gonna get the attention. Now he's got Tanomeo going on live TV to explain the whole program."

"Weird," I said, playing along as if I didn't know this was all MJ's doing.

"I'm really stumped on why he's including Tanomeo when he doesn't need to," Jim said. "Maybe he realized working together can be used to his advantage. He's got a thick head, so maybe it just took him all this time to figure it out."

Or maybe he got a call from the media threatening him to play ball or they'd find what they needed to know about this Dimitri guy on their own.

Jim went on, "It's like he's genuinely excited about it, talking about 'budget' this and 'the budget' that. He even mentioned morale as if it somehow mattered to him all of a sudden. At the end of the day, I think it's really just about him getting elected. Either way, it's still a good thing that it's happening, right?"

Jim had a point. Dirty politics aside, this was a positive development. "I bet you would've liked to have been a fly on the wall in his office for those meetings," I said.

Jim nodded and laughed, "I sure would have, buddy. Hey, do you mind picking him up from the back and escorting him to H-block at fifteen-hundred? I've got to meet with the facility manager and go over a bunch of farming stuff."

"Not a problem," I answered calmly. Inside, I was more than happy for the opportunity to walk with him a bit.

"No cuffs. Warden's orders."

» » « «

At three p.m. sharp I was signing Dimitri out of the hole. Up close I could see his beard had grown and he'd lost weight, but he was in high spirits as always.

"Hey, Officer Ogabi! How ya livin'? How'd you guys get along without me for all this time?" he joked as we walked down the corridor.

"We managed," I whispered. "The real question is, how did you do in there?"

"Honestly, it was glorious."

I knew it.

"The noise level there," he continued, "compared to mainline was night and day. I was able to get a lot of inner work done and dive deep into my meditation. How's Zach doing? I got the hit he needs to talk to me about something."

You got a hit?

"He seems to be doing all right. As a matter of fact, your whole gang was on cloud nine today after seeing you in the field with the warden. Hell, most of the prisoners seemed to get a kick out of it."

"I bet. For many, it was the first time they've witnessed conscious manifestation firsthand."

I purposely slowed the pace of our walk. "To be completely honest—"

He interrupted, "I know, Officer. It was the first time you've witnessed it as well. Pretty incredible, isn't it? To actually know that we can create anything we want. Blows you away, huh?"

"I'm still trying to figure out how all of this has happened so quickly," I said, wanting to say much more but unable to because of the guard/prisoner dynamic, which was wearing thin. I did throw out one question. "What did you mean when you said you got the hit that Zach needed to talk to you?"

"That one could take a bit to explain," Dimitri said. "I'll just say, we all have gifts. Some of us never know what those gifts are because they're buried deep under the muck of our lives. One of mine is the ability to tap into the energetic fields and thought patterns of others, especially those close to me. It's so complicated that even I don't understand it. Sometimes it happens when I'm not with the person, like a few days ago during a deep meditation, Zach showed up and it felt like he had something to tell me. We'll soon find out.

"The other type of hit I get is when I'm with someone. This one is more common because my senses are assisting. It's more empathic in nature. I can feel what another is feeling. I get a hit with you that's very specific."

"Really?" I said, surprised.

"It's that you want to say more than you say. You want to ask questions, make comments, and be a part of all of it, but you feel you can't because you are a guard at Carlton State Prison and I … we are prisoners. It's just because of the way our current so-called reality is set up that we appear divided."

Yes, you're right. The "hits" are real!

Part of me wanted to scream it out, but I couldn't. I just looked down at the concrete floor, reflecting on all the things I wanted to tell him but wouldn't. Like it was my spiritual girlfriend that made the call to the press that changed his whole situation. Then there was the act of treason I'd committed by divulging sensitive information to his sidekick, Zach.

"You might be onto something" was all I mustered.

He could see right through me, and he laughed at my lukewarm response. "Know this for now: Beyond this sham, this absurd act we are both playing separate parts in, I can see you and your struggle. I know who you are and what you really want. I get that you feel the need to play your role. Which, by the way, you are playing wonderfully. Also, know your support, albeit mostly energetic, is felt and appreciated. Thank you for that. You are included and a vital part of everything that is happening."

Mostly energetic? If you only knew.

He continued, "More than anything, brother, know this charade is a temporary one and will soon be over. You and I will walk side by side together. We will change everything."

He didn't speak another word for the rest of our walk. Nor did I, mainly because I couldn't. I was too choked up.

I'd felt like an outsider up until that moment. Now, I didn't have to feel that anymore. All I had to do was keep up my part in the absurd act as a guard at Carlton State Prison.

» » « «

The hoots and hollers were deafening. As we passed, the inmates came out of their cells to cheer him. Dimitri had become a hero. And not just to some. Judging from this welcome, I'd say most of the inmates were on his side.

He held his head up high, smiling and nodding to all of the men, careful not to leave any of them out. But as we passed through the dayroom, there was one group that wasn't cheering. Joaquin Flores and his right-hand man Ronny Ortiz Orozco, AKA Sleeper, sat on top of the table, surrounded by a few soldiers in chairs. The tension was palpable as we passed by. Dimitri felt it as well and just looked away from them. In prison, there's a deep conflict around power, and at that moment Dimitri had a lot of it. Before he was just a guy doing a good thing. Now he was *the* guy, and this threatened the leader of La Familia and shot-caller for all of Carlton more than anything had before.

We turned the corner, and there was Markland standing in the doorway, waiting to greet him with a huge smile.

"What up, bro!" he shouted as he grabbed Dimitri's roll and tossed it on his bunk. He reached out for the prison brug, prison-speak for brotherly hug.

"I'm good, brother. You've been holding it down, haven't you?" Dimitri asked, noticeably happy to see him.

I stood outside the cell and observed. This was one of those torturous moments where I just wanted to be one of them but couldn't.

"And you know this, D!" Zach exclaimed, pointing his finger at him. "Oh brother, I've got something I've been needing to tell you."

"I kinda figured you did," he said, turning to give me a wink. I just shook my head in disbelief.

Taking my leave, I said, "Hey, watch yourself out there. You know what I mean?" I nodded toward the dayroom.

"Thanks. Will do," he answered with a careless smile.

"How was it in there?" I heard Markland ask as I turned. "Not bad at all, man. I had a cockroach as a cellmate; we got pretty tight. With all of this new pull I seem to have, I was thinking I could get you a cell transfer and move him in here with me."

I glumly walked on, hearing them bust up laughing.

BEST LAID PLANS

ZACH

I didn't want to interrupt his silence, but I had to know if I'd made a mistake telling him about my experience. "Are you bent at me for taking the peyote, D?" I whispered.

He opened his eyes. "God, no. Don't be ridiculous, Zach. I'm trying to find the answer to the question you had in your download." He grabbed the paper I'd written on. "You wrote, 'The instrument that will accelerate the transition.' I'm checking if it's ready to come through. Let me do my thing." He closed his eyes and went back in, wherever "in" was.

This guy's a total trip.

I'd caught him up on a few things moments before. One was the sudden growth spurt of the program in spite of him being in solitary and how most of the members had and were using their own TAS mats. He really liked hearing that and picked up his own and held it next to his heart. It was odd to see how this raggedy mishmash of fabric touched him so deeply.

The last thing I updated him on was the notebooks and how Officer Ogabi stepped up and helped the cause by informing me of the cell toss. In turn, he gave me the rundown on the deal he struck with the warden behind closed doors. He said the warden wanted him to speak to the media about ERP and the support he received creating it. D said he felt he could say that but he wanted something in return. That was the day the Carlton Food Sustainability Project was born and all limitations on ERP lifted.

"It just came through, Zach," he said, clapping and laughing like someone who wasn't playing with a full deck. "Can you make those ... those ... you know?" He was making gestures with his hands.

"You okay? What are you talking about, D?"

"I've never been better. Those app things. Do you know how to make them?" He had an excited but serious look.

"Dude, what app things?"

He took a deep breath to calm himself and slow down. "Zach, can you create apps for phones? A simple yes or no will do."

What a question. "D, I'm what's known as a high-level maven in the arena of software engineering. Apps are a kind of child's play in my world, so I've never been interested in them. But to answer your question with complete clarity, fuck yes, I can write code for mobile apps."

He looked at me with a bright, mischievous grin and said, "That's what I thought you were going to say, Zachy my boy! I've got the answer to our mystery concerning the instrument.

"I've seen people talk to their cell phones and the phone talks back. I'm not talking about talking to another person. They talk and something speaks back that's not human but sounds like it."

"Yo, D, have you ever used a smartphone or even a computer before?"

"No, I haven't. My upbringing wasn't exactly like that. The only experience I had with phones was watching the boys on the corner use them. I wasn't really a part of their world."

"Why not?"

"I don't know, I never thought about it. Maybe because my mother was white or, even more likely, because I didn't talk and was *different*, I'm not sure, and it doesn't really matter now."

I wanted to drill him about his ethnicity, but he'd been vague in the past, so I just got back on point. "There are many systems, intelligent virtual assistants, where you ask something and get an answer. We set them up using NLP, natural language processing. It's a data bank that processes your question in real-time, recognizing not only your words but the inflections in your voice and other nuances. This data bank is constantly learning and growing as it's used more and more. It's pretty exciting, you know, with what's coming in with artificial intelligence. There are going to be advances that we can't even—"

"Slow down there, tech nerd. I just want to know if we can put what we're doing here in Carlton into app form." I waited for him to say more, but that was it. I stared, trying to figure out what he meant.

This is the first time I've felt sorry for him.

"You want to make an ERP app where teachings come through the smart-phone?" I asked with zero enthusiasm. "D, that kind of thing already exists. Whole libraries of videos people can go listen to on different teachings and stuff." I tried my best not to sound condescending.

He looked at me with a grin. "Is that all we do here with ERP, Zach?"

It didn't take long for the lightbulb to go on.

"Oh snap, I think I get it!" I pulled out an empty notepad and began taking notes as fast as he could speak. We lost the concept of time as we went back and forth with his brilliant idea, an idea that became both of ours as I added more and more. Behind the easy-to-use app would be a highly technical integrative system like nothing that ever existed. Difficult to build and code? Yes, but I knew I could do it once I was out of prison. What I didn't know was how we'd acquire the astronomical amount of content needed.

"There's something else." My tone had shifted toward seriousness. "What about the content?"

"The content?" he asked.

"Yeah, dude. We've got to have the sage guidance for many, many issues at several different levels. Where's that gonna come from?"

That same D grin, the one that, when you saw it, you knew he was already ten steps ahead, spread across his face. "You've already got it. The content is in the notebooks."

He was right. The notebooks carried countless personal issues that were dealt with successfully and logged.

"You gotta point, but how are we gonna get them outta here? First off, they're not technically ours; each one belongs to its corresponding inmate, and, in the past, we sent their books with them once they were released. Even if we kept them, prison rules say that we can't leave with them. Not that many, anyways."

"Don't worry about those details," he said. "The help will show up. You'll see."

"Okay, but we'll still need a lot more content once we're out of here. How's that gonna happen?"

His eyebrows scrunched while looking at me confusingly. He raised his hands in the air. "What am I, chopped liver or something?"

"Oh shit. We got you. Sorry, D. Of course you'll be able to come up with the needed content. But just know we are talking about a huge project here. A lot of work. No one has ever done anything like this."

"You do get that this is *the instrument,* don't you? It doesn't matter how much work it is. This is *it.*"

"When you say that this app is 'it,'" I said, making air quotes, "you mean the thing that's gonna change everything?"

"It's an app to start, Zach, but it will morph into something much bigger."

I thought of AI and its trajectory of rapid growth. The sky was literally the limit. This was the first time I imagined the possibility of a world being saved by technology rather than destroyed by it.

I nodded, "This *is* it, D. I can see that. Thank you."

"Thank *you*." He put his hand on my shoulder, and I got full-body chills. He saw the goosebumps on my arms and pointed. "This is what's called being in the flow, Zach. Truth bumps never lie. Let's keep it going, okay?"

The physical sensation, along with the rapid mental movement, affected my emotions as my eyes began to well up. "Yeah man, but I really don't understand this. A lot of ideas are coming very quickly. It's pretty trippy and awesome."

"This is the power of intention at work. Because you and I are both aligned in doing something for the greater good of many, The Universe is working with us. Get ready because this is just the beginning, amigo."

LIVE AT 5

MARCUS

"We are Live at 5 and this is Marianne Kelly. As you can see, we're here at Carlton State Penitentiary, where a new program has had quite an impact on the reduction of in-prison crime by aiding in the rehabilitation of prisoners. Warden Shady, maybe you could comment on the results Carlton's new program has had." The attractive news reporter looked to the warden, who sat across from her at one of the tables in the visiting area.

Carlton's new program?

"Thank you there, Marianne. Let me first say that I'm very appreciative of y'all coming out to talk to us about the unparalleled stats from one of our cellblocks. The test program we've implemented is called ERP, and currently we're seeing a thirty-two percent decline in overall crime a predicted thirty-five percent drop in the prisoner return rate."

The test program we've implemented?

My blood boiled as he rattled off statistics, the outcomes of a program he knew nothing about and had no part in creating. I wanted to speak up and say something, but I was just a guard guarding the members of the press, the warden, and his entourage from the potentially dangerous criminal, Dimitri Tanomeo, who sat peacefully at a table on the other side of the room. It was clear I was more bothered by the warden's blatant fraudulence than he was. He sat smiling, enjoying the interview.

"Thank you, Warden. According to our research, those remarkable statistics, albeit averaged out to a smaller scale, are the best in the nation," she pointed out. The warden perked up in his seat.

"Yes, Marianne. That's true, but I'd be remiss if I didn't point out that those stats and their ranking are not just representative of this year only. They beat out any stats in the history of any prison ever."

"That is phenomenal, Warden. Thank you for that clarification. What exactly does ERP stand for?"

The warden glanced over at Jim. I couldn't believe it. He'd forgotten. Or worse, he never knew. I, too, looked over at Jim, who was trying unsuccessfully to mouth the acronym.

"I say we leave some things for the man who teaches the program to talk to y'all about. I'm not one to hog all the air time. But I will say, come this November, I'd be much appreciative of the folks of this great state if they could remember my name at the ballot box. I want them to know that my promise, if I'm elected, is to bring the same level of improvement to this great state that I have here at Carlton."

"We are going to take a commercial break, and when we come back, we'll learn more about the program and how it works from the man who teaches it."

"And we are clear! Back in three on set," Phil, the producer, announced.

I could hear the news jingle in the background as Phil pulled off his headphones and laid them on the table next to me. I looked at the warden as he scolded Jim, probably for not reminding him what the acronym stood for.

How'd this guy ever become warden in the first place?

"Quickly, let's get set up in front of inmate Tanomeo," Phil ordered and the operation moved to Dimitri's table. He clipped a microphone onto Dimitri's shirt and tapped it. "Soundcheck please!"

"Hi," Dimitri said with a smile. Phil looked at him blankly, then back at the cameraman who gave him a thumbs up. Dimitri shrugged his shoulders.

Phil focused intently on Dimitri, "Just act natural and don't look into the camera directly. Talk to Marianne just like you would with anyone."

Easy for you to say.

At first, I wondered how Dimitri, a very young man who hadn't been close to a beautiful woman in a long time, would react. Marianne walked over and sat down in front of him. He smiled and said "Hi" again.

"Hi, I'm Marianne."

"I'm Dimitri. Nice to meet you. We watch you on TV in the dayroom."

"One minute out, quiet on set!" Phil shouted as a young woman approached the table to give Marianne's face and hair a last touch-up.

"That's nice. You ready, Dimitri?" she asked.

"I am," he replied with a huge smile, clearly liking the attention.

"Quiet!" Phil ordered before counting off, "Five, four, three, two, and ..."

"I'm here with inmate Dimitri Tanomeo, the teacher and creator of the ERP program, which has apparently helped several prisoners here at

Carlton. Dimitri, could you please start by telling us what ERP stands for and how it works?"

"Yes, but I'd like to first thank and acknowledge you for taking an interest in what's happening here at Carlton. This type of exposure around the positive things that happen in prison really helps support us all in so many ways." He closed his eyes, put his hand over his heart, and bowed his head.

"You are very welcome. Channel 5 is always interested in feel-good stories like this one."

He sat up straight and cleared his throat. "ERP stands for Early Release Program. As you can see, it's a play on words."

"Yes, I just heard a funny story from one of the guards about the first day."

"Well, we thought it was hilarious, Zach and I. But not everyone was laughing when they showed up and found it had nothing to do with actually getting out of here early. By the way, shout out to Zach Markland, my cell-mate and the organizing force behind ERP. None of this could've happened without him."

"Can you tell me what the Early Release Program is all about?"

"Marianne, what we are doing is basically using our time at Carlton to awaken to who we really are. But in order to do that, we must first discover what we are not. We have to release ourselves from the programming in our minds. The programming that ninety-nine percent of the population in our world is infected with. You see, there's a voice in our head that most of us think is us. It tells us things such as 'I can't,' 'that's just not possible,' or 'that's never going to happen for me.' All of this destroys possibility in so many areas, like being in a great relationship, living in abundance, co-existing in balance with nature—basically our contentment in general."

Marianne nodded. "I think I understand what you are saying. I could see how many of the men, if not most, here suffer from this programming, as you call it. That's probably what made them do whatever they did to get them into prison in the first place."

Dimitri looked her deep in the eyes and gave her one of his signature grins. The one where you know you've said something amusing to him but don't know what.

"Actually, Marianne, yes. That programming is what got us here, there's no doubt about it. But maybe you missed the part when I stated that ninety-nine percent of the global adult population is in the same predicament."

She paused. "I did hear that, Dimitri, but they're not in prison," she shot back with a condescending tone.

"Oh, but they are. All of them. They're in a different kind of prison. One that can be more difficult to leave. I speak of the prison that confines the mind. Lockdown twenty-four/seven, Marianne. And no one even knows they're in that prison because it's become so normal. This is what's at cause for all of the suffering in the world. You can only become free of it once you've identified that it exists and it is not your natural state. From there, you can begin to free yourself. That's why we call it ERP. These men, the ones in the program, are really doing the work. They are actually living life more than many on the outside in the so-called free world."

Phil gave Marianne the signal that they were going to a break.

"This is all very interesting, Dimitri, and I'd like to hear more. Let's take a quick break, and when we come back, we'll speak to one of the men who benefited from ERP and how it's changed his life."

"And we are out!" the producer announced as he yanked off his headphones. "I wasn't expecting that, Dimitri," he exclaimed, looking at the warden in obvious disappointment.

"I'm over here," Dimitri snapped, and Phil turned in surprise. "What were you expecting, and why were you expecting anything at all?" His voice had an authority not expected in an inmate.

"I don't know, but I wasn't expecting that. Can you just tone it down a bit?"

"Tone it down? I don't even know what that means," he replied with complete honesty.

"It means you don't attack Marianne."

"Attack Marianne? If that's what you call an attack—" Dimitri began.

"It's fine," Marianne said. "He's got a point if you think about it." Phil stared at her in disbelief before storming to the other side of the room where the third interview was being set up. Vinny, already seated, was eager to get started.

Vinny the Ham should really be his nickname.

Marianne leaned forward and spoke under her breath, "It's too bad for us on the outside who don't have ERP readily available. I guess we're going to be stuck with our programming forever."

Dimitri's head snapped up. "Oh, not at all. I hope I didn't give you the impression that ERP was the only way out. There are several different paths to liberation. Great books, powerful programs, amazing teachers. Too many to mention, actually. We could do a whole show just on that. If you want, I can make a list for you," he offered.

She blushed, reaching over to touch his hand, "I'd like that, Dimitri."

I took a few steps away, continuing to listen.

"Tell me, what's a guy like you going to do when you get out of here?"

Phil's hand went up. "Marianne, we need you over here. We're on in two!"

"I'm coming," she answered.

Dimitri moved forward in his chair. "Put me back on and ask me that. You'll be glad you did, I promise." He grinned.

"Uh, I'm not sure if Phil will go for that," she replied.

"Tell him we talked and I'm going to clean up the attack, so to speak. Show that we're all good. I also want to thank the warden and the others that are in the original ERP group."

She nodded. "I'm intrigued. I'll see what I can do."

Now it was just him and me on the far end of the visiting area.

"How'd I do, Officer Ogabi?" he asked slyly.

I stared soberly at the wall on the other side of the room and murmured, "Pretty powerful stuff there, kid. Not sure I'd label it an attack per se."

Dimitri leaned back and whispered, "She's a big girl. She can handle it."

"Yeah, but can the people out there watching handle it?"

He smiled. "Oh, them? Yeah, they're all ready, they just don't know it yet."

"You really think so?"

"That's why I'm here."

"That's why you're here?" I asked.

"To show them there's something to be ready for," he replied.

» » « «

After wrapping up the interview with Vinny, the crew started working around Dimitri's table again.

"We're gonna close it up with Dimitri in three minutes!" Phil announced. He leaned over the table, closer to Dimitri. "Marianne mentioned you wanted to thank some people. That's great. So, again, tone it down and remember, don't look at the camera."

Dimitri ignored Phil's words, instead flashing phony gang signs at Vinny, who was cracking up. Marianne made her way back to the table, and Dimitri got serious, well, as serious as he could get, given the circumstances.

"You ready?" Marianne asked with a teasing smile.

"Always," he shot back.

"Quiet on set. Back in five, four, three, two ..."

"We just spoke with one of the inmates, Vincent Palermo, and it sounds like ERP has really helped him. He mentioned that you have others teaching this as well."

"Yes, a total of seven of us are working within ERP, including myself."

"Sounds like you hold to the adage 'a great teacher creates more teachers, not students.'"

He nodded, "I've actually said that myself. The idea is that once we become clear, we need to help others do the same. When they're ready, of course."

"That's an interesting point. How many people do you think are ready for this?"

"I was just talking to a dear friend about this." He shot me a quick glance. His secret acknowledgment of me as a dear friend sent shivers down my spine. "He asked me the same thing, and do you know what I told him, Marianne?"

"What did you tell him?"

He looked her dead in the eyes. "I told him they are all ready. Every single person on this planet. They just don't know there's something to be ready for ... yet."

"Yet?"

"That's correct, Marianne. I say 'yet' because things are about to get very uncomfortable in this world of ours. Uncomfortable in a way that you cannot imagine, forcing everyone into that state of readiness. What I speak of is already on its way, created and sent by those who, up until now, have held power over our physical existence. This will be the beginning of a desperate, last-ditch effort to hold on to control as it continues to slip through their crooked fingers, thanks to a global population that's soon to be fed up with listening to their lies. Fed up with living in the shadows of darkness."

Marianne stared silently, visibly shaken by his words. Phil, however, waved his hands frantically, surely regretting having Dimitri on camera a second time.

Dimitri went on to praise the rest of the group as well as the participants who had the courage to step outside the norm and take the necessary steps to better their situation. He thanked the warden for his help and involvement, then went on to make it clear that everything ERP taught was available in several different formats, including books by living and dead authors, videos, courses, and even in the base teachings of most religions. "Minus the scare tactics," he noted.

"That's good to hear," Marianne said with a nervous smile. "That means I don't need to figure out how to break into this place just to get some of these teachings."

"No, but it would be great if you came back and checked in on us again. We're starting our own prison farm-to-table food program, and it might be something worth reporting on once it's up and running. I'll buy you dinner. How does that sound?" Dimitri joked.

"It's a date, Dimitri. I'll have the warden notify us when it's up and running. But now I've got one more question for you."

I glanced at the warden, and he was smiling, happy that it had all ended positively.

"You're a young man," Marianne said sweetly, "in the prime of his life. You'll be out in a few years. What's next for Dimitri Tanomeo?"

He looked down at his hands and began to softly bounce the tips of his fingers together. A silence filled the room. Even our minds became quiet as if the whole universe was waiting for his answer.

"Well, Marianne," he responded before turning and looking directly into the camera. "I'm going to change everything" His eyes shot over to me then back to the camera. He smiled. "I mean, what else is there to do, right?"

No one knew exactly what to do next. Finally, Phil began making overt hand gestures around his neck for Marianne to end the interview.

"Well, there you have it. We need more men like you in this world, Dimitri Tanomeo. Thank you for sharing with us today."

"I believe I can speak for all of us here when I say we truly appreciate your visit to Carlton," he responded kindly.

"Thank you and good luck with all of this," she said, and he gave her a slight nod.

"And we are clear!" Phil shouted. He was immediately at the table, beginning to disassemble the sound equipment.

"Jesus kid, you've got a set on you, don't you?" Phil uttered, shaking his head while angrily unclipping the mic from Dimitri's collar.

"Why do you say that, Phil?" Dimitri shot back.

"I told you to not look into the camera and you did. And what was that rant about some conspiracy theory of yours? What did you mean by you're going to change everything?" Phil inquired in a demeaning tone. "No one person can change everything. Especially not a convict."

Dimitri's signature grin began to grow, and I knew what was coming.

Phil went on, "I don't mean to burst your bubble, but do you know what that means in the real world? To be an ex-con?"

"Please go on, Phil."

"All of humanity is messed up, and it's going to be like that forever. It's just the way it is. It's always been that way," he continued to roll up the wires around the room while shaking his head.

"That's it? Really?" Dimitri asked, chuckling.

"I just thought you should know because you've been isolated, so you're not aware of how the world really works. You need to worry about getting a job when you get out and making a life for yourself. You know, so you stay out of trouble. Those in power, as you put it, they know what's best for us. They're taking care of us. Don't rock the boat. Things are fine just the way they are."

Dimitri waited, making sure he was finished.

"Now, I'm gonna say a few things, Phil," he calmly remarked, sitting up straighter than before. "You asked what I meant when I said 'change everything.' I'm going to tell you. This messed-up humanity you speak of, the one we shouldn't rock the boat with, is at a very interesting place right now. We've co-created a situation wherein this thing we call life, this beautiful gift, is not worth living for most. Consequently, the planet is nearly uninhabitable, and it's getting worse every day. All of this was done by design, crafted by your handlers, Phil. Those who, according to you, are taking care of us.

"We all let this happen. We are all responsible for co-creating this situation. But do you know who's responsible for keeping us in bondage?" Phil said nothing. He just stared at Dimitri as he stood up from his chair, towering over Phil. "Do you?"

Phil slowly shook his head. That's when I, not wanting such a glorious moment to be interrupted, moved to block the others' view of the table. I took it a bit further by crossing my arms and smiling at Phil. This was the first time I felt like I was doing something with Dimitri for the cause, and it felt great.

"You are, Phil. You and the others that currently hold the majority position. Those who speak like you, think like you, and act like you are expediting our demise. But you see, that's where I come in. As you and yours do what you do to prevent our transition to the Light, I will be there to expose every-thing." Dimitri began to laugh. "You were right in saying no one person can change everything. But I will be the one who gathers the others and starts the movement that will. This will eventually cause you and your people, the holdouts, to fall into the more fitting position of the new minority."

Phil was frozen. I could swear his skin was turning white.

"While at this moment you and others like you may hold the keys, I advise you to not get too comfy. Because that negative vibration, the one that's been in the driver's seat of humanity for far too long, is about to dissolve into the ether. So, enjoy it while it lasts, amigo." Dimitri sat back in his chair.

Phil had gone from predator to prey in just minutes.

"Well, I don't actually—" he began to say, scrambling to grab the rest of his gear.

"You know, I'm not finished yet, Phil." Dimitri said calmly, in a voice that was more friendly than the one I'd just heard. "You asked me if I knew what it meant to be an ex-con in the *real world.* My answer is yes. It means simply that I spent some time in this place and nothing else. You see, I, as well as the other men in ERP, refuse to identify with being ex-cons, meaning we know that's not *what* we really are. I am no more an ex-con than you are a news producer. We are both much more than those things, Phil. You just don't know it, yet."

Goosebumps broke out across my arms. They'd become a common thing for me by this point. I looked and Phil had the same on his arms. That meant, while Dimitri's delivery was harsh, it had an effect. What was even more surprising, I could see Phil was affected just like I was. It meant we had something very profound in common. It meant he wasn't the monster I'd made him out to be. He was only playing the monster role, just like the role I played as a guard.

I thought about all the parts I'd play throughout my life. *Whose side am I on?* There were times in the past, both recent and distant, when I felt like

Phil. But I'd found my way back home to my truth, hearing Dimitri and even MJ speak from that place of empowerment.

I realized there were no sides. I could see, in some strange way, I was both Phil and Dimitri, which meant that I was everyone and they were me. Separation didn't actually exist other than in our minds.

Phil squeaked, "What I meant to—"

"Save your breath. You don't have to backpedal now." Dimitri's tone had gotten softer, more compassionate. "I know what it's like to feel helpless, and I am aware that many feel that way. But a shift is coming. Remember this day."

Dimitri then turned and called Vinny over, leaving a stunned Phil to contemplate alone as he slowly rolled mic cords.

I was strolling toward the far side of the room when Marianne appeared at my side. "I noticed your journal. I love the hummingbird on it."

"You don't think it's a bit too girly, do you?"

She giggled. "Not at all. The hummingbird symbol has a lot of different meanings. At least that's what I hear."

Lady, you have no idea. "I actually believe that's true," I answered.

"What do you write in it?"

That's kind of personal. "I haven't put anything in it yet. My daughter told me I needed to get one, so I did."

"Kids can show us a thing or two sometimes," she said.

"I have a question for you. How is it that you just let him say what he said? Going against what your producer wanted."

She looked at me blankly. It was almost as if she didn't know herself.

"All I can say is, I think the world needs more dialogues with Dimitri. Does that make sense?"

Dialogues with Dimitri. I like that.

"It does," I answered.

She gave me a wink and pointed to my journal. "I'm sure you'll get inspired by something, Officer ..." She moved her head to see my name tag. "M. Ogabi."

A look shot across her face. "Where do I know that name from?" she asked.

Please don't put it together.

Her eyes widened and her mouth fell open. She looked from me to Dimitri then back to me. "You're the same one who ...." She was too polite to finish her sentence.

"That would be me, ma'am," I said coyly, hoping she would end it with that.

"I actually covered the story," she said, finally composing herself. "It was big news. How is it that you're here? What are the odds?"

"A really big coincidence, I guess."

She shook her finger at me as Jim motioned for me to get Dimitri up and moving.

"Nice meeting you, Marianne," I said with a smile.

"Same," she said, returning the smile before rejoining her news team.

I hovered near Dimitri's table. "Come on. It's time for you and Vinny to get back to the block," I said. Dimitri stood up and stretched. He looked fresh.

Just another day prepping to change the world for this guy.

As we passed Marianne, she looked at Dimitri, smiled, and waved good-bye. He did the same.

As Vinny, Dimitri, and I walked down the corridor toward H-block, Dimitri whispered to me, "I did okay on that one, don't you think, boss?"

He was obviously referring to the tongue lashing he'd given the producer. "Pretty harsh. That one could actually be called an attack."

He began to whistle. The melody was familiar but an odd one, even for him.

"He's a big boy. He can handle it," he said and proceeded with the jingle.

"Are you really whistling Kumbaya, man?" I asked.

"I am."

A FAMILY AFFAIR

ZACH

It was a full house in the H-block dayroom as we watched the Live at 5 segment on Carlton. The inmates booed and threw stuff at the TV when the warden came on and a few cheered for Vinny, but they completely lost it during D's part. Everything he'd done for the inmates, now he was giving shout-outs to all the boys on the core team and acknowledging the others in the program. This cemented him into hero status forever.

I liked hearing my name mentioned on TV for something positive for once, but it did bring an unexpected surprise: a visit from my twin sister.

Tess Markland, the semi-famous socialite, made the trip from LA for the first and only time since my incarceration. She was the only family member who'd come to visit me, and although I was stoked to see her, I was dying to know why. You see, Tess only cared about Tess. So, whatever this was about, I knew it was gonna be entertaining at the very least.

She sat at the farthest table in the visiting room, her legs crossed and hands tightly clasped in her lap while staring at the grimy tabletop in front of her. She was purposely frozen. She didn't want to stir up and breathe in more molecules than necessary. Her blue designer sweatsuit, Buscemi sneakers, and her perfectly ponytailed hair made her stand out like, well, a rich girl.

"Hey, Tess, what's up? I see you dressed down for the visit."

"What's shakin', Zachster?" she said in her casual tone as if I hadn't been locked away for all this time. "I wanted to fit in, so I figured what the hey."

She's so out of touch with reality. I couldn't help but giggle.

"To what do I owe this visit? Is there a fashion show in the area or a fundraiser for anorexic baby seals or something like that?" I snarked.

"No, silly. Can't I just visit my younger Z-bro?"

"I'm your younger brother by like fifteen minutes, Tess. And don't call me that. Seriously, I've been here for a good minute, and you've never come to visit. Why now?"

"Well, I saw the video online where your friend there, Dimitri Tanamoo, mentioned your name, and it just made me think, I need to fly over and see my Z-bro in prison as soon as possible." Then she whispered, "BTW, Zach, this place is revolting."

"It's supposed to be. That's why they call it prison. And his name is pronounced Tan-oh-mayo and—"

"Well, what kind of name is that? And where is he?" she interrupted, looking around the visiting room. "What's his nationality? Part black? Is he single? Is he on Instagram?"

I glanced up at the clock. *Is this almost over?* "Tess, I don't know, his name is his name. He's in cellblock H right now. He's a mix, and yes, he's single. I'm not even gonna answer the last one."

"Isn't that just like you, Zach. You need to learn to share a little more."

My poor sister is absolutely nuts. "Share? Share what?"

"Resources. Like this hunk of a human you're in here with who seems to think very highly of you. Does he know about your big sister?" she winked.

"Is there something wrong with you, Tess?" I asked with all the sincerity that existed in my being. Then I realized what she had just said. "Wait. You said you saw the video online?"

"Yeah. The podunk Live at 5 video got picked up nationally on GNN and then went viral on YouTube. Some of our friends must have seen it and posted it. You and I both got tagged, so it's really out there. I reposted it and have gotten thousands of likes so far. The end, where he says he's gonna change everything is the bomb. I edited it so he repeats it like ten times in a GIF. He's such the specimen, Zach."

Wanting to change the subject, I asked "How's mom and dad?"

She sighed. "Well, mommy wanted to come, but you know how she is. She wouldn't have made it past the front gate, so she sends her love. And with daddy, well, you know the story there. You really teed him off with your last stunt. He won't even mention your name anymore."

In the past, when she took pleasure in saying something like that, it would have made me upset. But now, I felt different about it. I felt sorry for her. But in a caring way, not a condescending one. It did hurt to hear my father didn't want anything to do with me, though.

"I have to reach out to him at some point and heal this stuff."

She made a fake sad face. "Ah, Zachster. I wouldn't bother. I'm pretty sure that ship's sailed."

I sat there, stunned at her level of coldness. But I had an idea. "You know, Tess, there's this different guy here that I think you'd get along great with."

"I'll tell you right now, I'm not interested in the Italiano who was also interviewed. That whole Italian thing went out years ago with the Sopranos."

I shook my head. "His name is Officer Tanas. He's a guard here. You two were made for each other, I'm tellin' ya."

"Oh, Zachy, gross," she chuckled. "Tess Markland with a prison guard. I don't think so. Now, that D-boy of yours, that would be a whole different story. Can you see it? The bad boy ex-prisoner turned healer, together with the Markland socialite. Now there's a power couple."

I refused to comment. "What else, Tess? The clock is ticking."

She talked about some of our mutual friends, most of it negative drama stuff. I was surprised to see I wasn't interested in hearing about it. I actually felt repulsed, whereas before I'd get caught right up in it. Something in me had really shifted.

My growth also allowed me to see a distinction between an ERP inmate's drama and Tess's. The inmates were there to do something about it, which somehow made it feel okay. But with Tess, it was just pure dirty gossip. Admittedly, in the past, hearing it would've made me feel better about my own life, but now I was able to observe that only my lowest self would want to hear about the downfall or struggles of a fellow human being. It made me feel even more for my sister who was so completely lost.

"Let's talk about something else, Tess." I interrupted her mid-sentence, which immediately made her uncomfortable. She started squirming, not sure what to do or say.

"You're looking for your phone, aren't you?" I asked.

"That's silly. Those SOB's made me put it in a locker with my bag before I came in."

But it wasn't silly. It was exactly what she was doing. She was hooked on social media and would turn to her phone every time things got uncomfortable. I noticed it because that's exactly what I used to do. One of the very few pros of being locked up, besides what I was getting from D, was ridding myself of that horrible addiction that has most people imprisoned, just in a different way.

"Yes, let's talk about something else," she said. The tension in her voice told me her lower-self was in control and felt threatened by a deeper conversation. I decided not to push. She wasn't ready, so I held out my palm, welcoming her to shift the topic.

"Have you thought about where you're going or what you'll do when you get out? Daddy sold your apartment in the city. I'm sure you saw that coming."

No, I didn't actually. I literally had nowhere to go. I'm sure I could crash at a few of my friends' places, but that would get old fast. I also wouldn't have the privacy or space I'd need to work on the app.

"I'm not sure where I'll go," I answered. "Dimitri and I will be working on a project together, but I've still gotta figure out a bunch of stuff."

Her ears perked up. "What kind of project, dear brother? Do tell."

I hesitated, but I had to tell someone about it. "It's a tech thing. It's ambitious but it's real. I'd tell you about it, but I should keep it on the DL."

"Now, Zachary Michael Markland, I can keep it on the DL. I promise."

From what I knew of her, when she used my full name she was usually sincere. I swore her to secrecy before explaining the rough idea of what we were planning, the cost, and work involved.

"What do you think?" I asked. Judging by her look, she seemed to genuinely like it.

"I love it. I'm in," she stated.

Oh shit.

"What do you mean you're in? This is mine and D's thing. There's nowhere for you to be in."

"Think about it. You and D—BTW, I love that you call him that—need me. I've got a place for you guys to live and work, right on the beach. I can fund *our* tech project with my own money, something you've never had really." She made another fake sad face.

Ouch. I didn't want to admit she was right about that last thing, but she was. She had the beach house in Malibu all to herself. My father had signed it over to her, his way of giving me a dig when she graduated and I didn't. But, most importantly, Tess had money. A lot of it. She'd started her own skincare line years before and had done very well. And as far as two ex-cons getting venture capital funding goes, well … let's just say we'd be turned down during the first round of due diligence. Tess knew all this.

"First off, you can't say 'our' project. It's just mine and D's. You're not even into this stuff."

"What stuff?" she asked.

"You see. Right there. I just told you what it was." I shook my head. "Self-transformation. Awakening."

"Oh, but I am into this stuff," she said. "I know mindfulness. I went to a talk about it in Venice with Taylor and Devin."

I looked again at the clock.

"I've got a secret," she continued, "that will prove I am indeed into it."

"What?" I asked.

She brought her foot up to the table and pulled back her pant leg to reveal a small, half dollar size tattoo on her ankle.

"It's the Om, the universal symbol for yoga. It represents the vibration that permeates the cosmos and brings us into the deep feeling of clarity and bliss."

My head fell into my hands. "Where did you get that?"

"True Tattoo. They're rated a perfect five on Yelp. It's where Jenna—"

"No," I snarled. "The definition of the yoga symbol. You said it like you were reading off a card."

"I actually did get it off a card that I picked up at the yoga studio. I go twice a week. I'm telling you, Zach, I'm perfect for the team."

I had to take a minute to process that my own sister had become a full-blown member of the pseudo-spiritual society, and for whatever reason, I was finding it very offensive. Like she had become a poser of the worst kind. This brought into question whether there had ever been a time when she wasn't a poser? She'd always been faking it in some way. So the bigger question I had to ask was why this one was bothering me so much?

Because you are identifying with this whole spiritual thing.

I was coming from a place of "how dare she," which, when examined, revealed a feeling of being threatened inside of myself. I could see it was my lower-self, my ego, trying to protect its position. With all the practice I'd had, I was getting better at seeing my own slip-ups, my own moments of forgetfulness and hypocrisy, and was able to drop it right there.

I looked at my sister and felt compassion for her. She had no idea she was already whole, so she continued to search, just as most others did.

"Let me talk to Dimitri about this. It would be nice to hit the ground running once I get out, and you've got what it takes to make that happen."

She smiled condescendingly with that 'I knew you'd cave' look.

"Don't," I shot back. "I didn't say you were in. And you have to promise one thing."

"Anything," she answered.

"That you won't get psycho on us. That's *if* we even do something together."

"I have no idea what you are talking about, Zach."

"Yes, you do. Just promise. And I'm not saying you're in. There are a million reasons not to go this route. Either way, I need to run it by my partner."

"I promise, Z-bro."

"I told you not to call me—"

"Visiting hours are now over," the guard announced. "All visitors please exit through the white door on the other side of the room. Inmates will remain seated until instructed to leave."

"Okay then. I'll call you when I know something."

"Perfecto," she said.

I laughed as she used her sleeve to push her chair back into the table.

"Oh, one more thing, Zach. Your D boy's right about what he said about something coming. Daddy's been making moves. Big contrarian moves. I guess he got 'the call,' if you know what I mean. He told me to get ready because it's gonna be much bigger than the last one they pulled off when we were kids. So I followed his lead and liquidated pretty much everything and parked it somewhere else for now. All that is to say, your big sister is about to have a hell of a payday. Cha-ching, cha-ching." She pumped her fist as she walked toward the exit.

"Wait. What are you talking about?"

She hid her mouth and whispered loudly, "You know. They're going to crash the market again, Daddy even flew to our 'survival island,'" she made air quotes with her fingers, "to make sure it's ready. Mommy said at least you'll be safe in prison, but after seeing this place, I'm not sure I agree. Love and light to you both. Make sure you tell D I said that. Namaste, Z-bro."

As she walked out the large white double doors, back to her life, a life that was very different from mine, I realized she'd left me hanging just like she'd done a thousand times before.

» » « «

When I got back to the cell, I told D about the visit with my sister. I gave him the rundown: her offering the funding for our tech start-up and how difficult it might be for us to raise money, considering our situation.

"When it comes to the business and technical side of this thing," D said, "I'd prefer to just leave that up to you. I have no experience with any of it. As far as I'm concerned, I can't see any reason not to do this with her."

"That's because you don't know her, D. She's a very different type of person."

"Aren't we all, Zach?"

"Yeah, but she can get crazy at times. I've seen it."

"Again, we can all get crazy at times, no?" he said calmly.

"She's sort of jumped on the pseudo-spiritual bandwagon. She's speaking that language, wearing the clothes, and even got a tattoo, but she's not doing the work."

He pointed at me. "You told me about this sort of trend that's going around. The fake boho thing right?"

"Exactly. Tess is now officially part of the craze."

"Tess is experiencing her own inauthenticity without even knowing it is part of her spiritual journey. Maybe that's where she'll hit her bottom—in her hypocrisy, her falseness. It will just be another opportunity for her to come back home. None of this is a reason to exclude her. You remember what I always say about this kind of thing, dontcha? If they are asking, we must take them with us ..." He put his hand out, asking me to finish his mantra.

I mumbled, "... no matter what that looks like."

"That's right. Either way, it doesn't sound like something that could get too much in the way."

If anyone can find a way to get in the way, it's Tess.

"So, what then?" I asked.

"You make the decision. I'm good with whatever." He returned to the book he was reading.

I was afraid you were gonna say that.

"She told me something else that I think you need to hear." He put his book down. "It appears, through his connections, my father found out the global financial market will soon be brought down, and it's gonna be bad."

"Your father has connections that would tell him before it happens?" D asked.

"My father is one of the richest men on the planet. He's connected in ways that I don't even understand." D picked up his book again. "You don't seem surprised."

"I'm not surprised," he answered, not looking up. "I've known it's been coming for some time now."

"I'm gonna take a shot in the dark here. Your knowing about this thing, does it have anything to do with those moments when you talk in Espanol with your dead grandmother?" I felt really lame asking, but he'd been having those conversations more and more lately.

He looked up and smiled. "Yes and no. Yes, it's coming through at those moments but not with my dead grandmother."

"You call her Nana, so I just figured. Are you ready to tell me more about that yet?"

He closed his book and rubbed his face in contemplation. "No, not really. Only that, like I said before, it's guidance. Also, what's coming has something to do with a sickness or something like that."

A sickness?! "Tess didn't mention a sickness. Maybe they're not related."

"Oh, they're related alright, amigo." he laughed. "We just have different feeds notifying us so we can ramp up our work, personal and collective."

I left it there. There were pressing issues at hand, and my trying to decode the mind of Dimitri wasn't one of them.

"Speaking of work, there is something we need to figure out, D."

"What's that?"

"In order for me to get all the logged information from the notebooks out of Carlton, I'm gonna need either a digital camera or a smartphone. There's just no other way."

Dimitri thought about it for a moment and nodded, "That makes sense. How do we make it happen?"

"This idea might be a bit out there, but remember how Officer Ogabi gave me a heads-up about the cell toss?" I said.

"I see where you're going, Zach. And while that was commendable of him, this might be too much to ask. He's no Tanas."

"No, he's not, but he does seem to be on our team," I countered.

"I could ask him and see what he says. It doesn't feel like the most fun thing to do, but it might be the best solution we've got."

He was staring at the wall in front of him. He wasn't comfortable with the idea, but he was the only one that could ask for such a thing.

I grinned, "Like you always say, D, it is what it is."

THE BIG ASK

MARCUS

"Let's watch it again! Let's watch it again!" Hope shouted, hitting replay on the YouTube video.

It was great having the two most important people in my life there together to watch the news clip online. Out of the three of us, I couldn't say who was happiest about the whole thing. MJ wanted to see the results of her phone call, and, with this being the first time she'd ever seen Dimitri, she was pretty blown away by his powerful presence. I was just happy to be a part of it, even if I was only a guard in the background shots. Then there was Hope, who'd switch it to slow-motion every time I was shown. She was proud to see me on the news. Like MJ, she, too, was impressed by Dimitri and began to ask questions.

"I like Dimitri, Daddy. He's cool."

"He is, sweetie. He's a pretty good guy too. He's funny and makes people laugh, just like you."

"Is he your friend?" she innocently asked.

"Well, he is in a way, but it's complicated."

"Why?"

"Because Dimitri is an inmate and I'm a guard. It creates a certain dynamic that makes it hard to be good friends. Does that make sense?"

She sighed, shook her head, and said, "Sounds like that programming thing he was talking about with the reporter."

A perfect silence filled the room as I spun around to look at MJ. She was already staring at me, nodding with her eyebrows raised. I turned back to Hope, not knowing exactly what to say next.

"You're right, Hope. Ultimately, that's what it is. So you understood what Dimitri was saying?" I asked, feeling my emotions creep up.

"I think so," she answered. "Am I programmed like he said most people are?"

I didn't want to scare her and looked at MJ for guidance. She shrugged her shoulders and smiled.

"He was talking about adults mostly, sweetie."

"But I don't want to be programmed when I'm older," she said with fear in her voice.

My eyes immediately welled up. I didn't know how to answer her, but luckily, MJ did.

"You won't be, Hope. Not to the extent Dimitri was talking about. Just by knowing you don't want that helps you to avoid it in the future."

"But how will I know when I need to avoid it?" Hope asked.

"You will know because you are growing up with something called awareness. On top of that, as your father becomes more aware, he will be able to guide you."

"You mean like Dimitri helps the guys in jail?"

"Just like that," MJ answered.

"You hear that, Daddy? you're going to be a hero just like Dimitri."

MJ cleared her throat. "Your daddy's already a hero."

I wiped my eyes and turned back to her. Hope gave me a smile that will be locked in my memory for the rest of my days.

"That's true, Daddy. You are my hero! Thank you!"

She sprang forward and hugged me with everything she had. This was one of those moments that made being a father the best thing in the world. We fell back on the carpet and laughed. I looked at MJ, gave her a wink, and mouthed "thank you."

"Let's watch it again, now!" Hope shouted as she jumped up. I kissed her on the forehead as MJ stood to see me off to work.

As I drove, the silence filled my head, and I was at peace. There were only good thoughts, like marveling at how a nine-year-old could comprehend the things she heard during the interview. I was also impressed at how MJ could love me, even though I wasn't anywhere near her level of awareness. This was only possible because she could see I was on my way. I thought about Dimitri, how he'd touched my daughter's heart the way he did, which had, in turn, touched mine.

I was struck by an overwhelming feeling of gratitude that would ultimately help me to help him in a way I never thought I could.

» » « «

"How's it going there, inmate Tanomeo?" I asked, popping my head into cell number 111.

"It is all good, Officer. How are you this fine day?"

I took a step forward, just in the doorway. "Same here. I've got no complaints," I responded awkwardly with no official excuse for being there. What made matters worse was the odd silence that went on for at least a half a minute.

"I'd ask you to sit down, but I don't think you would," Dimitri laughed.

"You know I would, but I can't, right?"

He responded by simply nodding his head. I realized my statement was the most human thing I'd said to him since my arrival at Carlton.

"Thank you for that, Officer," he responded, putting his hand to his chest.

"I came here to say something," I said, as he sat up straight in his bunk and put down his book.

"Okay?"

I was about to say something even more human, which made my hands sweat, so I put them in my pockets.

"Well, my daughter, Hope, saw your video and—"

"Our video," he interrupted with a huge smile, pointing at me. "You were in there too, Officer. I saw youuuuu."

Oh my god, he's just like a little kid. I was getting frustrated seeing how much it took just to get to this point of vulnerability.

"You'd get along with Hope, you know that? Mentally you guys are about the same age."

"Well, I can't wait to meet her then," he shot back, not missing a beat, unaffected or possibly unaware of my dig. "All of us need to return to being children again because that's what we are."

"I heard you say once that we are just children in big bodies and our salvation lies in us getting back to that childlike state of playing in the world."

"You remembered that? Impressive," Dimitri said, nodding.

"It's easier said than done," I responded with a smile.

"Only if you say that it's easier said than done, can it be that, or remain that way for you."

Here we go again, another Dimitri teaching.

"Are there moments," Dimitri asked, "when you let yourself say otherwise?"

I remembered, just hours earlier, I was rolling around on the floor with

Hope like a little kid. It felt good to just play, but he was talking about taking it to a whole other level.

"Yeah, yeah. I've heard you say all of this, I'm just not there yet. Maybe, I'll never be."

"That would be a real shame, Officer," he said.

"Let me get back to what I wanted to say. She really liked you and what you said. She's so young, and it was like she got your message somehow. It brought us together in a nice way. Not that we're not already close, it was just a really great moment. So I want to say thank you for all you do, for everyone. Even me."

He had closed his eyes, taking it all in. He slowly opened them again and said, "Thank you for that. You just made my day." He put his hand over his heart and bowed.

His mood immediately shifted to one of excitement. "Isn't it amazing how the new generation is coming in, ready to take over the new earth? It always astounds me to hear things like that because it confirms that the Divine Consciousness is at work in every way. It can be our proof that even with what the darkness has thrown at us and will throw at us in the future, together we will overcome it all and be victorious. Why else would these rainbow children be born into the world right now with a completely differ-ent genetic makeup? No wonder you named her Hope."

I had to take a moment for that one. MJ had mentioned something about this before but never went as deep into it as he just had.

"Tell Hope I said hello and to keep up the great work," he said.

"My girlfriend, MJ, is also a big supporter of yours. She's a meditation teacher in town and had heard about ERP before we'd even met."

"That's kinda wild."

"That's what I thought. She even talks like you, believes the same stuff and all."

"Well, send my love to MJ and thank her for the support as well."

Time to get moving.

"I should move on, I've—"

"Wait! Just a second," he said quietly, moving closer to me. "I need to ask you to do us a favor. It's a big one." His serious tone caused me to take a half step back.

"Normally, I'd say anything, you name it," I said, "but seeing how you are in here and I'm a guard, let's just start with, what's the favor?"

He nodded back, "Fair enough, boss." He prompted me to check outside and I did.

"Go ahead," I said.

"Zach and I will be creating a piece of technology that will help people, just as we are doing here in prison. It's a big thing. Global big. Zach's going to work on it when he gets out."

He paused just long enough for me to become aware that I was still envious of their bond.

I crossed my arms. "So, what does that have to do with me?" My bitter tone caught his attention.

"Well," he said slowly. "In order for us to make this happen, Zach will need all of the data that's been hand recorded in each one of the notebooks for each prisoner."

"Why doesn't he just walk out with them?"

"Firstly, there are too many to carry, and secondly, there are forces here working against us, so we can't risk them getting confiscated on a technicality. By the way, the origin of these forces is the same as the ones that will do their best to stifle the truth from the masses in the future. But I digress. Basically, we need to get the data that's in the books onto a digital format and get the data out of here."

I suddenly got very cold, hoping he wasn't about to ask me to do what it sounded like he was about to ask me to do. What he'd said about the origin of forces didn't even register, that's how nervous I was.

He looked at me directly and whispered coyly, "We need a tiny digital camera."

I closed my eyes. *I wish you hadn't said that.* I wanted to be a part of it all, to help where I could, but this could cost me not only my job but also put me on the other side of the cell bars.

I looked out the doorway and when I turned back he was staring at me, waiting for a response. *What have you gotten yourself into here, Marcus?* I felt trapped. As much as I didn't want to, I had no choice but to play tough with him.

"What are you talking about? And who the hell do you think you are talking to?" I hissed.

He leaned toward me, closer than he'd ever been before, and whispered,

"I'm talking to the guy who gave us the heads up on the cells being tossed. The guy who enabled us to save those valuable notebooks, ones that will continue to help others in the future. Thank you for that."

He continued, "I'm not sure about this one, but I might also be talking to the guy who had something to do with the media finding out about ERP, which in turn, forced the warden to change his tune. This move not only saved the program, but it also inadvertently brought a garden and crops to Carlton. If you had a hand in that, thank you.

"This is a favor I'm asking for. You can say no. But it is something we need. And I want you to know that it is not easy for me to ask this, just as I'm sure it's not easy for you to hear it." He sat down on his bunk and slid back against the wall. He calmly looked at the wall in front of him waiting for me to make the next move.

"How would I even get something like that in here?" I closed my eyes and dropped my head, knowing that by asking I was basically saying I was in.

"Zach looked into it and figured out how our favorite guard is smuggling in drugs and other contraband." I knew who he was talking about, making it all the worse.

"How does bringing him up *help* me?"

He looked at me confused for a moment before catching on.

"Come on. You can't compare yourself to Tanas. What he does promotes a low vibration and comes from his fear of lack. What we are doing is helping raise the vibration in everyone who is touched by our work. This is born from love and love only. All you have to do is ask yourself where you operate from when making your decision."

He explained how I could use a large, disposable coffee cup, making a false bottom in it. When I put my bag through the scanner coming in, I could pass my cup around it. This is exactly what I did when I came in every morning to work with the "Best Dad In The World" traveler's mug Hope had given me for Christmas. So, technically, I knew it could work.

What am I thinking? I couldn't believe I was actually considering breaking the law to this extent. "Are you insane, Tanomeo?" I whispered. "What happens if they want to look in the cup or make me put it through the machine? It's a felony. It's nothing like me warning you guys about the cell toss. Do you want me to end up in here with you? Do you think I signed up for this?"

He looked at me curiously as if he was trying to put something together in his head. "In the order of your questions," he said quietly. "One, yes maybe. Depends on who you ask. Two, according to Zach's research, the chances of that happening are very slim. Three, while I'd love to have more time with you, no, I think you are better off on the outside. And in answer to the last question, yes, in a way you did. Otherwise, you wouldn't be here."

He smiled, nodded once, and got serious again. "Listen, I know it's a heavy request and a decision only you can make. But let me leave you with one thought. If you look back on everything that has happened in your life, all of the synchronicities, or whatever you want to call them, since you and I met that night in the alley, you might see how it all led up to this moment. I don't know much about your world, but it sure seems like we've been put together here for some reason, wouldn't you say?"

I'd come to this same conclusion several times as well. "One could look at it that way," I reluctantly answered.

He went on to tell me there was an alignment at this level when doing something that is good for the whole and it comes with a shroud of protection. He shifted over to the back of the bunk, grabbing his book, sending the message our meeting was over. There was a lot to think about, but as I got to the doorway, it was clear that, for him, my mind was already made up.

"Zach says he needs a Yaeg minicam and a couple of memory cards. I don't know what that is but I imagine you do. He said you can find it in 'The Amazon' or something like that." he whispered casually, opening his book as I stood there, my mouth half-opened.

"Jesus, kid. For you, it's like ordering a pizza, isn't it? Phil, the producer, was right. You really do have some balls on you."

In the Amazon. Now I've heard it all.

I chuckled as I walked out into the corridor. "Thank you, Officer," echoed behind me.

IT IS WHAT IT IS

MARCUS

During the next two weeks, things really got done at Carlton. The greenhouses were fully functioning with vegetables and greens already planted. The library had been restocked with hundreds of books, most suggested by Dimitri and related to self-development and transformation. The warden was doing great in the polls, mostly due to the ERP program, which he had actually nothing to do with.

"At the end of the day, it's all a bunch of political crapola, buddy," Jim said. "The warden is doing all this for his own gain. He's even bringing back the Channel 5 people to show off the food program. I guess Tanomeo's suggestion to that reporter paid off, for the warden anyways."

I held my fork in the air while chewing the last bite of my pie. "I'm with you, Jim. Sometimes I really get disgusted, but if you think about it, does it really matter? The stats are improving, which means less crime and violence for us to deal with, and on top of it all, the guys will be getting good organic food. That can't be all bad."

"And for that reason and that reason alone, I'm good with it, Marcus."

And for your career advancement if the warden wins.

I was getting used to seeing the different faces people would wear depending on the situation. Through the ERP sessions I'd eavesdropped on, I was able to let go of a lot of my judgment. Of course, that didn't mean I didn't recognize it when it was staring me in the face. All I had to do was see the hypocrisy and inauthenticity in my own life, and that would snap me out of any bullshit I was telling myself about another. Who was I to talk anyway? I'd lied, cheated, leaked information to inmates, and was about to smuggle contraband into a state prison that I'd vowed loyalty to. It didn't matter that what I was doing was for a supposed good or not, I'd sullied my word. Pointing my finger at another, even if the motives behind their actions were different from mine, was the last thing I needed to be doing.

"Cheers to that," I said as I raised up my juice box and touched it to his can of soda.

As I walked through the corridors, heading back to H-block, I wondered what Jim would think if he knew what I was planning. Hell, if he'd known what I'd already done, I'd have been gone months ago. He liked Dimitri and what he was about, and of course, he could see right through the warden. But, for guys like Jim, the law was the law, especially with him being smack-dab in the middle of a political game.

» » « «

After spending two days pacing back and forth in front of the small camera and the modified Monty's coffee cup on the kitchen table, the moment of truth was approaching. The plan was I'd spend the night at MJ's, and she would have lukewarm coffee in a thermos for me to pour into an altered cup just before I got out of my car at Carlton. It looked easy on paper, but I was struggling and MJ could sense it.

"There are two forces at work here, dear one. Dimitri and the other six are working within The Light. That's Light with a capital L. This is the force that is appearing as the opposite of darkness, evil, fear, lower vibrational frequency, or whatever one chooses to call it. If you, if *we* help them, we will be working for what appears to be positive, good, and of the highest vibrational frequency. What comes with that is aid from the unseen realms. I know I just got a bit woo-woo there, but you can handle it." She patted my knee.

Confused, I shook my head. "Dimitri said something similar about there being a shield of protection around this whole thing, but I don't know."

"I do know," MJ said, "and I see you entering the prison safe and sound with the coffee cup in hand. I'm feeling what it feels like right now, to be the version of myself that feels so happy to receive your call telling me your mission was accomplished"

"I have no idea how I could see what you are seeing, but I'm glad at least one of us does," I said, nervously laughing.

"You'll be fine. Just use the same technique Dimitri and the others used to get better food in prison. It's the same thing, I just said it in a different way."

That evening, after we'd gone to bed, I did my best to feel what it felt like to have gotten in unscathed. I imagined myself inside the prison, walking quickly to the men's locker area to change my clothes and dismantle the inside of the cup, removing the camera and placing it into my front pocket. The more I did it the more it worked. I felt happy that I'd made it in, even though I was still in bed.

» » « «

Once I parked the car, I poured the coffee into the cup, sealed the plastic lid, and made my way toward the entrance. The same rookie that was there every Monday was working the X-ray scanner as I placed my bag on the conveyor and put my coffee on top of the machine like I had done every time I came into Carlton. I walked through the metal detector and reached for the cup when he grabbed it.

"What happened to the mug you usually have?" he asked, holding the altered cup in his hand, inspecting it.

"Oh, my Best Dad in the World cup? I lost it over the weekend. But don't tell my daughter. That would be the end of me," I said jokingly, feeling a knot form in my stomach.

"This coffee isn't hot," he said, looking closely at the lid.

I hadn't thought of a comeback to that one. I put my shaking hands in my pockets, which I'm sure made me look even more suspicious. My mouth dried up and everything went into slow motion. I imagined the worst, him finding the camera and radioing in for back-up. I glanced down and saw a book next to his chair: *The Secret Lives of Hummingbirds*.

You've got to be kidding.

"It's my teeth. I've just had work done and they're sensitive," I said to him while opening my mouth and pointing to them. Can't have anything that's too cold or too hot. It sucks but I need the caffeine!"

He shrugged and handed me the cup. No sooner had I walked away and let out a suppressed sigh of relief than I heard him yell, "Hey, Ogabi."

Oh shit. The blood drained from my head, again. I felt dizzy but still managed to turn.

"That does suck. I'm not sure what I'd do if I couldn't have a cold beer," he said with a snort.

"Have one for me then, will ya," I shouted, the blood returning to my head. I turned and walked quickly toward the locker room, breathing heavily.

My fingers shook as I spun the combination on my locker door. When I opened it, I found a note from Jim to go to his office once I arrived. *Really? Now?* I threw on my uniform and realized I needed to dump the coffee in order to get the camera out. There were a couple of COs in the bathroom so I couldn't just pour it anywhere. I had no choice but to gulp it down. I carefully dismantled the false bottom and pulled out the camera, neatly wrapped into a plastic bag. I left the cup and lid in my locker, tucked the camera into my front jacket pocket, and headed off to Jim's office.

"Come in, Marcus," Jim said. "Mind shutting the door?"

"What's up, Jim?"

"Pull up a chair." He motioned for me to sit close. I could tell whatever he had to say was important and probably not good. "You know how you and I talk about things here at Carlton?" Jim asked.

"I think so," I answered, not really knowing.

"Just to be clear, we talk about things that happen here. The behind-the-scenes stuff, right?"

"Oh yeah. I know what you mean."

"So, I can trust you when we talk about these things, can't I, buddy? To keep it just between us."

"Of course. It all stays in the vault with me, Jim."

"Thank you, buddy, I just needed to confirm before I tell you the latest. I'm grateful to have someone to talk to about these things."

I hesitated to ask, but what the hell. We'd gone this far. "What happened Jim?" I asked.

"This morning the warden got a call from our illustrious governor, W.H. Stages. He caught wind that the media's coming back to do a piece on the food program since they've been promoting it all week on TV."

Jim looked around to make sure no one was listening. He dipped his head down and I lowered mine as well. "He told Shady he needed to tone ERP way down, even if that meant closing it up. He said everything Tanomeo was doing would eventually put them, and us, out of business. He wants the stats to go back to where they were before, ASAP. 'The worse the stats, the more funding.' Those were his words, again, according to the warden."

"What?" I began to feel a coldness throughout my body.

"Yep, do you remember Charlie Clemans from the original ERP group and how he was trained by Tanomeo as one of the teachers?"

"Always liked that guy. He got a tough break. Twenty-eight years for that shooting didn't make much sense. But he made something of himself. He got transferred up to Fieldstat Correctional, right?"

"Yep. And do you know what he did once he got there?"

"No clue, Jim, but I've got a feeling you're gonna tell me."

"He started his own ERP program."

"Really?" I stammered. "So there's an ERP in another prison now?"

"Buddy, there are ERPs in five different prisons in two states. It's spreading like a virus, and the governor, along with the other wardens, are trying to figure out what actions are needed to curb the spread. The infraction stats are dropping in each of the prisons just like they did here. In all, there's close to a thousand inmates enrolled in the program nationwide."

The coldness in my body immediately vanished, replaced by goose-bumps—a lot of them. I sat with my mouth open in a happy state of shock.

"There's more," Jim went on. "You wanna hear it?" I could only slowly nod at this point. "Get this. You know Femington State Prison?"

I moved back in my chair. "The largest women's prison in the state. What about it?"

He just stared at me until it landed.

"No?!" I exclaimed.

"Yep."

"How?"

"That I'm not sure of, but the warden said they suspect that one of the ERP teachers at Fieldstat who got released was hooked up with the gal who started the program at FSP. They're trying to trace it, but it looks like it was passed, the curriculum that is, through visits and phone conversations. Do you know what they call it there at FSP?"

"Call it? The program? I don't know." I thought about it for a moment. "WERP?" I asked laughing.

"That's exactly what they call it. How'd you know?"

"Well, you know, with the 'W' for women, it's really not that cryptic, Jim." He chuckled as I put my hands on his desk and dropped my head down. My emotions were all over the place. I was so happy but pissed at the same time. "I'm amazed by all this. I know prison systems are ultimately for-profit entities, but I guess I never knew how deep the corruption went."

"I agree. If it wasn't for Shady needing Governor Stages to be on his side to win, we probably wouldn't be having this conversation. Who knows." He scratched his head, contemplating something.

"What do you mean 'who knows'? That is what this is all about, right?"

"That's the thing. It seems to go deeper than that. According to Shady, the governor got 'the call.' That's the term he used, and I have no idea what it means or who the call was from. I don't like to ask too many questions when he's on a roll like he was. I just let him spill his guts. What I do know is someone didn't like what Tanomeo said on camera that day."

"What do you mean?" I asked, suspecting there could be more to this.

"After that call, the governor got really serious about stopping the upcoming interview. He tried his damnedest to have Shady cancel it."

"All of this because of a few words from a prisoner?"

"Yep. But in the end, the warden convinced him that, with as close as we are to the very hyped interview, it would be best to just coerce Tanomeo into playing ball. The governor agreed but made the warden promise to control Tanomeo's words completely."

I shook my head, "Forcibly tone down ERP and control Tanomeo's words. I'm not sure that's even possible. How's the warden planning to do it?"

"I have no idea, but if he wants to be governor, he'll have to figure out a way. He's in a tricky position, between the media, Governor Stages, and Tanomeo."

"But why with Tanomeo? He could just not have him there at the interview, right?"

"The warden already committed to him being there. Haven't you seen the plug on Channel 5?"

I didn't really know how to say the next words to another man. "I don't have a TV right now," I said, looking down at my hands.

He looked at me with genuine concern and asked in a serious tone, "What do you mean you don't have a TV, Marcus?"

There was a part of me that wanted to tell him about all the things that went away since meeting MJ, but I just bit my tongue. There was no way he'd understand. "It's a long story," was all I said.

He paused for a moment, either trying to figure it out or imagining what it'd be like to live without a TV. Finally, he said, "Oh, well, I'm sorry about that, buddy. Anyway, they're beefing up the meal thing with Tanomeo. Remember, he joked with Marianne about buying her dinner at the end of the interview?"

It was starting to come together. "If Tanomeo gets wind of this, he'll divulge it to the media on live TV and that could threaten Warden Shady's chance of winning the election."

Jim shook his head while pointing his pen at me. "No. It wouldn't threaten his chances, it would destroy them. Shady's whole campaign is riding on Stages' recommendation and those stats, and even if the stats fall due to ERP's dismantlement they won't show up until after the election. He wins either way. If Shady pulls away in his commitment to the program, Tanomeo, using the press, will have a field day with it. If Shady goes the other way, against the wishes of the governor, he'll lose his support. And the governor wants a clear confirmation that ERP has been contained and is in the process of being dismantled and eventually eradicated. Shady's walking a very thin line. His plan is to have a talk with Tanomeo and get him on his side just before the interview."

"This all sounds so unbelievable," I said.

"There's more. I really struggled with whether or not to share this part with you." I moved closer as he hesitated.

"We're in this deep, Jim. We might as well go all in, right?" I said with a chuckle. It was one of those moments when, if a place called hell actually did exist, I knew there was a space reserved for me there.

"In addition to smashing ERP, Governor Stages ordered the warden to dismantle the food program in its entirety before he leaves Carlton. He told Shady he could tell the public after he was elected, that it was due to permitting oversights and there were health complications caused by something in the ground where the food is grown. All of it lies. He told the warden that he needs to confuse the public with misinformation. He even said the media could help if necessary."

Jim looked around and whispered, "Just to be clear, we are actually going to tear down the greenhouses and all, Marcus. No matter what happens."

What I felt at the moment is hard to describe. I'd liken it to how I would feel if someone threatened Hope. I could feel my blood pumping through my body as I clenched my fists.

"Did the warden really tell you all this, Jim?"

"That's word for word, buddy. He wasn't happy about any of it either. I guess he just had to tell someone, and I'm the closest to him. He trusts me. Hey, it's kind of like me with you, if you think about it." Jim paused, "But you're not going to …"

I couldn't hear him anymore. I was livid.

"I'm going to the bathroom real quick," I said blankly.

"Did you hear what I said?" Jim asked.

"I did. I'll be right back." I got up and walked quickly out of his office and into the men's room where I paced. I honestly can't even mention the thoughts I had at the moment about these men, Tanas included.

Calm down, Marcus. Let this be the bottom right now.

I looked at myself in the mirror and splashed cold water on my face, breathing deeply. I began to observe those thoughts, the first step in confirming that they weren't my own.

I could see the mental movie playing. Men were literally dismantling the greenhouses and breaking apart the soil boxes while a tractor destroyed the crops. I saw the inmates looking down from the window where we'd first witnessed the project get underway. Their hearts crushed, their dreams gone, everything they'd learned from Dimitri immediately forgotten. That's the moment I heard a voice shout in my head.

"Watch yourself when you are creating a reality that doesn't even exist! Ask yourself if this is the version you choose to embody into the physical realm of existence because that is exactly what you are doing!"

Those were the words Dimitri yelled out in one of his sessions in the chapel. I began to laugh as I dried my face.

"This shit's long from over, Marcus," I said to my reflection. "Anything can still happen."

» » « «

The patting of my own back would come to an end as I entered the cell-block area. The stress of smuggling the camera had returned knowing that I still needed to hand it over to one of the two cellmates. My plan was to do a walk-by first. I knew enough to drop it with only one of them present, that way if anything happened it would be my word against just one of theirs.

As I passed by, I could see I'd gotten lucky. Zach was alone in his bunk listening to music, air DJing with his headphones on. I continued down the line, doing my routine glances in each cell, most of them empty as the majority of the inmates spent their time in the dayroom at this hour. When I got to the end, I turned around and made my way back. I glanced around and stepped into cell 111. "Hey, Markland. Turn it off," I said, bumping his foot with my knuckles.

"What's up, Officer?"

"What's up, you ask? This place is a mess, get your shoes off the middle of the floor and straighten this shit up!"

He jumped down from the bunk with a surprised look. I stood above his shoes and quickly dropped the camera into one of them. I kicked it softly with my foot and said, "This place is a pigsty, Markland. Is this how your parents raised you?"

He looked in the shoe and joined the performance.

"Sorry about that, Officer Ogabi. I'm picking up some of my celly's bad habits. I'm pretty sure he actually was raised in a pigsty." He grabbed the shoes and put them under the bed and began to fold the shirts on top of it.

I continued, "Well, Markland, if you don't want to be written up next time, I suggest you pay more attention to the tidiness of your space." I was so nervous, I couldn't tell if I was overdoing it or not, especially with the load of caffeine that was hitting me. I took a deep breath, looked again at the door, and whispered, "I need to tell you something quickly, so listen up."

He continued folding while stealthily moving his head in my direction. I fired off everything Jim had told me, leaving nothing out. They'd need every bit of it to figure out how to play out the situation. "Did you get that, Markland?"

He nodded and I could see that some of the life had left his eyes. "Fucking politics," he whispered. "It's like that cure for cancer, you know. There's one out there, but will never be brought to market because there's too much money in cancer, too many jobs. This is the same and it's bullshit. Everything we've worked for, all of it, for nothing."

"I don't know about all that, but you might want to relay what I just said to your cellmate." I secretly took pleasure in knowing that I might be more of an optimist than Zach, even with all the work he'd done with 'the master.'

"I will, thanks," he answered with a look of concern, maybe not so much for the program but for more selfish reasons. He was one of those inmates that had a lot of fear around danger.

I stepped toward the door, turned again to face him, and shouted, "Just get this mess cleaned up!"

"I will. It won't happen again, Officer!" he said loudly as I walked out.

Before turning the corner, I stopped and took several deep breaths in an attempt to expel my guilt. I'd just betrayed my job, my friend Jim, my word, and, I'm sure some might say, my country.

I was in a mental paradox as the little voice in my head fought to make me feel guilty by questioning my actions. With the last deep breath, I decided I would stand up straight, walk forward, and do the job I'd been hired to do by corrupt men who'd also been hired to do theirs by others like them. At the same time, I would continue the treachery, knowing it was part of a bigger picture, a grander plan, one that might someday take down the corrupted system I worked for. As that little voice chimed in again, attempting to confuse me, I called on the louder, bigger one, the voice that truly represented me, to step forward and firmly state "it is what it is."

KNOW YOUR ENEMY

ZACH

"What a dickhead, right D?" I had just filled him in on our newest obstacles and hindrances originating from corruption, rooted deep in all forms of modern politics and greed.

"To be fair, Zach, we don't know exactly what he's going through."

"What do you mean, what he's going through? What about what we're going through and all the work we've done here? All of it's now at risk."

"We weren't there for his discussion with Governor Stages, but what we do know is that both of them are doing the best they can with the tools they have in their limited toolbox."

There, he said it. True to form. Always seeing things from the other's perspective, which, at times, really pissed me off. He referred to it as living in a state of compassion. I called it being a weak-ass pushover.

"At the same time," D went on, "this is really valuable information. Just so I understand, Officer Ogabi told you all of this and brought in the camera?" We had now stopped in the corridor on our way to chow.

"Straight up, D. He got us a couple of memory cards too. I'm gonna start taking the shots tomorrow. Robert's gonna help. He's gonna have the door while I snap the shots. It's gonna take some time to get them all logged, but we'll make it happen."

We began to walk again. I pulled my head close and whispered, "You've gotta figure out how you're gonna play this out with the warden. He'll be calling you in soon. The stakes are high on this one, D."

"I know. Let's not forget there's an opportunity in this as well. There always is. I've just got to check in and receive the guidance," he said quietly, with confidence. He put his hand on my shoulder and smiled. "Are we going to take a few *selfers* of ourselves while we've got this camera?"

I cracked up, "That's what I'm talkin' about, D! History's being made here at Carlton State Penitentiary. They're *selfies* by the way. And some shots of us with the boys, for sure." His energy had a way of pulling me back in, no matter how down I was.

"Prisoner number 52066, Dimitri Tanomeo, please present yourself to the Program Office." The voice boomed from the loudspeaker. "Inmate Tanomeo to the Program Office."

"Shit, D. That was fast. You can eat at warp speed and then go," I said as we walked up to the line.

"Yo, Tanomeo, I heard them call you over the loudspeaker," Vinny yelled from the front of the line. "Yous can take my place. I'll go to the back."

"Go, D. I'll catch you later," I said as he made his way toward Vinny.

"Bullshit, Tanomeo!" Tanas yelled from the back of the hall. "Get your ass to Admin. What part of 'present yourself' did you not understand?"

"Another dickhead," I whispered to D as he passed on his way toward the exit.

"Intermittent fasting, Zach. It's a good thing," he said, chuckling while walking out the door.

» » « «

When he returned to our cell later, he looked like he'd gone through some heavy shit.

"Damn, that took a minute, D. What happened?"

"It was the warden after all," he said.

"What did he want?"

"Mainly he wants to be the next governor and apparently will stop at nothing to get there." There was a seriousness in his eyes. "And I do mean nothing, Zach."

"Sit down, bro." I said. He took a seat on his mattress while I sat on the floor in front of him.

"I went in there and kind of played stupid," D said, "just to feel him out. In the beginning, it stayed pretty civil. He told me that I needed to cut our ERP meetings way down and that we couldn't use the public areas to meet anymore. At first, he blamed it on paperwork, bureaucratic stuff. I knew that it was all bullcaca. He said we can do what we want in our cells, but we have to keep it to two people max."

"That kills the program right there. How are we gonna spread the message of personal liberation with that kind of forced isolation?" I asked, realizing the full brunt of what was happening.

"I'm sure that's the idea, Zach. But there's more. He told me when the news crew comes back to re-interview me, he'd appreciate it if I wouldn't mention any of this or go off on any rants like last time. He wants to work on exactly what I'm going to say in front of the camera, and, because I'm a positive guy, we should say only positive, approved things. His words. He did say if I did that for him, he'd build a bigger library and extend the food growing area beyond the six acres we are currently using."

"We know that's bullshit after what Officer Ogabi told me."

"He doesn't know that we know that, so I just let him run with his lies for a while. When he was done, he asked me what I thought about his offer."

"Did you tell him to stick it up his ass?"

"You know me better than that. I actually felt bad for the old guy. I could see he was struggling. But, at the same time, I couldn't just jump on board. So I told him I'd have to think about it all."

"What's there to think about? That would have pissed me off so much. I would've told him to fuck off right then and there."

"Maybe that's why I'm in the position I'm in, navigating this big ship through the rough waters. I've seen you say things when you get angry. How's that worked out for you in the past?"

I smirked and nodded my head. "Yeah, yeah, D. I've heard this before. Just let me do me and you do you. Just steer us in the right direction, will ya?"

"Have I let us down yet?"

"True dat," I said.

"At one point," he continued, "he actually leveled with me and said there were outside forces that wanted our thing brought way, way down. He said he has to comply, and while things are going to become very restricted, if I help him he'll promise to lift the restrictions little by little until we get back to what he called 'a new norm.'"

I stopped him. "That part right there the governor's obviously not in on because he wants our thing gone, permanently. The warden is just bullshitting you to get you to work with him?"

"It looks that way. I still feel he's not loving any of this and just got himself boxed in a corner. Because of the inauthentic life he's been living, he probably feels he has no choice but to play dirty."

"What do you think he meant by 'new norm'?" I asked, finding it all really fucking hard to believe.

"I can tell you what it really means, even beyond what he's probably aware of."

He cleared his throat and looked at me in the eyes. "It means they are planning to break us with tactics that have been used throughout the ages. They are going to isolate us, silence us, turn us against each other, and, when we've had all we can stand, just before we really lose it, they'll return with a new norm."

I was getting it. "The *new norm* being a still more restricted life than we have right now, right? That's fucking evil, D!" I exclaimed. "So life in Carlton, which was never all that great to begin with, will never be the same once they roll this thing out, and there's just nothing we can do about that, right?" I asked, almost instantly regretting it. It seems I'd forgotten who I was talking to.

A big-ass smile came over his face. "That's where you have more work to do, *amigo mio.*"

"Sorry. What's your plan though, D?"

He looked at me confused. "Plan? Oh, I don't have one of those," he chuckled. "I just know that we are all on a hero's journey. That means there is always not only the possibility but probability that we come out on the other side of whatever the antagonist throws at us." He pointed at me. "Remember what I always say we have to do in order for this to happen?"

"How could I forget?" I whined. It's not that I didn't like his mantras; it's just that I got tired of repeating them like we had to in the sessions.

He rubbed his hands together. "Let's say it together, Zach."

"Yeah," I nodded while secretly rolling my eyes.

We chanted in unison. "I choose to be the hero of this incredible game that I have not only chosen to play but have created at will. I welcome all the bullcaca that is thrown my way, for I have designed my gameboard with the paradoxically perfect hurdles that, while appear to be hindering me, are actually guiding me to the finish line."

God, I hope no one heard us. I got up to look out the door; all was good.

"Just to start, Zach," he began.

Oh god, there's more.

"Let's feel what it feels like to be on that other side as we stand in the place of knowing the good things we want are there in the realm of the already accomplished. By doing this, we pave the way for the magic to happen as the mind and heart join together and create whatever needs to be created in order to ensure this outcome. From that place, the *plan* will show up when it's needed."

I know what's coming next.

"And what makes this so powerful?" he asked.

"Yeah, D, I know."

We chanted again together. "When two or more are gathered together."

"So, here's the not-so-great part," he said, lowering his tone.

"Oh no. There's more?"

"When I didn't jump on board with the warden, he got nasty with me," D said.

"What do you mean by nasty?"

"He reminded me that there was just over a week until the news crew would be here and said, 'Boy, might I suggest you take this time to reflect on what's really important to you. I hear y'alls' names might be on a piece o' paper. Looks like yo' little program be gettin' in the way of someone's profits. Sure would be a shame if somethin' happened to y'all, if ya get my drift. On the contrary, I'd be more than happy to have Officer Tanas make sure you boys stay real safe 'til the interview, as well as after. Like I said before, if we can do this together, I'll do what I can to get you an early parole hearing. What you think about that, son?'" D settled back against the wall.

For the first time, since the Earl incident, I was paralyzed with fear. "Sorry for asking this, D, but did he say 'y'all' or did he say *your* name was on a piece of paper?"

D shrugged. "He said 'y'all.' As in, you and me both." He nodded at me. "And he also said 'you boys,' which is plural, and—"

"Yeah, I get it. You can stop now." I was already in panic mode. "Fuck. Everything was going good. It's like we've been protected this whole time or something," I said, shaking my head. "I don't want to live like this again!"

"Then don't," he said calmly in the midst of my hysteria. I took a breath to slow my mind.

"A while back you mentioned you felt something with Joaquin Flores," I said. "Is that who you think is putting out this hit?"

He nodded. "If you think about it, it makes all the sense in the world. Just consider the number of men who no longer use or gamble, not to mention the other compulsive activities La Familia controls. I'd say we've taken a substantial bite out of their profit."

"We? This is your thing. You started it." I put my hands over my face. I knew I was being spineless, but I couldn't help it.

"Technically we started this thing together, remember? They could just come after me; there is that possibility. I'm sure I'm seen as the leader. Does that help?"

The question stopped me dead in my tracks. "No, bro. I don't want anything to happen to you. Sorry, I'm just losing my shit here. How can you be so mellow when we're facing death? I don't know why you didn't just agree to the warden's requests right there on the spot. Why can't you just play ball? There's still time to go back and accept his offer."

He just stared at me with a blank look on his face.

"Zach, you just told me that I should have told him to eff off, remember?"

Did I say that?

"No, what I said, D, was that's what *I* would have said. But *you*, as the captain, should have accepted, maybe. That would have been better, right?" My cowardliness had no boundaries at this point.

"Zach, are you coachable right now?" He'd asked this in the past. It meant he was getting ready to bring down some heavy truth.

I rubbed my face and gave it a few light slaps. "Yeah, go ahead. Lay it on me."

"Do you remember what I've taught you about those two emotions that pretty much run the show?" he asked.

I knew where he was going, but I really didn't want to go with him. But D was D, and I was his captive audience, so I dove in. "It's either fear or love. And, yes, I'm in a state of fear right now, I admit it."

"Thanks for owning that. Remember how I went over that it's natural for the human animal to have fear? It's a mechanism that was installed in us way back in the beginning and for good reason. We needed it back then. But, as you and I both know, the modern human mind hasn't got the memo yet."

"Memo?"

"The one that says, 'Attention user. You can put the fear away for the most part. Your chances of being eaten by a lion are nearly zero. You've made it.'"

I chuckled. "I guess I haven't got the memo yet, have I?"

"You got the memo alright. Living with me in this cell all this time, and doing the work we've done with others ... you've gotten it several times. You just haven't integrated it into your current reality."

"But how do I do that? I know staying in fight-or-flight mode when there is no immediate threat is damaging to me in many ways. I don't like the way it feels in my body, and that's a great indicator that I need to shift something within myself."

"Dang, look at Zach! Checking in with the body and all. I'm proud of you, amigo."

The praise made me loosen up a bit.

"Let's go back to love and fear and its relationship to light and dark," D said.

"I know this part," I said excitedly. "Love is to fear, what light is to darkness. You showed that to me in one of your books under your bunk. I know we can't just wish or force fear away."

"We can't, so let's shine the light of love right now by doing your work. I've told you the work you do on yourself is never-ending. What you are feeling with this current situation is a signal that there's more to do."

He got in my face. "Where are we right now, Zach?"

I looked up and around. "We're in our cell at Carlton."

"Are we alive, you and I, right now at this moment in our cell at Carlton?"

"Yeah. Right now at this moment, we are alive, I know."

He reminded me that this moment is perfect, right now, this second, because that's the only one that ever really occurs. Any stress or anxiety I bring in is on me. I was invited to choose to stay right there with him, in the now. Of course, I could certainly choose to remain in an imagined future or the nonexistent remembered past where I will continue to suffer.

He'd said this so many times before, and with the help of meditation and watching my thoughts, I'd been able to hang there, in the now, for long stretches at a time. But today was different.

"I get it," I said. "I really do. But with your way, it's like we're ignoring the danger at hand. Like sitting ducks waiting to be shot and made into tacos for the LF."

He was doing everything he could to not laugh at my taco joke. I went on, "I know you believe we never really die and we are eternal beings, but I guess I'm not there yet, so this feels like an irresponsible, reckless way of living."

"You know what would be reckless? You mentioning duck tacos and the

LF in the same sentence ever again. Besides, I'm pretty sure duck tacos don't exist."

He explained that abiding in the present moment doesn't mean you ignore potential danger. It means you do what is necessary to prevent or prepare for the possibility of it. The difference is you do it consciously, in the state of presence, where the soundest decisions can be made. If and when something were to happen, it also happens in the now, where you'll do your best to handle it.

"But dude, how the hell do you stay there like that, in the now, always?"

"Because I know there's no peace anywhere else. I've tried living the other way, and it doesn't work for me. That doesn't mean I don't have my moments when I feel what you're feeling, you know, for like a couple of seconds at most." He winked at me, and I just shook my head smiling. "I've just practiced returning faster."

He patted me on the shoulder. "You're doing great, brother. Just keep watching them thoughts, and remember, at the end of the day, it's you who chooses where, or maybe I should say 'when,' you want to be."

I was feeling better after our discussion, a confirmation that love truly does extinguish fear.

"So let's consciously, while in the now, bang out a discussion on how we might prevent, or reduce the possibility of, danger surrounding this newest threat," I said.

"That's what I'm talking about. Let's do just that."

» » « «

We contemplated the different moves each party might make for over an hour as well as our best options to survive the storm that could be coming our way.

We were able to surmise that Tanas was the warden's bitch. D said when the warden told him to leave his office, he overheard him radio Tanas to come to his office ASAP. We considered that Tanas could be the warden's distant connection to Joaquin and his gang. He was the dirtiest of all the guards and was often seen talking secretly to Joaquin or his right-hand man, Ronny Orozco, AKA Sleeper.

We knew even if we gave the warden what he wanted, which was basically our full compliance, it didn't necessarily fix the issue with the LF. For Joaquin, the damage was done. His business had been affected permanently, and he wanted revenge and to make an example of us.

Thankfully, D and I saw eye to eye on one particular point: that it was vital we both make it out of Carlton alive. For him, it was so we could move forward with his plan to change the world. For me, well, I just wanted to stay alive.

In the end, we came up with a plan. "Several measures" might be more accurate. One of them was to share with the remaining Mag Seven guys what was happening. Together, we would create a system of heightened awareness around our personal safety. No one would walk alone anymore, and we'd keep watch for one another when needed. We also agreed to tell Officer Ogabi everything, and to be on the safe side, we figured it might not be a good idea for him and Dimitri to speak directly. For the moment at least, I'd continue the secret communication with him on my own.

There were several other provisions put into play, all of them starting immediately. All I had to do was remember to stay present and not panic, which, at times, was easier said than done.

FEAR AND LOATHING

MARCUS

It had been a few days since Zach clued me in on Dimitri's meeting with the warden. Things felt different in H-block. There were no public ERP meetings, as we guards were instructed to write up anyone from the group that gathered with four or more in any one location. On top of that, the two-man cell restriction extinguished any possibility of furthering their work.

As far as Dimitri went, he was taking this whole threat thing that Zach told me about pretty seriously. He spent less time in his cell alone and would usually walk with at least two of the other guys. The rest followed suit. I could see the LF was on the move, members of Joaquin's crew cruising the corridors more than normal. Something was coming, but there was no way to know when or where.

I desperately wished I could've done more, but I had to keep playing my part as a CO at Carlton Prison. I couldn't tell anyone what Zach had told me. It was just Dimitri and Shady, alone in his office with no witnesses. The perceived imminent danger was all speculation at this point. It would be obvious I was in collusion with them if I came forward with details.

Even my closest ally, Jim, was too involved in his own career advancement by this point, and I was sure he'd turn on me if I spilled the beans. My hands were tied. The best thing I could do was keep an eye on both Tanas and the LF and my ears open for whatever important information I could get to Zach.

When I arrived in the mess hall, the ERP crew was separated at different tables. Tanas would move close, roaming from table to table, to discourage them from talking about transformational stuff. The warden and governor's plan was working on many different levels. Distancing the ERP members from each other and keeping them from doing what they loved seemed to kill their spirit. They were much easier to control and looked almost docile. There was something evil about it—you know, that just two men making up such a small percentage of the entire prison body could bring down so many.

I couldn't blame the ERP guys, though. They were surrounded by concrete, wire, and guns. Guns held by men who took their orders from psychopaths like Shady. When you think about it, I couldn't blame the guards either. They didn't know any better. They were just in their programming.

It was obvious how much more attention the LF table was putting on Dimitri and his crew. I could feel the tension from where I was on the other side of the room.

I needed to talk to Zach.

» » « «

Later that day, on my way for that chat with Zach, Dimitri and I passed each other in the corridor as he walked away from his cell. He was probably headed for the yard. I gave him a discreet nod, which he ignored and walked on, obviously knowing how to play the game better than I did.

"What's up, Officer?" Zach whispered while moving things around the room, acting as if I was harassing him again.

"I'm sure you're aware that the LF could make its move at any moment. I'm doing what I can. Wish I could do more," I said, bending down, pretending to inspect under his bunk.

The kid was already in panic mode. "Fuck, I still can't believe this." He did his best to play it cool, but his hands were shaking, and his voice squeaked on every fourth word.

"D told me he was still waiting for guidance. And please don't ask me what that means, Officer. There's still a lot of stuff I don't get." He shook his head. "How did the fucking LF get mixed up with the warden, anyways? How's this shit even possible? I'm seeing the end of my stretch in here. I just need to survive and get out of this hellhole."

Zach was definitely starting to lose it, and I wasn't helping the situation any. It was time for me to get out of there.

"If he is mixed up with them, and it sure looks like he is, then it has to be through Tanas. There's really no other way. I don't have to tell you, but how you guys play this is crucial to your survival. I'm outta here."

"Wait. Take this card with you. It's got a bunch of data on it." He reached into his pocket.

"I thought you said every three days," I said, surprised.

"What does it matter? Let's just get this one out. And we're gonna need more. We talked about this before, remember?" He was right. There wasn't much more for me to say.

"How then?" I asked.

"How what?"

"How are you going to pass it to me?"

"Really?" He asked with his eyes closed. "It's less than a square inch in size. I'm going to put it on the corner of the bunk, and then you'll put your hand on top of it and bail. It's a pretty minor event, Officer O."

I gave him a double take. Calling me Officer O was bad enough, but it was his tone as well. It was like we'd entered into a role reversal, one that I wasn't quite ready for. But what could I do?

He tossed the card on the bunk. I grabbed it and headed for the door.

"Watch yourselves out there," I said under my breath.

"We'll try," he whispered back.

I stepped out onto the tier and there he was, walking directly towards me, Ronny Orozco, Joaquin's main guy and second in command for the LF. Seeing him definitely wasn't what my nerves needed at that moment. The look on his face told me I was the last person he was expecting to see come out of cell 111. Stopping dead in his tracks, he put his hands in his pockets, spun around, and began walking the other way.

He was up to something and I knew it wasn't good. As if on cue, three of Joaquin's soldiers, Octavio Chavez, AKA Spyder; Pablo Hernandez, AKA Creeper; and Oscar Lopez, AKA Lil' Loco, entered the tier from the other side. Just like Ronny, they also turned around when they saw me.

I grabbed the handle of my club. My breath shortened and my heart raced. I'd just gotten between them and a hit on Zach.

I'd had enough.

LAS MANOS EN LA MASA

RONNY

"Inmate, hold it right there!" I heard ese pinche negro Ogabi yell out. I wasn't holding, so I didn't give a fuck. I stopped and turned around.

"What can I do for you, Officer?" I asked with my chin up and my arms out. He knew who I was and who I was with and that he couldn't do shit to me, but that didn't stop him from coming straight in and getting all up in my face.

"What are you doing, Orozco? You need some help with something?" he asked, breathing all heavy and sweating. I'd never seen this vato like this before. I could tell he was pissed.

"Help?" I laughed. "No sir, I'm just looking for my homie, but he ain't around. Must be in the dayroom. I'm just goin' to head over there, see what's up. Dat cool with you?"

"What's cool with me is you grab the wall, punk!"

Puto negro, pedazo de mierda.

I got up on the wall, and he put his hands on me, grabbing the back of my neck with one and frisking me hard with the other. This vato was acting different from normal, and I was getting pretty pissed off at his current level of disrespect.

"Punk? Who you callin' a punk?"

"You, Orozco. You're the punk. And hear this: Call me anything but sir or officer again, and I'll put your ass in the hole so fast you won't know what happened. Comprende, ese?" he yelled in my ear.

I didn't answer him. I was just breathing, waiting for it to end.

"Do you understand?!"

"Yeah, I got it, officer!" I yelled back.

"What the fuck you got on you, Orozco?" He was pushing my head into the wall so hard I had to turn it to one side.

"Take it easy! Whatcha thinkin'? I got nothin', güey."

"Where's your weapon, inmate?" I tried to move away as he grabbed my crotch harder than any guard had ever. "Don't move." I just stayed quiet and shook my head. He knew what that meant. He yelled in my ear, "What?! Whatcha gonna do about it, vato?!"

What I will do about it will be decided between myself and Joaquin. But something will be done, mi negro.

I just continued to nod with a little smile on my face. I didn't need to say anything else.

Then a call came on his radio. "10-29. Attacks in Alpha Yard. Code three. Several inmates involved, east end of track. South end behind the courts as well. All available staff respond immediately." He backed off for a minute and could see me smiling.

I felt power knowing more than he did, but he was a smart negro. He grabbed the back of my neck again.

"You assholes are synchronizing hits right now, aren't you?"

I was laughing on the inside but played the part. "I don't know what you're talkin' about, but it sounds like they need your help in the yard, Officer. That's a code three, right? Could be a riot or something, who knows. You better hurry, no?"

He turned and yelled, "Inmate Markland!"

The rich white puto popped his head out.

"What's up?" His face turned even whiter when he saw me up against the wall.

"Where's Tanomeo?" Ogabi asked.

"I-I-I'm not sure. He left a while ago."

"Close it up and stay inside, shit's poppin' off! I'll get someone over here," Ogabi yelled at him.

These putos are too familiar with each other. Why does this pinche mayate care so much about Tanomeo? It was like this shit was personal to him or something, confirming what I suspected that day in the yard, all of these fools were tied together.

The white boy went back in, and Ogabi got up in my ear again and squeezed my neck even harder. "I know why you're here, and it's not gonna happen today, not in this cell," he whispered.

"I don't know what you're talkin' about. Like I said, I'm just walkin' here, lookin' for my homeboy."

You see, Tanomeo was the main target, and on top of that, Joaquin wanted as many of them taken out at the same time as we could. I was to spot while Spyder, Creeper, and Lil' Loco carried the iron, handing mine off to me if both of them were in the cell. If Tanomeo wasn't there, my plan was to let them take out Markland while I got to the yard where I'd join up with my homies to hit him and the others.

He laughed, you know, like he knew I was lying. "Tell your handler it's not gonna happen. Not as long as I'm around."

I shrugged my shoulders. *Maybe you just need to not be around then.*

He must have read my mind because he slammed my head against the wall again.

"Yo, take it easy, ese!" I shouted as my face rubbed against the rough concrete wall.

"Yeah, I know how high up this goes and I'm not afraid," he said.

I could feel his spit hitting my ear. Then he said some shit that would eventually get his name on a piece of paper.

"What a life you've chosen for yourself, Ronald. I'm sure your son would be proud to see what his father's become." He slapped the back of my shoulder and backed up. "Now get the fuck outta here. Don't let me catch you around here again."

I turned around and looked him in the eyes, you know, in that way we do. I wanted him to know he was nothing but un hombre muerto caminando, but I couldn't say it so I just walked away.

» » « «

On my way back to our cell to tell Joaquin the news, I went back in my mind to a few days earlier when Joaquin gave me the order with the details on how he wanted it done. Up until that moment, I still had hope that I could get out of this shit and rebuild my life with my release date being just around the corner. But Joaquin, with his desire for more money and power, wouldn't allow for that. The last thing he cared about was my date. I asked him, "You sure we need to go this route, holmes?" hoping he'd reconsider the order he'd just given for me to hit Tanomeo and Markland while in their cell. "This fool has lots of friends, it's gonna stir up shit, carnal."

He stood up and motioned for me to do the same. I knew I'd fucked up by opening my mouth.

"Ronny, if I tell you that you are going to put in the work, then you know what time it is, right, fool?" he said in his quiet voice, the one that lets you know he's dead serious.

"I'm here for you, Captain, you know dat. But I think about this shit, ese."

"There's nothing to think about. There's only doing now. Nothing else. Unless you are getting soft, that is." Those last words, that's all he had to say, and he knew it.

"Shit, holmes, I'm down. You know me. It's LF for life, ese," I shot back, not missing a beat. You see, if you get soft in the LF, you're dead. It's just that simple.

» » « «

Walking back to my cell, on the other side of a failed mission, I knew Joaquin would be there waiting. I was really fucking lucky to have Creeper and the others to back up my story of ese negro CO Ogabi walking out of the cell right before we went in to put in the work.

All three walked out as I walked in, and I knew it wasn't going to be good. "I don't give a fuck about the CO, you should have been there earlier, Ronny!" Joaquin yelled before I could tell him the shit they'd just told him. With the lockdown siren blasting, I told him what went down with Ogabi and that it was all just bad timing.

"You missed both of those fools, the most important ones," he shouted. "What the fuck is wrong with you, eh? Then you let that pinche mayate talk to you like that! You should have done him right there on the tier. Fuck your date, ese!"

Maybe I have gotten soft.

He went off on me for a long time as I just stood there and took it. I realized my whole life had been like that. If I wasn't getting it from my father when I was younger, I was getting it from Joaquin now, and if I moved away from that side of the world, people like Ogabi were there to pick up where they left off.

There was nothing for me on that side, the side that many said was good because it was all the same as far as I was concerned. I knew I had to stand up like a man and get serious and make the move that needed to be made.

STRAIGHT OUTTA CARLTON

MARCUS

"10-29, H-21, Ogabi en route, ETA two minutes!" I shouted into the radio as I took off towards the yard. As I passed by Markland's cell, I glanced in to find him literally hiding under the covers.

"Copy that H-21."

The lockdown siren went off as I ran down the corridor. I worried they'd already gotten to him, and mental movies of a worst-case scenario played in my mind. My eyes welled up and a tightness gripped my chest from the guilt and anger I was feeling.

You shouldn't have said that. You went too far, Marcus.

Just before I arrived at Carlton, Orozco had lost his only child, a child about Hope's age, to a stray bullet in the barrio. We all know no child deserves that, and no father should be in prison when something like that happens, but more importantly, no one should put it in his face to make a point. I'd only wanted to affect him with my words, but somehow it backfired and ended up hurting me.

At the same time, I was worried about Dimitri and hoped he was still alive. It seemed like everything was falling apart all at once and it took all I had to keep my composure.

When I burst into the yard, I was still a couple of hundred yards from the scene. I could make out John White Eagle's husky frame, kneeling over a downed inmate. There appeared to be others hurt as well.

I kept running as other COs came in from all directions. In the distance, I saw a Mexican gang member stabbing someone on the ground. I sprinted, club in hand, and when I could see who it was doing the stabbing I ran even faster. It was Jerry Mendez, AKA Lil' Joker, the strongest soldier Joaquin had. He was in for ten and down for the LF cause at any cost.

When I got closer, I could see he was on top of Malik, who was barely conscious. I raised my club without warning and hammered it down on the back of his head. Instantly his bloody shank fell to the ground. His body went limp, falling on Malik. I kicked the weapon away and rolled him off to the side as purple blood flowed from his head, making a puddle on the dusty track.

I radioed for emergency medical assistance. "Stay with me, Malik. Help's on the way."

He was gasping for air and staring at me with a frightened look. There were puncture wounds around his neck and across his chest. I scanned for Tanomeo, but couldn't find him amidst the tear gas smoke.

White Eagle joined me on the ground by Malik. He'd been stabbed in the arm but didn't let it stop him from helping.

"I've got this," I told him. "Go post up in front of Markland's cell for as long as you can. He's alone in there."

He gave me a confused stare, surely wondering why I was thinking of Markland and ordering him to help like that. "Get on it, man!" I yelled, not concerned about blowing my cover. As he turned to leave, I asked, "Where's Tanomeo?"

"I'm not sure. He wasn't with us," White Eagle ran off while I applied pressure to a now unconscious Malik's wounds.

I jumped back as soon as the medics arrived. They went to work on both Malik and Mendez.

I joined the other guards just as Jim arrived on the scene.

"What's the situation over there, Ogabi?" he asked, pointing to the medics hovering over the two inmates.

"Inmate Mendez was on top of inmate Malik, sticking him when I got here. I warned him to get off, but he didn't comply so I had to use force." *Another lie. You just dug yourself in even deeper.* "I struck him once with my club, and he's got a severe head wound. This one has multiple upper body contusions. Medical's working on them both."

"What about with these guys? All work of the LF as well?" He pointed to the other ERP teachers, who were either on their backs waiting for attention or hunched over.

"I haven't asked anyone anything yet, I've only been right here, but that's what it looks like."

"Okay, we're on lockdown, so let's move fast. The quicker we make arrests the better chance of gathering evidence."

After the dust cleared, we had five injured men and zero arrests, except for Jerry Mendez, who was in an induced coma but expected to pull through. Tyrone Henson, AKA Malik Abdul Ali, was on life support and was also expected to make it. The other three were being treated and in fair condition.

Dimitri had been on his way to request a visit with the warden when it all went down. What did he and the warden talk about? That question and others had my mind spinning. Was Dimitri selling his soul for an early parole hearing? Did the warden, worried about his interview, have a hand in the attack, as he hinted in their last meeting? Or was it just the vengeance of Joaquin Flores?

Mostly, I was amazed at the luck of Zach and Dimitri, the main targets, coming out on the other side of the incident unscathed as they did.

» » « «

"Remember, dear one? There is no luck, just synchronicity," MJ said as I sat on her couch. "Dimitri, Zachary, and even you are synched up."

After what had been the most hellacious day I'd had at Carlton, I wasn't really in the mood for MJ woo-woo.

"I'm going through some serious shit right now, so can we take a break with the spiritual stuff, MJ?" I asked grumpily.

"Of course, dear one. Let me make us some tea."

In the kitchen, I proceeded to tell her everything. All of it. My suspicions of Tanas and the warden and how I'd made the mistake of alluding to their involvement to Orozco. I even threw Dimitri into the mix with my doubts around his suspected cooperation. Then there was me hitting Mendez like I did. And, worst of all, how I spoke to inmate Orozco in my anger. I told her how I felt ashamed I'd said it and even shared with her about my tears.

I also made her aware of the situation I'd put myself in by doing these things against the LF gang members. My life was in serious danger, and only now, being away from Carlton, was this reality beginning to sink in. I'd always laughed at Markland, thinking he was a bit of a coward, but now I knew what it felt like to be terrified.

She handed me a cup of tea and sat down with me at her kitchen table. "You can always apologize to him," she said innocently. I explained why that just wasn't possible and how, in the end, it would only make matters worse.

"Ho'oponopono never makes matters worse. It can only clean up those matters at their root. I know you don't want to hear anything spiritual right now, but guess what?" My forehead was on the table.

"What?" I whined quietly.

"I'm just gonna go with it."

Jesus, she can't help herself.

"As you well know, ho'oponopono is a major step toward peace in all of our lives, and—"

I stopped her and explained that, while she and Dimitri might believe this is the way to peace in the world, there was an exception, a place where that doesn't work. "And it's called Carlton State Penitentiary," I said.

"There are no exceptions when it comes to being your authentic self, dear one."

I remembered my first meeting with Ana, when she'd spoken of authenticity. I guess I still hadn't gotten it, because here I was, years later, hearing it again from my girlfriend and still not convinced.

MJ went on, "Listen, hun, I'm not going to bore you with my words, but you have only two options. You can see how you are synched up with the others and know that that synching is connected to a higher realm, let's call it The Realm of Intention. That's Intention with a capital I, if you get my drift," she winked.

"I'm not sure I do," I said, "but that's never stopped you before."

"You are all working toward bringing forth something that every person, every being on this planet wants. Peace, love, and harmony for all. Our birthright, our natural state, that's what I'm talking about. And that is what Intention wants as well, for us to come back to that."

"And how does this keep me alive in Carlton after all I've done?"

"That's where the choice part comes in. You can either keep on doing what needs to be done for this thing to happen. Or you can quit today, leave Carlton, move away, get a job somewhere else, and forget about it all. You can lead that life of quiet desperation you'd been living before. At least you wouldn't be alone, because, according to Thoreau, most are doing just that."

"You make it sound like it's the cowardly thing to do. Most women would tell their husbands, or significant others, to leave a place where there was imminent danger lurking around every corner."

She got serious and looked me in the eyes. "First off, I'm not most women.

You should know that by now. Secondly, it's up to you what you want to create at Carlton and in your life. You can either choose to live within the drama of danger lurking around every corner or you can trust in the synchronistic act that is playing out, not only in front of you but through you."

She slammed her empty teacup firmly on the table. The impact was loud enough to startle me. "You know what? Don't apologize to that Mexican fellow if you don't feel it's time, but at least admit that it's the only way out. If you can just do that, you'll be well on your way, and Intention will take care of the rest."

I couldn't tell if we were in a fight or what exactly was going on. "Are you mad at me? I don't get it," I said.

"I'm not mad, Marcus, but someone has to say these things. Sometimes it's hard not only to hear them but also for the person on the other side of the table who has to speak them."

"What about Dimitri? Where's he in all of this? If you're going to be so blunt, what about him?" I asked.

"What about him?"

I sighed. "I just wonder if he's given up. What's he doing, going to talk to the warden. Kowtowing to Shady's desires for political gain is repulsive. At the same time, I understand Dimitri wants to be safe and keep others safe. But MJ, there's no ERP, no plan, and there sure as hell isn't going to be any revenge if I know this guy," I said in a mild panic.

She brought the cups and teapot to the sink before turning to me. "How do you know he's given up? Are you sure there's no plan? There could be something going on here that you and I can't even see. Something much bigger at work. I told you about this year, the year the veil gets pulled back?"

"Yeah, but sounds kind of woo-woo to me though. I'm not sure I'm with you on that one." I wasn't in any mood to get into the conspiracy-based, spiritual stuff.

She put her cup down and patted my knee.

"I know you're not going to like this, because it might be a bit too woo-woo for you right now, but maybe our friend Dimitri is just waiting for guidance."

Oh, lord, please make her stop.

"And as far as revenge goes, you're probably right. I can't imagine him wanting anything to do with that," she added. Her ramblings were beginning to really annoy me.

"Well, I can't imagine anyone who *wouldn't* after they tried to kill your friends! How can he make sure it doesn't happen again?"

"Oh, dear one, there are some who wouldn't. You're with one in this house right now. Have you ever heard 'an eye for an eye makes the whole world blind'?"

"Can't say I have."

"Gandhi said it. Nothing is gained from revenge. It's only re-entering the cycle of suffering from another place when the idea is to leave the cycle completely. To walk away from the pattern of fear that begets more fear is the only way out of this mess we've created."

I was surprised to hear her say "we've created." She was taking responsibility for the big mess the world was in, just as Dimitri said we all must do. In my mind, she was the last person who needed to do that.

"I know I'm gonna regret asking this, but what did you mean by waiting for guidance?" I asked.

"It means he's waiting for direction or an answer from that higher realm I mentioned before."

Yep, I knew it. I'm regretting it already.

"Yeah," I said, "and in the meantime, he's gonna get himself and others off'd by not taking action."

"Maybe what he's thinking is that it's more important to get out of Carlton in one piece so he can fight the bigger battle on the outside. We don't know."

"It seems like no matter what I say you have an excuse for him. I've put so much into this thing working, with all the risks and everything. Whose side are you on anyway?"

She busted out laughing, which only pissed me off more.

"I'm sorry, dear one. It's just that you talk about sides like a child in a playground." She calmed herself. "The only side I'm on is that which is unseen, pure, and absent of evil. And while I don't want to get too deep right now, I will say it's not separate from you, me, anyone, or anything on this planet and beyond. You, on the other hand, are only interested in what works for your expectations, your attachments, and this will always fail, Marcus. I invite you to let it go now."

This is bullshit.

"I'm going home. I have to be back early tomorrow," I said harshly.

"That might be better," she said. "You've had a big day. You need to process it all."

I actually wanted her to stop me from leaving, but she wasn't like that. She didn't play those games. She'd called my bluff without even knowing I was bluffing. Now I had no choice but to go. "Oh wait. I've got that memory card for you."

"You've got it already?" I moaned, not wanting to deal with it, especially not then.

"I went to the mall and bought it instead of waiting for it to be delivered. There's no tracing it back that way."

"So, after everything I've been through today, I'm just going to smuggle that in tomorrow morning?"

"As I said before, you can always just give up," she said cunningly, knowing me better than that.

"No, it's just that, after all of this, I figured—"

"Did Zach send out a memo saying he was delaying the recollection of data until further notice?" she smirked.

"Give it to me," I snapped. "Here's the one Zach gave me today."

We did the exchange before she said, "I know I don't say what you want me to say all of the time, but someday you'll thank me for saying what needed to be said."

"You think?" I asked.

MJ nodded, "I know."

She gave me a hug and tried to kiss me on the mouth. I turned my head to the side, and she laughed loudly, which pissed me off even more. I walked out the door.

"You take care tonight, dear one. And come back when you feel better. I love you to the moon and beyond!"

I could still hear her cracking up, even after she'd shut the door.

CONSPIRACY THEORY

MARCUS

"Hey, Jim, gotta minute?" I asked as he pulled files from his case. I'd gotten to the briefing room early so I could privately feel out the post yard attack situation.

"I've got a few," he responded. "Just preparing. The warden's attending this morning's briefing. How you doing after yesterday? And what were you thinking, by the way, putting yourself in danger like that with the LF? I've seen them go after COs for a lot less."

I didn't know what to say so I lied. "Jim, it all happened so fast, I guess I just slipped up."

"You're lucky the camera clearly shows Mendez stabbing the ERP inmate, so you should be okay with the use of force, especially with the warden having his hands full right now. Governor Stages wants Shady to use what happened yesterday as an excuse to lock us down indefinitely."

My hands began to tremble. I was getting pissed off again. "That makes no sense at all. That wasn't a riot, it was an attack. They happen all the time. Where is the governor getting his information from and how does he think he can shut down Carlton due to one assault? Worse things happen all the time, and we don't lock down prisons long-term because of it."

"I know, buddy. The stats show that, but we're not just talking about Carlton. Fieldstat, Moebin, Femington, and Livingsworth, where they suspected transferred inmates started programs, are what's concerning them. ERP is still spreading. He's talking about an indefinite period of lockdown and attributing it to the dangers of the ERP program. He's working with the Bureau of Prisons to classify ERP, first, as a statewide gang and then, eventually, declare it a nationwide epidemic of sorts, if you can believe that."

I put my hand up for Jim to hold on for a second so I could gather my thoughts.

"What's going on? I don't know what planet I'm on right now." I said, wide-eyed.

"I'm with you there. What warden Shady told me was that when the warden over at Moebin tried to quell ERP per the governor's orders, there was a bit of an uprising. Not violent, but it got close. The members and a few non-member inmates didn't like being told they couldn't practice their rights, including freedom of speech, expression, and association.

"First they tried the legal route, complaining to the ACLU. When that didn't work because of some legal maneuvering by the governor, a small disruption broke out. A protest. Mind you, this was much less than what we had here yesterday, but nonetheless the governor used it to enact an institutional state of emergency. All rights of the inmates were suspended immediately, and they went on full lockdown. Says he won't lift it until he gets the gang classification. With that he'll be able to stomp out the program forever, making even ERP material illegal contraband in all state prisons.

"He's also going to require that all ERP members go through a deprogramming seminar if they want to return to any kind of normalcy once the lockdown is lifted. What he's doing, Marcus, is treating the program like some kind of virus and the classification as the vaccine. This part could be a rumor, but apparently, he's trying to figure out a way to identify the ERP members once they've been deprogrammed so that they can have their old privileges back, you know, like using commissary and going to the yard and dayroom."

"What, how?" I asked.

"I'd bet he'd tattoo them if he could get away with it," Jim scoffed.

At this point my heart was beating so fast I had to put my hand over it. *He wants to deprogram them from their deprogramming?* "Wait a minute, Jim. What the hell is an institutional state of emergency exactly, and how is any of this even legal?"

"I couldn't tell you, buddy; I've never heard of it before this morning. I know this is going to sound crazy, but I almost think it was made up by the governor, hand to God. It's just a feeling I'm getting. Who knows, maybe something does exist in the law, but to enact it over this relatively small attack makes no sense. It would be like shutting down the world over a flu virus, and of course, we'd never let that happen, but these poor guys don't have a choice. It almost seems like the governor and whoever he reports to don't want the inmates to better themselves, or *awaken,* using Tanomeo terminology.

"You know, Marcus," he said, a strange look coming across his face, "there's a part of me that wants to believe that my suspicions are crazy and it's all for the well-being of our state's citizens and the prisoners. But there's another part of me that suspects something fishy is going on. It's almost as if there's a conspiracy behind this whole thing that none of us are privy to. I just can't tell if it's benevolent or evil. The latter would suggest that our leaders are not working for the best interest of others, and I just can't believe that. I can't go there. I'm sure they know what's best. They study these kinds of things and can see far into the future." He took a deep breath in and sighed. "This level of control must be needed."

There, in the briefing room at Carlton State Prison, I witnessed a good man fall into the trap of acquiescence. His fear of accepting an uncomfortable truth opened the door, and once in, his past programming closed it behind him. I was numb, almost speechless. Seeing this come from Jim hurt inside.

"Now the warden is going to do the same here? How is that going to play into his election, shutting down the very thing that's getting him elected?" I asked, marveling at how, in the beginning, he wanted to control ERP for his own gain and how the tables had turned on him with a bigger shark now in the tank.

"That right there, buddy, is why the warden is not happy about any of this. Well, he's not happy about it, but he's gotta play ball because it's coming from the top down and he needs the governor on his side.

He says he's going to wait until after the Live at 5 taping to drop the bomb, seeing how Tanomeo's on board with the interview. He was meeting with Tanomeo when it all popped off in the yard. They came to some kind of agreement, and I think Tanomeo got a pretty good deal for playing ball. He might even be getting an early parole date, but I have no proof, just got a feeling. Of course, if Tanomeo found out what was really going to happen, post taping, he'd probably refuse to be a part of it."

Jim shuffled his papers around nervously before going on. "He wants me to get up there and hint at what's coming, to prepare the COs for the harsher measures against ERP and the prisoners. That's the last thing I want to do, but it's my job."

By this point, Jim's current reality of being the warden's lapdog didn't interest me. I was stuck on something else.

Tanomeo on board? Did he sell out?

"Do you have any more good news for me, Jim?" I asked sarcastically.

He hesitated, giving me a guilty smile. "Actually there is something else, but I'm not sure you really want to hear it."

I threw my hands up. "Lay it on me."

"Shady informed me this morning that he's been ordered by the governor to create an Anti-ERP Task Force."

"A what?"

"Yep, and can you guess who's going to be heading it up at Carlton?"

This was one of those moments in life where I really questioned if there was a God, and, if so, why he was so cruel?

I was livid as the door opened and the asshole, the head of the new Anti-ERP Task Force, walked in. He sauntered slowly down the aisle, torturing me by looking at each seat as if he was in a goddamn movie theater. Finally, Tanas took one on the far side of the room and sat up extra straight with his hands folded like a little tattle-telling school bitch.

"Not him!?" I hissed as if possessed.

Jim nodded. "Yes, him."

Jim went back to his files. I got up in a state of silent shock. Jim whispered. "Like always, mums the word, right, buddy?"

Within five minutes the rest of the COs piled in and took their chairs. The warden entered a few minutes later and began looking through the file Jim set on the table in front of him. The warden wasn't his normal jolly self. Normally he'd say hello to everyone in the room, like the good politician he was good at portraying. Today he glanced, giving me a fast but cold stare.

Once Jim finished briefing the group with mundane rhetoric, the warden stepped up to give a quick, canned speech. Shady acknowledged the COs who were on the front line during yesterday's incident. He mentioned the importance of riot prevention and praised the rapid response to violence at Carlton. He read the names of the guards that had rushed to help. I was one of the first to arrive at the scene, so expected my name to be called, but that didn't happen.

Done, he closed his computer and walked back to his chair. When he passed, it was obvious that he purposely avoided eye contact with me. I snuck a look at Tanas, who was giving me an evil grin. That's the moment when all doubt was stricken from my mind and I knew they knew, which meant they knew that I knew as well. I was sick to my stomach as Jim moved back to the podium and spoke of the draconian restrictions that would be implemented at Carlton if the ERP program continued to spread.

Jim's words became the garbled, unintelligible background music to the bad movie now playing in my head. It had several dark scenes, involving not only the warden and his psychotic sidekick, but the most powerful gang in the whole compound as well. I was so deep within my method acting, I didn't even know I was in the movie. There was no witness to bring me back to the present moment. I was so far in I'd forgotten it ever existed.

I wanted to go back to the simplicity of my old life, one of quiet desperation, as MJ had put it. I didn't care, because if going to work, watching sports, getting drunk, and sleeping it off was quiet desperation … well, that was beginning to sound pretty good.

TWO HEADS, SAME COIN

MARCUS

I walked directly from the briefing room to my car. I was sick and stayed that way for almost a week. I was sick of my life and everything it had become. I was sick of Tanas and the warden and all their bullshit. But, most of all, I was sick with fear and figured staying away from Carlton would keep me out of harm's way. So I took a proper sick leave, knowing I wanted to be back for the Live at 5 interview.

» » « «

I'd been gone for less than a week, and within that short period of time, "Carlton World" had changed so much it felt like I was living another life. There were so many tyrannical changes being pushed on the prisoners that I couldn't keep up. Guards were writing up inmates who gathered in groups of more than two, even if it was only for a few seconds. All of this was in response to the governor's idea of flattening the curve of PSG, positive statistical growth.

These restrictions weren't limited to ERP members. All inmates, gathering for any reason deemed nonessential by Tanas, the Anti-ERP Task Force leader, were subject to point increases. I tried to figure out why non-ERP members were being targeted as well. What were they worried they'd talk about? Their release dates, sports, girls, getting high? On top of it all, Tanas made sure the inmates knew the new semi-lockdown reality, and the harsh rules that came with it, were due to the rift between the LF and ERP. This caused a separation between the inmates, with most blaming ERP for rocking the boat that had never been rocked. More fights were breaking out, leading to even more restrictions as the two sides formed. One side, the minority standing with ERP and what it stood for. The other, wanting the old system to control with Joaquin Flores at the helm.

I never thought I'd see an attack in the yard, the kind that happens all the time, used to impose such repressive measures against other human beings. It became clear there was more to this scam than job security, politics, or money. The call the governor received that day was from someone, or someones, fearful of losing something very important. Whoever they were, they were threatened by Dimitri's interview and what he'd said when asked what he was going to do when he got out. Those five little words, "I'm going to change everything," were at the root of all this invented madness. It was also obvious that whatever that person or group was afraid of losing reached beyond the walls of any prison.

Carlton had become more of a concentration camp than a prison. I'd heard Tanas would sit in the control room, spying with the monitors. He'd wait for one of the inmates to slip up and greet others in the yard, or something equally as minuscule, and he'd call in his minions to swoop in and cuff the violators, pat them down, and write them up. I was even more disgusted by how the other guards jumped right into this new norm, treating the men worse than cattle.

I remembered Dimitri's teaching about the lower-self that abided in the unconscious human, how it would join in with like energies to feed off of the carcasses of helpless prey. "This type of cannibalism," he'd said, "will be short-lived in an awakening world. Those who turn against their own will eventually self-destruct or be ousted from the tribe. This is the way of true justice. It is Love in action, the path to our liberation."

Those words didn't mean much at the time I heard them, but they meant everything now. I was in a strange place. I still held to his words, his teachings, my only hope. But, at the same time, I had my doubts about him participating in an interview that only served the warden and, well, Dimitri, if he'd taken the bait about getting an early release.

God, I hope he didn't do that.

» » « «

I motioned Dimitri to come out of his cell so I could walk him to the interview. I was ready with all the things I wanted to say and ask. It had been a long time since we'd been alone, and I was planning on making the most of it, but there was something that got in the way. That something was him. He was different, more serious than before, more concerned. When he came out of the cell, I took three steps back, for *inmate distancing*. I then put on my face shield, both new requirements put in place by Tanas's Anti-ERP Task Force.

"Are you serious?" he asked, staring at my getup. I couldn't tell if he was disgusted, insulted, or maybe both. He began to walk, and when we got down the tier, I moved forward to begin my inquiry.

"It's been a while and I've got a few questions," I said.

"We're not going there today. It's time to get real. But I do have some questions of my own."

I didn't say anything. All I could think about was how much our dynamic had changed and why I couldn't ask him the questions I wanted to.

"Hey," he said, snapping me out of it. "What's going on with our food? They are over-salting it. It's almost inedible. There's nothing from the greenhouse or garden, just the same unhealthy products from before. And Zach got transferred out of the kitchen last week and put on bathroom clean-up. Due to the new regulations, we can't even talk to the men who are serving the food, so it makes it impossible for us to know what we're eating.

"Several of us got the word out to begin a long fast. We started it together, but that was squashed by another new regulation that says if we don't eat their food, we're restricted to our cell, no yard or dayroom privileges. They are literally trying to tell us what is going to go into our bodies. They've also cleared out everything in the commissary that has any kind of nutritional value. All that's there is soda, candy, junky snacks, and coffee."

I didn't want to answer him because he wouldn't let me tell him about my problems, but he'd think it childish if I told him that. "That would be Tanas and his new task force. Are you aware of it?" I asked begrudgingly.

He whispered in a direct, more to the point voice, "Most forms of communication between ourselves and the outside have been cut, so I'm only aware of what Zach told me you told him, about it being a political thing with the governor. Of course, that was confirmed during my meeting with the warden, but I had no idea he would take it this far.

"What I do know is that they're putting things in the food that weren't there before, and I can feel the effects of it. I can internally reverse those effects, but the other men can't. We never got that far in the teachings. Oh, and shutting down the library. What's that about?"

He paused and seemed truly frustrated. It wasn't like him. Finally, he said, "You know they set this whole thing up, don't you? This unjustified lockdown we're in? They're pitting everyone against ERP so we take the fall, which is making it almost impossible for us inmates to come together and figure out how we are going to deal with this. Keyword, almost."

Talking to him through the faceguard made it feel like we were more distant than ever. At the same time, it did mask the movement of my lips from the cameras.

"It's Tanas actually," I said. "He's adding pure sodium fluoride to the salt. He says it has a calming effect on the men. He also deemed the garden food unfit for consumption, citing phony health concerns regarding Carlton's yearly flu outbreak as well as a lack of precautions in the growing and handling. All of it is bullshit, of course.

"The library shut down is temporary. It will reopen today after the task force finishes removing the nonessential books. Those are the ones you had brought in. Oh, I've never read it, but I hear they're removing Orwell's *1984* as well. I didn't know about the commissary food. I'm just getting back from sick leave myself and I ..."

He stopped walking, dropped his head, and began to talk to himself in Spanish. I had no idea what he was saying, but it went on for almost a minute like he was on the phone, but he wasn't. He even laughed at one point, and I was getting nervous about how this looked on the cameras. I cleared my throat loudly, which seemed to work because he said "adios" out loud and started walking again.

"Tell me about the Tanas task force. What's it all about?" he asked, giving me no explanation for what had just happened.

"It's called the Anti—" My words were halted by the sight of a short man with perfect black hair briskly walking toward us.

"Where are you taking this prisoner and why wasn't I notified about this?" he shouted.

"I'm bringing him to the interview in the control room. Captain Devic ordered me to escort him. If you have a problem, I suggest you talk to Jim." I said. Dimitri just looked Tanas up and down almost as if he'd never seen him before.

Tanas pulled out a file. "Here is the new regulation that states any ERP leader that is to be moved by a correctional officer in and throughout the prison must have clearance from the AERPTF leader. That would be me. I'm sure you are aware of this, Ogabi."

"Let me see that," I demanded as he handed it over.

"Wait a minute," I said. "This is from today and it's signed by you." I started laughing. "The next thing you're gonna tell me is you created this document too." One of those long pauses showed up while I watched that wicked, trademark Tanas smile grow slowly on his face.

He nodded, "That's exactly what I was going to tell you next."

I looked at the paper then at him.

"You can't just write new rules like that; it's illegal. And what is AERPTF any-way?" I looked at the letters again and figured it out. "Oh Jesus, never mind!"

"I created that as well. See how I did that?" Tanas asked. I looked at him like he was crazy.

"You just put the letters for Anti-ERP Task Force together. It's called an acronym. There's nothing creative about that, Tanas," I scoffed, but my words didn't affect him. He went on with his chin in the air. I thought about punching it, but I knew if I did I'd be in big trouble.

"I can write new rules daily if I see fit. I've written more than twenty-one this week alone and there are more coming."

"It's illegal. It has to be illegal," I said, shoving the paper into his chest with no concern of wrinkling it. He smiled and placed it back into the folder after ironing it out with his hands.

"It's much bigger than you think, Ogabi. There's been a big shift on an administrative level. I'm talking executive-order big. Giving me all the pow-er I need to bring about the NCO." He paused and stared at me, obviously waiting for me to ask.

"Okay, what the hell is the NCO, Tanas?"

He got excited as if I was on my side. "It's the future reality here at the prison, hopefully for all prisons someday. But for now I call it the New Carlton Order, NCO for short." He started ruffling through his paperwork, smiling. "I created that name as well. I want to show you my outline for the NCO. It's not approved yet, but with that shift I spoke of, it will be a breeze to implement. It'll give those in power, myself and the warden, much more control over the inmates."

More control of prisoners locked up in a prison? What is wrong with this man?

I couldn't hold it in any longer. "That executive order, the institutional state of emergency, what a crock of shit that is!" I exclaimed, instantly regretting my words as his mood shifted from arrogant pride to genuine interest.

"Where did you hear about that, Ogabi?" He inquired with a sinister tone. I didn't answer, because I didn't know what to say. Jim had told me about it in confidence, and I'd just screwed up royally. "No one's spoken of it outside a very small circle of people. We're waiting until tomorrow to announce it."

"I-I-I don't know. I just heard of it somewhere, a long time ago, and figured that's what you were using to pull off this crap."

"You heard of it somewhere? I find that hard to believe." He stared, waiting for me to answer. When I didn't, he reached back into his folder and happily continued, "Let me draw your attention to this other document." I grabbed it out of his hand while he pointed. "If you look there in the middle, it explains how COs are not to engage in conversations with the ERP leaders in any form other than what is completely essential. I was watching you two on the monitor and could see the chitchat. Nice trick by the way, wearing the face shield, and while I couldn't see you talking, I got a perfect shot of Tanomeo rambling away when you both stopped walking right back there."

"He was speaking Spanish, and not to me. Ask him. And with the shield …" I was getting confused by it all. "Ah, never mind, Tanas!" I yelled, disgusted by the whole thing.

But he wasn't finished. "So you weren't talking to Tanomeo and you heard about the state of emergency a long time ago? Riiiight." He closed his folder. "Don't worry, I'm gonna let you slide on this one, Ogabi. But take off the face shield for the rest of the walk."

"You're going to let me slide? Is that what you said? You have no power over me. We're both—"

"If I may direct your attention to this document," he opened his file again and removed another paper. "It clearly states that as long as I am acting task—" I put my hand up.

"You can put that right back in your folder," I snapped. "I'm not gonna look at it. This prison used to take its directions from the warden, but now I'm seeing it's really being run by an entirely different entity."

"You have no idea," Dimitri whispered.

"Ssshhh!" Tanas snapped at Dimitri and then pointed to my face. "The shield. Remove it, please."

I glanced back at the paper I still had in my hand. "Look right here, Tanas. Above the restricted communication part. It says that we, the COs, must have protective face shields on while interacting with all ERP leaders and members. You don't even know the rules you yourself just enacted." He held his hand out, and I gave the paper to him.

What an ass.

He studied the document, looking a bit confused himself.

"Well, like I said, I've written a lot of new regulations within the last week."

"Okay, Tanas," I said, pissed off. "Now I'm confused about the whole face shield thing. Should I be wearing one? Because at first I'm told I need to, then I hear something completely different from you. Are you just trying to confuse people? Because if you are, you're doing a good job."

"How about I just walk with you fellas? That way I can make sure we are doing everything by the book," he said like the little prick that he was.

What could I do? We started walking. He quickly got in between Dimitri and me, which I thought was weird and imagined it looked funny as well, considering the size difference. Unlike me, Dimitri seemed to enjoy having Tanas next to him. He couldn't take his eyes off him. He'd take a few steps then glance over and down at him. It was almost as if he was intrigued by the little Nazi marching down the hall with us.

"So," Dimitri spoke up, "loading up the inmates on extra fluoride and removing bottled water from the store. Wow, I mean, wow." He pointed at my face, "And this shield thing here, depersonalizing the guards when they're with ERP members and all. Oh, and I imagine removing the channel buttons on the TV so the inmates are forced to watch only *fear-based* GNN is your doing as well."

Tanas said nothing and kept walking as if he couldn't hear him.

"Absolutely brilliant!" Dimitri exclaimed in what appeared to be genuine awe. Tanas, never looking at him, grinned smugly, giving a single nod of acceptance to what appeared to be a real compliment. My head snapped, confirming those words were actually Dimitri's. "No, really. Using fluoride as the dumbing agent. It's an old trick, but combined with the fear-inducing phony news channel, incredible work. Really."

Tanas shrugged his shoulders, joining Dimitri in admiration for the job well done. My mouth was wide open. I couldn't believe that Tanas was, in essence, admitting to all of this. At the same time, I was shocked to see him being showered with compliments by the very man who I'd never expect to see this from.

Dimitri continued, "Then, for the coup de grace, placing the blame like you did, creating polarization between the inmates so we fight between ourselves. Hats off." Dimitri had his hand over his heart.

What? It was as if I was watching two lifelong sports adversaries having a chat about their latest match.

"The whole problem, reaction, solution thing, a bit dated also," Dimitri went on. "But it's what you guys use every time. It's your go-to. I get it, it works."

We walked on for a moment in silence. "You didn't mention the cleansing of the library," Tanas whispered with a sickeningly sweet voice.

"I know, I know," Dimitri said, nodding. "I'm still processing that one, but a strong move for sure. And the removal of *1984*, icing on the cake."

"Why, thank you, Dimitri," Tanas said in the same sweet voice. It was killing me inside that he used Dimitri's first name. I don't even get to do that.

Tanas pointed up at Dimitri. "And you with inmate Mills that night in the kitchen. He's category J now. Impressive as well. Would you like to shed some light on what happened there?"

What the … ?

A big smile grew on Dimitri's face. "I almost forgot about that one. It's true, old Earl will never be the same again. But I wouldn't say he's mentally ill. Just different, happier now. But you know full well I can't divulge too much to you, but the words you just used, 'shed some light,' well, I'll just say right there is a big clue."

"Touche!" Tanas said, putting his finger in the air.

Dimitri whispered, "You didn't actually think that was going to work, sending him and Pete after Zach like that, did you?"

Tanas shrugged his shoulders again. "I couldn't have known until I tried. Sometimes you throw something out there to see where to go next." I looked around me to make sure I was really walking down the corridor at Carlton with these two guys.

Dimitri nodded, "I figured it must have been something like that."

"Speaking of next," Tanas laughed, "I've got some new ones coming for you."

"Wanna share any of them now?" Dimitri asked.

It took Tanas a moment to answer, like he was struggling with his ego. "Well, I probably shouldn't divulge too much, but here's a big clue: The next time you're escorted somewhere, the COs won't be the only ones wearing a mask," he giggled. I didn't want to play in Tanas's game, but Dimitri was deep into the riddle.

"Oh, I think I got it," Dimitri said, laughing with his finger in the air. "Oh, that's good!"

Tanas couldn't help himself. "Yes, full-face bite masks will be worn by all ERP members being escorted within the Carlton compound."

"Ah, a savage tactic indeed, Tanas. Very dehumanizing," Dimitri shouted. "Having both the inmates' and guards' faces covered is a double whammy with the whole psychosomatic, dissociation thing. Did you get that from the holocaust? I know the Nazis were working on these techniques for mind control over their victims, but ..." Dimitri paused and brought his finger up again as if he'd come up with a new question.

Tanas looked up at him with a hint of concern. "But what?"

"I don't want to make caca on your parade or anything, and while I can see it working with some of the newer ERP members ..."

"Out with it," Tanas said with a tinge of worry in his voice.

"It's a *no* with the advanced members or the teachers," Dimitri said. "They're just too clear. Not gonna work. I'm sorry."

I'd had enough. I stopped walking and watched as they both moved on without me as if I didn't exist.

What the hell's going on here? Dimitri complimenting the evil doings of a psychopath while the psychopath accepts the compliments with honor as if at an award ceremony. Then they discuss future and past wargame strategies, almost giving each other advice.

I ran to catch up as they walked on in silence. But even within that silence, I could feel a connection between them. Not a friendly, brotherly connection like Dimitri had with so many of the men at Carlton. More like a connection of familiarity that somehow went way back.

Dimitri then took a deep breath and moved his shoulders around and his head side to side, loosening up for something. "You do know I'm going to have to step in the middle of all this at some point, don't you, Gene?"

Tanas stopped just before the control room entrance and gave Dimitri a nod. "It's the game we came here to play. I mean, what else is there to do, right?"

What the ... ?

He turned to me and snarked, "The prisoner is all yours. And try to follow the rules for God's sake, Ogabi." Tanas then disappeared just as quickly as he'd shown up.

Dimitri started cracking up. "Oh, you gotta love that guy, right? I mean, not too much, but you know …."

I don't know what to call what I'd just witnessed, but it was real in a way I could never explain. I'm just gonna leave it at that. It was real weird.

GOING ROGUE

MARCUS

As we walked into the mantrap, the interlocking door controller sounded. Dimitri's eyes got big. "I've never been in one of these. What is it?" he asked.

"They're used to separate nonsecure areas from secure ones. We'll be buzzed in the second door once they've checked us out." I looked up at the camera and gave a nod. "We're going into the most secure area of Carlton. It's where all the cameras are observed through monitors. I'm surprised a news crew is being allowed inside, let alone an inmate. Hell, I've only been in once and that was during my orientation."

Dimitri looked up at the camera and whispered, "There's always an unseen reason for everything. There could be something else to this happening in such a secure place."

"Explain something to me. What did you mean when you said you gotta love that guy, anyway?" I asked, still perturbed by the remark. "No one loves Tanas. Probably not even his mother."

"There are things you aren't ready to know yet. All of it will come in time. But in reality, what's puzzling you is the nature of his game."

Wait, where have I heard that before?

The warden stood inside with a big phony smile as he welcomed Dimitri. He immediately pulled him aside and began whispering, ignoring me completely.

I nodded to Marianne and her crew, which consisted of just two others: a cameraman and one younger guy who looked to be the new producer.

Marianne smiled and said, "So here we are again, Officer Ogabi. I'm back for more 'Dialogues With Dimitri.' I see you still have your hummingbird journal."

"I do, and it's still empty. To be honest, I'm not sure what to write in it."

"Oh, but I do," she began. I was all ears, but her attention shifted to Dimitri as he finished with the warden.

So much for me finding out about what to write.

"And how are you today, fine sir? It's been a while, hasn't it?" Marianne asked joyfully as if she and Dimitri were old friends.

He looked into her eyes, saying nothing for what felt like a bit too long. I could see he loved her. Not in a romantic way necessarily, more as a recognition. Not that he didn't love everyone he was with, but this was a woman treating him like a human being and he could feel it.

"I'm doing well. Staying present through current life situations," Dimitri said. "And you?"

"Trying to do the same," she said. "It definitely takes practice. I've read a few books since our last meeting, and I wanted to say thank you. I don't know how to convey the magnitude of what's happened since meeting you and subsequently starting this process. But, somehow, I think you know."

She looked at him with a sincerity I'd never seen in a news reporter. I was seeing through the facade of the make-up, the hair, and the on-air personality. She was just a human being like any of us with problems and challenges, and that allowed me to see the beautiful person she was. Just as Dimitri could see.

"Thank you for the acknowledgment," he said quietly. "You just said it takes practice?"

"It sure does. For me at least."

"I understand. It's just when we put words like 'it takes' or 'I need to' in front of practice, it pushes us further away from the desired result we had in the first place. Instead, I invite people to remain in the state of practice. I invite them to 'become' the practice of presence itself. This is done by abiding in the constant state of deep inquiry, the kind that never stops, and doing the work from there."

I looked at the monitor and saw Jim in the mantrap, so I hit the button to buzz him in. He gave me a quick nod when entering and hurried straight over to the warden, who was with the producer, surely directing him on what he wanted to see happen. Jim pulled the warden aside and told him something. I could tell by his reaction it wasn't good. As they left the room, I heard the warden whisper, "Just don't start without me."

"We'll be right back," Jim said to me. "I removed the CO on monitor duty so we'd have more space in here. Just keep an eye on them and buzz us in when you see us. We've got to make some calls. There's an issue with the food. The interview starts and ends with us inside this room, warden's orders."

"You got it, Jim. I don't know how it could happen otherwise." I'd find out later that one of Tanas's minions from the AERPTF had destroyed all the food from the garden and greenhouse. They'd been dumping the grown food for days, forcing the inmates to go back to eating the old, prepackaged kitchen slop. This left nothing for the lunch between Marianne and Dimitri.

I was left alone in the room with the four others. Dimitri didn't seem to notice. He was captivated by the video monitors.

"Look, there's Vinny," he said to Marianne, pointing at one of the screens. She walked over as he waved at the screen. "Hey, Vin, can you see us? Hi!" he shouted.

"Do you remember Vinny? He didn't come today." Dimitri kept waving, trying to get Vinny's attention.

She spoke to him softly, as a mother would. "I do remember him, Dimitri. But he can't see or hear us. This is a closed-circuit system, hun."

I guess she loves him too.

"Oh. That kind of sucks." The wind had been knocked out of Dimitri's sails. It was comical. They laughed as I watched the warden in one of the monitors yelling into his phone while in the program office. I saw Jim in the kitchen frantically opening up the refrigerators, desperately trying to find something that looked like it came from the garden.

I watched Marianne get prepared while I periodically glanced at the warden, who was checking his watch constantly. Jim was doing the same. They were due to return shortly. I noticed Dimitri staring at one particular monitor, the one I saw Jim on before I buzzed him in.

I walked up next to him and could see the back of what seemed to be a very short and somewhat squatty, older female correctional officer. She was messing with a large set of prison keys, attempting to lock the first mantrap door from the outside, which made no sense at all.

"Who is she and why is she locking that door? I've never seen that CO before." I was talking to myself out loud. Dimitri just stared at the monitor, frozen, no expression or movement except the slight movement of his mouth when he dryly said, "I have."

I looked at him and then back at the guard on the screen. I grabbed my radio to call Jim, but Dimitri's hand shot up for me to stop. The woman finished and attached the keys back on her belt and just as she turned to walk away, she glanced up at the camera and gave it a wink. It was Ana, and just like the times before, my heart began to race.

"Oh shit!" I shouted as Dimitri made his way to the far corner of the room.

I looked back at the monitors, but she was nowhere to be found. She'd disappeared as quickly as she'd shown up. I looked at Dimitri. He was talking to himself in Spanish again.

What the hell is going on this time?

Marianne and the others were looking at me strangely. They'd seen my reaction, but not the person that caused it—a person that apparently only Dimitri and I could see but weren't supposed to talk about.

"Everything okay, Officer Ogabi?" Marianne asked.

"At this *exact* moment, everything is great," I said with a nervous giggle, using the present-moment thing to my advantage.

Dimitri spun and sat down in front of her. I looked at the monitors to find Jim and the warden on their way. I knew it would only be a few minutes before they got to the locked door.

"Marianne, you know how there's that moment in our lives that can show up and truly define who we are as a person? That moment where one has the opportunity to really help with something big?" Dimitri asked, looking directly in her eyes.

With zero time to clarify or even think about what he'd asked, she answered, "What do you need me to do, Dimitri?" She was in. It was full-body chills and watery eyes for me as I watched what had taken me a lifetime to embrace take her just seconds. I found myself loving her as well.

"Tell me, quickly, about what we film here and how it gets out to the people on their TVs," he asked, and she began a long, technical explanation. "Just tell me this: once we start, who can stop us?"

"No one really. I have a direct live feed that cannot be cut because we broadcast directly from the van to the viewers during my twenty-one-minute time slot, minus the two commercials. After that, we are automatically cut off."

"Who's in the van?"

"No one. We use remote broadcast technology from here with that." She pointed to a device on the table. I looked at the parking area monitor and saw the news van with the giant antenna off on its own in the southern corner of the lot.

"What if I give you a raincheck on lunch, and we go blow it out right now?" Dimitri asked excitedly.

"Without the warden?" she inquired with a suspicious grin.

"Definitely without the warden. Oh, and without commercials." The without commercials part caused her wheels to turn, calculating the consequences around the actions she was being asked to take. I looked at the monitor to calculate mine.

"You're really going to owe me on this one, Dimitri Tanomeo," she said with a smile. She adjusted her mic and got ready to do what needed to be done. I was in awe of her courage.

"We're up in five, Marianne," the young producer announced, unaware of what was really going on.

Dimitri looked at him, then back to Marianne and asked, "What about Phil, the producer, are you sure he's not lurking in the shadows somewhere and has some sneaky way to shut us off?"

"No, Phil hit the big leagues and got a pretty high-up position over at GNN."

Dimitri laughed. "Of course he did."

Marianne looked at me then at Dimitri. "What about him?" she asked.

"He's one of us," he said. All I could do was grin while Marianne nodded.

"I knew it!" she exclaimed.

I felt great again, being part of it all.

"One minute!" the new producer shouted while Marianne and Dimitri got settled. I looked at the monitor. The warden and Jim had arrived at the locked door.

"Thirty seconds!" I bent over the table to speak to him one last time. "They're at the door, Dimitri. Once they get a key, they'll be inside the mantrap."

"It's not going to be that easy. The keys have been hidden. If they find them, just make sure you don't buzz through the second door until we've finished."

I was too nervous to respond. What did respond was my stomach with the familiar pain that seemed to show up every time things got heavy, which seemed to happen more often since I'd met this guy.

"Quiet please, and we're on in five, four, three, two …"

SILVER FOR GOLD

MARCUS

"Good afternoon. We are live at Carlton State Prison with Dimitri Tanomeo, the young man we visited a few months prior."

I looked at the monitor. The warden was in a panic, beating the door with his fist while Jim frantically spoke into the phone, likely trying to locate the keys.

"Dimitri," Marianne said, "I was promised a meal but it looks like I'm going to be stood up. Tell me, what does it take for a girl to get a date with you?" Dimitri laughed, turning red. I'd never seen that happen before, and he rubbed his face with both of his hands.

"Well, Marianne, thanks for returning to Carlton today. Due to circumstances beyond our control, having a deeper conversation concerning the fate of the world could be the wiser play."

"Wow. The fate of the world. Those are some big words, Dimitri. But, since our last meeting, your words have helped me immensely, so I have no choice but to turn the floor over to you."

I checked the monitor again and saw Jim and the warden giving their full attention to one of their phones. *Oh shit, they're watching the live broadcast.* From what I could see the warden was mortified. I saw Jim pull his own phone out, and seconds later, the control room phone rang. I unplugged it as the young producer, whose name was Alex, looked at the outer mantrap door monitor and then at me in confusion. I just shrugged my shoulders and turned back to the interview.

"Thank you, Marianne. I have a lot to say, so let me start with this: The message I have is for every human being in the entire world. May it penetrate all arenas—political, social, racial, as well as religious. I call for this message to cross all borders, to infiltrate military institutions and governmental offices while it establishes itself in the hearts and minds of everyone it reaches."

Marianne sat up in her chair, unclasped her fingers, and rested her hands, palms upward, on her lap. Alex, the producer, plunked down onto the nearest chair, his eyes locked on Dimitri as if the rest of the world didn't exist. I'd forgotten just how powerful he was.

"The stage is yours, Dimitri Tanomeo!" Marianne stated with an authority I'd certainly never heard on the local news channel before.

"I've got some good news and some bad news. The good news is a change is coming, and the bad news is a change is coming." He chuckled as she squinted her eyes.

"What kind of change? And how can it be both?"

"Evolution, Marianne. Accelerated, deep, perfectly merciless evolution. Depending on how we look at it, individually or collectively, will determine if it will register as good or bad if we're using those somewhat inaccurate terms, which, for the sake of moving along, we can. The evolution I speak of is spiritual in nature. It has to do with our species shifting from a less-conscious third density reality into the fourth as some are already in the process of doing so."

I had never heard him speak of this. I was just as lost as Marianne. He continued, "We don't need to get caught up in that right now, but I do want to be clear that this accelerated shift is already underway. For a long time, humankind has been in a holding pattern. We've co-created a world that's been held together by a weak glue. Think of it as that cheap white glue that kids use. Let's call that glue 'fear,' or more accurately, 'egoic fear.' We fear that there's not enough of the things we need or want, so we trample others to get ours, never realizing there was never a shortage in the first place.

"Many point their finger at those who have but don't share, while others blame those who want but refuse to do. We've constructed governmental systems to serve the people and put individuals in place to run them who only take for themselves. We've idolized supposed stars, the sellouts who promote, sing about, or display greed, violence, and depravity in our entertainment industry. Then, there are our entitled children with the unchecked content in their technology that propagates all of this as they are raised on the training ground of violence, perversion, and separation. All of this due to our own disconnection from the Love that we are.

"We feed ourselves poison from big food companies who want us sick so that eventually we end up in the hands of their accomplices, the medical associations and Big Pharma. Those who, instead of our healing, will only ensure our eventual return to their loop of dis-ease.

"It gets worse. Less money in people's pockets equals more fear, their biggest weapon. Then they amplify this with their one-sided news media designed to hold people in distress. Add all of that to the movies and TV they're making, and you have the perfect recipe for caca soup."

He stopped to take a deep breath. "I almost forgot, we add fuel to the already burning fire as we treat each other with hate, self-righteous judgment, and indignation. All of it a symptom of the lost compassion that once made us human. How could we not be in a constant state of suffering in this world we've so unconsciously built and, worse, sustained?"

He paused to give Marianne a moment to respond.

"I'm not sure if I agree with you about us all being responsible. I surely don't participate in the perversion and violence and do my best to make sure my son doesn't watch it either."

"What I'm talking about is so much more complex than what you are doing or not doing. Imagine a world where the things that keep us away from our natural state of a high vibrational frequency don't even exist."

A doubtful smile grew on her face. "You mean a world where there are no bad things? How's that even possible?"

"It's beyond the subjective concept of good and bad and quite the complicated conversation to have right now. But, ultimately, yes, that's what I mean. The fact that it's impossible to imagine is the indicator of how deep the problem lies. As hard as it is to hear this, we've joined in with the darkness merely by being born into a reality where a low energetic vibration permeates our earth. It's our acquiescence and collaboration that allows that cycle of low vibration to continue and flourish."

I was concerned about him talking about energy and vibration. That kind of stuff always made me drift off.

"But first, before the people out there tune out," Dimitri said, looking into the camera, "I need to warn you about what is coming, so stay with us until the end."

Well played, Dimitri.

"What's coming?" Marianne asked. "It gets worse? I thought this evolutionary shift would be the remedy for the ills you stated."

"It is, but there are negatively oriented beings, architects of a very dark plan, that see this evolution as a threat to their own survival, which is exactly what it is. These forces feed off the fear-based, low vibrational frequency carried and sustained by unsuspecting and manipulated human beings, and they will do anything to keep their food supply intact."

Be careful, Dimitri. Remember your audience.

Marianne, oblivious to the odd silence, fixed her eyes on him. She grabbed and gulped down the glass of water on the table, not realizing it was Dimitri's.

"All that made sense in the most disturbing of ways, Dimitri. Is there a silver lining in any of this?" she asked as her nails dug into the vinyl of her chair.

"There's a huge silver lining!" Dimitri exclaimed, way too excited about what most would consider a depressing topic. "We are just in the calm before the storm phase. Imagine that, Marianne!" Her mood shifted as the lines on her face became more defined.

She shook her head and snapped back with, "I don't want to imagine that. I know you've been locked up for a while, but the divisiveness in our country, our world, has never been worse. Normal people are taking sides against each other with their political viewpoints, and when I say taking sides, I'm talking about visceral hate between them. So please tell me how we're in the calm. Because, if that's true, we are in big trouble when the actual storm hits."

"I can see by your reaction that maybe I wasn't clear," he said with a nod.

Marianne's face relaxed ever so slightly, showing renewed contentment at the probability of him retracting his statement.

"You can forget about imagining it. I now invite you to *know* it is coming! Every bit of what you described has been perfectly designed and executed by the very architects I spoke of minutes ago. They are the ones who hide in the shadows behind the supposed leaders of the world, playing all sides of the political arena in their giant game of chess in which you and I are pawns. They keep their white horse watered and ready for those who carry their forged messages, cleverly using the guise of moral virtue as their own trojan horse.

"Believe me when I tell you, what we're in now with the massive polarization, hate, disconnection to Self, and all the other caca is nothing compared to the storm of biblical proportions they have waiting for us. Think global financial meltdown, draconian censorship, savage rioting in the streets, famine, forced vaccinations, a tyranny that rivals the holocaust, and even another world war, just for fun."

He had a look of seriousness on his face that was light years away from the young man who had just been laughing like a child. He meant what he said, and everyone in the room knew it was real. I felt another sharp pain in my stomach. Even the cameraman was standing up and staring. But it was Marianne that was affected the most.

Dimitri motioned for the box of tissues on the shelf behind me. Conscious to stay off-camera, I quietly placed it on the table. She wiped her eyes and apologized. Her softness came back. I could see she'd let go of resistance to what he'd said.

"So what about the silver lining. When does that come in?" she said in a subdued, broken voice. I kind of teared up slightly watching her. Dimitri's mood shifted into one of positivity and softness and he smiled kindly. I'd seen him do this many times in the ERP meetings. He'd come on strong until he knew he'd beaten down the ego. Then he'd morph back into his nicer, gentler self. This was the mastery within his gift.

"The silver lining is in the middle of our divisiveness, just waiting for us to see it," he said quietly. "All we have to do is show up, join together in unity, exit their plan, and start a new one of our own before it's too late."

A bit of life returned to Marianne's face. "So, what you're saying is we don't have to necessarily get to a World War III scenario?"

"Not if we get busy, wake up, and take responsibility for what's going on in our minds and in our world. But I stand by what I said because until there is evidence that this great awakening has cranked up, their plan of evil will remain and advance. Our individual, as well as collective, transformation by taking responsibility for all of it is the only thing that will keep the red horse in the stable. But we must move quickly."

I wondered if I was the only one getting stuck on the white and red horse part.

"How do we wake up individually to the degree you speak of, barring a bullet in the chest and having a near-death experience, of course?" Marianne smiled at him innocently, knowing she'd taken a risk touching on a possibly delicate subject. "I imagine that's what happened to you and that's why you are the way you are."

Her boldness made him smile. "That's very astute of you," he said. "I can see you've been doing your homework. And no, we cannot go that route with the rest of the world. There are gentler ways for what needs to die in us, as well as in the world, so those many rebirths can happen." He snuck a quick wink at me.

"Then what can we do?" she asked.

"You and I are doing it right now by putting out this message. But we have 'miles to go before we sleep,' Marianne. We need to join together with people out there who are ready to do their part. For those who are undecided, or maybe not ready, I say step up and decide to be ready now! Because this is your invitation to awakening!"

I heard Marianne gulp as her head moved back a little. "I think I can speak for the others in this room when I say you have our attention. I imagine it's the same for those watching. Go ahead and give it to us." she said.

"First, we have to be ready to let what needs to die, die. As within every evolutionary process, what no longer works must go away so the new can be born in its place."

"I feel like the old me is dead somehow after all of this work I've done since our last interview, but I did have to let go of many different things and even some people."

Dimitri nodded. "Sometimes we have to *let go for love*, the love for ourselves and others, by not nurturing their sickness."

"Absolutely," she said. "Since then, I've been seeing how the mainstream media promotes this sickness, which actually led me to stop watching GNN and others like it, as funny as that might sound, you know, with me being a news reporter."

She's so natural, it's like she forgot she's on live TV.

"Yes, congratulations. One of my highest recommendations to everyone seeing this is to stop watching the news right now, well once we're finished here of course." They both laughed. "Another, which is just as important if not more, is that they rid themselves from the horrible addiction to social media which has been designed to manipulate and enslave us all." She was nodding in agreement. "And whatever you do, and I mean this with all of my heart, don't let your kids use it. The biggest threat to the future of this world is the irreversible damage that social media inflicts upon the young adults and children who are hooked on it."

"I agree with you there, Dimitri. It wasn't easy getting my son, who's fifteen, off of it. I actually had to get him therapy, you know, someone to talk to about what he was going through. But he's been clean now for nearly six months."

"That's great, Marianne. We've all got a lot of cleaning up to do, don't we?"

"Yes, we do, but it can be tough to take those first steps. Oh, and I also stopped drinking alcohol and ingesting sugar as well."

Energized by her words, Dimitri rubbed his hands together, barely letting her finish before jumping in. "That's awesome! If we look at what really happened, it was that you moved beyond your fear of making those shifts by diving straight in and doing it. And by taking those first steps, you found your fearlessness, another one of the required steps to awakening."

She nodded. "And you know what, the clearer I got about what I wanted in my life, with what brings me joy and happiness, the more shifts I made to better it. It's so interesting that we're talking about this, because I've been reading a book that talks about the fears we carry and how they originated from our fear of death."

"Exactamente!" he exclaimed. "And the cause of *that* is the false narrative we've recycled over and over from the first day we found out we were going to die. We've been told so many lies about death that living this beautiful gift called life has taken a backseat to merely existing in it."

Nodding and inspired, Marianne continued, "It was really difficult because I was afraid of being lonely, but I let go of some relationships that weren't serving me anymore. The unhealthy connection with my ex was first. Then, I cut way back on the communication with an immediate family member who's become toxic, only wanting to talk about what's wrong with the world, using pollution, racism, politics, and I don't know what else to make herself feel more than me and others. She's anti-this and anti-that, always accusing me of my privilege, and we grew up in the same house, same DNA!"

She went on, obviously triggered by the issue still. "At first I was doubting myself. I wondered if she had a point and should I feel guilty? But now I can see she's just a bit sick. Like a form of accepted mental illness. No one in the family knows what happened to her, but with the constant patting of her own back and verbal attacks on others, I had to put an end to it."

Dimitri nodded. "That's what I call 'loving from a distance.' We are about to see a lot more of that happening in the world. It's the flip side of enabling."

Loving from a distance. I like that.

"What happened after you finally let go and made those changes?" Dimitri asked.

After a brief chuckle, Marianne got quiet before answering. "Something better came around for me every time. There were moments I got lonely, but I just had to go through that. Even with the sudden death of my mother, my having to let her go and surrender to it changed my life."

As I listened to them, I was brought back to the moment I surrendered to the death of my relationship with Lisa. A space for my meeting MJ had opened up almost immediately.

"Thank you for sharing that. Just like you, many will have the tendency to resist this evolutionary transition and the many deaths, the endings that come with it." He paused to think. "And for good reason, if you really think about it. Let's remember it is evolution that's motoring this shift, and the acceleration of it is merely due to the imminent death of what no longer serves us individually as well as collectively. That can be uncomfortable. Meaning, we can no longer go on as we have. The old way is over."

He took in a deep breath. "So I want to be crystal clear because it's time we get straight about something. This thing we're talking about is really about the death of our disconnection to Spirit."

Marianne's eyes narrowed. He'd lost her as well as me on that one.

"It's quite simple," he continued. "We've lost touch individually and collectively with the essence of the Love that we are. That's a capital L for love, Marianne. The upcoming crisis will be the vehicle that brings us home. The question is, who do we want driving the car? Who or what we choose will determine the length and bumpiness of the ride.

"The architects of the dark plan have no compassion for us or what we feel because they are void of feeling themselves. This is why they promote living in victimhood, hate, entitlement, and all other low vibrational caca that ultimately must be purged from our existence if we want to thrive again. We, the awakened collective, not to be confused with the *woke* mess, must become the designated driver." He looked at the ceiling and started to laugh. "Think about how fascinating this all is. Every horrible move it's made so far, or will make in the future, is actually bringing us back home. It's like the gasoline that runs the car!" He threw his hands up while giggling. "What an amazing time to be alive, right?!"

Marianne wasn't laughing. There was a strange pause before she continued. "How is it these people you speak of have the power to make this shift a hard one?"

"The short answer is because we gave it to them. I touched on it earlier when we talked about them owning our food, the medical establishment, and pharmaceuticals. There are others in this group, and they own literally everything that sustains us. Because of time restraints, I will leave out the explanation of who these players are and how this all happened. What I'd rather do is get back to what needs to be done as soon as humanly possible."

He stopped, straightened up, looked at each one of us in the room, and then landed on the lens of the camera.

"Very soon, a series of events will unfold that will trigger immense fear in nearly every person on earth. This part *is* going to happen, Marianne. The events I speak of, brought on by the current owners of this world, are designed to whip us into submission, all because they are terrified of losing the illusory and temporary grip they believe they have over us. We, the ERP members here at Carlton and a few other prisons that host the program, have been liberated from our minds. We have reconnected with the eternal Life Force that is not separate from us but is us, as the rays of the sun are not separate from itself. We now know and have merged with what we are beyond the physical body, beyond our identification to our names, statures, titles, races, and occupations. That means we know without a shadow of a doubt that we never actually die, other than the transition out of our physical body and into our next experience, whatever that may be. We've reached this state of consciousness while in prison because each of us hit a bottom and have chosen to rise from that bottom, never to return again—all of this by recognizing and bringing to the surface the things within us that are not the Love we are.

"When we see the compassionless judgment within, we do the work to heal it because we stand for a new earth, a new way. We've even made mats called Wheels of Love. We stand on them when we are ready to pledge the truths I just mentioned. If we, as inmates can do it, then so can the world. All people have to do is acknowledge their current life's situation as their bottom and commit to rising up from there. This can be done right now, or one can wait until it gets worse. The good thing is you don't have to go to prison for your motivation because you're already there."

Marianne slowly crossed her arms in what I imagined was disbelief or resistance. I watched as he softly shook his head while motioning to her arms, another thing I'd seen him do in the ERP sessions. She got the message and promptly uncrossed them.

"You might doubt that this is even possible," Dimitri went on, "but I'm here to show you it is. I am proof, as are close to a thousand others on the inside, who would say the same. How is this done? By meeting the darkness with light. What makes that easier said than done is merely the fact that your light has dimmed so much. You must regain it now before it's too late, before they go too far. You, those who are ready, can only get there by diving deep into the shadows of your life experience.

"And just so we are clear, I'm not doing the spiritual bypassing caca here. The pretty woo-woo words and flowing boho clothing won't get you where you need to be to rise up and face what's coming. This means meeting the darkness within, something all of us carry, then transmuting it. There you will pull up the story you tell yourself about your life. You know the one. Where you're the victim of whatever and that's made your life rough. Or even worse, perpetuating the victimhood story onto another, in an attempt to hold them down while your out-of-control ego makes you the false knight in shining armor as you jibber-jabber about protecting them from social injustices and inequality. Here's where you acknowledge that each player on all sides of these stories was doing the best they could with what they had at the time.

"As strange or even as impossible as that might sound, it is a vital truth that must become part of your cellular knowledge before you are liberated from the prison of your mind. Once this step is accomplished, you will have no choice but to change what you say to yourself around the meaning of your story or that of another. This is where you die to your past, the past that carries the beliefs and concepts that limit you. This is where you become present in the only moment that exists, the moment of right now. Then, through your newfound compassion and outlook on life, you'll need to repair the damage that has been done along the way. As difficult as this part may seem, with the discomfort of leaving the old you behind and making amends where needed, you will not be trading gold for silver, but silver for gold. This is how much the Love that you are loves you, that it only has beautiful things waiting upon your return."

I could see that Marianne was getting teary again. I had to look away so

I wouldn't start to feel the same. "Well said," was what she finally said. "I feel like we could end with that, but maybe you can expound on how to repair the damage that involves others. This, I imagine, is the most difficult part, as there are so many facets to what's happened to so many people that—"

"You simply apologize to everyone involved," he interrupted dryly as if that's all he had to say about it.

"Everyone? Even those who did something to y—?"

"Everyone. There is nothing too great that has happened that an apology and taking full responsibility can't fix, no matter the facet or side of the table you're sitting on. Then ask for forgiveness. Thank them for their contribution to your growth, and say I love you. Because you do. As all children of The Divine Light love everyone and all things."

I was in awe, wondering how was it that this very profound message he'd just given, one that would normally take him hours if not days to get across to me and others, he'd thrown out in minutes. I would come to find out much later that what I had witnessed was what he would one day name *critical accelerated uploading.* When I snapped out of it, I saw a very nervous Alex with his phone in one hand and running his other finger over his throat while looking at Marianne.

He's getting messages from the news station to cut the feed.

He looked down at the broadcasting remote on the table, then at Dimitri, who gave me a slight nod. Just before Alex went to grab it, I slid it over to my side, just out of his reach, while simultaneously giving Dimitri the five-minute warning.

Marianne looked back at Dimitri and went on. "So it's time we trade silver for gold, huh? I can see that, but I wonder if it's because I've done some of this inner work you speak of. I'm concerned about the others out there who either won't understand this message or not move on it. What will this world look like as these events occur and many don't follow your words of wisdom?"

"Those who are ready to hear what they already know deep inside will act now because they are in the process of remembering that they are that wisdom itself and all that's left is the embodiment of it. But there will be many who will need a push, and believe me when I tell you that push is coming. Then, of course, there will be several who, through their own fear, will stay on the side of darkness and go through whatever their masters have planned for them. These folks will let the politically-driven, mainstream media direct their every move and, even as the information becomes more and more convoluted, will choose to follow it. These will be the same people who will twist personal freedoms, including freedom of thought, into their new delusional definition of selfishness, racism, or whatever nonsense they can think up."

Marianne chuckled. "I think I know a few people who will drop right into that part. Many in fact."

"There are more sheep in the flock than there are herders," Dimitri said. "And as for what this world will look like with people who remain asleep, that will become of much lesser importance the more you awaken. You will step into your own knowing that each person is on their own very special, individualized journey, and however that unfolds, or doesn't, may have very little to do with you and what you want to create for yourself. This means you will see past the imbalance of the extreme polarities at play. And because you can do this, you will come to see the perfection in all process, even in the destruction or death of whatever shows up and needs to die. You will know that all is just as it needs to be."

"That's a very intense way of looking at it," Marianne nodded. "What's next?"

I looked up to see the goon squad had arrived in full riot gear and were trying to pry the door open, the warden and Jim standing behind. Dimitri saw them too.

"So far we've got dying to our past. That's number one, and through that we become present. Second, we find our fearlessness in letting go of what no longer serves us. Then we repair the damage and finally see and accept the perfection in all process. Once you have awakened to your liberated self by exposing your story and have purged the toxic judgment you have around it and others, then and only then can you be touched by the Love that you are. This is when you step into your life's mission of *agency* and being in the state of service to others. From there, you will have little choice but to play your new role within the unfoldment of the transition. Here's where you will rise to the occasion and take a stand for the eternal Light and Love of all that is. The others, the 'holdouts,' will have no choice but to collapse into the arms of those who have only their worst interests in mind."

He paused to take in a deep breath. "Now I would like to speak to the chosen few who are ready right now." He looked into the camera. "Be aware, great warriors of Light, of the drunk-on-power government officials all too ready to control you and your every move. See the hypocrisy of evil as they make caca on the many constitutions of the world, stripping you of your human rights and freedoms. Appeal to those who carry the badges of authority within the military, government, and police, as well as their family members, so they may lay down their weapons when ordered to move against their fellow sovereign human beings. Because if not, they should know that they will be held accountable in the highest court, the court of karmic law, for any and all war crimes committed against humanity.

"Be clear in your *knowing* that the dark entity will keep the agenda of fear and separation alive by using the mainstream media to create a global hypnosis of fear and bondage as they invent schemes on top of scams to keep you fighting against each other. This is where the work you have done on yourself will pay off as you lay down the sword that you'd unjustly used in fighting against your brothers and sisters on the basis of religion, social activism, gender, politics, race, and any other form of separation the darkness has promoted within you. To win this battle, unity must become commonplace where it never existed before. This looks like you loving what you once hated and called your enemy. This looks like you seeing yourself in all others, especially those people or things you have a problem with, your biggest mirrors."

Marianne shifted uneasily in her chair.

"What's wrong?" Dimitri asked.

"I don't know how ready I am and what my role is in all of this. I think I still have a lot of fear in me, which probably inhibits me from knowing what I came to this planet to do."

He smiled warmly. "I look at you and see the Buddha, Marianne."

Her mood shifted instantly as a smile came to her face. He pointed to her eyes excitedly.

"Right there, that's the sparkle of Christ Consciousness pushing through you!" He stared for a long moment, apparently mesmerized by what he was seeing inside of them. Then he snapped out of it. "Why, look at all you've done here today, Marianne. You are already doing what you came here to do. Just keep up the good work, outer as well as inner, and you'll continue to open the channel for that Christ Energy to come through."

She was beaming, with her head tilted to one side.

I'm pretty sure that confused her.

"Okay, thank you, *but* there are a couple of things I'm not clear on, Dimitri," she said, looking at her pad. "First, when you said 'do whatever it takes to stop them,' what did you mean by that? How far should we go?"

"Once you have truly awakened, you will know exactly what needs to be done for the highest good because you will be using your heart before your mind in deciding how to take the power back." He hesitated for a moment to look around the room and whispered. "And here's another thing: Whatever you do, and I mean this, don't let them force their poison into you, ever."

"Okay, powerful stuff there. I don't totally know what you mean by that last part, but I won't," she said with a confused look on her face. "So, here's my second question. You spoke of the followers who give in to or even those who work for and act on the side of darkness. What do we do when they are friends and family?"

"For those who choose to abide in their deep slumber like the family member you spoke of, as a conscious human being, you will no longer have the energetic space for them in your life. And that's because they will be 'showing up' as working against Life itself. That's Life with a capital L. Once you have let them go, and yes, you will let them go, something or someone new will show up in the space they once occupied, just like we spoke of before. And because you will be working for a new world by loving Life and spreading light, what ends up filling that space will only add to the brilliance of your own."

Marianne giggled. "It's kind of funny because what you are saying, in essence, is that we have to cancel the cancelists."

"Well, we don't *have* to do anything, but if higher vibrational beings want to keep their frequency raised, they won't have a choice. So, yes, I see this happening on a huge scale wherein the tables will be completely turned around, and folks will see that all of this is just a narrative being pushed by the dark media, social as well as news, along with their shady cohorts in the entertainment industry."

"That would be something because I see so many good people confused and asking themselves if they are indeed guilty of this or that."

"Tell them they would only be guilty of their own acquiescence by not standing up for themselves and speaking their truth about what is going on. And if they are worried about being canceled themselves, to that I say, cancel me now!"

Oh, I like that.

"You'd really say that?"

"I'm saying it now. If you don't like what I'm saying, cancel me. I love it. Heck, if somebody makes me a t-shirt that has that on it, I'll wear it every day." He put his finger up. "When I get out, of course."

Everyone cracked up, even the producer, who was shaking his finger signaling us to stop laughing.

"You are bold, Dimitri, I'll say that," Marianne said with a smile.

"If we are going to turn this thing around," Dimitri said, "those who know the truth are going to have to get bold real fast and join the Sovereign Village."

Marianne nodded and said, "The Sovereign Village. I like that."

The kid was spot on, and we all knew it.

Dimitri pointed his finger at Marianne. "You know, the real challenge is to be okay with it *all* because it's just a part of the unfolding perfection. It's important to remember that each person will rise or fall in accordance with when they are ready. There's no right or wrong at this level. It's more complex than you can ever imagine. So, when you love from a distance, you don't make them wrong. That is the opposite of what they're doing.

"There's something else .... I want folks to know there will be a period of shock, disbelief, anger, and hurt when they discover the uncomfortable truth about what's happening with those in power. Those who they believed were there to take care of them while running the nearly fallen system. But it's what you do with that truth that's important. Once you accept what is, I invite you to go through the needed emotional release—cry, scream, yell, hit the pillow, whatever—but then at some point, let it go. Put in that space your new empowered role and mission, rather than continue to feed the enemy with the low vibration that comes from the anger and hurt. Become the practice of letting go, as this is where you will surely be put to the test."

He paused to contemplate, then began to nod. "Having said all that, I want to be clear about another rule to this game. This rule states that at any moment the darkness and anyone under its spell, may move over to the Light where loving care awaits. That spans the whole spectrum from big tech and entertainment sellouts to wife beaters, dog kickers, finger pointers, and informers. Not excluding warmongers, rioters, or constitution breakers, as well as your run-of-the-mill, deeply deluded social justice activists lost in cultural narcissism.

"This offer extends all the way to their boss, foreman, supervisor, owner, the CEO of Hades, the Prince of Darkness himself. All are welcome to return home to the Light of Divinity!" he said, raising his hands high in the air like a preacher.

He cleared his throat, composing himself as he eased back into his chair. "I just wanted to make sure that was clear."

"And I'm really glad you did, Dimitri," Marianne giggled. "I wasn't expecting you to say that, but it's nice to know there's a second chance."

"That's what Love does, it gives second chances and even third sometimes."

"What about a fourth?" she asked, laughing.

"There's always room in the home of the Great Spirit. This I know."

"You know what I keep asking myself, Dimitri? How is it that the darkness is the bringer of this evolutionary process?"

He chuckled. "A paradox for sure, but make no mistake, its only intention is to bring a thousand years of suffering to the people of this world. And know that its worst nightmare is us uniting to co-create a pleasant and beautiful path to move through this evolutionary process together. You see, that's where the paradox lies. In all its effort to separate us, with all the caca it's thrown our way and will continue to throw, it's actually pushing us towards unity. This is because it's in our very nature to join together in times of strife. So it can't win. There is only the illusion of that happening."

She sighed out loud. "It looks as if we've really got our work cut out for us around the coming-together-in-unity part with all the divisiveness in the world. Do you think we even have a chance?"

"It certainly doesn't seem like it, does it?" he answered. "That's the crazy part because the actual fix is a simple one. Just by us going back to the true compassionate nature of loving ourselves as well as all others would instantly return the power we relinquished a long time ago. For me, as the strategist that I am, I'd say they are at a disadvantage because they believe they've done a sufficient job of shrouding us in so much fear that we've forgotten we are actually the opposite of darkness, Light, their kryptonite, or kryptolight as I like to call it. But then I look at where we stand today as a collective and see that we have indeed forgotten, which makes it a tough call."

"So what can we do? They're so big and powerful, it's impossible to stop them, no?" she asked, a bit of panic in her voice.

It took him a moment to answer, but he came back with, "I can only say that, yes, 'they've got the guns, but we've got the numbers, we're gonna win, but we must take over.'"

Did he just quote Jim Morrison?

Dimitri giggled and moved forward in his chair, getting excited again. "In all seriousness, the Light always outshines the dark. I wasn't kidding, a fairly large number of awakened souls, say, one hundred and forty-four thousand, with just that, we could take the power back."

She put her hand up. "That's an interesting number, but wouldn't you say that amount of awakened souls already exists, with all the yoga and healing going on?"

"It is an interesting number, and, no, there are not. If there were, we wouldn't be where we are right now. Are there that number of people who believe they're awakened? I'm sure there are many more than that actually. But what I'm talking about is truly embodied fourth density beings."

"Are you one of those, Dimitri?" she asked in a more hushed tone.

He looked down at his hands and bounced his fingertips together as if he was contemplating what to say. "I am, mostly," he said with humble sincerity. "But you bring up an interesting point. Little by little, folks are taking care of their bodies and minds more than ever. They are exercising, looking at the food they eat, doing yoga, and meditating. They're even learning the importance of being present and observing the mind and its perceptions. Most of those people are just beginning their journey toward becoming fully aware. All of this brings in light and a positive vibration on the planet, and that's what has the darkness losing their caca, hence the chaos it's about to bring on us." He looked up at the ceiling and got all excited. "So, back to the numbers, it's kind of like what Jesus said about where two or more are gathered. Can you imagine two billion, Marianne?"

She didn't answer, because I think she wasn't sure if the question was a real one or not. He calmed down a bit.

"You know, the original number works as well, I was just playing with the number two." He looked down at his hands while fidgeting with his fingers.

Is he really trying to calculate the correct amount? I remembered how MJ joined in on global meditations and how powerful she believed they were. I wondered if that's what he had in mind. *Jesus, I hope he's not talking about some kind of militia or something.*

She threw her hands up. "Then we really are in trouble, then?" Her fearful face had returned and he could see it.

"The fear you carry right now is not a bad thing," he said, "It's actually bringing you back home by forcing you to remember the deeper truth of the fearlessness that you are. Once you truly remember this through your deep inner work and see what's happening from the bigger picture, you won't ask that question like that again." He took in a deep breath. "But to answer, there is one thing they've overlooked. Something that will greatly tip the scales in the favor of the Light." He froze and just stared ahead.

"Well, tell me, I mean, tell us what is it!" She was almost shouting, which caused him to snap out of it as he smiled again.

"It's me."

The cameraman's head came out a second time as nothing but silence filled the room. Even the distant pounding on the second mantrap door had stopped. I looked at the monitors and saw Jim holding his phone up for all of them to see, the warden with both of his hands on top of his head.

Dimitri continued. "I will utilize every bit of my being to reclaim what is ours and die a second or third time, if necessary. I will relive my own darkness, the one I lived in for most of my life, with the sole intention of uncovering their weaknesses so as to foretell and expose their next move on the battleground of the material as well as the nonmaterial plane. I will continue to give my life in service, inside these prison walls and beyond, as I proceed to assemble an army of awakened soldiers ready to do whatever is necessary to win back the sovereignty of our species. And in the end, as we stand in victory, we will salute the fallen soldiers on all ends of the battlefield, for without them there would be no mountain to climb, no game to play, and no journey for the hero to triumph within."

Dimitri closed his eyes and breathed deeply as if he was preparing himself. Alex held up his index finger, signaling one minute till the cut-off. We heard the rumble of the second mantrap door being broken open. We watched as the goon squad ran down the hall. I could tell by his height that it was Tanas in full riot gear leading the pack, the warden and Jim following behind.

"Well, Dimitri, thank you. It looks like we all have quite the adventure lined up for us, whether we want it or not," Marianne said with a not-so-convincing grin on her face. "I'd say, what I got from this is that we have to really take your invitation for awakening very seriously."

I could hear the distant stomping of the guards' boots as they approached. Then, out of nowhere Alex stood up and found the electrical connection to the video monitors and pulled them from the wall. All went black. He looked at me and shrugged his shoulders.

"All you have to do is your best," Dimitri said, "just like you have done here today. You keep doing that and all will work out just as it needs to."

"Thirty seconds," Alex mouthed as Dimitri moved right up in front of the camera.

"Thank you everyone for listening. I truly do love you all. So much that I will leave you with this …" He paused and looked at each one of us in the room with the eyes of a young man who truly cared.

I motioned with my head for him to hurry up as I knew the door of the control room was about to fly open. What happened after that would probably not be good for any of us.

"If you want to experience a reality different from the one you live in today, become that new reality now. If you want love, be the one who gives love. Start with yourself. If you want compassion, have that compassion for everyone on this planet. Be the shift you want to see in the world. That is all you have to do."

"Five, four, three, two …" Alex mouthed.

"Be the shift!" Dimitri shouted into the camera and gave a wink to all who were watching.

Alex jumped up and shouted with a smile on his face, "And we are off the air!"

A beautiful silence lingered in the air. The world seemed to stand still as we looked at each other with humility. It was Dimitri who closed his eyes and slowly put his hands on the table, ready for what was coming.

SHOCK AND AWE

MARCUS

The silence didn't last long. The cameraman yanked off his headphones as Alex high-fived him, shouting in victory. I was stunned by their excitement as they shook our hands and thanked Dimitri and me. It felt good to be on the team at that level for such a big thing. But the fun and excitement were short-lived as three COs in riot gear burst in. Tanas and CO Hopper both had tasers pulled and trained on Dimitri, the two red laser dots moving erratically across his torso. He looked down in awe, trying to touch them with his finger like a cat.

"Cool," was all he said.

Jim came in behind them while the warden stayed just outside, on the phone with who I imagined was a very irate governor.

"All cameras need to be turned off. Warden's orders!" Jim exclaimed.

Oh, shit, I'm in trouble now.

"Feed's cut. Cameras are off," the cameraman announced nonchalantly while gathering his cables with zero fear of any consequence.

The warden walked in and silently surveyed the room. It was as if he was disgusted, afraid, and pissed off all at the same time. I stood at attention, staring straight ahead, waiting for whatever was coming next. "No one move. This is a crime scene!" The warden shouted. Dimitri's hands were still on the table in front of him. He opened them to show his compliance.

"A crime scene? How's that?" Marianne asked, standing. "This man's done nothing illegal."

"But you have, Marianne," the warden scoffed.

"How? By doing my job and giving the interview I came here to give, in the room you asked us to do it in? By starting without you when you weren't here when our live feed came on? Where's the crime in that?"

"Check your damn phone, sweetheart," the warden said and turned his attention to me. I looked ahead stoically as he stared me up and down. I could feel Jim doing the same.

"I'm not sure what you were thinkin' there, boy, but we will get to the bottom of it. That I assure you."

Just play stupid, Marcus.

"Sir, I stood here the whole time. The prisoner has not moved or threatened anyone. I was ready to do whatever necessary if he did." I grabbed the top of my billy club and moved it from side to side, showing I was serious. "He's out of the cuffs just as he was when you were here earlier, sir. I didn't find it nec—"

"Are you playin' stupid with me or are you just that stupid?" I turned my head, feeling the rage creep in. "Which one is it, boy?" he demanded.

There was a part of me that wanted to jump across the table and beat the shit out of him. That was the part that hated hearing a white man call a black man "boy." But I could see he was desperate, and I know what it's like to feel that way. I also know what it's like to be ignorant with your words, as I'd done similar things in the past.

"I guess I'm stupid, sir," I said. "He's been—"

"We've been out there tryin' to get through them doors. Why the hell didn't you buzz us in when you saw us on the—" He pointed up to the turned-off monitors.

"My bad, Warden," the cameraman said coolly as he continued to dismantle his equipment. "I unplugged them for the lighting in the room." That silenced the warden as he began to pace back and forth.

"Let me see your phone, Officer Ogabi," Jim said impersonally. I reached in my pocket, pulled it out, and handed it to him. He pushed the home button to show me all of the missed calls and messages from him.

"I'm sorry, I had the ringer off. I knew this TV stuff was important, and I was just trying to be helpful," I said with a broken voice, acting as if I was actually fearful.

Jim looked at the side of the phone and nodded to the warden. "The ringer's off," Tanas scoffed loudly, shaking his head. I glanced over at Marianne who had her hand over her mouth as she scrolled down her screen. The warden stepped back outside to make some calls.

"I've been fired. And, by the looks of it, they want blood. Something about advertising dollars and not cutting to commercials," Marianne said with a cracked voice as tears began to well in her eyes. Then, unexpectedly a smile came to her face. One formed on Dimitri's next, and they both started laughing.

"What do you think will be filled in the space where my job as a news reporter was, Dimitri?" she said, cracking up.

"I don't know, but it's going to be really great!" Dimitri said, which sparked more laughter between the two of them. Tanas's face turned red with anger.

"The prisoner will remain silent and not resist arrest," Tanas ordered. The laughter stopped, and I turned to see Tanas with his taser again pointed at Dimitri's chest.

How do you arrest someone who's already in prison, you idiot?

"What are you doing? He's just sitting there. There's no threat," Marianne pleaded.

Dimitri spoke in a calm, neutral voice as he explained. "Don't worry, Marianne. Officer Tanas is acting exactly in line as the servant of the darkness he's been trained to be." It was as if he was protecting him from blame. "His orders have been given to him from the same force we've been talking about, and at this point, his ego, the energetic match to that force, has taken over. It's fine." He smiled while shrugging his shoulders, no big deal.

"This is your first and only warning, Tanomeo. I will taze you if you continue to speak. You will submit!"

Dimitri, true to form, started cracking up. The sudden clacking sound of the taser jolted us all. Marianne jumped out of her chair as Dimitri looked down at the electrodes buried in the skin just below his neck. The sounds of the voltage crackled, and he began to shake uncontrollably, his head thrust backward, his mouth wide open as he groaned in agony.

"Stop that right now!" Marianne screamed and began sobbing. This made Tanas hold the trigger down even longer as he smiled at his nemesis's suffering. He'd gone way past the authorized amount of time, and I put my hand on my club, trying to gather the courage to put an end to it all. But, before I pulled it out, something happened. With the voltage still entering his body, Dimitri sat down calmly and pointed at us.

"You should see the look on your faces!" he said, laughing hysterically. "I was going to start spitting and stuff, but I thought that might be too much!"

Every one of us had our mouths opened, including Tanas. He looked at his taser, at Dimitri, then at his taser again.

"This is not possible. It must be broken!" Tanas exclaimed over the sound of the shock waves that continued to enter Dimitri's body. He motioned for the other guard to fire his taser, but Hopper hesitated.

"It's not broken, Tanas. I can feel the energy. There's some serious wattage there. It's just not effective with me, sorry!" Dimitri, still chuckling, turned his attention back to Marianne. She was frozen in the same trance as us all, witnessing something that just couldn't be.

"No, this is not humanly possible. Hopper, I want you to line your laser up with his heart and pull the trigger." CO Hopper moved the dot over the left side of Dimitri's chest as Dimitri looked down in fascination.

"Gene, you're the last one that should be using that word, 'human,' and what's possible or not for us. A subject that by no means can you speak about from first-hand experience!" Dimitri shouted with a smile on his face.

Oh, please just shut up, man.

I was blown away to see Tanas respond with a smirk and a slight shrug of his shoulders, agreeing with him.

What the ... ?

"Fire!" Tanas shouted as the two wires ejected and landed where the laser indicated they would. Dimitri shrugged his shoulders and chuckled.

"I told you, Tanas!" he laughed, trying to speak over the sound of both tasers pulsating at twenty-six thousand volts each. "I gotta say, at this point, you guys are just wasting electricity." Dimitri stood slowly and removed the barbs, letting them fall onto the tabletop. Tanas reached for his club, and Hopper and the others followed suit.

"There will be no need for that," Dimitri said calmly as he held his hands up and walked toward Tanas. He stood in front of Tanas, brought his hand together and said, "Cuff me."

Tanas looked down at the back of Dimitri's hands and slowly returned his club to the metal ring on his belt. He paused before taking his cuffs out and looked up at Dimitri, who in turn smiled and flipped his hands over, his palms now facing upward. This made Tanas take a step backward.

"Go ahead. They're just hands. Cuff me," Dimitri said, moving his palms upward just a bit, showing his compliance.

Tanas studied Dimitri's face. "Ogabi, you cuff him."

I pulled my cuffs out. "Turn around, Tanomeo," I said, playing the part I was surprised I was still allowed to play. Nothing out of the ordinary happened as I cuffed him.

I saw the warden reenter and hand something to Tanas before leaving for the last time. Tanas kept it hidden behind his back as he returned to the table, presenting us with a full-face bite mask. It looked like the one Hannibal Lecter wore in *The Silence of The Lambs*, except made of white plastic.

"Put it on him," Tanas ordered and slid it across the table. I grabbed it just before it flew off the edge. Holding it up, I looked at Marianne as she faintly shook her head. Dimitri seemed interested, trying to get a better look.

"No, that's not gonna happen, Tanas," I said.

"Put it on him and bring him to solitary confinement, his new home."

"I'll take him to solitary, but, as I am the escorting officer and find no threat, I refuse to use that extent of force." Tanas smiled and nodded as if he had me.

"Sounds like over-familiarity to me, Ogabi. Maybe an investigation needs to be opened."

"It's not that at all. I'd say the same thing for any inmate. Forcing him to wear a mask isn't necessary and is nothing more than a power play of submission. If I'm taking him, it's my call."

"Then you won't be taking him. Hopper, put the mask on inmate Tanomeo and take him to the hole." Hopper hesitated, looking down at the ground just long enough for Marianne to stand up.

"Put that mask on him," she said, "and I'll be so far up this prison's ass with the ACLU and whatever other shitstorm I can stir up, you'll wish you were never born." Everyone looked at her. "I may not be a reporter anymore, but I've still got a voice and connections that extend throughout this nation and beyond." She grabbed her pad and pen, readying herself to leave. "We've all had our fun here, boys. Let's just call it a day, what do ya think?"

And just like that, I found myself walking back with an unmasked Dimitri, accompanied by the three other guards in riot gear. We couldn't talk and, even if we could have, I don't think I would. *What just happened in there?* It felt like the whole world changed after that. How could it not? The magnitude of what was said, along with the weight of the implications that could follow, was immense.

Did this guy just declare war? What did I sign up for here? Was that as big as it felt?

My mind drifted. I worried about my safety as well as the people I loved. I also thought about more basic concerns, like Dimitri and how long he would spend in the hole. And for what? Telling the truth? I wondered what

Jim was thinking. Now, more than ever, I wanted to share everything with him. But his behavior in the control room, along with his aspirations for career advancement, told me it wasn't a good idea. I thought about the elections and how they might be affected, how pissed the warden probably was having to deal with the governor. Did Shady and Jim buy my story and, if they didn't, how bad could it get for me? Getting fired would be a blessing at this point, but something told me the warden had bigger fish to fry.

"Hey," Dimitri whispered. "Would you think I was crazy if I told you I kind of wanted to wear the mask?" *What is wrong with this kid?* I glanced back at him with my forehead scrunched. "I thought it was pretty cool looking. I was hoping Zach could see me in it." He started chuckling.

"Hey, no talking up there!" Tanas shouted from the back.

When we arrived at the entrance of the segregated housing unit, I noticed the conference room door was cracked. Inside were two men in dark suits sitting at the table with the warden, who got up and came outside to whisper to Tanas. A chill ran down my spine as that sharp pain hit me in the gut for the second time in one day. *Who the fuck are these guys?*

"Ogabi, we'll take him from here," Tanas said. "Get back to H-block and finish your shift." My first thought was to jump down his throat for giving orders, but I remembered the new Anti-ERP mandate. I calmed myself and removed the cuffs, trying to get a better look at the men in the room. This prompted Tanas to hurry over and close the door.

A terrible feeling came over me as I stood in front of Dimitri. There was something not right about leaving him with Tanas and them, whoever they were.

"Thank you for your service, Officer Ogabi, and goodbye for now," Tanas snapped, trotting back toward us. I had to fight not to ask the little piece of shit what was going on with them and who they were, but after mentioning over-familiarity in the control room, I knew I had to be careful. That's an offense even the union couldn't get me out of if an investigation was launched.

Dimitri snuck me a look. "Don't worry. I'll be fine," he whispered.

As I walked away, I could literally feel my heart hurt as if I was failing him, myself, and the grand mission in general.

SHOUT AT THE DEVIL

MARCUS

The rest of the day was a challenging one, a far cry from when it was just us in the control room with the news crew. At that moment, it felt like we were creating a new world together, so much that I'd nearly forgotten about the not-so-great one I'd already created for myself outside of it. The kind of mess I'd made with the LF carried a heavy price, one that could require payment at any moment. I felt like a sitting duck no matter where I went in the block.

I saw Markland several times throughout the day but knew it was impossible to talk to him. Maybe it was my imagination, but it seemed like all eyes were on me as I made my rounds. Not just Joaquin's gang but other inmates, their allies. *How did my life turn to shit so quickly? Will it ever get good again?*

Feeling relieved the day was finally over, I was on my way to my car when I noticed a black suburban with no plates parked in the restricted area. I slowly walked by and tried to get a look inside, but the windows were completely blacked out. *This has to belong to the guys in the suits.* But that would mean they'd been in there for hours. The sick feeling came back to me as I walked to my car, worrying about Dimitri and what he might be going through. I grabbed my phone to call MJ before remembering we were in a fight.

I was at my car's back bumper, putting my phone back in my pocket, when I felt the data card. I'd forgotten about it. My plan was to drop it off with Markland, but I was so scattered it completely slipped my mind. I stood there and stared down at the white parking line on the blacktop, internally beating myself up for inadvertently getting the contraband in and taking it out only to have to repeat the process later. I was at a boiling point with it all: Tanas, the warden, Joaquin, Ronny, Jim, my problems with MJ, and now these suits with their damn suburban. I just wanted to explode, cry, and kill someone, all at the same time. "Shit!" I yelled out.

"Having a hard day, Ogabi?" a voice said from somewhere. I looked around to find Tanas sitting in his car, backed in right next to mine.

Oh, shit. He just saw that. I put myself back together. "I just forgot something, that's all," I snapped, fumbling through my keys, my face flushed.

"I feel ya, cuz. Must have been something important though. Looks like you're about to lose your shit there, dawg," he said, smiling. "But we all forget things sometimes, don't we?" Tanas was one of those white guys who tried to use ebonics when he was around a black guy or talk cholo when he was with a homie. It was just another unlikable aspect of his already revolting personality.

"Yeah, I guess so," I answered, trying to ignore him while unlocking the car door.

"Forgetting can get us into trouble sometimes, knowwhatimsayin', cuz?"

I pulled my hand off the keys as they tapped against the side of the car. My breath became short and rapid like a puma ready to jump its prey. "I don't, Tanas. I really don't," I replied, standing motionless, my back still facing him.

"Forgetting who we are and where our loyalties lie. Shit like that. We've got to remember who's really running the show. It's all about respect up in here, aight? This place can be fucking dangerous. You really gotta watch your back, cuz."

I turned to face him. He was wearing that same evil grin, the one he'd wear when he wanted to trigger me. It was working. I had so much to say, none of it good. I forced myself to pause and asked myself the question that in the past would help me. *What would Dimitri do?* But at that point, I didn't know and I didn't care. I took a deep breath and counted to five, a technique MJ taught me, but that didn't work either. "I haven't forgotten my loyalties. Not for a moment, you piece of shit. It's just that where mine lie appears to be in a very different place than yours ... *cuz*."

He started his car. "Damn, I hope that's not the case, for your own safety and all."

That was the straw that broke the camel's back. I lunged and yanked open his door as he frantically grasped for the shifter. I grabbed his shirt, trying to rip him from the vehicle, but he slammed on the gas and the car lunged forward. I kept my grip, and stumbled, trying to run with it. He hit the brakes, and I collided with the inside of his door. I felt my forehead impact the metal window frame. The pain was so intense, it caused me to release my grip on his shirt. I heard the plastic buttons tap against the cold blacktop before feeling the itch of blood run down to my brow. I grabbed my forehead with both hands, keeping my eyes on him as he took the car out of gear and pulled the brake handle.

"Oh, that must have hurt," he snickered sinisterly, slowly removing his left foot from the car. "Here, let me check and make *sure* you need stitches."

I backed up a few feet and pulled my hands from my head. I swear I could see the lump grow bigger every second as blood dripped into my eyes.

"I'm gonna fuck you up now, Marcus. Just a taste of what the homies are gonna do."

I had one eye closed as I raised my fists. I heard a whistle blow. I looked back but couldn't see anything. I was secretly relieved but knew I was probably still in trouble.

Tanas was up on his toes, looking over the cars. "Oh, of course. It's your boyfriend coming to save you."

"What are you talking about, you corrupt fuck?!" I shouted, holding my head and seeing Jim run toward us.

"Say what you want now, Ogabi. When your butt-buddy Devic gets here, you'd better figure out your story." He was breathing heavily. He wasn't expecting me to go after him like that. He was a pussy at heart, but he wasn't finished.

"By the way, are you trying to get him fired? That's what's going to end up happening if you keep getting into everyone's shit." I didn't answer him. My mind was spinning, realizing the corruption I'd long suspected had just been confirmed. "One more thing you should know. Using my new position, I made the TAS mats, or whatever they call them, illegal contraband. We will be burning them in the field where your crops used to be, during chow, of course, so the boys get a good view from the window."

What a piece of shit. Now I was really pissed. That's when the ghetto in me came out. "What happened to the black speak, cuz? Why switch it up now, nigga?!" I shouted. I shook my head in disgust, switched the tone up and casually stated, "Nah, you're just a wannabe-anything-but-yo-cracka-punk-ass self!" I paused trying to remember the last time I'd spoken like that. "Jim doesn't know what I know. Leave him out of it, motherfucker. But I swear to God, you and every one of your sick fuck friends that are involved in this will pay."

His eyebrows raised a little. He was obviously taken aback by my language and bravado, but that didn't stop him.

"The question you should be asking is, will you be around to see it, Ogabi?"

I couldn't take one more threat to my life. I went at him.

"What the hell's going on here?" Jim yelled, running up, wheezing. I froze dead in my tracks. Tanas remained silent and looked at me as if waiting for my reply along with Jim.

"Well, Jim—"

"It's Captain Devic. Address me correctly, officer!" he shouted. I felt a pressure in my chest. It was a sadness that came from realizing that this man, who I'd considered a great friend, was, at least at that moment, not a friend anymore.

"Captain Devic, I … I …"

"You what? You don't have to say anything. I saw it all from my office. You opened this man's car door and grabbed him."

Tanas spoke up, "We just had a misunderstanding." Jim turned to glare at him too. "I'm probably a part of it as well. It's hard for some of the men to get used to my new position, Captain Devic." I had no choice but to give him the finger, behind Jim's back.

"I don't doubt for a minute you were a part of it, Tanas!" Jim snapped. "But, Ogabi, you crossed the line."

I wanted to say it all then and there, but couldn't because of Tanas's threat to Jim's job. "Yeah, I did, Captain. I'm sorry, sir."

I'd never seen him this pissed before. He took a couple of steps, stood up straight, and, in an official tone I never expected to hear from him, asked, "Officer Tanas, would you like to file criminal charges against Officer Ogabi for the act of unwanted touching and assault?"

My head jolted back. *Jim's taking his side?* Then I remembered that there really were no sides for Jim. He was a by-the-book guy.

"No, Captain Devic, that's not necessary. We've got it worked out. I think we're both committed to becoming 'the shift we want to see in the world,' right Ogabi?"

Did you really just go there? I looked at Tanas, and he was still smiling. I gave him the finger again and reluctantly said, "Yeah, we're good now."

"I'm gonna get going if that's okay, Captain?" Tanas asked.

"Yeah, go ahead. See you tomorrow," Jim said, as he turned to me.

"I was just taking my break." He backed his car back into its spot while Jim looked at him confusingly.

Yes, Jim. Ask him why he's taking his break in his car which was, oddly, backed in next to mine.

"Okay," Jim said as Tanas opened his door.

"Make sure he gets his head checked, Captain. We need him sharp. It's a dangerous job we have." I couldn't believe this guy was doing it again, right under the nose of our superior. I snarled at him, which he seemed to love, as he gave me a wink when Jim wasn't looking.

"I've got it, Tanas. You just get back inside and do your job," Jim said as if he knew something without knowing it.

Once he'd left, Jim stood staring at me curiously. "You know, yesterday the warden asked me what I thought about you, if you were a team player. I told him you were one of the best officers I had. Then all of that happens in the control room and now this."

"Jim, I mean Officer Devic, it's just—"

"There's nothing you can say that will cause me to believe what I've just witnessed was justified." He came in close and whispered, "Look, I know Tanas is not of the best character, but you've got to control your emotions. I can't have this kind of crap happening right now. There's too much going on. Do you hear me?"

"Yes, but there are things you don't know about and—"

He held his finger up, signaling me to stop speaking. I'd already said too much.

"I'm sure there are and guess what? I don't want to know. I have no interest in rocking the boat because Shady could very well become the governor soon. Which means he'll bump me up, which means I can be more effective in making changes. So whatever you know or think you know, keep it to yourself and let things be the way they are until Shady's out of here. Copy that, Ogabi?"

Wow, really?

I was so disappointed. I wasn't buying that his motivations were about making changes. I took a deep breath and mumbled, "Yes, sir. Copy that."

"I've got to go deal with today's mess from the stunt Tanomeo pulled, which I hope you didn't have anything to do with, despite what was insinuated in the control room. Either way, go and get your head looked at. Off compound. The fewer people who know about this, the better."

"Roger that. See you tomorrow. And thank you, sir."

"One more thing," Jim said as I walked to my car. "Don't call me sir. Don't call me Jim either. Just Captain Devic from now on."

Those words hurt more than anything I'd felt in a long time. For me, it signaled the end of our friendship and that broke me. The only thing I could do was nod my head while staring at the ground and say, "You got it, Captain Devic."

» » « «

I went to the hospital and got a few stitches. They gave me some pain medication, and I drove toward home. The whole way I felt like I was falling apart. I glanced down at my phone and saw it had blown up after the interview. MJ, Hope, and even Lisa had called, but I didn't want to talk to anybody. I pulled into the grocery store to get some ice for my head, and on my way to the register, I saw the booze aisle. I hadn't gone into that area since the almost DUI incident in my car.

I stopped and looked down the row lined with glass bottles filled with a substance I swore never to touch again. It was as if each one was calling me to come and say hi.

What could it hurt? I'm just going to look.

OFF THE WAGON

MARCUS

I woke up to the distant sound of my phone ringing. *Why am I on the sofa?* As I pulled my head up, my mouth unstuck itself from the cushion. My face was swollen, everything was a blur, and my head hurt. I could barely make out the cat sitting on the chair in front of me.

"What happened, Lucky?" I asked, thinking I might get an answer.

I surveyed the dark room. Everything looked normal. Then I noticed something on the floor just behind the coffee table. I stood up for a better look.

"Oh shit, no!" I yelled, turning on the lamp next to me. There it was: an empty bottle of cognac. I looked in the kitchen and saw four empty cans of coke next to a plastic shopping bag. "No, no, no!" I shouted louder, realizing what I'd done. My stomach turned as I staggered to the bathroom, only to drop to my knees and vomit into the toilet. I stayed slumped over a while, trying to put together the events of the evening. I gathered I'd blacked out— that much I knew for sure. I grabbed my phone, mysteriously hidden in the clothes hamper. "No way. No fucking way!" I yelled, noticing I'd slept in.

I got to my feet, turned on the light, and looked in the mirror. "Oh, come on!" I shouted, only now remembering my damaged head and the cause of it. The recollection of all the dramas in my life came rushing in at once. *Maybe I should just drink some more, to forget again.* I studied my booze-induced, puffy face in the mirror, and as if that wasn't enough, my forehead looked terrible. I'd torn off the hospital bandage in my stupor and began frantically searching the empty Band-Aid box. *How am I going to go to work looking like this?* "How are you going to go to work *feeling* like this," I asked my reflection out loud.

I showered and cleaned up the best I could. I wanted to get rid of any evidence of what I'd done so I wasn't reminded when I returned. I searched the apartment for the hospital dressing and finally found it in the cat food bowl. I was late, so I carefully pulled off each bit of kibble and reapplied it to the nasty wound.

On the way to work, I kept looking in the mirror. It wasn't just how the wound looked that I was worried about. It was the wound combined with my swollen face, bloodshot eyes, and the fact that I was still somewhat intoxicated. I needed coffee, but seeing how MJ had convinced me to stop drinking it a week before, I didn't have any at my place. There was no time to stop, so it would have to wait until after the briefing.

Of course, when I showed up, all the COs wanted to know what had happened. I wasn't going to out and out lie because I didn't know who knew what, or whether or not Tanas would talk in the future.

"Just me being stupid, that's all. I don't really want to talk about it" was the line I used several times. Actually, I *had* been stupid, and I *really* didn't want to talk about it. But the real truth was I let my anger get in the way of my peace, more than once in forty-eight hours. On top of it all, I had no idea how Dimitri was doing and what occurred with the men in the suits.

Jim didn't show up for the briefing, which I found odd. No one seemed to know where he was. In desperate need of coffee, I went quickly to the staff program area.

» » « «

"It ain't gonna be ready for fifteen minutes. Just put it on. The old machine takes a bit," the trustee worker said as he rushed to put the pastries out.

"It's six a.m.! Why wasn't it made earlier? Every day it's ready at six and today it's not!" I yelled.

He stared at me, nervously pulling on his fingers. "Because the lieutenant unlocked the doors to the cafeteria kitchen late today. I'm doing the best I can, Officer."

"Okay, okay. I get it," I said as I stood and watched as the short, balding, middle-aged white man ran back to where the supplies were stored. Maybe it was the hangover, but I felt sorry for him and regretted yelling. *What would it be like to live in this prison, having to suck up to mean guards like me?* I noticed the familiar tightness return to the middle of my chest.

I turned to leave but only took a couple of steps before stopping. *There is nothing too great that an apology can't fix,* I heard Dimitri's voice from the interview say.

I noticed my hands were shaking. *Oh, boy.* He was in the kitchen so I had to yell, "Inmate, can you come out here for a moment."

"Yes, sir, comin' right now," he shouted. I heard some pans clank and he appeared. "It's still not ready, just a few—" I raised my hand. "No, it's not the coffee, inmate. What's your name?"

"Gilbert R. Sullivan, number 72348, sir."

I looked him up and down and took a breath. "Okay, well, Gilbert, I would like to apologize for snapping at you. I've really had a bad couple of days, and I kinda took it out on you. So I'm sorry for that. And I hope you can forgive me."

A noticeable stillness filled the room. Something had just happened, and, in a way, kept happening. I don't think I can describe it, but what I can say is something occurred in me and, I presume, Gilbert as well because a huge smile appeared on his face. I immediately saw him. Not as a prisoner or even a little man that I felt sorry for. I saw him as the good guy he must have been as if he was never in this place and we were just two people having an exchange of words.

"Oh, okay, Officer, well, I ... I ... I really don't know what to say about dat, sir." He put his hand in front of his mouth, trying to hide his two missing teeth as his smile grew. The silence was getting uncomfortable, but at the same time, it was nice. "You know, we all have hard times, Officer, and truth be told, we all can lose ourselves a little. I know I have. So of course I forgive you."

Any guilt, pity, or sadness I might have felt for him, toward him or toward myself had vaporized into the ether. What was left was what I can only describe by using a term I learned from Dimitri: the absence of separation. That means, at that moment, I could see Gilbert as a person just like me. I knew he probably had a family that loved him and, like myself, he had made errors and was paying for them. This made me feel much better than I had just minutes before.

"I'm late for my shift. See you soon, Gilbert. And thank you."

"Thank you?" he asked, looking confused.

"Yeah, you know, thank you for helping me see something I hadn't before."

He looked down at the ground, shaking his head in disbelief. "Okay, well thank you as well then, Officer." He chuckled. "First time I've ever seen a screw say he's sorry to an offender before." He looked at the coffee machine,

"Still not ready."

"Can't wait, gotta go," I said.

"You take care, Officer."

I grabbed a croissant for later and paused, trying to conjure up the courage to attempt yet another first. I moved my hand up to my heart and bowed ever so slightly while almost silently muttering the three words as I'd seen Tanomeo do in the past. It wasn't as clean as his, a bit rushed, but I got it done. I spun and left, never seeing the reaction of prisoner Gilbert.

» » « «

Knowing I was taking over the pod from Brenda, I hurried down the corridor, getting dizzier with every step. I hoped being ten minutes late for the shift change wouldn't set her off too much. Our friendship had shifted to a sort of uncomfortable, odd toleration after our drunken night of intimacy. I remember my father used to say, 'You cannot fuck your friends, figuratively or literally. So don't fuck your friends.' He also told me to 'never fish off the company dock.' I'd managed to break both of the rules in one regrettable night and was about to pay for it.

"You're late and I've got shit to do."

"I'm sorry about that, Brenda," I said. "I'm going through some stuff right now."

"It sure looks like it," she said hatefully, looking at my forehead. "Don't for a moment think that just because we fucked means you can walk all over me!"

Oh, yuck.

"I don't. I'm really sorry. It won't happen again."

"Better fuckin' not," she snapped.

For the life of me, I couldn't see why I had sex with that woman. Still pissed off, she grabbed her thermos and keys and said, "I heard you got your fuckin' ass kicked by Tanas yesterday. *Nice!* I also saw the interview. I heard you could've put an end to that shit and didn't." She looked me up and down. "I took you for more of a badass than that, Marcus." She laughed and shook her head. "Tanas. I bet even I could kick that weird cocksucker's ass."

"We actually didn't fi—. Never mind." My head hurt too much to explain, and I just wanted her out of there.

"Don't get too close to any supervisors. You smell like booze. God damn, I wouldn't let them see you either. You look like fuckin' dogshit."

"Thanks, I think?" I said, glancing at my reflection in the window. *It's true, I do look like dogshit.*

She walked away without saying goodbye.

"Sorry again, Brenda!" I called out. She never turned, just threw up the bird and continued.

» » « «

After forgetting the memory card swap with all of the craziness the day before, I decided to make Markland's cell my first visit. In all honesty, I was doubtful about what good the cards would do at this point, and whether they or the guys would even make it out of Carlton alive. Booze makes me pretty negative.

"Markland, hey," I mumbled as I stood in the entryway of their cell.

"So, you did *get* your ass kicked by Tanas?" Markland said, jumping off the bunk.

"We didn't actually … never mind." I put my hands in the pockets of my jacket and felt the memory card. I proceeded to walk right in and toss it on the top bunk like it was nothing. Zach lunged forward to snatch it up.

"What are you doing?" he snapped in a whisper, glancing at the door.

"I'm giving you what you asked for. It's a pretty minor event, Markland." I slurred. "Thank God this is the last one. Get it back to me sooner than later, so I can tie up this portion of the madness in my life."

The camera and memory cards were by far the most illegal things I'd done. I couldn't take the hit if they were discovered and my involvement found out.

Zach looked at me. "Oh snap. You're hammered." He handed me his coffee. "Drink this man. D probably wouldn't appreciate you coming in here like this." He looked outside and waved for me to hurry. He quickly passed me the memory card that was ready to go out of Carlton. I put it in my same jacket pocket while drinking the last gulp.

"That's terrible," I gasped.

"That's Carlton commissary, boss. Sanka is all we get. Sorry, no Monty's in here," Zach laughed as he grabbed the cup to wash it. "What happened anyway?"

"It's been a hard week," I said.

"Tell me about it, Ogabi," he said sarcastically, not concerned about the disrespect. "It's been intense for us all. I've got the Mexican Mafia trying to take me out, a cellmate who's MIA, and a warden who's closed us down completely. I'm not sure what happened, but there was no way the warden okayed what D said in that interview, which was fucking epic. I watched it on one of the illegal phones. Something happened to the dayroom TV. It's stuck on GNN, who would have never shown it anyway."

His face got serious. "Where the fuck is my friend, Officer Ogabi?"

I told him everything I knew. The color on his face changed when I mentioned the men in black.

"You say they were driving a black suburban?" he asked.

"It had to be theirs. Parked in the red, like they just didn't care."

"Sounds like the FBI, maybe the CIA, or *worse*. Why didn't you stay there with him? You could have just fucking refused to leave." His tone wasn't what I was used to, but I was in no position to do anything about it.

"It doesn't work like that," I said. "It would have been worse for all of us if I did. I'm going to dig and see what happened. Just go easy on me right now. I don't feel so great."

"You gonna hit the bottle every time things get challenging? This is just the beginning. It's nothing compared to what's coming and—"

"There you go, talking about what's coming just like he does, how big it's all going to be. But there's no evidence of that right now, is there?"

"You wanna explain what you're referring to?"

"Well, your program has been brought to a halt, and by the look of things, Dimitri's not going to be able to bring it back. You guys are all following the Anti-ERP orders like good little children. And there's no guarantee he'll even make it out of here alive to be a part of 'what's coming.'" I used air quotes and a stupid face. It was cynical, born from drunken frustration. I realized I'd maybe gone too far.

"You really are going through it, aren't you?" Zach asked.

I hesitated to say what I felt. I didn't want to sound like a victim, but I had to get it off my chest. "It's because of this thing that I'm doing with you guys.

It's causing everything in my life to fall apart," I pointed to my forehead. "It wouldn't be so bad if it seemed like the program was still alive. I just had no idea it would die off so quickly."

Zach shot up and squared off with me, ready to argue a point. "Yo, it's never dead. It's alive in the men who wish to carry it. As far as us not breaking the new task force orders, D's getting specific guidance. I don't expect you to understand what that looks like. Shit, I can barely understand it myself. We only ask that you have faith in the process. But know this, the most important thing is that we all make it out of here alive. This is just a testing ground. Outside is where the big work lies. Remember that the force that causes the doubt in you is the same force that doesn't want us to remain united. It knows we're here to put it out of commission. Do you get me?"

Jesus, he sounds just like Dimitri. "Not really, but I might in a day or two."

"It can take a little time to process," he said. "Speaking of staying alive, how you doin' with that? I heard something."

"What did you hear?"

"I heard your name's on a piece of paper like mine and D's, but you haven't been green-lighted, yet. How's that even possible? You're a CO?"

I told him about me taking it too far with Joaquin's main vato, Orozco, that day outside their cell.

After his initial freak out, with him realizing that he'd come that close to getting hit and not knowing about it, he calmed down. "You got your name on paper for that?"

"I said some things," I said. "I really disrespected him. I brought his kid into it. The one that got hit with that stray in the projects last year."

"Oh, you went there, did ya?" Zach asked, shaking his head.

"I let my emotions get in the way."

"There's not much I can say about how you are gonna perceive the unfolding of this thing, whether ERP's dead or not," Zach said. "You're gonna have to choose to trust or not, but with this thing with Ronny, you've gotta fix that. You know what you need to do. Not just for your safety but, you know, just because."

"It's a tough one to fix, that's all," I said.

Zach went over the whole apology thing. It was nice to hear it again, but I couldn't help but wonder if his true motive in encouraging me to make things right was his future safety.

"Just remember you are doing this with a person, not a gang. In this case, it's Ronny O. I get what you mean—he's a heavy—but I do know you need to fix it."

"Okay," I whispered. I breathed a silent sigh of relief. His words, genuine or not, calmed me. He stepped into Dimitri's shoes when he wasn't there. It was impressive.

"Just one more thing," he said. "I don't have to tell you how serious this situation is, but if what went down the other day in the yard and almost in my cell is any indication of how far these different players are willing to take things, you need to be very careful."

"It's even worse now that Devic and I have drifted apart. I'm all alone here." I took a minute to fill him in on the Devic story.

"Captain Devic has a good heart. D and I were talking about it the other day. He's just got his head up the warden's ass right now. Don't count him out just yet."

Our time was up, and I left his cell quietly, my head full of thoughts despite the hangover. I spent the next few hours dwelling on how quickly Jim's opinion of me had changed and how I might fix it. I wanted to tell him about the warden threatening Tanomeo's life. I wondered what he'd think if he knew who was really behind the attack on the ERP crew and all the dirty details. But he did tell me he didn't want to hear about it. On top of it all, I kept hearing Tanas in my head saying, "Are you trying to get him fired?" Either way, without proof I was dead in the water.

CAT OUT OF THE BAG

MARCUS

Just before lunch, I got a call on the radio that Jim wanted to see me. When I walked into his office, I could tell he wasn't happy.

"Close the door and have a seat," he said sternly.

I tried to make light conversation about the plants in his office. We'd spoken about them in the past, and he'd put many in the warden's office as well, which I thought was a kind of kiss-ass move. But in all fairness, Jim *was* a botanist. "What's this one called?" I asked, touching the leaves of one on his desk.

He pulled my file out of his desk drawer. "It's a *red aglaonema*," he answered coldly while opening it.

"So, what's the problem?" he asked. I gave him a curious look. "And please don't act like you don't know what I'm talking about. You're fighting with fellow COs, you show up for work unfit to do this job effectively, and then, this morning, the warden questions me about where your loyalties lie again, obviously referring to what happened in the control room. Oh, and because I've been seen fraternizing with you in the past, my loyalties have come into question as well."

I put together the not-so-coincidental coincidence of Tanas talking about loyalties and where they lay. "I'm just going through a lot right now," I said. "I'm sorry if I've caused problems for you."

"Why is it that the warden is suspicious of you?" Jim asked.

Why is it that our warden-soon-to-be-governor is so corrupt?

I wished there was a way I could just push a button and everyone would know the truth. But there wasn't, so that left me in the middle of it all, playing the part of the warden's silent opposer. No one watching my back, no one on my side.

"I can't say for sure, Captain Devic, but I'm wondering why he's even concerned about me or my loyalties if he's doing his job honestly," I answered.

There was an odd pause. I knew I'd either crossed the line in my veiled accusation or he was considering what I said.

"I'll tell you where my loyalties lie, Officer Ogabi. In my job, that's where." I crossed the line. "I can see," he went on, "there's good reason for me, as your supervisor, to take action. I am hereby putting you on notice and occupational probation. I highly suggest you don't make any further behavioral mistakes in the next three months. If you do, your employment here at Carlton will be in serious jeopardy."

I think it was the hangover combined with the bad news that made the room start to spin. My hands got cold and clammy, so I put them in my jacket pockets. "I really can't lose this job, Captain Devic," I pleaded as he filled out the paperwork.

"I'm sure you can't. Just don't mess it up and you'll be fine." He finished, signed it, and spun it for me to do the same.

I took my right hand out of my pocket, grabbed the pen, and signed.

"What's that?" he asked.

"What's what?"

"What's that stuck below your thumb?" he asked, pointing to the memory card stuck to the bottom of my sweaty palm.

This is not happening.

The spinning of the room was replaced with what I think was a panic attack. I actually had to catch my breath just to get some words out while trying to think of what to say. "Oh, wow," I said, grabbing it with my other hand. "It's the memory card to Hope's camera. She wanted me to download the photos she'd taken and give it back to her. I must have forgotten when I saw her. It's so small, I didn't even notice."

He reached over and took it out of my hand. "That must be a really small camera," he said, inspecting it while glancing at the side of his laptop.

Please don't let there be a port for it.

"Why does your kid have such a small camera, and how do you ... ?" He kept searching for the port.

"She's small, so she probably wanted small. Her stepfather bought it for her so I'm not really sure." *I don't think that even made sense.*

I had to keep going. "My girlfriend has the thing you use to take stuff off it. I'm not technical at all, so I just give it to her."

He looked at it and then at me. He slowly handed it back. "You've got two strikes against you, Ogabi. Don't get a third. Good luck," he said in a cold but fair voice.

My heart was beating so fast I worried I might have a heart attack. "I won't, you'll see. And sorry again. Thank you, sir. I mean, Captain Devic."

» » « «

It was only a matter of days before I got a call from Jim asking me to come to his office for a very different reason.

"Come in," he said, motioning me to close the door behind me. He seemed a little more like the Jim I knew before, not the angry version I'd recently experienced.

"You know I have my CIs, right?" he asked, referring to the confidential informants that would feed us information from time to time.

"I do."

"Well, one of them, Clyde Ratford, gave me a tip on a device that's loose in H-block."

A "loose device" with Jim meant there was an unauthorized piece of technology, usually a phone, in one of the inmate's cells.

"No shit. Who's got it?" I asked.

"That's not so important right now. What is important is what Ratford's been hearing."

"Oh yeah. What's that?" I asked.

"That a black CO has his name on a hit list with the LF."

While it didn't get easier to hear what I already knew to be true, the only good part was it was coming from Jim, which meant this was my moment. I took a deep breath and, for the next fifteen minutes, told him everything I knew and all I suspected. It was no longer about him taking my word for it. He had other evidence to go on now. I clued him in on my situation with the LF, all the way up to Tanas and the warden, obviously leaving out the depth of my relationship between Dimitri and Zach as well my own illegal exploits.

When I finished, he sat staring at the pen in his hand. I wondered what could be going through his mind. The election, his career advancement, all of which could be put in jeopardy if he were to make any moves against the players I'd just clued him in on.

"I'm buying what you are saying about the LF. You crossed the line with them, but the rest? I'm not saying it's not possible, but it's darn unlikely. Let me get Ratford back in here with the both of us. I told him to get as much info as he could. Now that I know it's you, I want you here for the interrogation. Let's see what we can pull out of him, together. He owes me anyway. We'll toss his cell tomorrow morning as a ruse to pull him in for questioning as if we found something. He can't come in on his own like he did yesterday. It would look too suspicious."

I nodded, relieved to know I wasn't the only double agent at Carlton, even if the other was an inmate. "Until then, keep out of harm's way. Go ahead and team up on your rounds with Ken Chiou. I'd like to get this wrapped up before I go on the last leg of the campaign tour with the warden this weekend. The election's on Tuesday."

I'd often wondered why the warden chose Jim to go with him to campaign events. I guess he knew he could trust Jim would always say the right thing about the prison and goings-on in it. Plus, Jim always wore his uniform and made the warden look good. It was probably all political stuff that I didn't understand.

"Copy that, Captain," I said as I got up to leave. I played it cool on the exterior but was more than pleased to know that the truth was about to reveal itself.

» » « «

The next morning we searched Clyde Ratford's cell. He acted surprised. Probably because he was surprised. We actually found several illegal items, all of it low-level contraband. Clyde was a hustler and moved things around the prison just to have a little more than nothing in a place where every little bit mattered. I quickly bagged and tagged the evidence as Jim hauled Clyde off to his office.

I was removing my black latex gloves with my back to the entrance when I felt a presence behind me. I turned, my heart nearly jumped out of my chest. Joaquin Flores stood just outside the entrance of the cell I was in. He stared directly into my eyes and there was nothing I could do but stare back. I reached down slowly for my club. He smiled and put his palms up, leisurely walking backward.

"Peace and looove, Officer Ogabi. Isn't that what *our friend* teaches us?" He spoke slowly, with confidence, with no accent or slang. It was like he was in charge. In a strange, unspoken way, he was.

"Take two more steps back, inmate!" He took his time complying as I moved toward the doorway and looked outside the cell. It was just him.

"Was it a good bust?" he asked with a grin.

"What?" I asked, confused by the question, still trying to recover from the jolt of fear, my heart still pumping.

"The cell toss. Did you come up with anything?"

I ignored him and walked outside.

"In all the years I've been here," he went on, "I've never seen old Clyde's cell tossed. Not once. You must have found something to move him out so quickly." He studied the evidence bag in my hand. I concealed its contents by shoving it under my arm.

"What we are doing here has nothing to do with you, inmate," I barked. "I suggest you get back to your world."

"Will do, Officer Ogabi. I was just taking a walk and wondered what you and the captain were up to. Just goes to show, one can't be too careful these days with guys like Clyde walking around." He slowly turned and sauntered away. The inmates in the corridor nodded respectfully as he passed.

» » « «

I closed the door behind me as I walked into Jim's office. Clyde was still cuffed, sitting in a metal chair in front of Jim's desk. I pulled a chair up next to Jim and dropped the plastic bag on top of it. Clyde dropped his head and asked, "What do you want?"

"What else you got, Clyde? You can speak freely. Officer Ogabi has been filled in on our talk."

Clyde looked at me, then at Jim. Jim gave him a nod to continue.

"Officer Devic, you asked me to dig a little deeper and find out who was the black officer on the list. Well, I did, and I'm not sure if this is some kind of coincidence, but," he turned and looked at me, "you're the one that's on the list. You're the black CO, Officer Ogabi."

"How do you know that, Clyde?" Jim asked.

"I got it directly from one of the top guys."

"Who?" Jim insisted.

"This is where I have to draw the line, Captain Devic. It's bad enough I've been in this office twice this week. There's no way I can tell you anything else other than Officer Ogabi is the target. It's just too dangerous for me."

He was right, and he didn't even know the worst of it. My interaction with Flores at Clyde's cell was not a good sign, but I didn't want to spook him, so I didn't mention it to either of them.

Jim wasn't convinced by Clyde's story. He wanted a name so he could connect it with what I'd told him. But even after pressing Clyde with the bag of contraband we'd found, the most he'd do was tell what the beef was about, which would be proof in itself.

"I heard you got personal with some family shit. Something about a boy who got shot. And you did it with the kind of folk that don't put up with disrespect from anyone. That's all I got. I'm done."

That was all Jim needed to corroborate my story. He grabbed the bag, opened a drawer on his desk, and dropped it inside. He tossed the keys over to me and I uncuffed him.

"You're free to go, Clyde. Any other details you come up with, please let us know."

"That's gonna take a dent out of my earnings. Sure you can't give me that back?" Clyde asked, pointing to the drawer.

"I'm sure you'll bounce back. I'll make it up to you at some point," Jim said.

I opened the door and Clyde shuffled out.

"There definitely seems to be a direct threat against your life," Jim said. "I'm gonna act on that. But nothing he said connected your claims to Tanas or Shady. So, what I'm going to do, while I'm away, is put you on desk duty here in my office. That means you will act on my behalf with anything happening in the office only. I was going to have Ken Chiou cover me after your write-up, which I'll hold off on filing until I return. I think it's the safest move, given the circumstances. When I get back I can figure out what to do with the LF. Hell, if I have to, I'll move them all to separate blocks."

But you won't do anything about the corrupt warden. Nice. That's how by-the-book he was. Or maybe he just wanted to get his bump in rank. Either way, I just needed to be happy with what I got.

"Thank you, Captain. I've been stressing about this."

He looked at me and pointed his finger. "You've only got to do one thing for me."

"Sure. Anything," I answered.

"Don't screw it up now, ya hear? Don't go getting drunk, and no fighting with Tanas, or anyone for that matter. It's just two days. Do you think you can handle that?" I was being spoken to like a problem child, or an inmate. "You're taking too long to answer, Ogabi."

"No. I mean yes," I said quickly. "I can handle it."

"Then it's settled. You've covered my office in the past, and you know how I run things."

"That I do."

He got up and put his hand on my shoulder on his way out. "Just don't make me regret this, Marcus," he whispered in my ear.

The fear of messing up, combined with the happiness I felt that he had again called me by my first name, made for a strange mix. I nodded, got up, turned around, and shook his hand.

"You won't," I said. "I promise."

HOMBRE MUERTO CAMINANDO

RONNY

It took me a fucking long while, but I finally got the huevos to make the decision to do it. I guess I had to do it. My fucking life depended on it.

I walked all the way to admin, the place where none of us usually go. The woman at the desk told me I could just go in. *That part was easy.* Before I opened the door, I looked around to see who was close by. Of all the shit I'd done in my life, this was the heaviest, the worst, the most dangerous.

I mentally prepared myself. *Get it done fast, get out of there, and then let the fucking chips fall where they will.* My fucking hands were shaking as I slowly turned the doorknob.

"One second, I'll be right with you." He was in a chair, crouched over the bottom file cabinet with his back to me. I moved to the side, trying to get a look at his face. I had to make sure it was him. I couldn't see anything, so I waited until he was through doing his filing shit. My heart was pounding out of my chest. He sat up straight and turned around.

What the fuck? It was the mayate, Ogabi, in Captain Devic's office. I hadn't seen him since that day he fucked with me outside of Markland's cell. I think he was just as surprised to see me because he flew back into his chair, hitting the file cabinet with the back of his head. He was all paranoid and shit, putting his hands up as if that could help him if I wanted to hurt him. This might sound kinda fucked up, but it was the first time I'd ever seen a mayate turn kinda white.

"What are you doing here, Orozco?" he asked with a kinda shaky voice. I guess he thought I was there to come at him, seeing how he was gripping the arms of his chair.

"Where the fuck is Captain Devic, eh?" I was giving him a hard look with a hard voice, you know. But it was more like out of habit. I didn't know how else to be, standing in front of someone who dissed me and my son like he did. What I'm sayin' is that I wasn't really trippin' on him. I just had to act like I was. You know, because the shit he said was really fucked up, but, in truth, it got me inside that office doing what I needed to do. So, in a way, you could say I owed him, but I could never tell him that shit, you know?

"He's out today and tomorrow, I'm covering for him. What do you need?"

I just mad-dogged him. I couldn't help myself. He was still afraid, I could see it. We just stared at each other. It was sort of fucked up and felt kinda shitty at the same time. *He who speaks first loses.* I remember Joaquin saying that to me once, so I kept my fucking mouth shut.

Once he got his shit together, he broke the silence like I knew he would. "Inmate Orozco, if there's anything that I might be able to help you with, fire away." I just stared some more. He'd already lost, but I wasn't there for that shit, so I loosened up a bit and took my hands out of my pockets.

"Not sure, eh. I think I'm supposed to talk to the Captain about this kind of thing," I said and could see his face change right away like he knew right there that I wasn't there to throw down. Like I said before, we never went to admin, so he knew something was up.

"Ronald, go ahead and take a seat, please."

Oh, now you wanna treat me like a human?

"Look, I need to say something about what happened the other day," Ogabi said, showing his emotions. I could see he was soft, he even had to wipe his eyes and shit. "You know, the other day when all that went down between us. … I just want to say I'm sorry for my part in it. I also need to ask for your forgiveness." He looked down at the desk, kinda like he was defeated but sincere, knowwhatimsayin'?

What the fuck? I was shocked this vato was apologizing to me for what went down. I knew he regretted it, but it didn't help me any. I felt the painful lump that would come to my throat at times like this when I had to think about my son. I bit down hard on my teeth and let my eyes get watery, knowing no drop would ever dare to come out. That's how hard I was back then. "Simón ese, you have it, claro que sí."

He kept talking. "Also, at the same time, I have to thank you as well for this opportunity for me to learn something and grow as a person." It was like he was spilling his fucking guts out or something, which made the lump sorer. It got worse with every word he said. You know it hurt but not in a bad way. Then he mumbled some shit in the end that I couldn't quite make out.

By this point I just wanted him to shut the fuck up. "Okay, jefe. You don't need to say nothin' more. We good." Plus, I was there for something else.

Now I just needed to get the pinche words out. Otherwise, I'd go back to what I knew I didn't want.

"I'm here to renounce my affiliation with the clique. I want to PC up. I'm done with it and ready to debrief." He must have gone into some kind of shock, or some shit, because he just looked at his desk and then up at me. Then he started fumbling around his desk looking for something to write on. The last thing he'd ever expected was that I was there to turn against my people and move into *protective custody.*

"What's your inmate number?" He went from being afraid to soft to now acting all clerical and shit. For sure he was nervous and blown away by what I said. I gave him my information.

"That's, that's great Ronald," he said, but then he looked at me more suspiciously or something. "How do I know you're for real right now?"

I stared at him for a good minute and shook my head. *Just like everyone in my life, this mayate doesn't trust me either.* "Listen, I think I made a mistake here, eh. Why don't you just forget I ever came here. It's better." I got up.

"No, no, please sit down. What I mean is, how did you come to this choice? You sure didn't seem like someone who was done with it the other day on the tier outside of cell 111. You had something else on your mind then, right?"

I just shrugged my shoulders and smiled, still acting like a gangster, even though I didn't want to be one anymore.

"So, let me just be clear about how this works, Ronald. In your debriefing, you will be required to give up everyone and everything that you have been involved in that was crime-related while in Carlton. You will need to inform us about any and all pending hits as well as who you use and how the contraband gets into Carlton. If we even feel that you've left anything out, you will not make it into the protective custody program."

He was talking about the special needs yard. That's where I'd be put for the rest of my sentence once I debriefed. There the LF wouldn't be able to get to me, and I could start to think about a new life.

"I know what I have to do, and I'll take it just like that, holmes." *Agree to be a fucking snitch, Ronny.* But there was no other way. The last thing I wanted was to give anyone up, especially not Joaquin; he was like the brother I'd never had. But it was either him or me and, for once in my shitty life, I was choosing myself. "Listen, I've been goin' over this shit for a long time, holmes. I'm sick of this life, knowwhatimsayin? I've got just under a year left on my stay, and I can still make somethin' of myself when I'm out. That shit you said to me the other day really fucked with me, you know, like in my head, eh. It, like, pissed me off and everythin', but it was true." He just looked at me like, you know, like he was stunned or something. "You don't believe me, do you?" I asked.

"I'm not sure what I believe anymore. What about the hit on me?"

I looked down again and nodded. *Fuck it.* I breathed in and sighed loudly. "It's real. Joaquin is expectin' me to do the work with a couple of others. He wants it done fast. That's why I leaked it to El Soplon."

"What? Who's that?" Ogabi asked.

"Your informant, Clyde. That's what we call rats. We've been feeding him stuff for years. Many of the shakedowns you end up doing come from us. Joaquin says it keeps you off of the LF."

"Wait a minute, what you're telling me is you guys leaked to Clyde that I was on the list?"

"No, not 'you guys.' Just me, ese. I leaked it because I wanted it to get to you, knowwhatimsayin? And by the looks of things, that's why you are here in this shitty office." I watched him shake his head like he was still confused or something.

"So, let me just get this straight. A hit's on me just because of what I said to you?"

I thought about how I would answer his question, a question that had a lot of angles to it. "That day you disrespected me in the hall, sayin' what you said. I took it bad, eh. I gotta admit, I wanted you dead. I went to Joaquin, and he told me to wait it out a bit. Every night since then, I've thought about my hijo and what he'd think of all this shit. Holmes, I'm done killin'. I decided I wasn't gonna do it. But when you hit Mendez like you did, well it didn't matter what I wanted or didn't want anymore. Joaquin called it, and just like that, your number was up. Now it's on me, and I'm too high up to show weakness. I need to get into protective custody, for reals."

"What about inmate Tanomeo and Markland? he asked.

"Joaquin doesn't like that huevon. Says he's a threat to his livelihood or some shit like that. He kinda blames me for not hittin' him sooner. Says that he's done irreversible damage by helping the inmates."

"What do you think?" He was asking my opinion about something I really didn't understand but knew to be good. His asking made me feel like he and I were on the same level in some way. It was like we were just talking, not a guard and a gangster, but just two vatos chattin' it up.

"You know, holmes, I think that guy is pretty straight up. I've heard some of the shit he says, and believe it or not, it kind of helped me make this decision. I mean, it wasn't that his words made me understand this or that because I've never really listened to much of it. It's just that I see other inmates doin' better, and somehow I know, if I could just get out of this situation, I could do better too. Plus, not to sound like a maricon or anything, but just seein' him makes me feel good, knowwhatimsayin'?"

He was nodding, I was glad he didn't think I was a gay or anything like that.

"I do know what you mean, Ronny. I'm going to do everything I can to get you in the program, but there is a process involved. You know about it, right?"

"Simón, I do, and I agree to all of it. I'm going to get mami out of the house. She'll go to Mexico with my aunt for a while. I know Joaquin and what he's capable of."

He asked me some shit about Tanas and how high up the corruption went. "I don't know how high up that shit goes, but I do know the warden gets in it sometimes. Most of the time Joaquin deals directly with Tanas. I don't like that puto. He's got no loyalty to nothin'. Knowwhatimsayin, Officer?"

"I do. I don't like him either."

"I heard he did that to you. Is it true?" I pointed to his forehead.

"No, I did that with the car. We never got down. Captain Jim got in the middle of it before I could get to him."

I closed my eyes and nodded. "I pray that you have another chance then, holmes. That pendejo needs to get his shit handed to him in a big way. He's got no loyalty to nothin'," I said a second time because that's how I roll.

The officer smiled, "You never know." He picked up his cell phone and made a call.

"Whoa, who you callin' there, holmes?" I asked. Now I was the one who was all paranoid and shit.

"Don't worry. I'm trying to get a hold of Jim, I mean Captain Devic. He'll know what we should do. This is a first for me."

I nodded. "Simón, it's like me with Joaquin. I have to do the same, ask him shit before I do anythin." I laughed. "No answer, eh?"

"No, but I know I can take you off the mainline and put you in solitary if you want to exit right now. That's probably what we should do. You'll be in there for at least a month, pending reclassification for protective custody, maybe longer."

The hole for a fucking month? I'm not ready for that shit.

I told him that I would just go back to mainline and wait it out until Devic was back.

"Hey, be careful with El Soplon, ese. He's the weak link in all of this. If Joaquin even suspects anythin', it would be easy to get it out of him. That would make me a dead man walkin', you know, holmes?" I got up to leave.

"Maybe you should just go into solitary right now. Safer that way." He looked paranoid again.

"No, holmes, I'm good. I'm just gonna play like I had to sign some paper shit in here today. I'll be fine." He nodded again.

"Thank you, Ronny."

"Órale pues, Officer. Thank you too. All of it seems like it's good in some fuckin' strange way I don't even know how to explain, but I think good things are comin' my way. Maybe for you too." I'd never said anything like that to anyone before, but it felt like it was true.

"I believe they are, man. Watch yourself out there, and I'll do my best to make this happen for you."

"Gracias, Officer. You watch yourself as well, eh." I grabbed the door handle and turned around. "Or just stay out of H-block and the yard for a minute, knowwhatimsayin?" I gave him a nod and smiled. "Life's pretty fucked up, eh?" I walked out the door.

CLEANING HOUSE

MARCUS

The next morning I woke up at four a.m., an hour before my alarm would usually go off. I guess I was feeling better about it all. I'd be safe in Jim's office, Orozco was now on our side, and things were looking up.

I saw my cell phone light up. It was a message from Ken, who was on night shift at the prison.

KEN: YOU UP
ME: YES, WHAT'S UP
KEN: CLYDE RATFORD FOUND DEAD AN HOUR AGO.
TORTURED THROAT SLASHED. CAN YOU GET HERE?

Oh, shit, no!

ME: GO TO CODE RED LOCKDOWN. ON MY WAY
KEN: COPY THAT

I splashed water on my face and saw my hands were shaking. I gasped to get some air into my lungs.

In the car, it took several attempts to get the key in the ignition, dropping them twice and fumbling to find them on the dark floor. I slammed the bottom of my fist three times on the dashboard. "Fuck, fuck, fuck!" Flores connected the dots, just as I'd feared.

I entered the prison lot, parked, and walked hastily through the security checkpoint. The lockdown siren was still sounding.

The same rookie at the X-ray table passed my things through. "They're suiting up for the cell extraction. You'd better hurry if you're going in with them."

"What do you mean cell extraction? Ratford's dead already."

"Not that. Something just popped off in H-block, cell 269. One of the homies, a shot-caller, jacked his own cellmate. Sorry, I don't know all the names yet."

"Motherfucker!" I yelled as I ran down the corridor past admin. "Buzz me in!" I yelled, entering H-block.

When I got there Ken Choiu and three other COs were suiting up. "What happened?" I asked.

"Orozco's down. We don't know if he's alive. CO Franklin was doing a headcount and came across Flores jabbing away at Orozco's neck. Franklin tazed him through the bars. He said there's blood everywhere and couldn't tell if it's just Orozco's or both of theirs."

Flores hit him in his sleep. Fuck, I should have insisted he go into solitary yesterday.

I pulled my radio's shoulder mic, "10-27 to Dispatch. Officer Marcus Ogabi, acting captain, requesting immediate medical helicopter assistance. Inmate down, critical blood loss, severe lacerations to throat and neck area."

"10-27, copy that," the dispatcher responded.

"Whoa, Ogabi. Protocol says we must physically assess the situation before ordering a medevac. They probably just got into it, and Flores got the jump and pulled his shank."

I tossed my bag on the ground and pulled on my vest. "It's Orozco's blood. Flores attacked him when he was asleep. Don't ask me how I know, just get in there and get Orozco out. I'll take full responsibility for calling in the bird."

Ken put his helmet on while shaking his head. The others took off toward the cell, Ken following close behind.

As I ran toward their cell, I passed the kitchen entrance and saw the yellow tape wrapped around the door and handle. I imagined Clyde's body was there, waiting for forensics. *This is on you, Marcus.*

The prisoners banged their cups against the metal bars, hollering slurs as I sprinted past. Turning the corner, I slipped and landed on my hip. I quickly bounced up, the volume of the hoots, now mixed with laughter, shot up a notch. There was a pain in my hip, forcing me to limp-run the rest of the way.

When I arrived at Orozco's cell, they had already extracted Flores. He was on his stomach and cuffed. He'd been pepper-sprayed and was breathing hard, spitting and trying to rub his eyes unsuccessfully on the concrete.

I pulled the t-shirt under my uniform over my mouth and moved over him and into the cell.

Orozco was still on his bunk. I choked as I knelt behind a masked CO who was searching his neck for a pulse.

"I've got nothing here!" he yelled.

"Check his fucking wrist!" I shouted. My heart was pounding so hard I could barely breathe, and when I did, I choked on the gas. I was brought back to the day I shot Tanomeo. Even though I wasn't the one to stab Orozco, I was the one who let him go back knowing Ratford could be in danger with Flores.

"Is he alive or what?" I screamed.

"I'm not getting a pulse, but with these gloves on I can't be sure."

"Move back!" I shouted as I grabbed Orozco's arm and pulled it towards me. His head seemed lifeless as it dropped. I searched for a pulse with my gloveless hands.

Please, God, just help me on this one. I was praying to a god I didn't believe in but hoped existed in a time like this.

I thought I felt a throb, but couldn't be sure. I moved close to his neck, inspecting the lacerations to see if his main artery had been cut. There were over a dozen wounds with blood oozing from most of them. I saw a deep, three-inch gash with minimal blood flow just under his neckline. I pulled it open slightly and could see the carotid artery pulsating. It had not been severed. The CO patted my back as I turned to see his masked face nod, acknowledging Orozco was still with us.

The prison medical team arrived, and I moved quickly out of the cell. Ken had a bottle and poured it over my face.

"He's barely alive," I gasped, trying to catch my breath.

Ken nodded. "The copter will be here in five."

I looked at Flores.

"You were right," Ken yelled, his voice barely audible over the shouts of inmates. "I checked him. Not a scratch."

"Stay here!" I ordered and walked to Flores, still face down with his hands cuffed behind him. I could smell the drying blood that covered his hands and arms as I kneeled. I grabbed the back of his sweaty neck and felt for the pressure point just behind his ear lobe. I dug the point of my thumb deep into it. His cuffed legs convulsed and he screamed. I glanced back at Ken, who immediately turned his back. I didn't know if he didn't want to be a witness or was blocking the view of the others.

Flores twisted his head, trying unsuccessfully to get me off the pressure point. I released the tension to let him speak.

"Puto negro!" he screamed. I got down next to his ear.

"If this man dies, you'll do life in prison, you piece of shit!"

"Perfecto. I don't care, güey. LF for life! That ratfucker's dead, ese!"

I smacked the back of his head with my palm as hard as I could. "No, Flores. He's alive. You failed, ese," I shouted into his ear. I pressed my knee into the center of his back, using both my hands to reach the same nerve on both sides of his neck. I pressed hard, causing double the pain.

I'd crossed the line again and didn't care. The rage that was buried deep within, the pain of injustice as well in my own fear, released. I was torturing a prisoner, just like Ratford had been by whoever Joaquin sent. That's how he was able to piece together that Orozco purposely leaked the information on my hit.

I looked down at his face and could see his tongue extended out of his mouth. His body jerked back and forth. For a moment everything went silent. I was completely engulfed in my demented actions.

"Marcus!" I looked and saw Ken, his gas mask pulled up onto his head, screaming at me. Everything was in slow motion as I looked at the other COs and the medics, all of them watching me.

Suddenly, I was shoved from behind and tumbled over Flores. I jumped to my feet and turned to find Tanas, with Brenda right behind him. "That's enough, Ogabi!" he yelled.

I lunged at him as Ken held me back. Tanas came at me, throwing punches, landing none of them. The COs pulled us apart and held me pressed against the wall. I watched from the corner of my eye as the medics wheeled Orozco away.

"Calm yourself, Ogabi," CO Mike Rodriguez shouted. He had completely pulled his mask off, which helped snap me out of my trance-like state. I looked at my hands, finally realizing I'd gone too far.

"I'm done. I'm good. You can let me go." I relaxed my arms, then my torso, sending the message I was compliant.

"You need to get out of here. We'll handle this," Rodriguez said, glancing down at Flores who was now laughing.

"It's blood in, blood out, ese. Ronny knew that," Flores hissed at me. "And another thing black pig! Tráigate una cobija güey. Eres el siguiente!"

"Callate, güey!" Rodriguez shouted as he pressed his foot on the back of Flores's knee.

I was huffing and puffing. "What did he say?" I asked looking at Rodriguez, who ignored my question. He glanced at the other COs, most of whom spoke Spanish.

"Horvac, Sims, you guys take Flores to the hole," I ordered. "Tanas, maybe you should go with them."

The two men picked Flores up, each one grabbing an arm. Flores smiled as they led him away, Tanas following close behind.

"What did he say?" I insisted.

Rodriguez hesitated, then came out with it. "It's an expression the cartels use. It roughly translates to 'bring a blanket because you're next.' You know because when you die the body gets cold."

At that point, nothing more could affect me; I was numb.

"Look," Rodriguez was saying, "I witnessed the threat. We can get it added to his charge. In the meantime, you need to go cool off, Ogabi. The warden will be here in less than an hour, and there's going to be a lot of questions. Get your head clear."

As he walked away, I noticed the prisoners watching me through the bars. They'd seen the whole thing go down, which oddly quieted many of them. I had to keep my head up as I walked in the opposite direction. Something worse than shame engulfed my entire being.

Drenched in sweat, I was filthy in so many ways, and all I wanted was to get some water on me. I ducked into the empty inmate bathroom and frantically washed my hands. I watched Joaquin's sweat mixed with Ronny's blood swirl down the drain as the mental movie of my latest actions came full circle. A jolt of angst pushed through me as the tears flowed. I looked at my reflection in the plastic mirror while scooping handfuls of water onto my face. I dropped to my knees and silently cried. I coughed and spat on the floor, fighting the urge to vomit brought on by me suppressing the necessity to wail. I slapped myself several times, dried my face, and walked out of the bathroom.

On my way back to the office, I saw Zach standing against the bars. Like most of the inmates, he was trying to get a read on what was going on.

"Officer Ogabi, what's up? What happened?"

"Don't worry about it, Markland." I said, stopping at his cell door. I was still an animal that had just fought his enemy. There was no happiness or sadness in me, just the reality of war for whatever I was fighting for. I was dirty and evil, just like Flores. I went after him with the same anger he and his boys went after Orozco and Ratford. There was no difference. I looked at Zach with zero emotion and walked away.

THE FAT LADY SINGS

MARCUS

A week had passed since the incident. I sat, jobless, at the same round, blue kitchen table I'd sat at before. But things were different this time. I was in a different mindset. Instead of holding a gun in my hand, I held the local newspaper with the want ads open. Before, I would've made my lack of employment equate to the end of the world. This time, I only made it mean that something new was happening, which was true.

I owed this newfound way of perceiving the happenings of life to the words I'd heard Dimitri speak. His teachings, albeit received sporadically, helped me see things in a different light. Where there were holes, MJ helped fill them.

I was still struggling with all kinds of things. Like the guilt around the moves I didn't make that could have saved Clyde's life and kept Ronald Orozco, who was still in a coma, out of harm's way. MJ continued to assure me things happened and would happen exactly as they were supposed to, which sort of matched up with Dimitri's theory that there was a deep perfection in all process.

If I'm honest, I wasn't ready to buy into that, nor did I think I'd ever be. However, the process the warden used to get me out of Carlton and ultimately win the election was a piece of perfection in its own right. He started by making use of the three-strike rule, the third strike ultimately being what I'd done to Flores while he was in cuffs on the floor.

The warden had me right where he wanted as each step played out. An immediate two-week suspension with pay while they evaluated the situation. Then, I'd formally resign, in essence taking responsibility for everything, and for that, I'd receive a one-year extension of my current benefits. The only caveat was I had to sign a nondisclosure agreement stating I couldn't speak or relay any information regarding Carlton's employees, policies, warden, or damn near anything that could cause harm to the institution's reputation of good standing. If I rejected the deal, Tanas, using Brenda as a second witness, would file several complaints concerning my criminal behavior toward the Latino prisoner. That could land me in jail.

Taking a break from the want ads, I went to the local Channel 5 website to see how the warden would bullshit Richard Simpson, the news reporter covering the incident. I hadn't watched any coverage because MJ told me it was disgusting, and I had been too affected by everything that had happened up until now.

"Warden Shady, can you tell us what happened here at Carlton that ended in the death of one inmate and left another in a coma last night?"

"Rick, we really don't want to comment until we have all the details, but it looks like it's a gang-related incident."

"Is it true both incidents occurred within hours of each other?"

"It appears that way, but again, the investigation is ongoin', so I really can't say much more," the warden answered.

"Just one more thing. We heard you and the captain in charge were both away dealing with the last days of your campaign."

"That would be accurate, son."

"Is it also true that the officer you placed in the captain's stead was not up to the task, and if so, do you think it could affect your chances of becoming the state's next governor?"

"That there was two questions, Rick. But I'm gonna go ahead and answer the both of them." He smiled and, just like the ultimate politician, looked directly into the camera.

"First off, I was not made aware that this individual had been coverin' for Captain Devic, as I should have been. If I had, I woulda changed some things around and put someone more responsible, more seasoned, in that position while we were gone. This officer has had some issues with drinkin' and fightin' here at the prison, and, as I said before, we don't have all the details, but that officer has been put on suspension while we figure this thing out.

"If I discover that he wasn't in full compliance with this institution's guide-lines, well then, I'll just have to take the appropriate actions to keep this kind of thing from happenin' again. And about the election, Rick, as far as the voters of this great state are concerned, you need only look at the recent stats, all of it a result of the programs instituted during my tenure. Now, I've gotta get back to winnin' an election and of course runnin' this here prison, which, by the way, even with these most unfortunate of incidents, still holds the highest stats in the nation. Thank you."

"There you have it," the reporter said, "direct from the warden, straight out of Carlton. If you're just joining us, we are here at Carlton State Prison following up on our story concerning the violent death of inmate Clyde Lucas Ratford, shown on the screen. There are no named suspects in his death as of this moment. In addition, a violent attempt on the life of another prisoner, one Ronaldo Ortiz Orozco, occurred just hours later. Orozco is rumored to be the captain and number-two man in the Latino prison gang La Familia. Channel 5 has confirmed the active suspect, in this case, is none other than Orozco's own cellmate and alleged general, first in command of the same crime syndicate, Joaquin 'El Capitan' Flores. The gang allegedly runs the majority of criminal activity within Carlton as well as on the streets of this state. Orozco is on life support and in a serious condition."

Then the screen split and Stacy Leposa, Marianne Kelly's replacement, was in the studio. "Richard, as far as the elections go, what Warden Bill Shady alluded to concerning the stats seems to be correct. To date, even with these incidents, the data we've gathered at Channel 5 still shows Carlton miles ahead of every prison in the country."

They showed footage of gardens and greenhouses from their first visit while commenting on the programs that, to this day, the warden was still taking credit for even though they were actually shut down.

What a bunch of bullshit.

They rolled the whole thing into the current polls which showed the corrupt Bill Shady way ahead.

I was beginning to feel that something wasn't quite right. It was as if our local news channel and the Live at 5 news team were partial to Shady winning the election. In a good world, the news would be impartial and focused on great stories like the somewhat hijacked interview and the empowered speech by Dimitri regarding the state of our world. Instead, after that initial interview went viral, the news channel downplayed it, saying he was mentally ill and the warden promised to get him the help he needed. Many tried to copy and replay the interview, only to have it taken down from YouTube, who labeled it misinformation and warned that it put people at risk.

What *did* gain traction were the many spoof videos made, some doctored, showing Dimitri with a tinfoil hat. His fifteen minutes of fame were sharply challenged as many jumped on the anti-Dimitri bandwagon, guided by the media, both social and TV, and with him not around to defend himself, he was quickly forgotten.

But not by everyone. MJ had created a website that sold t-shirts with some of the quotes I'd heard in his sessions. My favorite was "There's no such thing as a happy victim," and the runner up was "You ain't woke if you're still asleep." Many of them, along with the quote, would have some kind of geometric woo-woo design or a special tree of some sort, along with the brand Be The Shift.

MJ was quite industrious and came up with several different products for the one thousand (according to her numbers) true fans he had, who would buy anything Dimitri. The idea was she'd hold a portion of the profits for him once he was out. She even posted a countdown ticker on the website for his release date, which was years out.

But she knew that site would someday have another purpose, as a time would come wherein he'd need a platform from which to speak, as they'd surely censor him on the social media channels. She put everything she had into the site, saying it would someday be a landing place for sovereignty, truth, and freedom.

» » « «

The media's partnership with the warden and the part they played in the cover-up of Dimitri's interview seemed to do the trick because, in under a week, our state had a new governor-elect named William Shady.

I hadn't found a job yet. They were out there but they were low-level. I was beginning to realize that if I wanted to remain in the area close to my daughter, low-level would have to become an option.

Hope Ayishat Ogabi was my rock, and I was her … well, I'm not sure what I was for her. I only know she loved me. She always knew the right thing to say when I needed it most. Not only mushy "I love you, Daddy" stuff either. There was some straight-up wisdom coming out of that child. On the Dimitri level at times. I'd find myself questioning how a child could know things I didn't.

I struggled with the concept that maybe we all know these things when we're born, but the world makes us forget. It was a crazy idea, but it fell in line with Dimitri's concept of programming. If we are all programmed, what was there before that programming? Does the blank slate that a child is before they're programmed have answers, and if so, how?

It was deep inquiries like these that kept me sane during a time that, in the past, I would have been experiencing the opposite. This was especially true after hearing news like the new governor of our state was Bill Shady. The news of the former warden's election win made me wonder how Dimitri, Zach, and the rest of the gang were doing. I regretted that I wasn't able to get the last memory card from Zach. I couldn't visit either. Part of my agreement was I couldn't set foot on Carlton property ever again.

I was also curious about Joaquin Flores and his gang and whether or not he'd been transferred to a different block or out of Carlton all together. I heard Ronald Orozco was doing better and off life support, so I was relieved about that. I still hadn't spoken to Jim, a man I once considered a good friend. I figured he'd gotten his promotion and was getting used to his new position. I wondered if he ever became aware of the level of corruption surrounding him.

I was thinking about all these things when there was a knock at the door. I parted the curtains to see a Carlton Prison issue cruiser in my driveway. My heart began to race and panic set in. *They've found out about everything you did for Zach and Dimitri.* I imagined being arrested before realizing there would have to be actual city police units with them if that were the case. I looked again, searching for marked and unmarked police vehicles. There were none.

"Hello," I said, my hand on the door handle.

"It's me, Marcus, Jim. Can I talk to you for a minute?"

It was the first time he'd called me by my name in a while, but, then again, what else was he going to call me? I opened the door.

"Hey, Captain Devic. How are you?" I put my hand out. Completely out of character, he grabbed me and pulled me in for a brug. This made me laugh and smile, and instantly we were friends again.

He rushed past me and sat on the sofa, excited about something. I took a seat on the chair in front of him. "Marcus, just call me Jim like before. Things are different now."

Yeah. I'm jobless, and you're not my captain anymore.

"How are you, Jim? It's really great to see you. I was literally just thinking about you and Carlton just minutes ago." I moved forward on my chair and looked him up and down. "I gotta say, there's something different about you. You seem happier. I guess being promoted has gotta feel good, right?"

Jim looked down and shook his head with a smile. "Shady ended up promoting someone else."

"What? That doesn't make any sense! What happened?"

Jim laughed, "Politics happened, Marcus, politics. It's the most disgusting, corrupt thing you could possibly imagine."

I couldn't help but smirk inside.

"There needed to be a second fall guy behind the scenes after you were gone. The warden needed to show the governor he wasn't the one who left you in charge. In all fairness, he hadn't. It goes much deeper, but that's the gist of it."

I sat in silence, going back to that place of guilt. "I'm sorry about my part in all this, Jim. There was so much going on in my head. I didn't mean to let you down."

"I know you didn't, buddy. Just like it says in Proverbs, 'Trust in the Lord with all your heart, and do not lean on your own understanding.' Suffice to say, things are as they should be. I hold no bad feelings. As a matter of fact, I'm sorry for being so harsh with you when you probably could have used a friend more than a boss. I was so caught up in being promoted, I guess I really lost my way."

I didn't know what to say. I thought I'd lost a friend forever, but here he was again. I felt my eyes begin to water. He must have noticed because he quickly changed the subject.

"Hey, I've got something for you." He reached into his jacket pocket and pulled out a folded tissue and began to unravel it. "Close your eyes and let me see your palm," he said. I suspiciously complied. I could feel my heart race.

The moment I felt it in the palm of my hand, I knew what it was. "How in the world?"

"Well, that's a bit of a story," he whispered as I opened my eyes to see the last memory card. "But first, can I get something to drink?" I told him all I had was reverse osmosis water because MJ encouraged me to remove all soda, beer, and anything unhealthy from my place. He laughed and said water would be fine.

I fetched his water from the large, glass dispenser that MJ had filled with crystals and different colored, gemlike stones. I maneuvered my body so he couldn't see them. I didn't want to explain.

"Do you remember," he continued, "when you and I were interviewing Clyde and he had mentioned the tip he'd given me on the contraband in one of the cells?"

I paused. "'Yeah, 'the device,' as it was referred to."

"None of it was very clear at the time, but later it came together," Jim said, as I got more nervous with every word he spoke.

I handed him his water and remained stoic, not wanting to implicate myself anymore than I already had by asking.

"Listen, I want you to know you're not in any trouble. Hand to God. So you can take that kooky look off your face." He grinned and went on. "That first day I talked to Clyde alone, he mainly came in to tell me about the planned hit on a black Carlton CO, but like always, I asked him if there was anything else he had for me. He gave me the name Zachary Markland and a mini-cam. Wondering how I tied this back to you?"

I breathed in deep and let out a sigh, happy not to be in any trouble but still curious. "Humor me."

"It came down to that one word, mini-cam. I remembered the day when that card was stuck to the bottom of your hand. You told me it came from your daughter's mini-cam. Something told me to keep it to myself, to find it on my own. So, once we lifted the four-day lockdown after the attacks on Orozco and Ratford, I did my own private shakedown, knowing all the inmates would rush to the chow hall. Can you guess what I found hidden inside Markland's mattress?" he asked sarcastically.

With a smirk, I responded, "My daughters Yaeg X21 mini-cam?"

Jim laughed. "Of course, I wanted to know what was on it, so I brought it home. Lots of pages from the notebooks I assumed were used in Tanomeo's ERP program. It was impressive to see how much work those boys had done at Carlton over the past years. And the level of organization with this Markland kid is really something to behold."

I looked down at the card, then back up at him. I had to get one thing straight. "It's not actually my daughter's mini-camera."

He grinned. "I figured that, buddy."

"There's a good reason for all of this," I said, prepared to explain my actions.

He stood and walked toward the door. "Actually, I can see it. I've put the pieces together, and I've got a pretty good grasp on what happened as well as the intention behind it, but I don't need to know the details. After what I know now about politics, whatever you did and why you did it was for some kind of good, even if I couldn't see it at the time."

"Wait. You came all the way over here to give me this?" I asked.

"And to see how you're doing, of course," he said with a laugh.

I looked at him suspiciously. "Jim, is there something you're not telling me?"

He smiled big. "Just take a look at the card. Go all the way to the end." He downed the rest of the water.

"Okay, I'll do that," I said as he opened the door and walked onto the porch. I was confused, not knowing what to say about the strange and oddly cryptic visit from my ex-boss.

"You take it easy, Marcus. And tell your girlfriend the colored rocks in the water make it taste pretty good." He walked down the steps.

"Just one thing before you go," I yelled. "What's happened to make you so happy? You didn't get the position you'd been waiting for all this time. I don't get it."

"Just take a look at what's on the card, then you do what you do. What's right and correct. And if you don't know what that is, just ask what *he'd* do."

"What who would do?" He stopped at his car door and laughed. "What would Dimitri do? From there you'll know."

What would Dimitri do? I like that.

He got in his car, lowered his window, and yelled out, "What do they say? It ain't over 'til the fat lady sings. Apparently, buddy, she's getting ready to sing!"

» » « «

I ran to my computer. I saw the many shots of the pages Zach had snapped, just as I'd seen in the first card, but then I came across several shots of Dimitri sitting on his cot reading and a few of him smiling.

They used the camera for this?

As I scrolled there were more, but with Zach and him together. The last one was a group photo of the remaining members of the Magnificent Seven squeezed into their cell.

Idiots, this is how you get caught. "I can't believe this shit!" I said aloud as Lucky jumped off of the desk. I paced back and forth, pissed off at their ignorance. It wouldn't take long for me to realize I wasn't really mad about them putting us at risk, because there was no risk. "In the now," the card was out of Carlton and all was good. I was just living in an imagined past. As childish as this sounds, I could see that what was really happening within me was I was hurt that I wasn't part of the group, or in the photos, with the camera I'd bought.

I scrolled to the end and saw there was a video. I almost didn't click on it because watching videos of them laughing and carrying on couldn't be good for my ego. But I couldn't help myself. I clicked on the play icon, and much to my surprise, it showed Warden Shady enter his office and sit at his desk. He was looking toward the door and said, "Shut that thing, and come over here and sit down." Tanas appeared in the shot and took the chair in front of him.

"He's gone, chief. It doesn't matter how it happened, he's not coming back."

"Boy, sometimes you're just as dumb as a stump. The real problem we have here is Tanomeo. I told you to let them stupid Mexicans kill him and that porch monkey Ogabi if they had good reason, and accordin' to you, they did! But you couldn't even make that happen, could you, Gene? This whole thing has turned into a fuckin' shitshow!"

"What more could I do?" Tanas was saying. "They had to get Clyde to know what he told Devic, and when they found out that Orozco was leaking unauthorized information about the hit on Ogabi, he had to go. I helped them set it up because, if Orozco turned, I could go down. I've done a lot of work with those guys. They've got serious dirt on me that could lead back to you."

I threw my hands in the air. "I knew it!" I yelled.

There was so much damaging evidence on film I couldn't believe it. I jumped up to my feet, pacing. "Oh shit, oh shit, what do I do?" I said quietly to myself. Finally, I decided to call MJ.

"Can you come over here right now? I've got something to show you. ... No, not that. Be serious, MJ. ... Be The Shift dotcom can survive without you for an hour. Just come over. ... No, I'm not drunk. I don't even have any more coffee, remember? Just get here. It's a good thing. ... Okay, bye."

I ran around in circles until I got tired. I grabbed Lucky and kissed him on the top of his head. "And that's the way we do it, Lucky my boy!"

Once MJ arrived I pulled her into the kitchen and sat her in my chair. I started the video from the beginning and let her watch it to the end. She sat silent and motionless as I danced around the living room.

"Well, say something!" I shouted, now dancing in the kitchen.

She shook her head. "I had no idea the warden was a racist."

I stopped. "I didn't either. That's the first time I've heard him cuss like that as well," I said excitedly, now doing jumping jacks.

"These people disgust me. Is that the one who kicked your butt? What was his name? Tanson?"

"No, baby, we didn't actually ... never mind. But yes, he's the one and his name's Tanas." I started dancing again, laughing out loud.

"I guess what I'm not getting is why you are so happy about this."

I stopped again, frustrated by her lack of enthusiasm. I closed the laptop and replied, "Because this means we won, baby. Don't you see it?"

"What have we won?"

"First off, my suspicions were right."

"Is that it? You were right?" she asked, downplaying the win.

"We've exposed some serious corruption at a very deep level." She nodded in agreement. "That you have, but the fact that this kind of thing even exists in our world isn't something to celebrate." She took a deep breath. "To be completely transparent, I'm also feeling bad that you had to hear him say that word about you."

I stopped dancing. I'd never processed it like that. I mean, it didn't bother me at all, which was kind of blowing my mind, but I had to act cool about it. I pointed to her. "Like water off of a duck, baby. I've been with a master for some time now, what did you expect?" That made her smile.

"Wow, dear one, you *have* come a long way, haven't you. But there are no masters, really."

"Yeah, yeah, but they're going to jail. That's a good thing, right?" I asked, snapping my fingers and moving my head to a beat that was only playing in my head.

We're going to party, karambo, fiesta, forever! Wait, Lionel Richie? Really?

"I'm sure that's a process in and of itself, with an investigation and such.

What good does it do when there's another corrupt politician waiting to take his place? What I do know is the warden can kiss his career goodbye. The governorship as well. Nowadays using words like those doesn't fly with the public. You say Jim recorded this? How'd he get the camera hidden like that?"

I reflected on it for about a half a minute. "I hadn't even thought about it till now. I guess maybe he hid it somewhere around the warden's plants. He's always fidgeting with them. Jim's a botanist you know."

"Smart guy. Courageous as well. Why do you think he gave it to you, dear one?"

I sat down next to her. "I was wondering the same thing. All I could come up with was he knows I've got nothing to lose. The problem is, I can't do anything against Carlton. That was in the deal I signed."

She stood up and looked at me suspiciously, then held her hand out. "What?" I asked as she kept her hand outstretched.

"Oh, I think you know," she said.

"No, I don't."

"Put it in my hand."

"Oh, MJ, that's not it. I hadn't thought that far forward. I'm really not that clever, I promise. You don't have to do anything, really."

"Yes, I do. I did it last time the media needed to get involved and I can do it again." I almost teared up. "You see, dear one, this is what is called us doing our part, just like the hummingbird and the fire."

"And this is why I love you, Mpenzi Wangu," I said.

"I mean, what else is there to do, right?" she said with a wink.

What the … ? At that moment, time stood still, and as I stared into her eyes, I saw Ana, Dimitri, Hope, Zach, and even Tanas deep inside them. I could feel my heart race as the dots began to connect, and I could see how everything had led to this moment. It was as if we were all part of a great, invisible orchestration playing a sad but beautiful melody, one that the whole world might hear someday.

» » « «

Later, I sat and reflected on what might happen after this video made the news. A void could be created at Carlton without Shady or Tanas, which would mean a lot of changes. I smiled thinking of Jim, sitting in the perfect position for a promotion after all. *That's why he was so happy.* It appeared Jim had learned to play the political game after all, and he'd just called checkmate on the warden. Now, all there was for me to do was let the chips fall where they may. And fall they did.

Whatever MJ did, she did it quickly. Within days, the video was on every local news channel, and in less than a week, it made national news. I watched nightly as the investigative news teams stood in front of the prison while protesters demanded action against the warden and Tanas. Interestingly, folks appeared more upset about the racial slurs than the cloak-and-dagger stuff. I had a feeling that if I would have been white and was called some other derogatory name, there would be almost no fuss. It was as if people were using me and my race to create a drama for their own benefit. *What's wrong with this world?*

Then came the day I watched the news and saw the authorities escort Gene Tanas and Bill Shady from the building in handcuffs. I stood in front of my TV with my arms raised in victory. I'd won or, at the time, I thought I had. It was a glorious day, to say the least.

ATTENTION SHOPPERS

MARCUS

The rest of the year wasn't so glorious. I'd taken a security job at the local Walmart. Pretty low-level, but it kept me close to my daughter. There was also peace in not having to worry about my life being in danger anymore.

Several months went by, and I'd finally settled into my new job. I stayed in the *knowing* that there was no use in walking around angry because I'd been dealt a bad hand. I had accepted my new life, knowing the correct way to raise my daughter was to stay close and be a part of hers. It was almost a practice in itself to find the things that were positive about it, like having a paycheck and getting to know different people outside of the prison setting. I was choosing to change my perception by shifting my internal dialogue around, and it was working.

As far as Dimitri, Zach, and all that happened in the prison went, it was almost like a dream. Not having communication for so long made me think the plans they'd made were dead and buried. Zach was probably out by now, and I'd all but let go of how I was going to get the data from the last card to him or if he even wanted it.

While in the breakroom having lunch, I was scrolling through my phone when I came across an article that immediately grabbed my attention: "IN-MATE PARDONED FOR BEING A MODEL PRISONER. Governor Catherine Trejos announced her decision today to pardon one single prisoner, Dimitri Cato Tanomeo. 'After careful review, I've decided inmate Tanomeo is the most qualified candidate for this executive order. His record at Carlton as well as his actions in creating programs that have helped many other inmates establish him as a model prisoner.'" I continued to skim through the rest of the article, which said the process could take up to six months and during that time the inmate must keep his record clean.

I immediately called MJ to update her, knowing she doesn't watch TV or follow the news in any way.

"Amazing news, dear one. I'm so excited for him," she said after I'd read her the article.

I felt goosebumps all over my body. "Right?"

"Isn't it ironic how the guy who invented the Early Release Program got the early release in the end?" she asked, giggling.

"That's true. But there's a part of me that wonders if the real reason for this might be political—them wanting to quash ERP, if it even exists anymore, or just to get him out."

"I'd hate to think it was that, but after what we've seen, I guess anything is possible. Either way, it's a beautiful thing he's getting out. Let's celebrate more later. I've got to get to my lesson."

"Okay, love you."

"Love you too, dear one."

I wondered how the remaining Magnificent Seven members were celebrating inside and what Carlton would be like without Dimitri. With the pardon, he could be out at any moment. Just thinking about both his and Zach's release dates inspired me, which was a feeling I hadn't felt in quite some time. Then I got the call on my radio. "Security, this is Wilma up at the front. A bird just flew in the store. Can you help find it? It just went down aisle seven heading toward the back."

There was no way I was going to let a bird in the store interrupt my lunch. MJ was away for a yoga teacher training program, so she didn't pack my lunch, which meant a chicken sandwich for me today. "Wilma, copy that. Did you call maintenance?"

"I did but only Stevie is available to help you. He's on his way," she whined.

I'm pretty sure having an attitude was a prerequisite to working as a floor manager at Walmart. I called Dave Vidick, who was working in the security cameras upstairs.

"Dave, go ahead and leave the monitors for a bit and help Stevie catch a bird that flew into the store."

"Copy that, Marcus, but I'm tracking a possible shoplifter. I was just getting ready to call you about it."

Perfect timing.

"Alright, I guess I don't have a choice then. I'll go help with the bird and take a closer look at the suspect. You stay on the monitors and feed me the intel. I'll put in my earpiece."

"Copy that, boss."

I speed walked over to aisle seven and found nothing. I radioed maintenance and told Stevie to check the aisles on the back end of the store while I checked the front. I moved quickly past eight and then nine, looking up and down with each pass.

"Marcus, the suspect is a Muslim female," I heard Dave say into my earpiece. "She's wearing one of those black gown things and is moving around the store from aisle to aisle. I've lost her but she's close to you I think."

"It's called a *burqa*, Dave," I radioed back, giving the eye in the sky the thumbs up. I'd never heard of a Muslim woman stealing from Walmart, but I figured one could really hide some stuff under that type of garment.

A voice came over the earpiece, "Wilma, this is Stevie. What kind of bird is it we're looking for? I mean is it big and black or is it, like, a tiny finch or somethin'?"

"Oh for god sake," I mumbled as I walked toward aisle ten. *It's a damn bird. If you see a bird, that's the one. It's not that difficult. Only at Walmart.*

"That would be a sparrow there, Stevie," Wilma moaned back. "They're fast little buggers so good luck on y'all capturin' it."

I slowed my pace as I turned onto aisle eleven. My mind didn't have the time to put it all together, but in front of me hovered a green and red hummingbird.

That doesn't look like a sparrow. That looks like a Huitzil. He was at eye level. We both stared at each other. Then, in my peripheral, I saw the Muslim woman enter at the far end of the same aisle. From what I could see, she appeared to be pulling things off the shelf and putting them into her sleeve.

"Marcus, she's right in front of you." I gave another thumbs up while still staring at the hummingbird. "She's definitely putting things into her burky or whatever you called it."

The bird turned and buzzed down the aisle, stopping to hover above the shoplifting Muslim. I followed, moving closer to the small, crouched woman whose back was to me as she arranged items under her gown. She stood up straight, turned, and took two steps towards me before stopping. I couldn't see her face, so I had no idea what she was thinking as I blocked her path. I looked up for the hummingbird, but it was gone.

"Ma'am, I'm chief of security here at Walmart. We have reason to believe you've concealed items from this store on your person. I'd like to ask you to come with me to our office. There I will have a female employee assist us."

She stared at me as I looked her up and down, trying to decipher where the contraband was hidden. She softly shook her head and in a faint whisper said, "No."

The quiet, frightened voice of Dave came through my earpiece again. "Marcus, do you need backup? I mean, I could come, but I really think we should call the authorities. Who knows if she's got a bomb under that thing."

I looked up and shook my finger. "It's a difficult situation we have here. I can't search you, and we don't have a female security officer here to do it, right now. So, I'd like to show you the video of you putting the items into your clothing. But you'll have to come back to the office with me."

She shook her head again. "Not going to happen, security ... officer ... at ... Walmart." She spoke slowly in a dull, monotone voice, overly spacing out her words. I couldn't detect an accent, but when I looked in her eyes, there was something about her.

I was getting impatient. "Listen, I've got a job to do here lady, and—"

"Some job, security ... officer ... at ... Walmart." I took a step backward and studied her, wondering why she was trying to get under my skin. *Who are you to judge, shoplifter lady from the Middle East?* I raised my right hand up and showed Dave our three-finger code. He called me on my cell phone. I put him on speaker.

"Confirming that I should call the police?" I gave the thumbs up. "Should I let them know it's a possible terrorist threat?"

Everything's a conspiracy with this guy.

"No, Dave. She's just an uncooperative shoplifter, that's it."

"Got it. Negative on the bomb squad then. Calling now."

I sighed and wondered how my life had gotten so strange. "The police are coming," I said to her calmly.

"I heard. My English is not all that bad, security ... officer ... at ... Walmart."

"I'm going to ask you to stop saying that." Her hand came up to cover her already veiled mouth and I heard a faint giggle.

We stood there in silence for a while. Finally, I asked, "Are you really a Muslim or just someone with a sorry-ass scheme to steal stuff?"

"I'll answer you if you answer something for me afterward," she said.

I thought about it and nodded. *What do I have to lose? I just won't answer if I don't want to.*

"You ask if I am a Muslim. My answer is, I am all things. I am the fire, the water, and the ground with its dirt. I am the you, the me, the every-one, and all things together, and ultimately, I *am* the shoplifter with the sorry-ass scheme but not to steal stuff. It's for me to ask you the question I came to ask."

She reached up and pulled off her burqa, exposing a face I knew well. It was Ana.

"Marcus Angbo Ogabi, is this what you came to this planet to do?" She gazed deep into my eyes, waiting for an answer.

"I think I'm going to throw up again," I mumbled.

She stepped forward. "No, you're not. There's no time for that." She waved the back of her hand past the top of my stomach and the nausea vanished. "I'll ask again, is this it?" She stared into my eyes and for a moment I got lost in what seemed like the cosmos. I had to blink hard to get out.

"What do you want from me, Ana?" I asked sternly.

"It's not your turn to ask questions. You have to answer mine. And besides, you already know what I want, and that's nothing. I only know. I know what you are here to do with him. You once knew it as well. That *knowing* is still in you. I'm here to bring it back to the surface, for all aspects of you must be on board. Otherwise, you can stay right here, there's nothing wrong with that. You can remain in your job as the security ... officer ... at ... Walmart."

"Please stop saying that."

She raised her hand and the hummingbird returned, hovering just above her head, seemingly looking right at me. "I will ask this just once more, Marcus. Is this what you came here to do?"

Standing in front of her, something began to happen to me, or maybe for me. It was like a high-speed video of every aspect of my life flashing in front of my eyes. I saw my fears as well as everything and everyone I loved. I could see that they and we were one and the same. I knew that everything was perfect, good, and righteous, including any and all changes that might happen for me to live the life I truly came here to live. I closed my eyes as tears of joy ran down my face. I nodded, and for the first time in a while, the air I breathed in felt fresh as if it were cooled. I felt taller. I was ready to give her a hug, all I needed to do was reach over.

I heard the sounds of footsteps and opened my eyes to her walking away. The hummingbird stayed looking at me a moment more before turning and following her.

She was nearing the end of the aisle when I yelled out, "Hey, what's next? If you can read my thoughts, you know I'm ready!" She kept walking as if she heard nothing. I figured I'd throw a Hail Mary. "Hey, Ana, I'm sorry, please forgive, thank you, and …"

She made a sharp left at the end of the aisle and was gone, hummingbird and all.

"And I love you," I whispered. Suddenly the hummingbird popped back at the end of the aisle. It hovered, giving me one last look before jetting off again after her.

At that exact moment, a young male turned the corner. I could barely make him out, but he was walking toward me, strutting in fact, with his hands open. *Definitely not from these parts.*

As he got closer, I could see the stylish man was smiling in my direction. *Is he looking at me?* I looked behind me. There was no one.

His hands went up as he yelled out, "What up, dawg?"

My mouth fell open as I realized it was Zach Markland. "What? Wait a minute. Where's Ana? Did, did she send you? You should have run right into her!" I asked in a daze. What had just happened left me in a state that I can only describe as utter bewilderment. I could barely stand.

"Who's Ana, Officer O?" he asked.

"She was right there, where you came from, with a hummingbird. Didn't you see it?" I asked as I wiped my eyes.

He just looked at me with zero expression. I could only imagine what he must have thought.

We turned to see Dave run up on the scene. "Is he okay?" Dave asked Zach as he grabbed my arm and handed me a water bottle.

Zach looked at Dave, then at me. "I'm not sure. It depends on what his current version of okay looks like nowadays. It's been a minute since we've seen each other, but as of right now, I'd say, so far, so bad."

I took a drink of water and tried to catch my breath. I picked up Ana's headscarf from the tiled floor and showed it to Zach.

"This was hers," I whispered.

Zach glanced at Dave with a worried look on his face.

"I'm not sure what happened," Dave said. "I was watching it all on the live feed, then all the monitors shut down." Dave pointed to the ceiling camera. "When they came back on, you were here and the Muslim was gone."

"Just to be clear, he's usually not like this, right?" Zach asked in a concerned voice.

"No, I've never seen him like this."

Zach looked back at Dave, "That's good, we need him bueno y sano, like D says. Do you have a place he can lie down?"

"We've got a small sofa in the security office."

They walked me to the office, and I lay down. "I'll make him some coffee," Dave said, headed for the coffee maker.

"Hey, chief, don't give him that," Zach said with an authority I'd never heard before as if he'd taken over the situation. "You got any herbal tea?"

Dave walked away to make the tea and cancel the police call while Zach pulled up a chair next to me. "Did you say you needed me?" I asked like an insecure little child.

Zach laughed and patted me on the shoulder. "I did, and we do. D sent me for ya. Damn, I thought for a minute I was gonna have to tell him you went J-cat like Earl. You know, turned into some kind of nut job or something." He moved in close and whispered, "That's not the case, is it Officer O?"

"I'm good. It's just … well, never mind. It's probably better I keep this one to myself."

"Whatever works, bro. So, what do you say?" he asked.

"What do I say about what?"

"Can you get on a plane and be at my sister Tess's beach house by next Friday. That's when D will be arriving from prison. It's gonna be EPIC!"

I stood up. "You want me to come to your place? For how long?"

"Oh, you know, like indefinite. We've got space, no worries there. My girlfriend is a chef … a vegan chef, so you'll have to adjust. It'll be good for you, I promise. The agency is forming, and according to D, you're one of the original superheroes."

It was all happening. My dream, or maybe my purpose, was back after I'd thought it was gone forever. All I had to do was say yes. I thought about my daughter and what my moving away might do to her. I worried about my relationship with MJ. We'd come so far so fast, and I didn't want to slow the momentum. But then I thought about the bigger picture and how I could help in a way that would, in turn, help many others, including them.

"I'll be there, Zach. Thank you."

"No, thank *you*. D says we need you. I would've never returned anywhere near this place if it wasn't for having to come get your dizzy ass." He smiled as Dave returned with the tea. "I gotta bounce, gotta get back to the real world. I'll leave my number with Dave. You call me when you're better, and we'll get it all worked out."

I nodded.

"So, just to confirm with your integrity, because I know D's gonna ask, you'll be there by next Friday afternoon, right?"

I was smiling so big I swear my cheeks blurred my vision. "With full authenticity as well as my integrity being completely intact, that is confirmed. I'll be there. I wouldn't miss it for the world, bro."

He chuckled and reached out for my hand, pulled me up, and gave me a brug.

"There's just one thing," I said. "It's Lucky."

"We would say it's more like Divine Intelligence than luck, actually," Zach answered.

"No, I'm talking about my cat, Lucky. I've been with him for years." There was a long pause as he studied me.

"Bring him!" Zach exclaimed. *That was easy.* "Tess is gonna love him."

He was cracking up, which led me to believe that might not be the case.

Then Dave chimed in, "I'm Dave. Are you the Zach Markland and is D, like, the Dimitri D?"

"That would be a yes to both," Zach said, readying himself to leave.

"Whoa, I know you. Marcus used to talk about you guys all the time." It was true. I shared a lot with Dave during my first months on the job.

"Easy, Dave. I don't want to get uninvited," I said.

"No worries," Zach said. "I as well as D are open books." He stood up and pointed at me. "You're looking better already. Keep smiling. We need you at a hundred percent starting next week."

"Zach, thanks for coming. I really appreciate it."

He put his hand over his heart and nodded, then shook Dave's hand.

Zach was putting his jacket on when Dave blurted out, "So, you guys are gonna save the world, huh?"

"Something like that," Zach replied. "In truth, there's really no world to save, but it's the game we've chosen to play."

"Ah, I like that. I mean, what else is there to do, right?" Dave yelled out.

Really? I angrily tossed my empty cup onto the table next to me. They both looked over at me as I lay back on the couch and at the ceiling with my arms crossed.

Am I the only one who doesn't get to say that?

CASTLE OF SAND

MARCUS

Driving my economy-sized, two-door rental down the Coastal Highway, the stark night-and-day difference between where I'd lived all my life and the beautiful landscape of beachfront mansions was blowing my mind. It was the middle of the day, the weather was perfectly cool, and the sun was shining. *If this isn't paradise, then I don't know what is.*

I pulled up to the entrance gate. It had a beautiful carved wood design molded into intricate metalwork of bronze, or maybe gold, for all I know. It opened automatically and I drove in. I came to a second gate where a well-groomed, grey-haired gentleman in a dark suit wearing an earpiece walked up to my window.

He looked down at his phone then at me, "Hello, Mr. Ogabi, and welcome to the Markland Beach Home. My name is Stan. I'll open the gate, just pull in and keep to the right. You'll see the guest parking, and the entrance door is just down the path. You can't miss it, sir. Zachary and Mr. Tanomeo have just arrived as well."

"Thank you," I said, stealing a look at his phone screen. A roster photo of me when I was on the police force was there. He stealthily inspected the inside of my car as he walked away and spoke into his lapel. The gate opened and I continued on. *These people are beyond rich.*

I parked the rental next to a white convertible Porsche and a dark blue four-door Bentley. I heard the waves crash against the shore and the sound of what seemed to be Indian or some kind of Middle Eastern music playing in the house. The sea breeze blew the scent of saltwater and ocean life directly at me as I walked down the manicured pathway, brushing my fingers along the home's fine redwood siding.

At the entryway, I noticed several pairs of shoes resting outside the door. *Just like MJ's house.* I looked at the doorbell, nervous, knowing that just on the other side of it was a whole different world, one I'd never known before. I pushed it.

The door opened quickly and a stunningly beautiful caucasian woman in her late twenties, dressed in all white with a kind of turban on, stood in front of me smiling. She had burning sage in one hand and a large black feather in the other. She fanned the smoke all over me. I didn't mind, MJ would do the same thing every time I came to her house directly from the prison. I never understood why, other than it had something to do with the energies.

"Namaste, Marcus. Welcome. I'm Starseed. Please remove your shoes and come in." Her tone was peaceful and smooth, a combination of MJ's and my late grandmother's.

I bent down and untied my tennis shoes. She hugged me as I entered. I noticed, under her long flowing sleeves, she was covered in tattoos. I couldn't make them out, but they were intricate, unlike the ones the men had at Carlton or back in the city where I'd grown up and worked.

"Come quickly. He's walking out to the sand for the first time." She grabbed my hand and pulled me through a short corridor leading to a large room with a massive glass window overlooking the beach just feet away. Zach and another young woman, I presumed his sister, stood gazing. Both looked back as we entered the room.

A big smile grew on Zach's face when he saw me. Unlike his sister, who instead, looked me up and down suspiciously. As far as first impressions go, I didn't get the best one from her. And, if I'm going to stay honest, I'd say I was intimidated by her for several reasons, mainly because she exuded wealth, power, and authority, three things I'd never had.

"Hey, Officer O!" Zach shouted.

I put my hand out to shake his hand, and he pushed it away, giving me a hug instead. Not a prison brug. A real one. Like the ones I'd get from my grandmother or even MJ, but maybe not as close. It felt odd hugging a man like that. I patted his back and pulled away as soon as I could.

"This is my sister Tess. Tess, this is Officer O" She darted her hand out making it clear she didn't want to hug, which was fine by me.

"Nice to meet you, Tess. This is a beautiful home you have. My name is actually Marcus. Thanks for having me."

"Welcome, Marcus. Zach has told me a lot about you. Thank you for taking care of my baby brother when he was on his 'little vacation.'" She used air quotes, and the tone of her voice was lifeless like she had to push her words out, only speaking from a sense of obligation.

"Look, look, check it out, Officer O!" Zach shouted, motioning me to come to the glass. "We just got here, straight from the airport. His first time flying."

I walked over and stepped onto the huge, vibrantly colorful handwoven rug.

"He's going out to the beach. First time seeing the ocean as well. He wanted to go alone."

Dimitri was standing on the edge of the wooden deck, his back to us, staring out at the massive blue. We all stood there in silence, witnessing the barefoot young man, who'd grown up in a hell only he'd known, step onto the beach for the first time. The cold sand caused him to shoot his hands into the air with every other step as he slowly walked toward the shore. He stopped to scoop up a handful and studied it closely as it fell through his fingers. He continued, picking up his pace, stopping just before the moving tideline.

"The water's butt-ass cold right now. About fifty-four degrees," Zach said smiling with his arm around Starseed, who I surmised was the vegan chef girlfriend.

Dimitri took two big steps, and the water splashed against his feet, wetting the bottoms of his old faded jeans. He jumped backward, turned, and ran from the coldness. We all cracked up and could see he was laughing as well. He began to run around on the sand, back and forth, side to side, like a child. It reminded me of Hope the first time we'd taken her to the beach. He dashed after a couple of dogs, and I smiled as their wealthy owners quickly leashed them before scurrying away from the crazy guy wearing tattered jeans and a faded flannel shirt.

I glanced at Tess. She was shaking her head while looking at Zach, who was by now almost in tears. "It is a private beach, Zach," she said with a serious tone that only made him laugh harder.

"Chill, sis. It's good for them to experience the D-ness at least once in their smug existence."

I looked back to see Dimitri sitting on the sand, legs crossed, facing the ocean.

"Is he … ?" I asked, wondering if I was seeing correctly.

"It sure looks like it," Zach said, as we watched him remove his shirt and stand up, his back still to us.

"Okay, now this is getting interesting," Tess whispered, moving closer to the glass.

"Come on," Zach snapped.

"What? It's good to experience a little D-ness. Isn't that what you just said?"

The guy's physique was something to behold. I never saw him workout at the prison, just yoga in the yard, but somehow he'd always maintained his build. Tess pulled out her phone and was taking shots. "Really?!" Zach snorted.

"Instagram, Z-bro, Instagram. It's what makes the world go 'round," she answered with a grin.

I almost laughed as I watched Starseed silently mouth "DM me those" to Tess.

Dimitri looked back at the house. He must have seen us looking through the window because he waved his arms with a huge smile on his face.

"Ew, what happened to his chest?" Tess whined, the scars visible even from afar.

"Cigarette burns. It was his stepfather. Started when he was just five," I answered, relieved to have found my way into the conversation. "One hundred and nine of them."

Zach looked at his sister, "It's actually a hundred and eleven, counting the other two, one from an Aryan gang member and the other from the shooting."

A strange kind of silence took over, the kind that shows up when someone says something they shouldn't have.

"Open mouth, insert foot. Sorry, Marcus," Zach said, giving me a nod.

Tess spun around and whispered, "You're such the lame-o, Zachary."

I smiled and gave him a thumbs up. "No problem." I pointed at Dimitri. "Like he says, it is what it is."

It got quiet again as we returned our attention to the man of the hour. Truthfully, I'd almost forgotten I'd shot him years before, and it really didn't bother me to remember now. Mainly because I knew that it didn't bother him, and if he was fine with it, then so was I. That was all in the past, and here we were in the present, doing something good.

"Get a shot of that one, Tess," I said pointing, consequently changing the subject, as Dimitri stood at the shore with his arms open.

She saw the shot and began to snap away. She swiped her screen, looking at the photos. "That's an iconic photo right there if he's going to be what Zach says he's going to be," she said, showing me the best one.

"He already is, Tess, he already is," Zach said as he leaned over to take a look.

Dimitri turned back to the ocean and removed his jeans, leaving him in just his white underwear. Unexpectedly, he took off running into the frigid water.

"No way!" Zach yelled and began laughing hysterically .

We watched him dive in and get thrashed around by the waves, shouting and hooting, surely due to the cold combined with the excitement of his first plunge. I laughed as he tasted the saltwater and spat it out.

Tess abandoned her photography to make a call. "Stanley, can you send someone out to the beach with a warm towel and robe? We seem to have lost one of our guests to the surf. See what you can do to get him out of there. He's in his underwear, so let's try to make it happen before the police show up."

Zach stopped laughing and turned to look at his sister, "Really, Tess?"

"It's a private beach, not a prison yard," she snapped.

That made no sense, rich girl. No one wears just their underwear in the yard.

In less than a minute, there were two clean-cut men in matching blue polo shirts and khaki pants coaxing Dimitri out of the water, one with a robe and towel in hand.

» » « «

Starseed showed me to my room. The wheels of my large, weathered red suitcase clacked loudly against the polished wood stairs with every step. If that wasn't embarrassing enough, Lucky cried from inside his carrier all the way while I lugged my police academy-issue duffle bag on my other shoulder.

"Go ahead and get cleaned up from your trip if you'd like. We'll be getting together for dinner after sunset. Do you have any food allergies I should know about?" she asked as she petted Lucky, who purred happily now freed from confinement.

"I'm good with whatever."

"We are plant-based here. I trust that will be fine with you."

She was so pleasant, I was just happy to hear her talk.

"That's fine. My girlfriend eats the same way. I've learned to deal with it," I said and she laughed. "Thank you, Starseed. That's your name right?" There was something strange about calling her that when I kind of knew that probably wasn't her given name.

"Yep. Hasn't changed since you got here. I'll let you know if it does."

Touche.

The room was beyond perfect. The view, the temperature, the smell, all of it was first-rate. I sat on the edge of the bed then fell back. It was the most comfortable bed I'd ever been on. I pulled back the layers to feel the fine smooth sheets, and the pillows were soft as clouds.

I walked around, examining each part of the room.

"No way," I said out loud and pulled out my cell phone and started videoing the bathroom that cost more than the home I grew up in. I sent it to Hope, and she rang me instantly.

"Is that their bathroom? Really?" she asked.

"Well, it's *my* bathroom, in just my room."

"No way!"

"Yes, way. I'm pretty sure there are many more like it in the house. Look at the view." I pointed the camera towards the beach.

"Oh, well, then these people are mega, Daddy."

"Mega?" I asked.

"They are mega-rich. Just like on MTV cribs."

"Actually, I think they're more mega than any celebrities that show their homes on TV. They even have a guy who's like a butler, but not really a butler. He seems like a guy that just makes things happen when they need something. His name is Stan."

A thought crossed my mind. "Hey, Hope," I said, "can you not share what we are talking about with anyone please?"

"Why?" she asked defiantly as I turned the screen around, going face to face with her.

"Because I think these kinds of things are personal." There was a pause on the line. "Hope?"

"Yes, whatever."

"Yes, what?"

"Yes, I won't share what we are talking about with anyone, but I want to declare that I say that under distress," she stated.

"Gotcha, drama princess," I said mockingly and she laughed.

"Hey, did you give him the shirt yet?" she asked.

"I'm going to wait 'til tomorrow. I want to make sure no one's around when I do it." MJ had put "cancel me now" on one of her designs, and I didn't know how the others would react, especially Tess, who I imagine could be set off by nearly anything.

"Gotta be bold, Daddy, just like D said in the interview. Look. I'm wearing mine." She showed her pink shirt.

"She's made a kids size in that one?"

"Straight up. We kids gotta stand up and represent. We're the ones that are gonna take over this mess you've left for us." She was cracking up. "Just kidding, Daddy. It's a beautiful mess, and I know it's the game I came here to play."

Wow. I looked at the goosebumps on my arm and then at the clock.

"I gotta go, babygirl. Gotta take a bath and get ready for dinner. It's vegan food. I'm sure I can handle it, right?"

"Okay, now I'm jealous," she said.

"For the bath?"

"Both, actually. More for the good food. I wonder if it will be as good as MJ's. If I had my way, I'd eat like that every day."

"What you talkin' about, girl? You sound like MJ."

"Good, I want to be just like her when I grow up. I want to do my part, just like the hummingbird in the story. Do you know it, Daddy? MJ shared it with me the other day when she was explaining to me why you left."

"I do," I said with a knowing grin.

"That's all we can do sometimes, our part. Just like you are doing over there at the beach. I mean, what else are we going to do, right?"

There was nothing else for me to say, so I stayed silent and wiped my eyes.

"Have fun tonight, Dad, and tell your friends thank you for me."

My first reaction was to ask her for what, but my heart knew the answer, so I just answered with, "I will, baby. Goodnight."

"Wait, have you started writing in your journal yet?"

The truth was, life had gotten so crazy after the interview, I hadn't picked it up since. But I did bring it with me. "Not yet. I don't know what to write, but there it is," I said showing it to her on the desk.

"You gotta get busy, Daddy? That's how you'll really do your part, just like the hummingbird, like the one on the cover. If that's not a sign, I don't know what is."

You have no idea, babygirl.

"I told you what you were supposed to write about, remember?"

"You just told me I was supposed to get a journal," I said.

"Really, again? I said you needed to journal *what he says*. Anyway, I gotta go. Mom's calling me. Pet Lucky for me. Love you. Hope out. Oh, and be the shift!" She shouted in a deep voice while giving me a military salute just before the call ended.

Be the shift? He's really gotten to her!

I wished she would have elaborated on what she meant by "what he says." I sat down and looked at the journal cover and closed my eyes.

"Come on, Hutzi, or whatever Ana calls you, give me some inspiration. What does it mean?" I waited silently for something to come. Nothing. "That's what I thought. You only work for Ana." I did feel a little strange when I realized I was talking to a journal.

I opened the cover and saw that someone had written at the top of the first page in bold letters, Dialogues With Dimitri. Marianne had used that phrase the first time I met her. She must have secretly written it at some point during the last interview. *That was pretty bold.*

There was an unexpected tingling sensation on the top of my head. It almost felt like it was vibrating. I grabbed a pen. An idea came to me about the book I would write using the name Marianne had given. This was the first time I'd ever known what true inspiration was and I loved it.

I turned the page to begin and found Marianne had already started by writing the first line. I got choked up reading it. "And this is how we change the world ...."

HOME AT LAST

MARCUS

I made my way down the stairs well before dinner time. I was nervous about seeing Dimitri after so long, especially outside of Carlton. I figured being in the space first would help me feel more comfortable, but when I turned the corner, he was already there, standing on the beautiful rug with Starseed, who looked emotional. He hadn't seen me, so I stood back and examined him.

He looked fresh, wearing what appeared to be brand new clothes, a pair of beige cotton pants and a light green long-sleeve with some kind of geometric pattern on it, very similar to MJ's shirts. I figured they'd sent one of their people to get him new clothes.

He looked over at me and smiled, the same genuine smile he'd given ever since our day in the courtroom. Starseed walked into the kitchen to give us our privacy, and he thanked her before turning to me.

"My dear brother," he whispered. "I've been looking forward to this day." He stood in front of me, closed his eyes, and put his hand over my heart. I trembled before he fell against me, hugging with his entire being. Tears poured down my face, but I didn't care. The feeling was deep and real but hard to define. It was the sense of being home.

He stepped back, and I wiped the tears from my face. "Thank you for everything, Marcus. Truly there are no words but so much to say. We've got time now, something we didn't have before. I'll get you caught up very soon."

"That would be great because I don't know exactly what I'm supposed to do here," I said.

"Right now there's nothing specific for you to do, except to be present." He put his hand on my shoulder and looked me directly in the eyes. "I gotta ask something. Are you ready for this, amigo?" There was a silence. I could hear the sound of the waves crashing outside and the seagulls crying, but everything was still as if all of humanity had stopped just long enough for me to answer a question that I somehow knew extended far beyond the mere idea of me getting caught up.

No, he was asking something much more poignant. He was asking if I was ready to give my life to this thing. He wanted to know if I was ready to take the hits that would come our way, doled out by corrupt men and women in much higher positions of power than Warden Shady. He wanted to know if I was ready to take on fierce opposition by the forces of a system much more savage and violent than the likes of La Familia. But what he wanted to know more than anything was if I carried enough light within me to stand in front of the darkness that was about to make its biggest play yet, on the world stage, against all of humanity.

My hands began to shake as my old, familiar pattern of worry returned. Right on cue, the nausea came right behind it. But then the voice I'd heard in the hospital that day long ago returned. This time, I didn't wonder whose it was, because he was standing in front of me. It was bigger than us, and at the same time, it was us and every being in the world because it was the world, the Universe, and beyond. The voice simply said "trust."

I nodded, searching for words. "I am, Dimitri. I'm all in," I said finally, putting my hand on his shoulder. He looked down and brought his head towards mine as I teared up yet again.

"We are going to change everything, Marcus," he whispered, our hands on each other's shoulders, our heads touching, looking down at our bare feet on the colorful rug. "Not just those of us in this house but the many other agents that will show up. And believe me, brother, show up they will. The numbers will grow to hundreds, thousands, then millions and beyond. What we will do is no less than lead humanity towards its inevitable awakening. And do you know how we're going to do that?"

"No," I answered, keeping my head down, nervous about what he might say.

He raised his head. "Look at me, brother," he said with a hint of sternness.

I brought my head up slowly and looked into his eyes.

"We're going to start a revolution," he said.

That's what I was afraid of. I felt my stomach drop as the old fear crept back in.

"Do you like my shirt? This pattern is the flower of life. It's an actual thing, Marcus. It represents the truth that everything is interconnected. Feel how soft it is. It's made of bamboo. Says so on the tag." He reached behind his neck and stretched it around to show to me.

I didn't answer him right away. I was trying to figure out how he'd jumped from starting a revolution to a bamboo shirt in seconds.

"Yeah, that's nice, kid," I mumbled, watching my life pass in front of my eyes.

Zach walked in, finding Dimitri and me standing close with his collar still pulled out.

"Oh, sorry. I can leave you guys alone if you want." They both laughed, but I saw no humor in the innuendo.

"Come over here, brother Zach. Let's do The Three Musketeers thing!" Dimitri yelled.

ALL FOR ONE

ZACH

"I'm not really sure what The Three Musketeers thing entails, but you only live once, right? Present company excluded," I said, hitting Marcus on the arm while D stepped to the side to create a triangle.

"What up, Officer O?" I asked, seeing how he was still frowning, obviously dissed by my joke insinuating something was going on between the two of them.

D must have picked up on it as well because he grabbed both of our hands and dipped his head to pray. "We are gathered here today to marry these three men ...."

Marcus yanked his hand away as D and I cracked up.

"Wait D, I got you a homecoming gift. This is the perfect time." I ran into the kitchen and, as I returned, I held it high and let it fall open.

D was blown away and put his hands over his mouth. "Un ruedo de amor!" he shouted. I shrugged. The whole wheel of love still sounded kinda lame to me.

"I still like Take a Stand mat better, but it's your gift, so call it what you want. Tess connected me with her designer in India, so it's custom. It's a bit different than the one you had on the inside, a lot bigger. I had them make it from hemp. Check out the crystals and gems woven into it. Those are Herkimers at each of the four directions of the spoke and one large one in the center cairn. The colored gemstones represent the seven chakras. You've got Black Onyx, Sunstone, Amber, Pyrite, Rose Quartz, Lolite, and Amethyst. The outer ring and the filled-in colors are made from handmade dyes. We even got your spirit animals in there."

I handed it to him. He was all teary-eyed and shit, and when I looked at Marcus, I could sense the envy vibration coming off of him. *Mellow out, dude. It's just a gift.*

"Gracias, Zach," D said. He placed the mat on the ground, lining up west with the sun just outside of the room. We both stepped onto it, but I had to coax Marcus a bit.

"Just stand right there, Officer O. Come on, it's easy." After a moment's hesitation, he finally joined us.

Dimitri looked at the ocean and took a deep breath. "Here we are. And what a ride it's been for all of us. The perfection of every aspect of our lives and our life experience has brought us together for something bigger than can even be spoken of. But we can try, right?" He chuckled and I nodded in agreement. "Let's each take a moment and meditate on what it is we want to see in the world for ourselves, others, Mother Earth, and beyond."

We stepped off the mat and sat on the rug. D was in a full lotus, myself half, and Marcus was sitting with his legs crossed.

I closed my eyes and felt into my life, how grateful I was for my freedom, my connection with D, and all that we were about to do. I was thankful for my sister letting me live in her house as well as my reconnection with Star, who I'd been hanging out with since I'd been out.

D took a deep breath in and let it out. "Okay, let's keep our eyes closed as I invite us all to just play with the idea that a reality already exists wherein whatever it is that we want to see in the world is occurring right now."

I'd done this with D before and remembered how difficult it was to get my head wrapped around the "just play" part. My mind told me it was crazy to just play with something that wasn't actually happening. I struggled until I finally chose to let go and play. Once I did, something very interesting happened, something that would change my life. I realized, remembered, or knew, I don't know which, that there were indeed multiple realities where every possibility already existed. This realization happened by me just letting go and playing with an idea. It's like something was freed once I surrendered.

I opened one eye to peek at Marcus. His forehead was scrunched. *Yep, he's struggling, alright.* But D, the wizard that he was, picked up on it.

"The key is to relax and let go of the thoughts that say it's not possible. Play with the ideas that could be. See what you want as already done, and be in there with it, within it."

I looked again and Marcus's forehead looked better.

"Feel what it feels like for you, for your wish to already be true. Are you experiencing joy? What does your body feel like? How are you breathing?"

I peeked one last time, and Marcus was smiling, which made me smile. I looked at D. His eyes were closed and a grin grew on his face as if he could see me, and he probably could. I closed my eyes and witnessed the already accomplished reality of us going big. All of it gave me chills, or truth bumps.

"I invite you to stay in the knowing that whatever it is you have envisioned already exists. All you have to do is remain in the feeling of what it feels like for you to be in that reality and live your life from that version of yourself that's already there living it."

Easier said than done.

He invited us to stand and get back on the TAS mat. "Let's close our eyes again for a moment, and if you'd like to share what you know already exists and are now living in the feeling of—that already accomplished feat—please feel free. By doing this, it gives us, as a team, the opportunity to jump in on that reality with you."

I spoke first, "So, I saw how the three of us had launched an app that was changing the world. We were high-fiving each other in celebration while walking into an interview around the success of a technology the world has never seen."

"Zach, talk in the present tense," D said.

Good point.

"Yeah, okay." I cleared my throat. "I see you, D, in the spotlight wearing a headset microphone, speaking in front of a mass of people, I won't even try to calculate how many."

"I like that," D snuck in and we all laughed a little.

"The earth is healed, the waters are crystal clear, the people are healthy and loving, not only to themselves and others but to all of life's beings." It felt good to share it with them both. The only thing I didn't say out loud was how I saw myself hugging my father and us sharing a meal together.

"The reality I see myself in is with you both as well," Marcus said shyly like he'd never talked about something like this. "And like Zach said, whatever it is that we've done is really something in the world. I see Dimitri as the leader of something big with many more leaders moving up, just like you guys did in prison but on a massive scale. I feel pride that I was able to help with something that was bigger than anything I'd ever imagined. I see my daughter playing in the world, remaining joyful throughout her life. I see my mother calling me on the phone to say she's proud of the way I turned out and can see that I am helping people. I see MJ and myself very happy together."

He hesitated. "Now here's where it gets weird."

"Weird is good," D whispered, which gave Marcus the courage to continue.

"I saw myself at a book signing for a book I'd written. It was in a large building full of people. I'm talking auditorium-large. It was as if I went to a place where the idea, or even the book itself, already existed and was successful in helping many people."

D let out a loud "hmmm" followed by a long pause.

"Thank you both for seeing the reality that I have already stepped into as I stand on that stage of global attention at this moment. Thank you, Zach, for heading up this technological empire, the most utilized on the planet. Your work has helped many to awaken, and you can be proud of that, now. Star has done so much as a bridge for people to move out of an old paradigm and into a new one as she stands by your side while doing her part as well."

Oh shit, he's really seeing it as already done. I snuck a look at Marcus, and his forehead was scrunched again. I don't think he was getting it.

D went on, "Marcus, be proud now as the one who has handled so much to get us here as leaders in the newest wave of global spiritual awareness. Your daughter and the work she's doing with us is amazing as a young adult. I see your partner, MJ, helping. What a beautiful soul she is."

I snuck a peek again and tears were running down Marcus's face. "This book you speak of has already changed the lives of so many. And those auditoriums are packed all over the world, as you've become a major player in the game yourself."

I looked again and now he had a huge smile on his face.

"I feel so alive on this stage as my heavenly Father, the infinite source of all creation has supplied me with the needed energy to hold space for the rebirth of so many."

Whoa, this is getting heavy. I heard D move, so I peeked one last time, only to see his arms up and open with his head facing upward.

"I hereby answer the Father's call, along with the Spirit Mother's, as I stand here with my brothers, the original agents of change, victorious in a battle already won. Our hearts speak to all those who have listened and joined us in agency. I love you all. Thank you, Great Spirit, Father Creator, ... God, for this and for giving me my life's purpose where I had none before. Thank you for all the messages, delivered by angels of both polarities in the illusion of duality. I love this awakened planet and the beings that populate it. We give thanks in advance for any and all work that wants to be done in the future as we remain humbly at service, in absolute servitude of the Divine Light and its mission." He took a deep breath and stated with command, "And so it is."

I heard his arms come down and took a deep breath myself. *This shit just got real.* I opened my eyes. Something had changed. There was a calm that wasn't there before, not like this one, anyway. I was completely and utterly present, beyond any meditation I'd ever done, even more than when I'd taken the peyote.

At that moment, the sun dropped just enough that a glowing light emerged through the glass, turning the now visible dust particles into flakes of floating gold. It was surreal as time stood still. I couldn't tell if what I was witnessing was real, but when I looked at Marcus, it was confirmed. His mouth was wide open as he surveyed the magic.

Our heads turned in unison toward D. His eyes remained closed, and I swear I could see his aura. It was white with a hint of gold at the edges. I wondered if the world had actually shifted, even outside this room. My first instinct was to call out to Star and ask if she felt it, but I heard two dogs barking at each other out on the beach. *If this is a new world, dogs still bark in it.* Marcus must have seen it as well because he was crying ... again.

His attention shifted from D to the glass slider behind me as if he'd seen a ghost. "Look at that!" he exclaimed, pointing and wiping his eyes.

"Yeah," I said, "that's UL1 bullet-resistant glass. Standard issue on all of the Markland homes."

"Not the glass. Don't you see it?"

D's eyes were now open. He was straining to see what obviously wasn't there for either of us to see. He walked to the window, examining it closely, giving it a few knocks with his knuckles before nodding in approval at its thickness.

I was more concerned about Marcus's mental state. I could see he was becoming agitated, just as he'd been at Walmart when he thought he saw a lady and a hummingbird. *Oh god, please don't be crazy.* I hadn't told D about the weirdness I'd witnessed that day at Walmart and hoped I wouldn't have to now.

"Okay, this is ridiculous. It's still right there. Just hovering!" he shouted.

"Oh look at it!" D yelled, pointing.

"Finally!" Marcus shouted.

"The sun. I think it's coming down!" he exclaimed with his forehead now up against the glass.

"What?" Marcus asked. I think he believed D had seen whatever he was hallucinating and was not happy finding out otherwise. "Oh, whatever. Forget it," he grumbled, throwing his arms up.

"Would you like some tea, Officer O? That seemed to help last time," I whispered, careful not to let D hear. I wanted him to know I was down for keeping his issue on the DL. He turned and plopped down on the couch, crossing his arms like a kid that didn't get his way.

"Hey, guys, I'm goin' up to hang with Star for the sunset. I think she got rocked by the D. See you guys in a bit for dinner," I announced. "Thanks for the Three M experience. Glad to have a new group I can identify with now that I'm not in the Mag Seven anymore. It's all about The Agents of Change now, baby."

Dimitri was cracking up. "See you at chow."

Marcus, not getting the joke about ego identification and still pissed that we couldn't share in his hallucination, just gave me a weak thumbs-up.

D turned to him and said, "Let's go outside, just you and me, to watch it go down." D pushed the button for the sliding door to open, and they walked out onto the deck, as I ran upstairs to my lady.

A STAR IS REBORN

ZACH

"We just had the dopest session, the three of us downstairs," I said to Star as I walked into our room. She had a look on her face that told me something wasn't right in Starlandia. She lit some sage to smudge the room. "What' up, babe?" I asked.

"It was just really strong what your friend said to me earlier. I'm still processing. I need you to hold space for me, Zach." Starseed Bliss, formerly Eve Fischer, was a part-time fashion model, spiritual life coach, and vegan chef. But her passion was in being an outspoken social justice activist and cancel culturist. These were people who would try to destroy the lives of others, using social media, because of some past wrongdoing, no matter when it had occurred in the past.

The WABM Movement, Women Against Bad Men, was one of the first on the scene. The original idea made sense in that it was giving a voice to those who'd been abused. But once the unconscious ego of some of its members had a taste of the dark, ill-gained power, it expanded into something sinister, going after anyone who didn't buy into its narrative. It was so bad that when I returned from my little vacation, I had to watch what I said around her, fearing I might get canceled myself. You see, before I went inside, I was right there with her on the front lines fighting what I believed to be the good fight. Then, of course, I met D and got straightened out about the concept of compassion and how energy works. Apparently, she'd just got a taste of that process as well.

"Do you wanna tell me about it? I spent years with the guy in a cell, so I might be able to help you process quicker."

"I'll try, but it's a lot," she said, breathing deeply.

"That's the way D rolls. He goes straight in. Doesn't pull any punches," I said, surprised he unloaded on her within his first hours in the house.

"He did ask me first if I was willing to dive deep. I told him, of course, that's what I'm all about. I guess I didn't realize how much work I still had to do." She started crying and I let it happen, knowing the importance of emotional release. "That fucking guy. He knows just how to push the buttons, doesn't he, Zach?"

"That he does," I answered, rubbing her shoulders. "But what he's really doing is speaking to the already fully awakened version of yourself. You do get that it's all in the name of love, yeah?"

"That's what I'm having the biggest problem with. I know he's right, but I don't know how to go there, you know, fully accept it."

Since I'd gone away, Star had become a kind of guru to quite a few people. She appeared to have the life everyone wanted, with the look, the walk, the spiritual lingo, all of it. It was weird to hear her talk the talk about the subjects that had become my life. The difference was I had D pushing me to walk that talk. She spoke constantly about the divine feminine and referred to herself as a goddess, which for me, she was, but behind the curtain, there were old wounds that hadn't been healed, and D had just pulled off the dirty bandages.

"He started with this whole victim mentality thing," she said, wiping her eyes.

"He always starts there." I was already chuckling inside. "Did he tell you that there's no such thing as a happy victim? I love that one." Her face remained somber, obviously bothered by my flippancy.

"He did," she said, "but, you know, I thought I had healed everything and was done."

There's that word, done. Like a turkey in an oven. Star was one of those who believed they were finished, with no work to do on themselves because they meditated, went to some plant medicine ceremonies, or had the pseudo-spiritual lingo down. She was a spiritual bystander and wasn't ready to do the work. But D had a way of making people ready.

"He pushed until I was able to see some things that had happened with my uncle, abusive stuff when I was young, and how I was carrying the blame for him around that and men in general. As hard as that part of the conversation was, and all the tears that went with it, it was very positive. I'm going to call my uncle Chet and actually apologize to him, as crazy as that sounds."

"I know all about it," I admitted. "When are you planning on making that call? Timing is everything, babe." She nodded in reluctance. Truth was, I'd waited too long with my father, and now I didn't know if it would ever happen. She went on.

"I told him I'd make the call tomorrow, figuring that was the last piece of work I had to do on myself. But he wasn't satisfied. He wanted to know who else I blamed. So I told him about my role as an activist and how I was sure that this kind of blaming was warranted, unlike with Chet.

"That's when he sat straight up, almost like my statement energized him in some way. His voice got serious and real and he said, 'Actually, Starseed, the social justice activists and anyone else who stays busy pointing their finger outward is acting out in victimhood, and that helps no one,' which totally triggered me because, the way I saw it, we're making changes in the world. Then he laughs and says, 'Just look at how you guys are giving energy to the very thing you speak out against. You act as if you want a world where none of those things exist but continue to hold humanity hostage with your holier-than-thou gibberish born from your own shortcomings and unresolved guilt carried by the culprit within. I often wonder what it's like to be so strongly identified with what you're doing that you can't even see the destruction in it.'

"I was so pissed off. Probably because what he said was true and I didn't have a logical answer, so I went to my first line of defense. I said, 'Excuse me, Dimitri, but you just misgendered me. My pronouns are she and ze. You just said *you guys*.'"

"No. You didn't say that, did you?" I asked as she nodded.

"I did. And do you know what he said to me? He asked if I was joking and if so, it wasn't that funny and we should stay on topic. Zach, he never recognized that there are more than two genders. He just continued on, never acknowledging my pain!"

She whined so loudly, I couldn't help but laugh out loud. She stared at me with a pissed-off look on her face.

"I'm glad you find this amusing. You're not being very sensitive. I thought this was a safe space."

Oh god, I forgot about the nonsense around safe spaces.

She sighed deeply and went on. "And he just kept going. He said, 'So back to you and your self-exalted friends. You know, the social justice activists, cancel culturists, *woke* people ... all those who've gone the opposite way of Love and Truth by pushing an agenda of mind control, telling others whose lives should matter, what they should do, say, and think. I call it PVT, the *parasitic victim triad.* There's the perpetrator, the victim, and then you guys, the false champions, there to save the day that never needed saving. The problem with that setup is that you need a never-ending supply of victims to feed your sorry attempt at self-validation. All of this done through deviously contrived, ego-driven, virtue signaling.' He actually paused to give me a look of disgust, Zach. No one ever does that to me. Only I to them. I was literally mortified.

"Then he goes on, 'I think it's important to get the word out about how damaging this blaming and finger-pointing really is and the evil that lurks behind it. I know all of this is hard to hear. And don't get me wrong, I am fully aware of the other forms of dark human behavior on the other end of the spectrum that are responsible for the current world's situation and what's coming. Neither of the two extremes work. It's just that the people we're talking about here and the bottom they'll eventually hit take humankind with them for the ride, and we can't have that, now can we, Star?'

"I was glad he admitted there were others responsible besides us. He laughed and said that the term 'woke,' in the incorrect way we use it, was probably a clever hoax planted by the dark entity to confuse unconscious people like me into thinking it is a synonym of 'awakened' and that a truly aware person would see right through it. All of this triggered me of course, so I took a deep breath, sat up straight, and told him who I really was, a high priestess, a goddess, and light warrior working within the divine light of consciousness and love."

Oh no. "What did he say to that?" I asked, already knowing the answer.

"He told me if that was so, then I sure wasn't representing that truth by pushing my own guilt and unresolved issues of prejudice and victimhood onto others. That really pissed me off. I actually had to walk away from him for a minute. It was a helluva strong moment for me, Zach. When I came back, he asked me something that got me even more. He asked how I felt in my body when I was attacking those I've gone after. Like, does it feel like it's flowing from a place of love or does it feel constricted, coming from anger or divisiveness?

"That's when I cried because it felt terrible every time. I'd gotten so used to it, feeling shitty became so natural, that I couldn't feel it anymore. That's when I said, 'You know, Dimitri, I can tell you right now, you wouldn't be very popular at any university campus. Most of the students see themselves as heroes, fighting the good fight.' Then he jumps up and says 'That's it right there. You see there's no fight to be fought, especially not between us humans. Fighting is exactly what it, the dark entity, wants us to do, mainly because of its parasitic nature that can never satisfy its need for negative energy. It just keeps the cycle going, stockpiling lost souls to further its sadistic cause, all fueled by the deeds of your woke friends. I removed you from the equation because I can see the eagle has almost landed, Starseed.' I was so impressed by his energy-reading skills I told him he could just call me Star.

"Then he nodded and went on. 'Do you really think self-entitled millennials and other broken victims dealing with their hidden guilt around whatever it is they're attacking, have what it takes to fix a broken system? How could they if the first word out of their mouths is "no"? Those who dwell in resistance to what is are the last ones who should be sitting at the table discussing something as complicated as us shifting into societal self-governance. Only awakened citizens can recreate an awakened world, and this must happen in the individual first. That means you, Star, have to clean up your act so you can stand in presence with me and the other agents of change.' Then he laughed again. 'Because, like they say, united we stand, divided we fall, and I'd say we've fallen enough. If we can just do this, there will be no room for the ills of our world to flourish. That will be the moment it will perish from existence and the game will end.'

"I was blown away by his words, Zach. But I was still struggling inside, so I told him I was having a hard time accepting that what I was doing wasn't helping and, in fact, maybe hurting.

"He had a response then too. 'Strong attachments to identity, whether it be mental concepts or what you've told yourself you are, can be challenging for some to let go of, but on the other side of it lies a peace you haven't felt since you were a child. That I can promise you.'

"I could feel what he was saying was right, but it's like my mind just wouldn't let me go there.

"He said, 'That's because your heart already knows. The mind is where the corrupt data is stored. All you have to do is remove it. This will happen through your own surrender and by listening to your heart from here on out.'

"'But if I jump on board,' I told him, 'that means I've done all this for nothing.'

"He smiled at that. 'Don't you see, Star, you're already on board. All you've done, albeit negative for the most part, has brought you here. The question is, how do you want to show up in this world from now on? If you want to show up as your true, authentic self, then start by letting go. Or not, and continue to hold on to that false narrative. It's entirely up to you.' He paused for a moment to let it sink in, but the struggle was still there and he knew it.

"'What you will tell yourself mentally, as well as your identification to it, will depend on your perspective, or what you choose to say about it, to yourself that is. It can be a huge part of your growth, seen as the perfect piece to a very complex, even more perfect puzzle that's about to be solved. Or you can deny it all and stay in it. Just know, if you choose the latter, you will remain in the current state of hell on earth along with the social justice warriors, cancel culturists, and all others who have their fingers pointed outward.'

"Then he got real close to me and whispered, 'This is exactly where the darkness wants you, Star. This is where its control lies. Only when that finger gets turned around and the deep shadow work gets done, will you, along with the others, be able to recognize the diamond within, thus opening the gates to the domain of its exact opposite, that place I call home. That's H-O-M-E, Star. Heaven On Mother Earth. Your birthright.'

"Zach, I'm telling you, I had goosebumps all over my arms."

"Truth bumps never lie, babe," I said and she nodded.

"So, get this, he starts laughing. 'What's so funny?' I asked him.

"'Oh, I was just thinking again about the irony with that term "woke." It's really the opposite of that, to be so wrapped up in the ego, attacking others like that. That's not what it looks like to be awakened. That's not what Love does. Do you think we can change it to sleeping or napping culture, or something like that?'

"While I didn't really want to show it, Zach, I was laughing on the inside. The guy had a point. There's part of me that feels like such an idiot, but the other part isn't sure that I can let go of that way of thinking. You know, with conservative people, male energy, our president, racism, all of it."

Male energy?

"Oh, I hear you, babe," I said. "The president was a big one for me. I finally saw that the hate I was carrying for him was propagated mainly by the media, both mainstream as well as social. That hate was something I had buried deep inside myself. For me to get as wound up and come unhinged about him as I did showed how wounded I was. I feel sorry for those people out there doing the same. The sad part is, once you've opened yourself up to that low vibration, others come into your field that have done the same, which creates a hatefest of sorts, spiraling all into the cycle of never-ending doom."

She smiled and started nodding. Star was getting it.

"Zach, I can see for the first time how much my vibe lowers when I'm in it. I'm done with that shit. I'm ready to lay down my sword like Dimitri said in the interview. That really stuck with me, Zach, but I guess I just needed someone to spell it out for me in no uncertain terms. I feel like I have to post and let my followers know what's up. Invite them to lay down theirs as well.

"I think it's gonna take more than a meme, babe." I started cracking up, but she didn't like my joke that much.

"How's anything gonna change then?" she asked.

The answer was so clear to me, but I hesitated so she'd think I actually had to give it some thought. I was considerate like that.

"There's no political solution to the spiritual issue at hand. Remember, during the interview, what D said about us losing our connection to our own essence? The solution is in us regaining our connection to Love, capital L, just like D says. When I say that, I am talking about a universal, unconditional love for everyone and everything on this planet."

"Isn't that what I'm doing when I'm pushing others to stop doing what they're doing?" she asked.

I readied myself to go in with the angle I knew she wouldn't like. "We have to go even deeper than that, and I invite you to look at where that's coming from. We must get all the way to the knowing that what we believe about others who trouble us is connected to something that hasn't been worked out within ourselves."

She gazed at me with a look of horror. "It's true, babe. This couldn't have happened otherwise. That's how manifestation works. I couldn't see it until D showed me these types of complaints, and the way I felt about them, were a deeper reflection of myself. This one I had with the president had to do with my father and was around unfairness.

"That new insight changed my life." I paused because her mouth was half opened, and she was staring at me without blinking. "So, what you need to know, Star, is that what you don't like in the other, or anyone you have disdain for, is what you don't like in yourself. You have to see yourself in them because that's what they are there for, even the president, as crazy as that sounds."

She fell back on the bed with her hands over her face and groaned, "Nooo." That's what transformation looks like sometimes.

"Don't worry," I said. "It took me a while to get there, beyond all the isms and blame, but it will happen. It's got to because we are at a crossroads with humanity right now and it's literally do or die time. D says we must put an end to polarization and return to unity, the dark entity's worst nightmare."

She looked pretty affected by the very real pill she'd just forced herself to swallow.

I went on, "How about when the unconscious, woke mob brings up people's past shit and tries to cancel them?"

"Oh, I've been a part of that too, Zach."

"D says, 'Only the dead asleep will use the weapon of past transgression against another while stumbling down the path towards their own demise.'"

She looked down and fiddled with her hands; there were tears in her eyes. "I see it, but why is this all happening? Why are there so many big companies behind the woke movement and even the media? Why are they so much a part of this polarization?"

"I have the answer, but I'm going to give it to you as a question. Would it not be the greatest hoax ever pulled off if the dark entity was able to bring down humanity under the false guise of moral virtue? Can you imagine that?"

That one got her, and she just sat there staring at the wall. "That means those people working at GNN and those big companies, as well as many politicians, are poss—"

"Not all of them are infected completely," I interrupted. "It's more like a spell has been cast on them, the same one that we once fell under. Like us, they were carrying a low vibration to begin with. Now, by buying into this lie, they are having their own darkness presented directly to them. What happens is they project it outward onto another, just as you did with the president and, apparently, *men*. I did it with my father and others. It's actually a great opportunity for them to purge it by doing their work, like you are doing right now. They just can't see it, yet. But Star, there *are* those who lurk behind the mainstream media, politics, and those big companies. They are the globalists, the ones pushing the narrative onto the sheep, and they're a different breed. They've let themselves become completely compromised."

Her mouth fell open. "That is some heavy shit, Zach."

"I'm glad you can see it finally. I was waiting for D to get here. Thank God it worked, otherwise ..."

"Otherwise what?!" She shouted, half laughing.

"How long do you think I could've been around that energy, babe? I was *this* close to loving you from a distance, as Dimitri would put it," I answered.

We both laughed. "I can get pretty toxic with this shit, can't I?" she asked. I just smiled, stoked that it was over. "So I can stay then?"

"Totally! Welcome to our village, Star." I shouted as she fell back, covered her head with a pillow, and screamed.

"Anyway," she said, popping back up, "so then I asked him, 'If we are the Love and the Truth that you speak of, then what's up? Why do I have to be dark like I am?'

"He told me that it's that whole original sin thing, but not as I'd learned about it through religion. I told him that, while I'd grown up in a very religious home, I'm not so down with the whole religion thing anymore, with all of the hypocrisy I'd seen.

"'I get you, sister,' he said. 'But I'm not coming at you with the twisted words that carry the sin of fear designed to control the masses.' He made the distinction between those teachings and the true teachings of Jesus Christ, which are perfect and full of Truth with a capital T. I agreed but told him that him suggesting I and others had been infected by the devil reminded me of the church.

"'That's because you're still seeing it as a goat-man with red horns and a tail. It's actually energetic in nature and much more powerful. As far as you go, how do you think a woman who is pure Love at her core had the seed of hate planted so deeply in her that she fell blindly into its plan of evil and attacked others? The darkness knows it can only attract those who forgot, or never discovered, that the only true power that exists is the power of Love.'

"I asked him about this thing he called the darkness and who or what's responsible for it."

I raised my eyebrows.

"I know, Zach. It's a big conversation, but I had to ask.

"He said, 'Star, a long time ago, and I'm talking way, way back, it, the thing we're calling darkness, decided to separate itself from us, the Light. It did this by choosing to step into its exact opposite. It forgot who, or better said, what it was. Because all is One, in a sense, we forgot as well. But, from that point of forgetting, a push was created for us to remember again because, in that state of forgetting, there is no peace. Love cannot abide where it's been forgotten.'

"I told him to stop for a minute so I could process before he went on.

"'So, through your fall, your own forgetting, you made yourself right and others wrong. You became compassionless, the opposite of Love. This, by default, made you better than the other from an unhealthy twisted world's perspective. Now, because none of this was actually true, the unhealthy, infected, ego-mind, the earthly representative of the darkness in its parasitic nature, went out to find other falsehoods. It did this because of its need to latch onto and feed off of negativity. This is how the cycle works within the distortion of victimhood, its most seductive weapon. It can only take hold of you temporarily because we are all here to remember and we're all going home. That's why Love has put us together here today.'

"Now you can imagine, Zach, I was already completely floored by it all, but he went on.

"'Are you aware of what I'm saying when I tell you this, sister?'

"This was the moment the conversation turned around. I'd given up resisting. I just folded. All I could do was nod.

"Then he asked, 'Do you see the perfection in your falling as well as the deeper perfection in your return? The return that is occurring for you right now as we sit on this rug in this mansion in Malibu? The return that will bring you back to your Truth as the goddess that you are—the goddess that helps instead of hurts, loves instead of hates, includes others instead of ousting them from the tribe. You see, through your return, you will assist others in finding the way to theirs. That will be the moment when you will be working truly for the Light rather than against it.'

"Then he stands up and grabs my hand and looks into my teared-up eyes and says, 'Welcome home, sister Starseed Bliss.'

"Zach, I was bawling. I was having a complete, transformational experience. I mean, who is the guy?"

"Trust me, I know. Been there," I said.

She relayed the rest of his download. "'Going back to what you said about the church. I get it. The Love I speak of, or God, is something your church

and many others falsely claim exists outside of you. Something you need
to strive for or be good enough for, bow down to, please with your prayer,
money, or whatever nuttiness they tell you. In truth, you've been that Love
all along. Christ said the kingdom of God is within you, and I know this
to be true. Sister, you are that Love of God. You've always been it, and you
will never be anything else, just like everything in this Universe and beyond.
This is how we know there's no separation other than the one our forgetting
and our fall creates. The trick is to stay in that knowledge of the truth, that
place you are in right now. Don't waiver or be sucked in by the opposite's evil
wares of separation and its allure of the desire to blame. That's a surefire way
back to hell on earth, and you've had enough of that.'"

I began massaging her shoulders. She'd gone through it with D and, for
some, D being D is hard to handle.

The room was getting dark fast. I grabbed her hand and led her out onto
the deck to catch the tail end of the sunset. We looked down and saw D and
Marcus on the lower deck. D was laughing and acting goofy, waving at the
sun and the people on the beach. Star just shook her head.

"How does he act like a child but carry the wisdom of an enlightened
elder?" She was asking a question that wasn't easy to answer.

"It has something to do with his awakening when he died in the hospital.
But to him it ain't nothin' but a thing, Star."

"I don't understand it, but I'd like to. How could a near-death experience
create that?" she said, pointing at him, now sitting in the chaise lounge,
pulling the back up and down.

"Give him a break, Star, he's never seen one of those before. In a way,
he's still a kid. Or maybe it's that he was never able to be one. So here we
have *this*."

At this point, he was actually standing on the lounge chair mimicking the
surfers in the water.

SHOW ME THE WAY

ZACH

We were walking along the beach, watching the sunset on the horizon, when Star suddenly asked, "What's this Agents of Change thing? Who are these agents, and what's it all about?" Her conversation with D had obviously activated her curiosity about what we were doing here.

I'd never talked about it with anyone before. It felt kind of trippy to say some of this stuff out loud.

"D loves to create new ideas and visions, you know, like The Sovereign Village. It's actually a real thing he's working on bringing into the world. He also plays in otherworldly realities, beyond what most people can even understand. I'm pretty sure that's where all this talk of the 'darkness' comes from as well. Now, in his mind, with the Agents of Change, he's created a group of superheroes that are here to neutralize those dark forces bringing equilibrium back to our broken world. He says the original three are him, Marcus, and me." She stopped walking.

"The guy with the cat? He just looks so, so … Republican," she said.

Wow. I shook my head. "Really, Star? After everything you've just learned? I can't believe you just said that. That's pretty lame, you know."

She put her hand over her mouth.

That wasn't very compassionate of you, Zach.

I recalled how long it took me to put down my judgment of others, how much I slipped up during that period. Plus, what talk would I be walking if I judged her for judging?

"D says each and everyone one of us has a glowing diamond light within that, once activated, will annihilate every limitation and boundary set by the lower self. Officer O's working on that activation right now."

She put her prayer hands to her forehead.

We started walking again. "He's gonna write a book," I said. "D says it's gonna be huge."

"Really? That's awesome." She got suddenly excited. "Remember how I told you D told me about standing in presence with the Agents of Change? Maybe I can be one of the superheroes too. *If* you guys let girls in, of course." She winked.

I cracked up. "You're in like Flynn, babe. No worries."

She took off running and did a somersault. Star was a gymnast before we met.

We walked on in silence. The sand was cold under our feet, but the warmth of our newfound admiration of each other kept us from even noticing it.

"I had a lot of questions about sin," she finally said, "its origin and what I'd been taught growing up. Specifically, something he said in the second interview with Marianne Kelly. So I asked him, 'When you mentioned the white horse and the red horseman, you were referring to the Four Horsemen of the Apocalypse, weren't you? How are they connected to what you were talking about?'

"'You are sharp, aren't you, Star?' was what he replied. 'I wondered if anyone would figure that one out.'

"'Remember, D, my father's a preacher,' I said."

My head popped back in surprise. *What?*

"Yes, I'm calling him D, Zach. We're tight like that now." She winked a second time. "Anyway, he told me that it was a hidden gem he'd planted for the overly astute. We both cracked up. Once you get past his harshness, he's a pretty funny guy, huh, Zach?"

"Yeah, yeah, yeah. Then what did he say?" I snapped, foolishly a little hurt that she was calling him D too.

"So, then he just goes into the whole explanation. 'I see the rider on the white horse, noted to enter first, as the counterfeit of Jesus, the anti-Christ, bringing to our world the false message of what 'should be.' It does this by insisting that its way, which always motors separation, is right and points its finger at everything and everyone it says are wrong. This rider, the anti-Christ, lures more and more broken soldiers, of which there are many, by utilizing the dark energies of guilt, anger, shame, and blame as it gains ground on Battlefield Earth every day.'

"'Isn't the anti-Christ supposed to be a man?' I asked him.

"'It's been interpreted that way, but the Bible is full of metaphors. Jesus had to use them constantly because of what was going on around him. For me, here in this moment in time, it's the crusade of narcissism brought about by the individuals who are infected by those dark energies and use them to create and take sides against others. The evidence of this happening right now is what we just went over regarding the whole woke culture and finger-pointing thing. Because *that* action, the one they are perpetuating, is the opposite of Christ energy, which is Love. They are operating from the polarity of hate. That is the anti-Christ at work.'

"It took a minute for me to get there, Zach, but when I did, I told him I could indeed relate to his theory, seeing how the energy I was in was definitely not of love and light. That was so hard to admit, Zach, you know, to be a part of something so wicked. So, then I asked him about the next horseman.

"He said, 'The red horse symbolizes bloodshed, this will come from the anger and hate, all brought about by the works of the white horseman. As I spoke of earlier, by using the core result of separation, the ground is laid for the materialization of anarchy in the streets, looting, rioting, civil unrest, destruction, violence, and, ultimately, war.' I mean, he was going deep, Zach.

"And there was more. 'Then there's the black horseman, which is many things but most of all famine and can only enter as a result of the works of the two previous horsemen. The social and cultural war they created, along with the ensuing violence, will cause a great financial depression leading to hunger. This is all within the plan of garnering control, as they, the dark controllers, present their people, their followers, with a solution. A new system of economy and the cost of survival is their acquiescence, which they've mostly given through their participation and creation of separation. In a sense, they already wear the mark, but there will be one more step, and it has to do with the physical body, as they will need to brand them. This is when the reality of their new slavery becomes crystallized, and those broken soldiers realize they've been duped.'"

Star stopped. She was breathing hard. What D said really shook her.

"I was actually shaking," she said, "picturing what was coming our way. He noticed it and said, 'Star, because we truly are the creators of our reality, this could all go down differently. We could literally recreate the black horseman metaphor to symbolize the starvation of Love, which could be considered a form of famine that has already taken place.'

"'Wait, how can you just *consider* it another way?' I argued. 'In my father's church, the famine as well as the other three are the prophecy.'

"'Yes,' he said, 'and that's the norm when it comes to the explanation for most people because that's the way the Church of Control explains it. But, because the teachings in the Bible are cryptic and open for interpretation and we know that Jesus was a good guy, we can choose to see them differently. We can agree to go a step further and acknowledge we've been fooled enough by the first white horseman, starved sufficiently of the Love we are and have shed the bloodshed of a thousand apocalypses. Has not the fourth horseman, the pale one, already brought hell on earth to our doorstep? Now is the time we saddle up to return on the real white horse as the true second coming. You see, Star, Jesus isn't coming back. He's already here. He abides in the spirit of Christ Consiousness buried deep within all of us.'

"This is where I had to stop him, Zach. Not only was what he was saying dense as hell, but I was also conflicted because a part of me really disliked what the church represented. There was another part of me that was fearful that what he'd just said would be considered blasphemy. So I told him."

"Really? Tell me what he said," I begged as she giggled and shook her head.

"He said, 'How's that fear been working out for you so far, Star?' Just like that, Zach, with no hesitation.

"It took me a moment to answer. 'Not so well, Dimitri. For the first time, I'm seeing how they use fear at the Church of Control.'

"'That they do,' he said. 'And if they just listened and told the truth about Jesus's own words, the world would be a better place. People would know the power they have, or, better said, the power that they *are*. Jesus said, "I tell you the truth, anyone who believes in me will do the same works I have done, and even greater works because I am going to be with the Father." The last thing the Church of Control wants you to know is how important his words really were. Not all of the church leaders, of course. There are some who are there to empower folks.'

"'My father's definitely not one of those,' I told him.

"And do you know what he said? He said, 'But *you* can be, Star. You can be the one that helps assist others in moving into the fourth density. I know you have it in you. All you have to do is continue in your process of ascension, which is happening right now with this conversation.'

"He's really empowering and kinda weird at the same time, Zach. So, as I'm going through all of this in my head, I had to ask him what would happen if the collective didn't choose to see it his way. You know, they stay in their victimhood mentality or wait to be saved by Jesus.

"'I don't know what that looks like exactly. None of us do. But you could expect censorship, mind control, being tracked, spied on, and anything else it takes to keep you in line. Look at it like this, Satan, I know you can handle me using that name, if it were to have its way ... imagine complete subjugation and what that looks like. Going out and gathering with friends as freely as you can now will no longer exist. You will be told where you can go, when you can drive your car, what for and when. All businesses not under its control will eventually be gone. I could even imagine them using depersonalization tactics, like forcing people to cover their faces. Demoralizing as that sounds, it could actually happen in an insane world. It did it with us at Carlton.

"'Even what you think and speak will be governed, similarly to how it is now with Satan's minions, the zombified cancel culturists dragging the name of those who won't submit through the mud of social media. But it will be even worse in this dystopian future because the dark entity will have eliminated cash. With its own digital currency, it's lights-out for humanity as starvation becomes the weapon of choice against those who resist. In the end, what it looks like is a low vibrational feeding trough for the wicked as folks sit in their boxes, interconnected to its evil artificial intelligence that has, through their taking of the mark, become them. So, Star, you can see that by our nonaction on a collective level, we would be leaving the fate of the world in the hands of the four horsemen. We can't let that happen.'

"Then he starts to laugh and shake his head like he's over it or something. 'And you know what, Star, whichever way it goes, I'll be at peace. Because I'm here to do thy will instead of my will. Ultimately, it's the Universe that's in control. I'm just following the guidance and am here to help people speed up the process by assisting those who are ready to move forward in their awakening. And again, this can only be done by first throwing hate, judgment, disunity, and self-loathing into the lake of fire where it belongs.'

"And that's where he left it because your friend Marcus came into the room. He's an interesting character as well. I don't think he likes my name or something. He also doesn't seem to be on board with how we eat. Is Tess really down with him bringing the cat?"

I laughed. "No worries with Officer O. He's good stuff, just a little stuck in his ways."

She was smiling and I stared at her, amazed by the huge shift that had taken place in just hours. She was peaceful beyond the facade of peacefulness she carried within her identification with being a spiritual goddess, high priestess, or whatever she was calling herself that week.

She plopped down on the sand.

"Why does this happen to us, Zach? Why are we doing all this?"

I took a deep breath, knowing her question was a big one. "D's explanation is very simple: It's the game we came here to play. For him, us transmuting our darkness back into Love is the goal of that game. Just like he talked about it during the interview."

She nodded and pointed at me. "That was EPIC!"

I nodded in agreement. "By doing this, we get back to what we really are, we heal our disconnection, we become whole again. It's actually more correct to say we begin to remember the wholeness we've always been but couldn't experience fully."

I looked her in the eyes. "How am I doing so far, babe? Do you see it?"

"I must be getting it, otherwise I wouldn't be tripping," Star said, nodding.

"Basically the world is waking up because we've nearly hit a bottom. Since that's happening, it, the darkness, is freaking out. It's been throwing all kinds of shit at us, working within the realms of polarity and division as we continue to move toward unity. What it doesn't get is that the more shit it throws, the faster the awakening, which means less food for it. According to D's theory, this should starve it out, hence, saving the planet."

Star was cracking up. "Um, I'm a little blown away by how you've advanced so much further than me, but I'm not going to be lured by it, the unhealthy ego. I'm just going to let the truth of Love speak through you. Capital L, right?"

I was loving her more than ever. The authenticity was beaming through her eyes. "That's right, babe. I'm not any more or less advanced. I've just improved my memory. And I wanna help you and others improve theirs as well."

"I know, right?" She said while wiping her eyes and then vowed to step away from any old pattern that brought forth the destruction of our world, its people, or the positive vibration that she truly was.

IN OR OUT
MARCUS

I followed him out to the deck, "Look at it, Marcus!" he shouted, pointing, more excited about a sunset than anyone I'd encountered before, with the exception of maybe Hope. "This will be my first one! How about you?!" he asked.

"Actually, it's my first as well. Over the Pacific, anyway," I answered quietly.

His eyes were wide with wonder. "I've never seen one anywhere!"

It felt strange to be there with him, happy as he was while I felt conflicted. The things he'd said in the house were so powerful. They were everything I wanted to hear and be a part of. But there was one thing he mentioned, right before Zach came in, that scared the shit out of me. It made me wonder if I'd made a huge error quitting my job and leaving my daughter and girlfriend to travel across the nation for this thing. I didn't know him well enough to know if I should take what he said with a grain of salt or not.

I stood next to him on the deck and placed my hands on the rail just like his. He was staring directly at the sun, almost in a trance.

He pointed to the edge of the surf. "Why do people wear masks on the beach?"

"What? Where?" I asked.

I followed Dimitri's pointing finger to find a man walking in the wet sand at the ocean's edge. He was in fact wearing a type of mask, the kind doctors wear.

"I have no idea," I said. "Never seen that before."

Dimitri let his hand fall to his side, nodding his head knowingly as the easy silence again overtook us. After a moment, I mustered up the courage to interrupt his bliss.

"So, you want to revolt, huh?" I asked quietly like it was no big deal.

He slowly looked over at me, and I'm pretty sure he could see right through my phony smile. He pulled a bag of peanuts out of his pocket, looked back at the sun, and laughed. "Yeah, but peacefully." He extended his hand. "Cacahuates?"

I literally breathed a huge sigh of relief that he couldn't help but notice. I took a few peanuts.

He's not insane after all, thank God. "Yeah, that would be better for sure, D."

He started cracking up. I couldn't tell if it was because I called him by his nickname, my inauthenticity, or maybe both.

"Maybe peacefully. We'll see," he whispered, remaining silent for a long time while gazing at the sun disappearing on the horizon.

He's messing with me, right? Remember, present moment, Marcus. There's no revolution right here and now. You're at a mansion in Malibu. All is good.

He leaned in, still looking at the waves. "So, you in?" he asked in a low tone.

I closed my eyes and saw the events of past years flash before me. *What a bunch of insanity.* I opened them back up. There was only one answer to that question.

I nodded and quietly said, "I mean, what else is there to do, right?"

He started clapping, hit the rail hard with his right hand, and shouted, "You see. Now you're speaking my language, hermano!"

As if on cue, the same hallucinatory hummingbird buzzed at us twice. This time I didn't even move my head to watch it go by. I was done with it and making a big deal out of something only I could see. It hovered just in front of the deck, looking at us. I was trying to ignore it, so I forced myself to look at the surfers just north of us. *This is ridiculous.*

"Cute, huh? Dimitri chuckled. "But he can be a real pain in the culo, you know," he stated nonchalantly.

My head snapped between the hummingbird and him.

"Wait, what are you talking about exactly, Dimitri?" I asked.

He put his finger out and pointed. "Huitzil. He seems to always show up at the weirdest moments."

The bird dropped in close as if it knew Dimitri was talking about him.

"You can see it now, but you couldn't before?"

"Marcus, I can always see Huitzil. But I don't talk about him when others are present that can't ... yet."

Knowing there was something I had in common with him that others didn't, no matter how much further along they were, gave me a sense of contentment. He held his palm up and the small bird flew over and lowered itself onto it. He walked onto the sand, just out of earshot, and spoke to it before throwing his hand into the air. Huitzil buzzed off towards the falling sun.

"I showed him who was boss, didn't I?" Dimitri said, walking back onto the deck and we laughed.

He rubbed his hands together, trying to warm them, and asked, "Oh hey, do you wanna know what they're gonna call it?"

"Call what?"

He gave me an odd look like I should have known what he was talking about. "Oh, initiating the turning point in humanity's evolution. Humankind's greatest achievement ever, that's all," he chuckled.

"Oh, that?" I smirked, giving him a wink. "No, I don't. But, as usual, I have a feeling you're about to tell me."

"That I am, brother. That I am." He pointed out to the ocean. There was a golden afterglow from the sunset that sparkled like diamonds on the water. I swore I could see Huitzil dancing over the top of it while seagulls squawked in the background.

My heart was beating so hard I could see my chest move as he leaned toward me and got very serious.

"This thing, this movement we're putting together, it's going to shake our world so hard that all people will come together in loving harmony, ready to do what needs to be done. And it shall be written into history and known throughout the ages as The Essential Revolution."

AND SO IT IS

EPILOGUE

MARCUS

In a very short period of time, the true owners of our world, those who controlled what we needed for our basic survival, would make their most evil play ever. The hidden globalist would start by pushing partisan, identity politics that would pit politicians against each other in a way never seen before. Then, similarly, those drunk-on-power politicians, along with the darkness-owned media, would manipulate the public by using polarizing ideologies such as sexism, racism, and culturalism to tear apart the fabric of society. Soon, the collective would come to behave like children on a playground fighting for toys while their cities burn, squabbling for their egos and isms, blinded by the very wool that had been pulled over their eyes.

But Dimitri had a plan of his own. First, he would pull back the veil, showing me and the others on the team the cold, hard truth. Then we would work together to expose it to the world. Like clockwork, many would begin to step up and join, making us a force to be reckoned with. That's when the darkness would amp up and unleash something to instill even more fear into the masses, a last-ditch effort to hold on to their illusory perception of control. Little did they know, he would use that against them, inspiring others to step into their boldness by saying no to hate and yes to Love, putting them right the fuck out of business.

It wouldn't be long before I entered into the knowing that all of the trying events in my life were perfectly synchronized to bring me to this moment, right here, talking to you from a beautiful future. The shooting, losing my job, my divorce from Lisa, and my turmoil in Carlton were all deaths. On the other side of them was life, new life. And not just for me. You see, only through Dimitri moving through his own death and rebirth is it possible for me to stand here on the other side of a deeply troubled world after it moved through the same. There was a time I'd cursed the dark entity's players for bringing about the pain in our world, but standing here now, post Summoning, I know differently.

I hope you join us again as we recreate the next leg of this journey, the most critical. We will endure the pains of labor together as the dark entity pushes us toward our re-birth of Unity and peace on Earth, thus eliminating the collective's doubt and confusion surrounding the true nature of its game.

ACKNOWLEDGEMENTS

First and foremost, to those who helped me directly with the creation of this book, I appreciate each one of you and what you gave to this project more than you will ever know: Nichole Netaya, who was there in the very beginning to help and push me to write this novel when I didn't think I could. Andrina Hutter, who joined in to support me through the completion of the initial draft amidst the forces that seemed to try to stop this from happening. Uma and Sandra De Vos who showed up at the end to contribute a layer of Love that made this piece just that much better. A profound thank-you to Amanda Johnson of Awaken Village Press for being the orchestrator of orchestrators, holding it all together while being put through the test of her own transformation throughout the process. You rock, sister!

Thank you to her team members: Artist Daniel Holloway, who did an incredible job tightening up the manuscript and putting together the layout design. Carrie Cojocari for organizing all the madness on the back end of the process. Artist Tim Murray for working within my vision in creating the awesome cover. Marianne Johnson, Amanda's mom, for being a joy to work with as she went the extra mile during the final editing stage. Juliet Davey for her assistance in proofreading. Amy Odland, the reviewers, and the beta readers for their book-launching support. And last but certainly not least, Christina Luna for appearing out of nowhere right when I/we really needed her to.

A special shout-out to those who helped me with the research: Brooke Hyman and Brittney O'Hara for working with me on all the medical information. Akshay Sachdeva for the tech terminology as well the Hindi translations. Monica Mosapor for the latin linguistics. David Ayotte for the help with the Ra Material. David Lema for his contribution with the financial content. And to Charlie Clemans for being so generous with his time in sharing the facts surrounding life on the inside of a state penitentiary.

Within my transformational experiences, I'd like to thank Eckhart Tolle, whose simple but profound words in his book, *The Power of Now*, came at a pivotal moment, saving my life at a time when it seemed it wasn't worth saving. Ana Huya Escavia, my surrogate grandmother who helped me to open my closed heart, changing my life forever. Marcus Ogabi, who brought me to experiential wisdom, showing me the clear distinction between believing in a thing and knowing it. Lastly, my initial meeting with the master of masters, Dimitri Tanomeo, and the realization I received, impacting my life forever. Gracias, D.

Then there was the inspiration that came from so many beings that it would be impossible to list them all. Thank you, Neale Donald Walsch, Charles Eisenstein, Doshin Roshi, Jordan Peterson, Carlton Pearson, Joel Osteen, Byron Katie, Teal Swan, Michael Bernard Beckwith, David Icke, Dr. Hew Len, Paramahansa Yogananda, Sri Nisargadatta Maharaj, and Sri Ramana Maharshi.

Thank you to anyone and everyone who ever taught me something, said an encouraging word, or had been there for me when I needed you. Thank you Adam Fischer, Stephanie Downing Verderber, Mr. Kawagoe, Sat Yoga, Carlos Arias, Steve Torchia, and the Scialdone family. Y gracias a Karol, Valverde, Barboza, y Canela.

Gracias a mi gente en El Valle, especially the few wisdom keepers that live in service for an awakened world.

I thank my earthly mother, Linda, for the heartfelt love she exudes and am grateful for any portion of that quality that has been passed on to me. I give gratitude to my earthly father, whose name I bear, for his genius and desire to bring about a world that works for all. Witnessing him dedicate his life to this planted the seed of inspiration so deeply within me that I chose to do the same. Then, there was his mother, Nana, who blanketed me with her Light from the moment I was born and continues to do so in the afterlife.

Lastly, I would like to acknowledge the co-author of this book, the ever mysterious, infinite, nameless power that has created and continues to move through all of Existence. I thank It for the gift of this life and all that's been given to me within it.

Aho!

FROM THE AUTHOR

Something very special has brought you to this planet during the most remarkable moments in known history. That *something* has put this book in your hands, and if you've gotten this far, then you should know you've been *chosen*. Chosen to make this story not only one of possibility but also of certainty—the certainty of your own healing as well as the world's. This is an official call to action for your entry into *agency* as we stand together for the intrinsic righteousness of heart-centered action and justice.

The mere fact that you are here, reading this now, means that you have already accepted the *invitation for awakening*. I know this to be true, only because that very special *something*, the One that brought you to earth and put this book in your hands, is the same One that wrote it through me. So, in essence, you wrote this, it's yours, and you are It, that's how special you are. So, what do you say? Let's do this thing, together. We got this.

I mean, what else are we gonna do, right?

Be the shift,

Mike

Let this symbol stand for your right to live free of oppression. Know that where you see it, freedom of thought, expression, and positive oriented action is not only protected but promoted. It represents the intrinsic Light that you and all other awakened beings are shrouded in.

¡Viva la revolución!

Find out more about Mike McGinnis and his books at

www.theessentialrevolution.com

and

www.awakenvillagepress.com/mikemcginnis.

Made in the USA
Monee, IL
09 April 2021